Corbett

The Novel

STEVE WHITEMAN

Copyright © 2021 Steve Whiteman.

All rights reserved. No part of this book may be used or reproduced by any means, graphic, electronic, or mechanical, including photocopying, recording, taping or by any information storage retrieval system without the written permission of the author except in the case of brief quotations embodied in critical articles and reviews.

This is a work of fiction. All of the characters, names, incidents, organizations, and dialogue in this novel are either the products of the author's imagination or are used fictitiously.

Archway Publishing books may be ordered through booksellers or by contacting:

Archway Publishing
1663 Liberty Drive
Bloomington, IN 47403
www.archwaypublishing.com
844-669-3957

Because of the dynamic nature of the Internet, any web addresses or links contained in this book may have changed since publication and may no longer be valid. The views expressed in this work are solely those of the author and do not necessarily reflect the views of the publisher, and the publisher hereby disclaims any responsibility for them.

Any people depicted in stock imagery provided by Getty Images are models, and such images are being used for illustrative purposes only. Certain stock imagery © Getty Images.

ISBN: 978-1-6657-0071-9 (sc)
ISBN: 978-1-6657-0069-6 (hc)
ISBN: 978-1-6657-0070-2 (e)

Library of Congress Control Number: 2020925351

Print information available on the last page.

Archway Publishing rev. date: 01/22/2021

1

This is not a western, but it is about the West. The 1880s and early 1890s were a time of rapid expansion. The railroad companies led the way for westward expansion. They borrowed heavily and raced into both the mining districts and the cattle, wheat, and timber industries of the Pacific Northwest. The Native Americans had been decimated. Their dwindling numbers were moved onto reservations. There was nothing in the way of westward expansion. This period piece dwells on these times and how these individuals adapted to a rapidly changing environment. Some were crushed by chance, while others reveled in their good fortune.

Our story begins two miles south of Animas City, Colorado, in a place called Durango. In 1880, the D&RG Railroad had chosen the sagebrush flats to build the train station and roundhouse over Animas City. The terminal would serve as the base for an aggressive charge into the mineral-rich Silverton mining district. The mountain south of the town became the location of the gold and silver smeltery, hence the name Smelter Mountain. Durango came alive. The money and the workers began building the dangerous and adventurous rail up through Animas Canyon to a flat terminus at nearly nine thousand feet in elevation—a massive undertaking. For some, gold and silver fortunes flowed down the rails to the smeltery. Others who were not as lucky fell on hard times.

Anyone with money and elegance stayed at the Strater Hotel when visiting Durango. The Diamond Belle Bar offered the finest hospitality in Durango. In the back of the Strater, in a room next to the coal-fueled boiler, was the laundry. Our story begins with the two laundrywomen. Ramona, a Navajo, and Ann, a Texan of sorts, led similar lives, but they had different stories. They both had babies early in life. Ramona had Ajai, now nearly sixteen, and Ann had Corbett, now eighteen. Together Ajai and Corbett celebrated their youth on the south side of Durango. Ramona's husband, Hok'ee, a renegade Navajo, showed up only when he needed her. Ann's husband, Laddie, a drunken card player, stayed around only to use her. As both Ramona and Ann were new to the area, working the laundry room was the best job they had ever had. They hoped for better.

The laundry was an afterthought use of space. The back side of the boiler kept one laundry wall warm enough to dry sheets and other linens. Linens were stored against the wall next to the door, with the tall folding tables taking up part of the opposite side. The huge washtubs and a mangle completed the room. With barely enough space in the laundry room, the women eked out a living. When those in the hotel needed heat, the boiler would radiate volumes of heat through the wall. The sheets would dry, Ramona would sweat, and Ann would wither. They hoped for better.

"We've been eating the same ham hocks and beans for three days now," Ann complained. "When we get paid Friday, I'm going to buy me a chicken and make some noodles."

"Oh, I love your noodles," replied Ramona. "Bring some to work. I'll make some fry bread, and we'll sneak some butter and honey from the restaurant. Corbett likes my fry bread."

"I think Corbett likes everything!"

A shawled woman staggered through the open door, aided

by a small, white-haired Native American woman. "Ajai, what happened?" Ramona dropped the towel she was folding and raced across the room to her daughter. Ajai's face and hair were covered in dried blood. Her body was bent in pain. "Sit, sit, *aw'e'e*" (my baby girl). Ramona wrapped both arms around her daughter as they both cried. "Who did this?"

"Shizhé'é," she sobbed. The depth of her sadness was even greater than the pain in her body. Ajai's grandmother, along with two of Ramona's uncles, had ridden two days by wagon to bring Ajai to her mother.

Ann arrived with a wet rag. "Who's Shizhé'é?" Ann asked. She had never heard Ajai or Ramona speak of this person.

Ramona turned and locked eyes with Ann. "*Shizhé'é* is the Navajo word for father."

Ann's eyes widened. "Hok'ee did this?"

Ramona's eyes answered Ann's question. Ann knew of Hok'ee. Every month or so, he would come up from the reservation in New Mexico and see Ramona. He would stay a few nights with Ramona down in the willows, where she had a small tepee she shared with two other Native women. He was bigger than most Navajo and quite traditional. He did not like the *bilagáana*—the name Navajo called white people—and he definitely did not like Ramona working for them. His intense eyes mated with a wide masculine jawline. His thick neck and shoulders made his constant anger more pronounced.

Ajai vomited violently and painfully. Ramona spoke to Ajai in Navajo, her hand on the girl's forehead. Ajai was wrapped in her grandmother's wool shawl. Grandmother had traded a buck lamb and three pieces of turquoise for the fine quality of a Two Gray Hills shawl, which was now splattered with vomit and blood. Grandmother stood just outside the doorway. She knew her place.

"I'll get a towel!" Ann went to the laundry cupboard and came back, only to stop abruptly. Ramona's attempts to wipe the vomit from Ajai's legs had stopped. Both sets of eyes were fixed higher on Ajai's legs. She was bleeding badly.

"Ramona," said Ann, "take her over to the bed in the hay shed. I'll finish folding up the last of the sheets and will get the pillowcases up to the maid on the second floor."

Ann, a hard-luck story from West Texas, was thin, white, worn, and sickly. Ramona, a Navajo from the Chaco Canyon area, had made the long forced march to Bosque Redondo on the Pecos River, where all the Navajo were quartered for five years. She was what the cowboys called a squaw. She was short and wide with coarse black hair. Ramona and Ann shared a closeness and loyalty that came from the heat and expectations of the laundry, knowing they could be replaced at any time.

The D&RG train tracks ran behind the Strater Hotel, on to the train station, and then farther south to the roundhouse. On the other side of the tracks were several small buildings, including a corral and hay shed belonging to the hotel. The shacks, lean-tos, and tents of the hotel workers lay along the river. The workers often used the hay shed as a place of respite between shifts. Ajai struggled to the hay shed and collapsed on the only bed. Ramona was sitting crying next to the bed, when Ann came into the shed.

"How is she doing?" Ann asked breathlessly. Her lungs were questionable on her best day, and today the run across the tracks to the hay shed had taken her oxygen reserve.

"It is very bad," Ramona said, slowly shaking her head as she lovingly watched her teenage daughter sleep.

"Sit, Ann!" Ramona's tone sounded grim; her eyes were tired and cloudy. "Corbett must leave!"

Hearing her son's name startled Ann. She slowly slumped on to a bale of straw, eyes wide with a sense of fear. With her husband, Laddie, mining sixty miles away in Silverton, Corbett was all she had. "Hok'ee is coming to kill Corbett!"

"Why?" Ann whispered, her heart racing.

"Ajai is pregnant," Ramona blurted out. "No," Ramona corrected herself. "She was pregnant, but Hok'ee found out and beat her so badly that she lost the baby." Only Ramona's strength allowed her to make it through the explanation.

Ann stared at the sleeping girl. "But why?"

"Ajai had to tell Hok'ee that Corbett was the father. He is bringing the Begay brothers and others to kill Corbett." Ramona looked at Ann with great sadness. "It is too bad he is a bilagáana."

Ramona and Hok'ee had both endured the long walk in which the US government moved the entire Navajo Nation to Bosque Redondo, a new reservation along the Pecos River, far from their historic roots. For the sake of convenience, the government had previously planted four hundred Mescalero Apaches at that location. The Mescalero Apaches were the traditional enemies of the Navajo, and they were still there. The government's goal was to restructure the Apache and Navajo tribes, suppressing their cultural identities. Wool was replaced by cotton reservation clothing. Horses were taken away, and men were no longer allowed to hunt. They were given gray mules and windrows to plow, and women were given flour and portions of beef instead of corn and lamb.

Ramona became passive and withdrawn. Hok'ee joined an angry group of rebellious young braves and escaped west, never to be bound by barbed wire and fence posts again.

Hok'ee took from Ramona anytime he was in the area—sometimes without her consent, sometimes not. She left for work in Durango, but he found her anyway.

Ann leaned forward, covering her face with her hands. Her

cry was silent, but the heaving of her body spoke volumes. Her reservoir for handling stress and anxiety was limited at best. She went from numb to blank.

To Ann and Laddie, Corbett was like a gift from God. Tall with blond hair, which turned golden after days in the sun; not yet grown; rangy; and ready for an arm full of muscles, as if propagated by different parents, Corbett took after neither Laddie nor Ann. Ann had come to Durango from Appalachia by way of a dirt farm in West Texas. She had expected nothing from life. Her most redeeming feature was her long, luxurious red hair. But that was years ago. Her hair was now a sorry orangish bit of flyaway with many strands missing. Given that she was always thin with shoulders hunched forward, there was nothing there anyway. Laddie, now mining in Silverton, was small and scrawny. His face was pinched, and his black hair was slicked back with pomade. Having an anxious disposition, Laddie was always looking to make a dime or to prove himself. His failure in life came from a lack of focus and hard drinking. It was a chicken-or-the-egg sort of thing.

"When will Corbett get back?" Ramona asked, anxious and worried. She stared at Ann, who was frozen in time. "Ann!" she shouted. "When will he get back? This afternoon or in the morning?" Corbett and an Italian kid named Nick made three trips per week by wagon to the coal mines fifteen miles away—one day up and one day back. Both the Strater and the D&RG depended on these trips.

"Today, but I don't know when." Ann wept. "Lord, Lord. My Lord!"

"Find Manuel!" said Ramona sharply. "He can warn Corbett before they get to the bridge. Maybe they can hide on the other side of the river." Ann just looked at Ramona, staring right through her.

"Ann, find Manuel!" It was almost a scream. "He might be down at the train livery!"

Durango was established along the north-to-south run of the Animas River in 1880 by the D&RG. It had become a bustling railhead. A fortunate bit of luck for all involved were the coal veins west of town. The last part of the trip back was the long, slow descent down to the Animas River Bridge, and then it was just three blocks of open space to the corrals next to the tracks and the Strater.

Earlier in the day, Hok'ee and the Begay brothers had begun their ride north from the reservation. They had returned the week previous from a raid to the east into the great forests of northern New Mexico. During their campaign to dislodge homesteaders, they followed the Piedra River north to the Pah Gosah and soaked in the healing waters of the Utes, keeping a sharp eye out the whole time.

Upon their return, Hok'ee went to Ramona's home in Chaco Canyon, where Ramona's clan still lived. Finding Ajai with a fat belly, he became angry that he had not the opportunity to choose the warrior that would wed her and make further alliances. He beat her, demanding the name of the baby's father. When Corbett's name finally came forth, he left her for dead.

It was a fast and easy ride along the flat plateau just east of the Animas. Grass, sagebrush, and cottonwood trees were intermixed with a few grain farms and their fields of mature wheat and barley. Hok'ee might burn them later, on his way home. His goal was to kill the white boy who had contaminated the insides of his daughter with white blood.

Within sight of Durango, Hok'ee and his companions dropped down the plateau and followed a trail through the breaks between the sagebrush bottomland to the south and the elevated flats of

Durango. He had taken this route many times to get to Ramona. Out of sight from Durango, the willows where she lived had a campsite near the water. It was a perfect rest stop and rendezvous point during the search for the blond Corbett. Leaving their horses, they crept up the incline and waited.

Ann, drained with the emotion of the moment, found Manuel sitting at the train livery, polishing the leather traces on one of the showy carriages used by the D&RG to move patrons about. The livery area was busy and dusty. A wagon full of soldiers from the Twenty-Second Infantry Division posted at Fort Lewis was preparing a return to the fort after a leave in Durango. Three carriages were tied as well.

"Senora Ann," said a rotund Manuel, "you are a long way from the laundry. Have your sheets flown away?" His large stomach jiggled with his joke. Then, without rising, he said, "You look sorrowful!"

"Some Indians are coming to town to kill Corbett!" Ann said, holding a cloth to her mouth and nose against the dust.

"Into Durango to kill Corbett? How could that be?"

"Can you meet him on the other side of the bridge and warn him?"

Manuel, still sitting, said, "Have you gone to the sheriff? I think you should go for the sheriff."

"Manuel, please!" pleaded Ann, her hands and the sleeves of her light blue work shirt now shaking uncontrollably. Her concern did not translate into a quickening of Manuel.

With the Animas River Bridge in sight and the freshness that came with it, the coal wagon and its young riders, Corbett Jones and Nick DeMasi, were finishing their trip run from the coal mine at Hesperus.

"I like your hat," said Nick, as he snatched it off Corbett's head. He adjusted it this way and that. "I think I'll get one."

"Why would you want a hat? You don't even wear a shirt most of the time," replied Corbett, glancing from his team to Nick's shirtless chest and skinny arms.

"You're just jealous. My brown skin in the sun brings on romance in my women."

"Last week you told me it was your curly hair that brought romance to your women. Give me back my hat!"

"I'm still trying it out."

Nick's family arrived with the D&RG's expansion into the area. When the mines opened to the west, Nick's father had become a coal miner. Now with the father weathered and drawn by consumption, and ill and old, Nick was working to keep the family in food. Nick knew his station in life and enjoyed just being the funny Italian kid. With wonderfully curly black hair, dark skin, and two bright eyes separated by a big honker, he often held court in the brickyard behind the roundhouse.

Corbett halted the wagon on the bridge overlooking the Animas. The view of the powerful thrust of energy flowing downward from the high country was always captivating. The see-through water, lower in the summer, still splashed over, around, and against the impeding rocks and boulders, southward.

"It's so clear today," said Corbett, admiring the water.

"Yep, grasshopper time!" exclaimed Nick, ready to do some afternoon trout fishing. Brown trout and rainbow trout readily rose for grasshoppers floating along in the river.

"All right. After we unload the coal," said Corbett, "we'll go down to the river and wash all this coal dust off us, then catch us some grasshoppers and fish the rapids down by the willows." He popped the reins. The wagon creaked across the bridge.

Hok'ee, the sentinel, watched while the Begays dozed behind him in the brush. His attention was focused on soldiers gathering around troop wagons near the railroad station. They seemed so young and carefree. His next glance was to the bridge, where a tall wagon had stopped. He looked and then looked again. One of the two riders was wearing a brown hat. The other was a blond. It was Corbett!

"Tsxiilgo!" (Hurry up quickly)! said Hok'ee as he raced to the horses. The gods had given him good fortune in the hunt.

The four-horse hitch pulling the coal wagon left the wooden planks of the bridge with the D&RG railway station in sight. Hok'ee's anger at the blond boy sent him and the Begays into a full charge, a screaming Indian attack, shooting from their horses.

Both Corbett and Nick saw the approaching rush of horses and were unsure as to the reason for all the running. Native Americans raced horses all the time, but when the three fired their rifles at the pair, Corbett whipped the horses forward.

"Hurry, Corbett!" screamed Nick as he watched the Natives approach. Suddenly, he fell forward out of the driver's box. One of the front horses raised up and kicked as it was shot in the hip.

Hearing shots, the paunchy Manuel said, "Señora Ann." Struggling to his feet, he continued, "I think those damn reservation Indians are here!" He stepped to the livery fence and looked between the top two rails. He saw that train employees, as well as the soldiers, were motionless, frozen by the events unfolding in front of them. "The soldiers will kill them dead!"

"Can you see Corbett?" Ann asked, looking through the rails, trying to make sense of the chaos before her. Two of the carriage horses were in turmoil, running loose, pulling the carriages this way and that.

"There!" Manuel pointed to the yellow and black freight wagon pounding across the empty lots toward the livery corral. "Run!" he said, stumbling past Ann then running up the tracks toward the Strater.

The freight horses, screaming in terror, were in dead aim for the corral gate. Corbett, with his feet set, was pulling hard on the reins, the wagon brake already set. Nick was lying lifeless on the wooden evener between the horses' back feet and the front of the wagon. The four powerful draft horses crashed into the corral gate, stumbling and twisting, with the wagon piling in on them.

Corbett flew over the fallen horses and the gate and onto the relative softness of the corral's mix of manure and dust. In a half-run, half-crawl motion, he slid between a wooden water trough and the thick rails of the corral.

The three attackers rode hard toward the staggering wreck. Then there were two. A soldier stepping out of the back of the military wagon leveled his rifle and shot one of the Natives off his horse. Then, as the remaining two leaped from their horses, rifles in hand, several soldiers fired. The second Begay was hit.

Hok'ee stepped into the corral, searching the wagon and the injured horses for Corbett. As a third round of shooting rang out, Hok'ee went from predator to prey. Ann and Manuel, from their hiding place, could see the large savage eyes of Hok'ee coming at them between the two buildings.

Corbett rose from behind the water trough that had hidden him. Amid the dust, the freight horses were scrambling, trying to reach their feet, only to discover the pain of hooves and legs all asunder. Corbett, the soldiers, and the roundhouse crew started cutting away leather straps and parts of the corral fence. The wagon, well inside the corral, stood atop the crushed animals. None of the horses could stand.

A shot was fired, then another, and finally the third and fourth. The cries of the horses and their suffering stopped.

"Help me find Nick!" Corbett knew that Nick was buried somewhere beneath the pile. As it turned out, Nick was very dead, hardly recognizable as a former human being.

"Goddamn Utes," said the boss of the D&RG roundhouse crew, witness to the two minutes of terror. Rail workers and soldiers closed around the freight wagon. Others went to stand around the dead Natives. "Damned bunch of renegades."

"Weren't Utes," said Corbett, bent over trying to comfort a dead Nick. "They're Navajos. I know one of them."

"What in the hell were they tryin' to do," asked a soldier, his gun still at the ready, "steal your coal?"

Another soldier, a corporal, came into the group. "I just telegraphed the fort. They'll—"

"Damn it!" a young soldier proclaimed loudly, stepping into the group and interrupting the corporal. "I joined the infantry to come out here from New York and shoot me an Indian. And don't you know it"—his skinny voice got louder—"three rode by me and I froze up like Johnny Christmas."

"I got the first one, right off his horse," said the corporal proudly, looking back at the area where the oldest Begay had fallen.

"Damn," said the loud young soldier as he looked down at Nick, his first dead person. "Oh God!" He groaned, tumbling away, vomiting down his uniform and all over his gun.

Everyone who was able had armed up and hurriedly joined those at the corral.

"Soldiers!" shouted the corporal, realizing that all were looking at the soldiers for guidance. "We don't need an officer to form us up. Form a line to my left."

"Hell, did anyb—"

Several shots pounded the sky. "It's over behind the Strater!" said Corbett, getting to his feet. The soldiers and the mob all broke ranks and raced up the tracks toward the sound.

Corbett took several steps to follow the others, then stopped. Nick needed him to stay. Corbett's mind was flashing back and forth from the fun times with Nick to the terrible sight before him.

Corbett shooed away the first of the manure flies from Nick's face. Nick was not the type of fellow who should die this way. Why were Hok'ee and the Navajos attacking Durango? Corbett knew Ramona was deadly afraid of Hok'ee. And when he'd taken Ajai back to the reservation, she feared the worst. Ajai and Corbett's relationship ended just like that.

"Corbett!" yelled Mike, running down the tracks. "Your mother's been shot!" Mike's bartender apron was smeared with blood. "Some damned Indian shot Ann and Manuel." Overwhelmed and in a dazed state, Corbett raced toward the laundry.

The three old Navajos, a grandmother and the two uncles, sat nervously on a bench far from the door into the hay shed. Soldiers and townsfolk crowded to see inside. Others, with guns, were flying hither and yon, most chasing the assailants west toward the river.

Corbett saw the crowd at the front of the hay shed. His mother would not be there this time of day. She would be finishing the ironing of the table linen for the bar.

"In here!" shouted Mike, waving Corbett to the hay shed door. He violently made space for Corbett to enter.

Just inside the door, Corbett stared for a moment, his eyes adjusting to the darkened room. His eyes caught the motion of two women huddled around a visible blue sleeve and a small, pale white hand showing along the dusty floor. He brushed by the corporal and another soldier. The women separated as Corbett went to take a knee between them.

"She's gone, son," whispered one of the women in a motherly tone. The shot from Hok'ee's rifle had hit Ann in the chest. Blood had found its way through Ann's blue shirt and onto the bales of straw. The other woman closed Ann's partly opened eyes while Corbett's head was bowed, Ann's hand in his. Corbett's thoughts lay in a dark recess. It was bad enough that his mother lay dead. The ultimate sadness was that she had never lived. Her life with Laddie was one of betrayal and hardship with only the pretense of love.

A cry and a thrashing of straw came from near the bed where Ajai and Ramona were lying. An army medic was tending to Manuel, who had fallen, half sitting and half lying, into a darkened corner. Those inside the shed saw the results of Hok'ee's quick rifle shot, Manuel's upper arm was shattered with bone fragments mingled with muscle tissue. His left hand was shaking uncontrollably with an unfired pistol still in his hand. The medic knew that an amputation was Manuel's only help, as a tourniquet had only slowed the blood loss and nothing more.

Ramona, upon seeing Corbett, fought her way up from the bed and the bloody shawl that lay on it and ran to him. "Corbett, I am so sorry," she cried. She hugged him hard, something she would have never done before. "Your mother tried to save me." Ramona's eyes wanted this truth to be out. "She stepped right at Hok'ee." Her head fell against Corbett's chest as she moaned and wept.

"Why did Hok'ee do this?" Corbett moved Ramona's head away gently so he could see her eyes.

"He wants to kill you!" Her pained eyes looked into one of his eyes and then the other, realizing that Corbett was aware of nothing. "You don't know?"

"Know what?" Corbett was at a loss.

"You were the father of Ajai's baby!"

"Baby?" Corbett was stunned. Ajai and Corbett had lain together once, just days before Hok'ee had taken her back to the reservation. "No, no, that's impossible." Corbett did not know why it was impossible, but he believed it was impossible.

Once, under the cottonwoods, just once. He remembered the feel of her skin, soft, warm, and enticing. Corbett thought of the rush and heat that had risen from his body. Afterward, they were too embarrassed even to look at each other. It was just the once.

"Is she still down in Chaco?" asked Corbett. He had not seen her in nearly four months.

Ramona's eyes were blurry with tears as she pointed to the bed where a cocoon lay on the far side, against the hay shed wall. Ramona had shared the shawl to keep Ajai warm until her daughter's last breath. A bucket of bloodied strips of bedsheets sat at the foot of the bed. Ramona and Ann had stuffed clean strips far into Ajai, but the bleeding had continued. The two-day trip by rough wagon had gotten her to her mother but had taken away her life.

"Ajai," said Corbett as he quietly leaned down toward her face. He fully expected her to jump up to him. He turned down the shawl to see her face. The white pallor against the light brown skin of her face caused him to pull back. She was still and dead. It was unlike Ajai to be still and dead; her warmth and smile had made her friends with those who lived along the river. Being a Native in Durango was hard, but then she had met Corbett, whose loneliness ended when he found her. Both Corbett and Ajai had been surprised at how well they fit together.

Corbett had never seen a dead person before, but in less than an hour, he had witnessed the souls of three whom he needed to comfort him. He was lost.

When Corbett awoke late the next morning, he was nauseous with a terrible headache. It took him some minutes to figure out where he was. By the pictures on the wall and clothing spread about, he figured he was in Mike's room. Mike had captured Corbett near the hay shed the afternoon before. By that time, Corbett was in shock and fumbling to be away from the hay shed and the day itself. Mike, a bartender with a bartender's frame of mind, did what he did best: he'd gotten Corbett passing-out drunk.

Sick and with a head that was pounding off his shoulders, Corbett staggered to Mike's window. He could tell it was early afternoon, but the amazement did not finish there. Downtown Durango was an armed fortress. Soldiers were posted on the corners, and two horse soldiers were passing by. The Twenty-Second from Fort Lewis, upon receiving word of a Native attack at Durango, had sent a full company immediately east by horseback and by wagon. Fort Wingate, to the south, had scrambled a company of cavalry riders, who were a day out. Every Native in the area was marched to flats and interned near where the Twenty-Second was posted.

Without an idea of what to do, Corbett dressed and went downstairs to find Mike. The vagueness of the previous day allowed him to process the flashbacks, one at a time. The horror of each death added to the fact that he had no strategy that he could utilize to move forward.

"There you are," said Mike from behind the bar. "I'll get you some coffee."

"Thanks. God, I'm sick."

"Sorry about Ann," Mike said quietly. "She was a good woman."

"Mike, what do I do?" Corbett did not know where to begin or how to begin. He needed to find Ramona and better understand what had happened. "Has anyone taken care of my mother's body?"

"Well, Corbett," said Mike, returning with the coffee and a

piece of berry pie, "the big dogs were in here for breakfast. Sheriff Harris, Major somebody, Jim Macon from the funeral home, and Father Pat from Saint Columba."

"This morning?" asked an astounded Corbett. "You should have come and gotten me."

"Remember, these fellows are trying to clean this up quickly, before somebody misreads this mess and starts an Indian war." There had been talk that the Navajos were brooding and looking for a fight all along the southern Colorado border and that the hot-breath whites wanted some action of their own. "Besides, your little roll in the grass with your Indian princess started this." Mike had just come out with the cold truth. "They didn't need you or want you here."

Corbett was hit with the blame for yesterday. He and Ajai were nobodies to everyone; that is what had attracted them to each other. The thought never had occurred to either of them that they would marry each other. Ajai would find and marry a Navajo warrior, and Corbett would marry a young woman from one of the ranches in the area.

"By the way, Corbett," said Mike, returning from serving a barfly at the far end of the bar, "overnight, your mother became a Catholic." Mike waited.

Corbett sat up a bit. His mother never had gone to church, let alone a Catholic one. "I don't think she's a Catholic." *How does that happen?*

"When the Catholics went to retrieve Nick's body, they noticed that no one knew what to do with Ann's body." Mike opened his hands, expressing the way things were. "No money, no body, and a pauper's grave. The priest just took her to be given the same burial as Nick. I think it is tomorrow morning."

Corbett's shoulders slumped as his eyes focused on some

unusual dark red blotches on his boots. Again, it was he who had brought about the deaths of those he loved.

"Did they catch Hok'ee?" Surely they had; he could not have gotten away.

"No. If it's the Indian you are talking about, I'll bet he's long gone."

From the glass front door of the bar, Simon, a friend of Corbett, made eye contact and approached Corbett in a hurry. "I'm taking a wagon down to the flats. The army is using it to escort the Navajos back to the reservation."

"Is Ramona leaving?" Corbett wanted to ask about Ajai as well, but he could not bring himself to do so.

"That's what I am saying!" Simon was obviously in a rush. Simon was the fireman on the Durango and Rio Grande railroad train to Silverton each day. "Coming or not?"

"Yes, yes, I'm coming!" Corbett reached in his pocket to pay for the coffee. Mike just waved him to the door.

When the wagon reached a viewpoint where the flats could be seen, Corbett saw newly planted army tents as well as a small gathering of Natives, nearer to the road.

"That's them." stated Simon, pointing to the group. Simon only spoke when something needed to be said. The job of shoveling coal into the train's firebox for hours was a task made just for him. "Looks to me that the Indian bunch is about to pull out. I know a couple of 'em—good workers."

"Thanks, Simon, for getting me!" said Corbett, staring at what was ahead of him in order to gauge the situation. "I can't believe what's happening!" Ramona had been strong enough to leave Hok'ee, but was she strong enough to lose Ajai? Corbett should never have looked at Ajai in that shawl. That memory of her would now be locked forever in his mind. His tears were freely flowing.

There were several wagons in a row, one of them containing the two dead Natives covered with tarps. Grandmother's rickety old wagon had the uncles on the backboard seat, and Grandmother, Ramona, and Ajai in the back. The other wagons held Navajos who were being returned south.

"Ramona!" called Corbett, running to her wagon.

"Corbett, yes!" She smiled for the first time in many hours. "I hoped you would come."

They hugged and cried, he on the ground and she leaning out the wagon. It seemed forever. They separately went through the agony of the day before in their minds. The comfort of being held gave solace and peace, if only for that minute.

When they separated, Ramona kissed Corbett on the cheek, saying, "Be strong, my son."

"Please care for my Ajai." His tears blurred his vision as his head dropped and he stumbled away.

From behind oak brush on Smelter Mountain just west of the flats, Hok'ee watched. The sight of Ramona hugging Corbett was not one he would forget. Soldiers from the Twenty-Second, milling about their tent area, and the horse patrol along the river, were all that was keeping Hok'ee from venting his anger again. He was surely *jish-cha* (among devils).

The next morning, the funeral home was a quiet and emotional place. The name above one of the doorways was that of Nickolas DeMasi. Corbett could sense a lot of quiet movement. From where he was standing, he could see Nick's mother. Her eyes were open, but she was not seeing. Although her family and friends were saying condolences as they passed by, her ears did not hear. Was Corbett strong enough to enter that room? Would it be better to be unseen? Would they already know that Nick's death had been brought on by Corbett's behavior? He owed it to Nick to suffer the eyes that would be upon him.

As he entered the room, Corbett kept his eyes focused on the closed coffin. He felt the stoppage of all movement. Even the air was still. The coffin was plain. Although it was nailed shut, Corbett could see through it to the terrible image of Nick from yesterday. That image would override the remembrances of Nick at the brickyard laughing at himself and everyone else. The world never had had a chance to meet Nick; had they done so, they would have loved him.

The other doorway read "Ann Jones." Corbett entered quietly as if she were just asleep. To his surprise, a nun was putting a little color on Ann's face, more kindness than Ann ever had received in real life. When the nun saw Corbett, she laid some daisies into Ann's arms and bowed out of the room.

Ann seemed very restful. Corbett knew that, truth be told, Laddie would not have wanted a Corbett or any other bit of responsibility. Ann had nothing and had given it all. Her time was done. Given that it was not very much time, it was not very fair.

Corbett moved to the wooden chair across from her coffin. There he sat, just him and her.

That night, Corbett returned for the first time since the murders to the shack that he and his mother had shared. He gathered the valuables, of which there were essentially none save a pair of earrings from Laddie that he'd given Ann after a big night at the poker table and a small coffee can of money that Corbett and Ann kept stashed for the road should they need to move on. There was no need to tuck away one of the pictures of Ann; there was none to tuck away anyway. Corbett's coal-blackened coat was still good, and so were the two blankets that Ann had taken from the Strater.

Corbett lay on the bare mattress, holding his life's belongings, waiting for the next day to come. Twice during the night, horse patrols passed by.

The funerals were both the next morning at the cemetery on a small, flat mesa above the Animas. Nick and Ann were buried only a few yards apart in the pauper section. A large group of mourners, mostly from the Strater and the DeMasi family, moved from one site to the other. Corbett had never been to a funeral. After each of the coffins was spoken over and blessed, Corbett watched while the long wooden boxes were lowered, a final statement.

He felt the compassion of those who came by. They spoke kind words, but Corbett sensed an underlying sentiment regarding how all of this had come about. He slowly slipped away to be alone.

From the brush and cottonwoods on the western edge of the mesa, angry eyes analyzed the possibilities of killing Corbett from that distance. Dying himself was of small cost if the blond devil died, but if Corbett were to survive, then Hok'ee's soul would never be at rest. In Hok'ee's mind, it was imperative that Corbett see and recognize him as the warrior who had caused his death, Hok'ee's contorted manifestation of counting coup.

After the funerals, Corbett made his way down to the roundhouse, where the day's run to Silverton was being steamed up and greased. The train would start late as the coal car was not yet full. Nick and Corbett usually helped after their coal run.

"Corbett," said Simon, looking up from his shovel. "What are you doing?"

Corbett, in a familiar position in the wagon bed with shovel in hand, answered, "If I don't help, you are never going to get up that hill."

"Not in that good shirt!" Simon said, talking through the dust. "Stay out of the way. I'm almost done."

A few shovelfuls later, done and leaning on his shovel, Simon asked, "Heading back to Texas?"

"I hope to go up to Silverton with you. I expect I'd better tell Laddie. I doubt that he's heard yet."

"Hell yes, ride up here with us. I'll get you someplace where the soot and ashes won't get to ya."

Taking a last look at Durango through the cinders and dust, Corbett put an end to his many thoughts when he saw a Native American rising from a red cliff and holding his arms open wide, a rifle in one hand and a knife in the other.

2

Silverton

With his bedroll stashed at the line shack, Corbett made a visual examination of the town of Silverton. Having arrived at dark the night before, Corbett helped Simon shovel out the ashes and clinkers from the engine's firebox in preparation for the next day's run back into Durango. Filthy from coal dust, Simon collected steamy hot water from the train's boiler and carried it by bucket to a partitioned little room next to the line shack where a crude shower system allowed them to shower with hot water.

Tired, but at least clean, Simon led Corbett through his early evening routine. The two walked along the boardwalk to the alley behind Blair Street and, farther on, to the back of the Blair Street Bakery. Included in the walk was a small, shiny pail. Corbett noticed but did not comment. Waiting inside the bakery's kitchen was the baker's wife, Mrs. Johansen, a portly woman of about fifty with white hair and a ruddy complexion. As was the ritual, Mrs. Johansen prepared a heaping stack of pancakes and eggs. She now did so for the pair of them. After a thanks and a good tip, Simon went into the back of another building and came out with the small pail full of foamy beer.

"You do this every day?" asked Corbett, laughing at Simon and his sloshing nightcap.

"Except on days that I don't." Simon grinned.

Inside the line shack, Simon's demeanor was calm and relaxed. His wooden chair was tipped back next to the coal fire that glowed, casting out a share of the light in the room. An oil lamp on the table provided the rest. "How you doin', Corbett? It must have been an awful day for you."

"If I could rest my mind for just a little bit, it would sure help." With every normal thought came flashes of the wagon wreck, images of Nick's crumpled body, or pictures of his mother or Ajai's empty face. "Ajai and I loved each other," Corbett cried in a whisper, "but we knew our future was the minutes we had at that one moment. Two days later, Hok'ee took her down to the reservation. I never even got to say goodbye!"

"What will your father say?"

"I would hope that he and I would hug for a long time, thinking of my mother and the sacrifices she made for us." Corbett wiped a tear from his cheek. "But he won't. He will think of himself and leave me standing, in trade for a drinking spell at a bar."

"So, you don't think you will be staying up here with him?"

"I expect that in a few days you will see me here at the line shack, waiting for a ride back to Durango, to a home that isn't there. Wherever I'm at is my new home, I guess."

Simon, standing and heading toward his cot, said, "I paid for your breakfast at the bakery. Just knock on the back door. Good night." And he was gone.

In the high mountain air of Silverton, Corbett watched the engineer and Simon bring the steam up on the train's boilers. He thought of Simon, the last strand of Durango, leaving. Without even a close acquaintance, Corbett was on his own. He looked around to arrange his mental compass. It was obvious that the morning sun arrived at this location very late because of the huge mountains to the east and the west, but seeing that the sun, rising high in the eastern sky, was now sliding down the shadow on the western mountain, he now knew his east–west–north–south.

Two blocks up and down the alley, following yesterday's path, stood the back door to the bakery. Corbett knocked. "Come in, come in!" said Mrs. Johansen. "I've got you an egg sandwich and a nice loaf of bread for later. I'm glad you like Simon. He is almost a son to me. You know he has nobody." She looked up from kneading some dough. "You know what that would be like?" Corbett thanked her and left, knowing exactly what it was to be alone.

Looking west above the houses on Blair Street, Corbett saw a mammoth stone building with windows along the top floor. Drawn by such a large building, one even larger than Durango's Strater, Corbett wandered up the board sidewalk.

"Hey, boy!" shouted a female voice. Corbett quickly looked around.

"I could run my fingers through that blond hair!" said another voice, laughing. Corbett saw three young women sitting on a bench across the street from him.

"Come over and talk to us," the first voice beckoned.

"Where in the hell's your hat?" asked the second. "That yellow hair has me worried."

Corbett, somewhat confused about the three young women and the yelling in his direction, crossed the street. Two of the women were wrapped in shawls, and one was wearing a man's heavy coat. The shawl covered the shoulders and arms of the first young woman, but nothing much covered her breasts. It was easy to determine from the first that the young women were young and frisky.

The smaller young woman in the heavy coat did not fit with the others. This was not her game, and she was not playing it well. Her ugly brown teeth matched her withdrawn demeanor.

The middle one was bulky and had a fat face and body to match her bulk, but her hair was a beautiful auburn color and draped down her shoulders. Her dress seemed an awkward choice; it had a high collar and was very plain. Physically, she was a woman, whereas the others were not. *Her genetics have given her big bones,* thought Corbett, *and you cannot make petite out of big bones.*

"Listen, blondie, what's your name?" the woman in the middle asked. "I'm Esther. This loud one here is Lilly," she said, pointing to the attention-hungry, well-rounded young woman to her right. "And this poor little mouse is Mabel, just now coming of age and broke as hell."

Nearly every day these young prostitutes sat on the same bench, both evening and morning, to analyze the new arrivals from the train. With three bawdy houses in town, this was a chance for the young and inexperienced to snag a customer before the experienced hookers uptown outhustled them.

"You girls know where the Irish Rose Mine is?" asked Corbett. "I need to find it." His mind, which still contained the shock and cloudiness of the previous days, was driven by a single goal: to find Laddie and tell him of Corbett's mother's death.

"Oh, honey, I'll be your Irish rose, your English rose, or whatever rose you want me to be," Lilly said, laughing. She had the breasts, the smile, the face, and the personality to be a dandy trollop. Her giddiness and naivety in the new profession were like dynamite, not necessarily toys to play with.

Corbett smiled, but his heart was not in it. Young men his age often talked about the gaslight girls, as they called them, explaining, without experience, how it would be to rent one for the night. From the time it really mattered, Corbett had had Ajai as a companion. With both mothers working at the Strater laundry and both new to the area, their friendship of convenience had become a tight bond. Sex came much later. First was pinch-and-giggle, then the first kiss. Ajai's pregnancy was the result of the pair of them knowing she was about to leave and their emotion of not wanting to lose each other.

"I'm Corbett Jones," said Corbett. "Up from Durango." Even though Corbett was ready to move on, he knew his politeness. These young women did not know that the only time he had ever had sex, three people died as a result.

"Well, Corbett Jones," Esther said, standing and pointing, "go up to the Grand Hotel and take the stairs to the second floor." She sensed that he was not quite focused. "That's where the mining offices are. They can tell help you find your mine." She touched his arm. "Then come back to me. It looks like you could use a friend."

"Doesn't Miguel work at the Irish Rose?" whispered the little mouse into the conversation.

"Do you know where it is?" asked Corbett, looking at Mabel and following a different trail.

"You and your little Mexican," said Esther to the mouse. Turning to Corbett, she added, "Mabel won't know. Hell, I don't think he speaks English. They tussle the night away every time he's down from the mine." The mouse began shrinking back from the conversation.

"Well, thanks," Corbett said, bowing a bit to all three young women as he began to pull away.

"You can stay at my place tonight." Lilly winked. "I could run my fingers through that blond hair. You know I could." Corbett, already walking, did not turn, but he lifted his hand in recognition.

"Get a damned hat!" shouted Esther, laughing. "You're in Silverton now."

After a few yards, Corbett began thinking about his hat. For a couple of years, he had been wearing a brown felt slouch hat. It was nothing fancy; it just protected his eyes from the sun. He tried to contemplate what had happened to it. That took him immediately to the wild coal wagon crash and Nick's falling from the driving box. Rather than search through those memories, he just marked the hat as lost.

The Grand Imperial Hotel opened into a large ballroom affair. There were fancy tin tiles on the ceiling and beautiful wood all the way to the tin. He did not dare sit on the furniture; it was obviously too good for his clothes. The stairs were wide and grand.

Each of the five offices on the second floor had lettering on the heavy doors. An important-looking man with gray hair, a mustache, a white shirt, and a blue bow tie stepped from one of the rooms, on the way to another.

"Which way to the mining office?" asked Corbett quickly.

"The one that says San Juan County Mining Office, you idiot."

Well, there was the rub. Corbett could do numbers, but he could not read a lick. Neither West Texas nor Durango had taught him to read. Neither Laddie nor Ann could read either. Their Bible did not have words printed in red. His parent's Bible was survival, nothing more, nothing less.

Corbett picked a door at the end of the hall and entered. There he encountered a woman who was quite nicely dressed in a high-collared white lacy blouse and a flared blue skirt with evidence of a bustle.

"Can I help you, young man?" she said, friendly but rigid.

"Yes," said Corbett with the best dignity and manners he could up come with. "Is this the mining office?"

"Yes it is. Now how can I help you?"

"I'm trying to find the Irish Rose Mine. I need someone to aim me that way." The walls were lined with maps. This seemed to be the place.

"John!" said the woman loudly. "We need you!"

A tall bony man with a full head of red hair came from the back. His wire-rimmed glasses were set far down on his long, pointed nose. "Well, what's the problem, young man?" His voice, high-pitched, carried a touch of Irish brogue.

"This young man needs to find the Irish Rose Mine, and I haven't a clue."

"The Irish Rose is up above Animas Forks." He walked over to a wall map and beckoned Corbett to follow. Corbett assumed that the red dot was Silverton from the manner in which the lanky man moved his hand up to another point higher on the map. "From what I have seen so far, the Rose has produced a pretty skimpy amount of silver. Some magnificent crystals of quartz and even some acanthite have shown up." He looked at Corbett over his glasses to gauge his level of understanding.

"I believe my father works in that mine," replied Corbett. "Just how far is that?" Map reading was not something Corbett had ever experienced.

"It's ten miles up to Animas Forks," the man said, his voice sounding as if he were giving a lecture. "Then it is four miles straight up to the mine. The road is good for a spell. It is the main road to the new tunnel they are boring. After that, good luck."

"Got a job up there?" asked the woman, now interested.

"No. My father works up there. I'm hoping to see him."

"With a good horse, you could make it to Animas Forks in a couple of hours," said John, obviously a direction giver. "Then figure out if you want to make a run for the mine before dark.

"I must tell you that the tunnel project has pulled a lot of miners away from their mines for better pay in the tunnel," John said as a warning. "Your father might be at the tunnel instead. Not much loyalty up there."

Because of the flat surface, Silverton had rectangular city blocks, some with houses and buildings, others empty, waiting for buyers and reasons to be. Lumber was available from the sawmill at the south end of the valley. Green Street held the main buildings in Silverton, the large rock-built town hall and the Grand Imperial. East, near the river, was the train station and the ore cars at the railroad siding, in various states of readiness.

Corbett, noticing how traffic had picked up while he was inside, stopped in front of the hotel and surveyed the energy of money being made. He saw wagons and horses moving this way and that, and a produce wagon bringing foodstuffs from the train. Meat, in the form of several steers, was being herded across town to the butcher's corrals. Two wagons with lumber passed, going north to the mines.

Corbett thought, *Money is here just like in Durango, and everyone wants a piece of it. The little man breaks his back for a good day's pay and the big companies make gold off the little man's back.*

With his backpack, his bedroll, and a stomach full of the fried egg sandwich that Mrs. Johansen had prepared for him, Corbett started his walk north.

At the edge of town, Corbett collapsed to his knees. A yellow and black D&RG freightliner, just like the one he'd driven for two years, passed. The whole set of his Durango memories swept by him again. It was a picture book of blood and death: his mother, white and dead from loss of blood; Ajai and Nick, his best friends, their eyes staring up at him; and Hok'ee, damned Hok'ee. Corbett's eyes moved back and forth as he replayed the events. He stumbled into an alley and went to lean on a fence post, nauseous and weak.

"Hey, Corbett!" shouted a voice coming up the alley. "It's too damned late for you to still be hungover." Esther, now in men's pants and a man's blue work shirt and carrying a brown derby, smiled as she stepped up to Corbett. "I've been looking for you." She took a closer look and saw that Corbett's face was wet with sweat. "What's going on here?" she asked, now concerned. Besides being a big-boned woman, she was tall, almost as tall as Corbett. Her eyes were right there, but he could not meet them. The freight wagon was the same, color and all.

"You, sickly boy, sit over here." Her hand led him to a nearby log in the shade.

"I can't. I've got to get to the mine before dark."

"Why the hurry? The mine will still be there tomorrow!" In her trade, calming a man and listening to his problems was first on the list.

"Two days ago, my mother was murdered. My father doesn't know yet!"

"Oh, darlin', I'm sorry!" Esther pulled him to her chest, a gesture she used many times over, but never for a reason so legitimate. Concerned that a young man this masculine would be drawn down so far, she asked, "What can I do to help?" She often used that phrase too, for a different reason entirely.

"Thanks, Esther. I was beginning to fade. Where, I don't know." Corbett noted Esther's manner, figuring she could be a sister, a nurse, a priest, or a bartender. He even surmised that her caring spirit might someday make her a good wife. "Better be off. Thanks!"

"I won't hinder you any, but I did find you a hat—a good one too. One of my men heading back down to Durango left this in my room." She handed him a rich man's felt derby.

"Won't he return to get it?"

"Let's just say he owes me."

"I can't take this. It's too fancy for me."

"If it brings you back to me," she said, winking slyly, "it will be a good investment."

"Well, thanks, Esther."

"Oh, I think it makes you look like a fine gentleman. Oh, I do believe it does." She squeezed his hand and turned to head down the valley, quite pleased with herself.

Corbett was an hour into his walk when the problem of elevation got his attention. At over ten thousand feet, he noticed the air was rare. Loading coal for years had given him strength, but this kind of fatigue drew a man's soul down to the basics of maintain the heart rate and the breathing. He watched the horses, the wagons, and the walkers like him, who were doing quite well. He was not! If he ever got to Animas Forks, that would be the extent of his day. Besides that, Corbett remembered John, back at the mining office, mentioning that the last four miles to the mine were steep.

The main road followed the Animas River north. The two ran parallel, often with just a few trees and rocks between them. Corbett moved off the road where a windfall of aspen trees lay on their sides. He broke out the loaf of bread from back at the bakery. It had a good smell to it.

"Hey, neighbor, what would you trade for a chunk of that loaf?" The voice had come from a vagrant-looking follow sitting atop a two-wheeled cart pulled by what looked like a small mine pony. Corbett stood and walked toward the old man.

"I know that anybody who has a fancy derby like yours would spare some grub." The old man nodded his thanks as he took the bread. "My name's Peabody. Everybody calls me Peabody." He had a few teeth, but the crust was being gummed to death. "Going mining, are ya?"

"No. My father works up at the Irish Rose," replied Corbett. "I hope to get up there today."

"Son, that ain't going to happen unless you catch one of the supply wagons heading that way." Peabody examined Corbett closely. "You ain't been in the world long, have ya?"

Corbett pondered the question. "What do you mean?"

"Up here in this bunch of high mountains is the world. If your lungs ain't broke in well, you can get real sick, even die from the 'high death'!"

"Think I can make it to Animas Forks?" Corbett's plans had gone to hell. A walk all the way back to the D&RG line shack did not seem appealing.

"Since your hat says you got money a-jingling, you can stay up at the Kalamazoo in Forks." There was a moment of silence. Corbett knew he needed a ride, but a supply wagon was out of the question. Corbett's hesitancy to catch a ride on a better wagon was interesting to Peabody. "Get on, and we'll get you there."

Peabody was diminutive in every way. His head was small, his body was slight, his fingers were small, and the weight of the world seemed to lay on his tiny shoulders. His bowler seemed many sizes too large, and his chin was understated.

"Want some wine?" Peabody asked, holding probably the dirtiest wine bottle that had ever been offered.

"No thanks. This high country is already toying with my mind."

Corbett could not tell whether it was the bad wine that made Peabody's breath smell or whether it was his breath that made the wine smell foul. Peabody might be right: until Corbett warmed to the altitude, going anywhere far or fast was just a dream. And for that matter, was Laddie still even in these mountains? Corbett missed Laddie, but not in the regular father–son way. Rather, he missed a model for how the game of life was played. What Corbett did learn from his father, he had learned by observation. Those times when Laddie did come home, he was either deadpan drunk or distressed and antsy. As Corbett, with his bigger bones and wider frame, approached Laddie's height, Laddie had begun to pinch and poke, followed by the days when Laddie pushed Corbett to fight back. Corbett took shots to head and body while Laddie teased him. The things he learned included how to block an overhead right which his punch of choice. According to Laddie, the overhand roundhouse right was always the first punch thrown in a barroom brawl. This was to be blocked with the left hand and followed by a bitterly powerful hook to the ribs. Laddie lived somewhere between needing to show his dominance and wanting to teach what he knew.

In those early years, Corbett, sent by his mother to bring Laddie home, spent hours in the Blue River Bar in Durango, watching Laddie drink while trying to win back another paycheck. Corbett began to read the players' eyes and mannerisms. Without even seeing the cards on the table, he could pick the winners.

While in deep thought, Corbett noticed that Peabody, because of the ebb and flow of the cart and the rush of the water, had slipped off to sleep. Corbett had concluded Peabody to be a lonely soul. He waved at every passing horse or wagon, but none responded. A time or two, there was a subtle negative facial feature or movement from the passerby.

With the quiet, methodical movement of the cart, Corbett thought of how Laddie might react when given the news of Ann's death. Would he go slobbering off to the bar to lament, or, if sober ... Corbett had not seen Laddie sober enough to contemplate that option.

Animas Forks was different from Silverton in that it lacked the room between the mountains to set out a normal city plat of ninety-degree angles. Buildings here were set at different elevations, some near to the river and some on nearby foothills just below the rise of the surrounding mountains. The Kalamazoo Hotel seemed to the centerpiece of the short, tight main street.

Peabody rose from the dead. "This here is the Forks. Used to be nothing here but the gold panners looking for gold in the summer, hightailing it downriver in the winter." Peabody stopped in front of the Kalamazoo. "I reckon you want set off here. They got food too." Corbett's grubstake from the can of savings that he and his mother had put together did not allow for fancy hotel stays.

After seeing Corbett's hesitancy, Peabody tapped the pony on the rear. "I can use a visitor, every once in a while, to keep me from going out of my mind." Peabody grinned with the remnants of what he had left. "You can bunk with us a day or two."

After a few minutes, Peabody's pony took a turn off the main trail and onto a narrow cart path. The trail weaved back and forth between trees and brush, sealing it from the view of the main road. Finally, the path offered an open area, a long, very narrow pasture bound on the left by a sheer blackened wall face and, on the right, with a small willowy stream. The width between the wall face and the willows seemed to be fifty yards or less, but the length of the pasture followed the stream up the canyon for some distance. The wall was sheer and smooth, except the bottom ten or so feet, where Peabody had built a shack into it. There was another opening farther along the wall.

"This here's the first patent mining claim in this country. I lived up here when no one else could."

"I don't understand *patent*."

"A claim," said Peabody, looking at the tall grasses of his pasture and enjoying the showing off of his world, "is owning the right to the minerals. A patent claim means you own the land as well."

The mine shaft, with a cabin in front, was a hodgepodge of different materials. One wall was made of stone mined nearby; another wall, slab wood from the sawmill. A fireplace, somewhere inside, further blackened the steep rock face above the cabin. A south-facing window stood like a one-eyed cyclops dead center in the outside wall.

"There you go, Tony!" Peabody watched as the pony nearly disappeared into the tall grass.

Peabody walked to the wall, then pointed. "A vein of sulfides and quartz lies just along the base of the wall," said Peabody, pointing at the place where the rocky material changed, behind and beyond the shack. "I've mined here for years. Called it the Peabody Mine, after me, of course." Corbett could sense a dry, quirky personality hidden in the forlorn figure. "We all came up here for gold but found silver instead. I've found enough gold to fill a tooth or so, and enough silver to pay the bills."

Peabody, for a moment, observed his pony Tony again, loose in its willowy empire. He invited Corbett inside. The large one-room estate had a rock fireplace settled in one corner, a round table in front of the window, and two chairs. A cowhide covered his lie-back chair. Another hide, maybe bear, covered the small bed opposite the fireplace. A thick, heavy door dominated the back wall.

"This big door goes right into the mine." Peabody chuckled to himself. "I thought I was mining in a straight line until I popped right out into the field again. Tony uses the other entrance for a barn in winter. Damned good idea, I believe it to be."

Peabody stepped back outside and excused himself. He began walking down into the tall crowded willows next to the stream. Corbett, uninvited, sat on the stone entrance to the shack. Not long after, Peabody returned with a dead rabbit.

"We'll eat good tonight," he said, holding up the furry beast. "I snare two or three a week all year round. They love my willows."

The meal went quickly and quietly, Peabody in his world and Corbett in his. The afternoon was spent. A world of shadows began gathering around the darkening cabin.

"I have to spend about a week back down in Silverton moving wood about," said Peabody, smoking an ancient pipe at the edge of the fire. "If you don't find your father in a day or two, I could pay you some eating money to come down and help."

Peabody surely did not have many guests, but he was patient with Corbett, whose eyes lingered on the fire. Corbett's mind wondered why he was in a mine shaft and why he was looking for Laddie, who would not care a bit if he did not find him.

It was morning; the lie-back chair had served him well. Corbett saw that Peabody had water boiling next to the fire. Boiling along with the water was a mixture of leaves and berries. The smell was sweet and fruity. Seeing that Corbett was awake, Peabody suggested, "You might ask at the bar in Kalamazoo about your father, if he's the drinking type. A month in the mines makes for an episode of drinking after coming down off the mountain."

"Sorry," replied Corbett, rising from the depths. "Yeah, I bet that's exactly what he would do. And you are right about the altitude. I might go up the road a spell, but I was kind of sick all day yesterday. I probably wouldn't get far."

"I never drink this water, no more, without boiling it good." Peabody's day had begun. "Several years ago, I drank, a big face-down kind of drink, from my stream. Calling it good, I walked ahead upstream for a few steps and saw a dead deer right in the middle of the creek, with maggots above, on the ribs, and with pinkish-white meat below the waterline. Gagged for a week."

3

Peabody's idea of checking at the two bars for Laddie, or at least a sighting, was the day's first plan of action. Sitting on a bench in front of Newton's General Store and Bar, Corbett did not feel a bit well. Even though a wagon passed now and then, a wagon trip higher to the upper mines would have to wait, if he were to take one at all. Peabody was already on the road down to Silverton. If nothing else, he was a survivor. He was intrinsically happy with himself, caring not what others thought.

When the general store opened, Corbett entered, first seeking a bit of food, but mostly hoping to find some information. Inside the store were canned goods, beer, and miner's supplies. It was naked for a store, but it was a hell of a place to have a store to begin with, Corbett thought. The owner was busy taking the chairs down from the tabletops and arranging them around the three poker tables.

"Can I help you?"

"I was hoping you might know a miner named Laddie Jones," Corbett said, lifting down a chair to help.

"Don't know about the Jones part, but I know Laddie," said the owner, spitting into a nearby brass spittoon. "I hear that he's a pretty damn good miner, but down here he's just trouble."

Corbett said in disgust to himself, *I just found him.* "Is he in town now?"

"Naw, I think I saw him flat-assed drunk in the back of a wagon going north yesterday," replied the owner, now wiping down the tables. "I imagine they'll be up there now, until they're snowed out."

"Is he still at the Irish Rose?"

"I wouldn't know that, but you can go next door to the Kalamazoo and ask for Sharon. When he is not drinking and gambling, he's up at her cabin screwing like a rabbit." Ever disappointed, Corbett dropped his head and began to walk out the door. "If he owes you money, you'll have to get in line."

When Sharon came out of the kitchen, drying her hands, Corbett knew that he had seen a hundred just like her. Once she had been a prime whore with a big chest, a small butt, and long hair that looked good on any man's pillow. Now the chest had given way to gravity, and drunkenness had stolen her shapely butt, leaving her with thin chicken legs. The south side of Durango was loaded with women like this.

"Well, hello, tiger. Whatever can I do for you?" Sharon could still talk the talk. Who knew if she could walk the walk.

"I understand that you know Laddie Jones."

"That sorry son of a bitch!" Sharon's demeanor was incensed. "He comes down here and steals my money when his runs out. Comes up to the cabin and rides me like I'm the rodeo." It was not that Corbett was speechless; it was just that she had a lot to get off her chest, mostly Laddie Jones. "Guess what he said when I told him I was knocked up? He said, 'Get on down to your mama, 'cause I ain't going to take care of ya! I am catching the train out of here as soon as I can afford it.' The bastard! Now what do you want with him?" Her were teeth clenched; her jaw was set.

Corbett had spent his whole life being let down by his father. It would end someday, hopefully. "He owes me money. I came to collect," Corbett lied.

Since he was unable to bring himself to catch a ride on a freight wagon passing by, he had begun to walk south toward Silverton. If the truth were to be told, Corbett was feeling sorry for himself. He had nobody. His friends and his mother were dead; his father, no more than a bad memory. In the three-hour walk, his melancholy turned to depression. Surely there was a reason for his being, but he could not think what it might be.

After three hours of Corbett's walking toward Silverton, the road split. To the left was the bridge across to Silverton, and to the left, back off the road, stood a mansion nestled among pines and aspens, just before the foothills that rose quickly up to the giant mountains. A fenced pasture followed the lane to the house. The house was huge with gables this way and that. The cedar shakes were perfectly aligned. The window frames seemed freshly painted, as did the porch rails. The large barn, livery, and woodshed matched in every way. The road to the house was crushed rock, not dirt.

Corbett thought little of the mansion until he saw Peabody driving a lumber wagon up the lane toward the house.

"Peabody!" Corbett was happy to see the little fellow. "Need some help?"

"Oh my gosh," said Peabody, pulling a slab from the wagon. "I'd rather be mining, where at least there is some shade and a chance for a nugget." Instead of dragging each slab to the saw-horses, Corbett carried each slab. "Damn, you're strong." Corbett appreciated being appreciated at this minute. He had altitude sickness, but the work seemed to refresh him.

The slabs Peabody and Corbett were unloading were about ten feet long and heavy. Some were green and heavier. With tree trunks being round, the lumber derived from the trunks needed to be square. The rounded part of the trunk that was sawed away was the slab. It dried better this way and was easier to handle.

"Did you find your father?" Peabody stopped, concerned about what Corbett had been concerned about earlier this morning.

"It didn't work out so good," said Corbett, moving yet another slab. "He is more of a jackass up here than in Durango. I don't even want to meet up with him anymore."

"That's too bad. You're welcome to work here with me until you're ready to go off the hill."

"Is the pay good?" said Corbett, smiling.

"You're working for me," replied Peabody. "What do you think?"

With Corbett's help, the slabs were turned to firewood at a record pace. Each night the two men received a fine meal from the house, prepared by an oriental woman, with beer. The hefty meal consisted of meat, vegetables, and rice or potatoes. Fresh straw brought up by the train covered the floors of all five stalls in the livery. Corbett and Peabody slept well.

Toward the end of the week, Peabody's cart was loaded with firewood and his pony was ready for the trip home. Corbett watched from the woodshed as Peabody talked to an older woman on her porch. He had noticed that this woman watched him and Peabody work from time to time.

Suddenly, Peabody waved, beckoning Corbett up to the house. Corbett was wearing the dirtiest of his two shirts. With his hair unkempt, he felt poorly presented, but a "How do you do?" before leaving seemed natural.

"Corbett, this is Mrs. Portman." Peabody and Mrs. Portman seemed good friends, he with nothing but a worthless silver mine and she in fine clothing, wearing a necklace and earrings that were as valuable as some of the mines.

"Corbett, nice to meet you." She had a rich southern voice, and she was much older than he would have thought from his view at a distance. A large woman who stood straight and proper, she had a friendly persona, but something about her made Corbett feel that she was not to be crossed.

"Thank you, ma'am," he replied, shaking her hand.

"Please, sit." The couch was larger than many homes. Their seats at the linen-covered table gave a great panoramic view of Silverton and the tall, majestic mountain range that surrounded it.

"Peabody told me all about you and your last few days." Corbett stared briefly at Peabody, not knowing where this was going. Corbett, over the course of some days, had told Peabody about Durango, Laddie, and his uncertain future. It had been an outlet, and Corbett had taken advantage of it. "How you have been able to handle all of that at such a young age is beyond me. I lost my husband three months ago, and it's nearly killed me."

"Sorry, ma'am," Corbett responded. She was not looking for sympathy, just stating a fact.

"This is my home. I am trying to put the pieces together. Peabody has done our wood for a couple of years, and I trust him to give advice on making a life here." One would never guess that the dirty little man who lived in a mine would be a confidant to those who lived in this house.

She continued, "I asked him to be on the lookout for a man to do odd jobs around here, someone I could trust." She looked at Corbett with a smile on her face. "He said that man is you."

This was a revelation. Peabody, that poor fellow who several days earlier had asked for a crust of bread from Corbett's cart, had just given Corbett a place from which to start a new life. This was only the second job in his life. Laddie had provided the first when he was too drunk to drive the coal wagon and Corbett covered for him.

"For a while, that stall would be your home, until I see how this works out. Two meals a day just like this week." Mrs. Portman had thought about this. "Seven dollars a week."

Two weeks past, Peabody collected his pay in wood and delivered that wood home twice. Orders each day were delivered with Corbett's breakfast. Emi, the cook, provided good food but little dialogue. Her English was marginal at best. Her Japanese dress seemed out of place at the livery.

The work was ordinary and mundane, basically serving as a gardener and maintenance man. Corbett's only trial came as Mrs. Portman needed a driver to attend a meeting at the Grand Imperial. Harnessing and preparing the covered carriage was not the problem. Touching the reins and sitting again in the driver's seat was. Anxiety and panicky flashbacks overtook Corbett as he waited for Mrs. Portman. Somehow, her no-nonsense appearance relaxed him a bit and drove away the ghosts.

As time went on, Corbett was surprised at the number of expensive carriages and important men who came daily to the house. From their drivers, Corbett learned that the late Mr. Portman happened to be a rich mine owner and a chief investor in the Sultan tunnel located in the high mountains to the north. The word was that other mine owners in the area were attempting various takeover scenarios. Mrs. Portman was not yielding to the pressure in the least. The drivers sided with their owners, believing that her late husband's job was just too powerful a position for a woman.

Mrs. Portman's first lieutenant was Miss Wallace, thirtyish, the mansion's bundle of energy, small but mighty. Serving as secretary and main confidant, she had black curls and big brown eyes, with look-over-the-top wire glasses that added to her age and took away from the potential of beauty. Single and married to her job, she welcomed guests and saw them off.

Each Friday, Corbett received seven dollars in an envelope from

Mrs. Portman, by way of Emi, delivered with breakfast. Corbett had yet to speak to Miss Wallace directly.

The other oddity about the Portman mansion was the arrival each day of two covered buckboards full of children. Peabody knew no more than Corbett. Both thought that schooling of some kind was done inside, but that was just a guess.

Except when Peabody was there, Corbett's only outlet was Haruyo, the housekeeper. She had tea about the same time as Corbett had his evening meal. She often invited him to eat at a picnic table on the lawn near the house. Homesick and yearning for someone of her own nationality, Japanese, of course, she spoke passable English. Her conversation was limited to the weather, the beautiful surroundings, and Japan. Mount Kita in Japan, she believed, was superior to any of the mountains in the United States. She and Emi were twin sisters. Corbett had not known that for about a month. He just thought it was one busy Japanese woman who changed clothes two or three times a day. Their thin, boy-like bodies and diminutive stature made them seem like young boys from a distance.

The job was satisfying, giving Corbett a stable existence, until the night it took a turn.

"Corbett! Corbett!" Emi screamed. "Bad men!"

Corbett was awake in a second. Emi was wide-eyed, pointing to the house. Without a gun or a knife, Corbett reached for the hatchet used that morning to chop kindling. He saw lights in the main living area. Peering through the window, he saw two men, each carrying a lantern yelling and threatening Mrs. Portman and Miss Wallace, who sat frightened in the same overstuffed chair. The changing shadows caused by the lanterns added to the terror. The larger of the two men stood in front of the women, demanding money, while the other looked about for something to steal.

Corbett reached down, found a rock, and handed it to Emi, who was just behind him. "Go throw this rock through that side window." Emi looked at the rock and then at Corbett, not understanding. "Emi, go throw the rock, then run."

Corbett stepped to the front door and waited for the crash of the window. When it came, he hesitated until the larger man shouted, "Go see what in the hell that is!"

By the time the bigger robber had turned to face the noise behind him, Corbett hit him solidly in the ear with the blunt edge of the hatchet. The man's gun went off. Corbett, not having seen a gun, fell back toward the door. The gunshot caused Hok'ee's face to appear for an instant. The fallen lantern darkened the room. The smaller robber reentered the room but could only see the brightness next to his partner. His subconscious move was to bend down to aid his fallen friend.

Corbett, uninjured and somewhat recovered from the shock of the surprise explosion from the gun, attacked the remaining gunman. His momentum carried both of them to the feet of the screaming women. Like Laddie once said, an overhand right is always the first fist to come forward. Corbett's right fist smashed into his opponent's face, rearranging those bones forever. There was no second shot. Both men, moaning, had been disabled.

Miss Wallace raced to the kitchen and returned with a large butcher knife. In her state of daze, she was about to carve into the two robbers like a Thanksgiving turkey. Haruyo, in her nightclothes, grabbed both Miss Wallace's arms from behind and held on.

Corbett bound both robbers, who were still out cold. With trepidation, the twins applied clean dressings to both faces. As the night progressed, each of the robbers awoke in pain and delirium. Mrs. Portman had found a used bottle of laudanum, an opioid used for pain, in her husband's medication chest. She gave each man a dose. The pain and delirium subsided as the men fell into unconsciousness. With both robbers tied and bound, they lay in the foyer, ready for removal to the San Juan Jail in Silverton in the morning. Corbett and the four women sat at the large dining room table, exhausted.

Before this night, the idea of having the Japanese women or Corbett ever sit at this table would have been absurd. Two guns lying on the table also would have been absurd.

"I have never been so frightened," said Miss Wallace in a whisper. Both she and Mrs. Portman were on their second hot toddy. "The gunshot terrified me, and then I saw Corbett fall back." She looked directly into his eyes. "I thought you were killed."

"You must know how thankful we are that you were here to save us." Mrs. Portman grinned, her gray-white hair falling unceremoniously to her shoulders. "Just like Peabody said you would be."

"I have two thoughts on this." Mrs. Portman thought everything through. "You must have a gun. Take these. Or, if you would rather have a different one, I will buy it for you." Corbett considered both guns. He had never had a gun before and was unsure if he really wanted one. But then, thinking of Hok'ee, he took the smaller revolver.

"This night brought to my attention the need to have a man in the house. Haruyo will prepare the large storage room next to the back door for Corbett."

"Yes, ma'am," replied Haruyo, pleased with the decision.

"At first light, take these two to the jail," Mrs. Portman said to Corbett. "Breakfast will be served in the kitchen, where you will take your meals from this time on." She rose from the table. "I am off to bed."

As foul weather up high began to bring ore wagons from the upper mines, the tunnel filled with miners done with the year's work. The mobs of golden-leafed aspens on the hillsides surrounding Silverton signaled that the mining season was over. Over half the men would catch the train and return to their homes off the mountain. This was the point in the year when they had the most money, some ready to drink it up or gamble it away.

Subconsciously, Corbett observed the wagons from the mansion grounds. No longer interested in Laddie, he still looked. There was a scarred place somewhere down in his soul, still yearning for Laddie to be a father.

"Corbett!" shouted Miss Wallace from the porch. "Mrs. Portman wants you!" Most days Corbett carried out his chores without any contact with Mrs. Portman.

"Corbett, I understand that you cannot read the orders that you get each morning." Mrs. Portman was quite perturbed. "Emi has to read them to you. She can barely speak English, but she can read!"

Corbett was taken aback. "Sorry, ma'am. I just never learned." Where would that have happened, the West Texas dirt farm ten miles from a semblance of a town? Or might it have taken place sometime during his middle teens, when Corbett had gone from helping in the laundry to hauling coal? "I guess it just never happened."

"Starting tomorrow," Mrs. Portman said, being very definitive with her instructions, "you will help me with the children." To the previous two covered buckboards was added a third, which arrived midmorning and left after a good lunch in the early afternoon. "These are miners' children learning to read and write. As you help them, you will learn to read and write as well."

The astonishing nature of Mrs. Portman's pronouncement sent Corbett reeling. With no experience with children, and with no appetite to gain any, he was going to school. A tiny smirk played on his lips.

"Then at seven each evening you are to go into Mr. Portman's library and read for an hour. Understood?!"

Corbett hoped for many picture books.

Snow removal in Silverton represented the ultimate challenge to the community to keep the place a year-round town. Corbett's task was to keep open the lane from the house to the main road. Ashes from both coal and woodstoves were spread along the lane. Those moments when the sun was out, its rays were absorbed by the black ashes, melting the snow. During every storm, Corbett used a two-horse snowplow to shove the snow to the side of the lane. Mrs. Portman had hired unemployed miners to hand-shovel certain areas along the road, as had the business owners in town.

By the time the children arrived, Corbett had worked several hours so their wagons could make it to the mansion. The kids dug their way out from under the heavy quilts and then climbed down from the buckboards, walking in through the side door of the house.

After some warm tea, the children sat at the tables, where white-covered books lay in front of them. Corbett looked at the large lettering on the front cover of the books. It would be weeks before he would be able to read the words *McGuffey Readers*. Emi and Haruyo moved about the room, helping the children. Corbett sat with the youngest of the students. He was astounded by the fact that each one of these marks made a sound, and if one put the sounds together, then a word came about.

The sight of a strongly built young man surrounded by youngsters who were enunciating the same sounds made Mrs. Portman proud and happy. Her only child, years ago, was stillborn. Money had bought her everything she wanted but a child of her own. These children this late in life were grandchildren of a child that might have been.

Mr. Portman's library smelled of stale cigar smoke. Beautiful brown paneling and bookshelves provided the ambience of a different world, a serene environment. By the third night, Corbett read out of a picture book for the first time: "We go. Do we go? We do go. We do so. See us go. We go so. Go as we go."

Having broken into the magic of reading, Corbett felt proud as he'd never felt before. As he moved through the McGuffey Readers, each day learning different rules of the road, it was like a blossom the first time it was exposed to the sun. He excited the young students about reading. He and Emi struggled through *Heidi*, a popular new book, during the evening reading time.

Mrs. Portman, a powerful mining figure, took such pleasure in these students each day that during the mealtime, she read to them. *Gulliver's Travels* was the first, followed by *The Adventures of Tom Sawyer*.

Given more responsibilities each day, Corbett was often sent into Silverton as a messenger to pick up supplies. However, this day he was to find men to help with the collapsed coal shed. Mr. Portman always used to order two wagons of coal in the fall from Durango. By coincidence, this was from the same mine for which Corbett had hauled coal for in Durango. The last heavy snow had brought the storage shed down.

Midday Silverton in the winter was quiet and slow. Men who wanted to work were shoveling somewhere for someone. Corbett decided to check the bars for prospects. He had not been two minutes in the Kendall Mountain Bar before he saw Laddie, who was comfortably slouched in a chair next to the fire with Lilly sitting on his lap.

"Hey, blondie, you still up here?" asked Lilly, tucked in comfortably. She remembered the day at the station when she and the other young women had met this handsome boy.

"Hell, is that you, Corbett?" Laddie did not rise. Neither did Lilly.

"Hello, Laddie." Corbett no longer wanted this conversation.

"How did you get up here in all this weather?"

"I've been here for about five months." His voice was slow and measured; his emotion, flat and obvious.

"Who you mining for?" Laddie raised his arm toward Corbett as to show him off for the first time. "Look how damned big this kid is!" Anything or anybody new to the bar took attention away from the boredom of being drunk.

"I work for Mrs. Portman."

"So do I. Which mine?"

"I work at her mansion."

"You a servant or something? I'll bet she is a bitch!"

"No, she's a fine lady." Corbett had never questioned Laddie's word before. This was not father to son; it was man-to-man.

"Bullshit!" Laddie roughly moved Lilly off his lap and stood, making a scene as he did so. The bar quieted as Laddie stepped toward Corbett. "You come up here to kick my ass?" he asked, cocky as a bantam rooster.

"No, I came up here to tell you that my mother is dead. I looked for you until I met Sharon. She convinced me you were a bastard and would never change. Nothing new. So I gave up on you."

Laddie said the first thing that came to his mind: "Hell, your mother was dead before I ever left her!"

"Laddie, you're an ass," Corbett said flatly.

As Laddie always predicted, the overhand right was the first fist to be thrown in a bar fight. The problem with the punch was that Corbett had grown up dodging it. Corbett blocked the punch and landed a powerful right hook low into the ribs of Laddie. He watched his father drop to his knees, waiting for a counterpunch. Whatever was to happen, this would be the end of it. Laddie came up with the legs of a wooden bar chair, preparing to swing the chair at Corbett's head.

Again, using his father's advice from long ago to load up and throw an overhand right, Corbett did just that. The blow lifted Laddie up and over the table behind him.

That was that.

"I understand that you were in a bar fight yesterday." Corbett knew this was serious. Mrs. Portman was sitting at her husband's desk in his study. Corbett had never been in this room before. "One of my mining superintendents said it was all over town about you being in a brawl. Is that true?"

"I don't know about it being all over town, but I was in a fight."

"I can't have you working here and setting a bad example of us out there."

"It was my father whom I fought with." Corbett's eyes and head dropped a little; his father was going to ruin something else in Corbett's life. "I told him about my mother's death, and he got smart about it. Now that I am a little bigger than him, he wanted to show he could still whip me."

Amazed by the story, Mrs. Portman asked, "Did he hurt you?"

"No, I'm fine. I don't think either of us will want to see the other."

Mrs. Portman knew the story and thought this might be the end of it. The superintendent's story about the fight was told from a different perspective. He'd said that a muscular young man had come into the bar looking to fight a drunk a bit smaller than he. Knowing the full story eased Mrs. Portman's worry. In fact, she wished she had been there herself. She had heard the last punch was a dandy.

The work order this day at the breakfast table was unusual indeed. Corbett sounded out the words *Peabody* and *coal*, and already he knew the word *food*. He had Emi read it for clarity. Corbett was to check on Peabody and take him a wagon of sacked coal and food. The past week happened to be sunny and warm. The road north to Animas Forks was open and sloppy with old snow and melted water. The relationship between Mrs. Portman and Peabody was unusual except for the fact that Mrs. Portman had a kind heart and appreciated the honesty and hard work Peabody put in just to survive.

The trip provided Corbett with the spectacle of the high mountains of Colorado in winter. The aspens were dropping clots of melted snow, the willows becoming upright after dropping their snow. The road displayed one set of wagon tracks used by both coming traffic and going traffic. When wagons met, both parties worked together to solve the impasse.

Corbett stopped off the roadway. Peabody's cart path showed no signs of having been used. The snow was four feet high, whether on the cart path or not. Corbett snowshoed in through the maze of trees and brush. Peabody, in just his long underwear, was sitting with his back to the great stone wall, his eyes closed, sunning himself. The pony was lying on dry ground four or five feet from the wall, doing the same thing. Acting the part of watchdog, the pony stumbled to its feet and shook itself.

"Peabody!"

Surprised by the voice, Peabody nearly fell out of his chair.

The cabin and a good share of the ground beyond to the mine shaft used by the pony had been stomped down by use.

"Peabody, I was worried about you."

"Oh, I'm here till I die. Then I hope somebody will take my body into the mine and seal it up." Peabody walked to the edge of the stomped-on snow. "How are you, Corbett?"

"Mrs. Portman sent you up some grub and several sacks of coal."

"Bless that woman's heart. I think my appetite could use a good change." Peabody walked toward the door of his cabin. "Want some tea?"

During their chat, Corbett admired the warmth radiating from the tall rock face. The snow level in the Silverton–Animas Forks area was four feet or higher, but next to this south-facing wall, the ground was dry.

"How did you find this place? It's amazing."

"Ah, just luck." Peabody watched his pony topping the willow sprouts that showed through the snow in the field. "The first two years up here, I was the last gold panner to leave in the fall. The third summer, I filed on this claim and overstayed in the fall. I was trapped by the heavy snow. Did you ever hear of blind luck?"

Corbett liked this place; he could live here. The vista east along the wall was maybe half a mile, and the sun, magnified by its absorption and reflection, warmed it all.

"Some deer survive through the winter up here. They do so by finding little places like this. Right now, there are probably six or eight living up the valley there." He smiled. "My mine just happened to be here. I always have meat—rabbits and deer mostly. I have a nice buck hanging in the mine right now."

"Your pony is really getting after the aspen starts." What seemed to be a grassy meadow dotted with year-old willows and aspens in the summer was, in winter, tasty tops presenting themselves just above the snow.

When the talking was done, the two men pulled a sled from

the mine and walked it out through the maze to the waiting horses and wagon. Fighting the wagon through all the snow into the hidden valley was not going to happen. Instead, the horses were unharnessed and led through one at a time, pulling the sled and a wagon sideboard loaded with supplies and coal.

While Corbett was harnessing the horses for the trip home, Peabody made his final exit from the valley with two white rabbits.

"Tell Emi to make some good rabbit stew. I snared them this morning. They love my willows."

Using teams to pull snowplows and Mormon boards, Corbett kept Silverton's heavy snows at bay. Coal he hauled in during the summer from Durango, along with aspen and pine from the area, kept the potbellied stoves and fireplaces full and warm. Animas Forks was still trying to be a year-round town. Newton's General Store and Bar, along with the Kalamazoo Hotel, was able to stay open, barely. Snow finally stopped the D&RG winter train from coming up the Animas Valley to Silverton.

It was Christmas.

Aged elk, wild turkey, venison, and cutthroat trout all made it to the tables of the miners' Christmas bash. With the fear that the miners would not return the next spring, the mine owners sponsored dances and bingo nights to encourage the miners to stay the winter. The return of any miners who wintered in Silverton was a sure thing.

The whole Portman household was going to the Grand Imperial. The twins were taking a Japanese dessert for the first time. They called it *dango*, a grilled floury gob skewered on a short stick and dipped into Emi's berry and honey sauce. Mrs. Portman had packed jars of honey, and Jenny Wallace had made bowls of buttery taffy. Corbett prepared the carriage and even had his derby brushed and ready. Hot stones placed beneath the pile of blankets made the carriage trip more comfortable.

The young Japanese women were being silly, speaking to each other in Japanese, delightfully happy to ride in the main carriage to the strange religious festival. It was not an accident that Miss Wallace, now on a first-name basis like Jenny, had chosen to ride at Corbett's side. Corbett had sensed for a couple weeks now that she was watching him more and more. During schooltime in tight quarters, she had brushed by him more than once. However, just like the three young prostitutes Lilly, Margaret, and Esther, Miss Wallace lit no fires. Corbett, now nineteen, still struggled with the constant notion that he must not ever become interested in women. Once he had had a chance to be happy, but now Ajai was gone.

"Thanks for having the stones ready," whispered Jenny, climbing in next to Corbett. Jenny had not been around men much during her adult life. Mr. Portman had lived in the same house as Jenny Wallace, but their relationship was lifetimes apart. Jenny Wallace had wondered at times if Mr. Portman knew her first name or where she lived.

Jenny had grown up in a staunch Pentecostal family, an only child to old parents. Anything having to do with men was a sin and disgraceful. Feelings erupted in her late twenties, entirely in juxtaposition to her early upbringing. Even though no one cared enough to call her a spinster, she felt like one. A yearning to feel a kiss or to touch a man's skin ran deep within her, both mentally and physically.

Every table and chair in Silverton seemed to be present. The crowd seemed to be wearing their best. For some, this was just one step up from rags. Mrs. Portman, the only mine owner who wintered in Silverton, might as well have been the queen. Her long table was open to all. She showed affection to all who wanted it.

Laughter and good food made the hard lives of the community disappear, at least for this one day.

Corbett had just gotten settled with a second helping of turkey gravy and mashed potatoes. "Corbett!" came a female squeal. "You're wearing my hat!" Esther, standing to the side of Corbett, bent over and surrounded him with her hug. "I can't believe you're still here. Did you find your Irish Rose? Is this her?" Esther leaned around to see Jenny sitting on Corbett's other side.

"I'm doing fine, thanks." Corbett liked Esther, kind of like a sister he didn't know he had. "And you?"

"First off, I'm starving. Can I sit here?"

"Sure." As Corbett reached out from his sitting position to pull the chair out for Esther, he noticed the enlarged girth trying to fit between the table and the chair. As Esther settled, he asked with a smirk, "What happened here?"

"Well, that fellow who left his derby that you now have …" Esther made a "Guess what?" kind of face. "He left me a gift as well." She immediately got distracted with food plates coming her way from the other end of the table.

"Who's she?" whispered Jenny, a little testy. She had not chosen to sit next to Corbett to be upstaged by this loud, uncouth sort of young woman.

"Oh, I met her when I first got here. She's a friend of mine," Corbett replied, laughing at Esther's antics. "She even gave me this hat."

"She's pregnant," Jenny said, again whispering. "So young."

"If you are going to play in the pond, she plays in, sooner or later you are going to get wet."

"Did you find your father?" asked Esther, rejoining the conversation.

"I did," said Corbett. "That's him over with Lilly." Laddie and several of the others from the bar were knee-deep in elk steaks. Lilly was the only female with the group.

"That's your father?" Esther, nearly shouting, repeated, "That's your father?"

Corbett glanced again at Laddie as if to make sure. "Yep, that's him."

"He's a bastard. He treats Lilly so mean. I think he even pays off his gambling debts with her."

Jenny looked past Corbett and toward the group. "The one with the beer in his hand?"

"Yep," said Corbett, sopping up the last of the gravy with a piece of sourdough bread from the Blair Street Bakery.

Both the young women thought the same thing at the same time: *How could this handsome, polite young man have come from the drunk across the way?*

Esther leaned forward and across Corbett to Jenny, saying, "You take care of this fellow. He's a keeper."

Jenny's chest rose in surprise. Esther actually thought that she was Corbett's woman!

"I w-will," Jenny stuttered. "I will," she said, this time more assuredly.

After the meal, there was time to mill around and visit with old friends. Jenny stayed right with Corbett, even when he stood talking among a group of miners. When Corbett spoke of an outhouse call, Jenny almost followed.

Mrs. Portman called Jenny to aid her in the handing out of hot cider to the multitudes.

Corbett milled about, looking for people he knew. He waved at Mabel, the little mouse. To her right, offering her some cider, was a young Mexican, quite short but muscular. *He must be Miguel,* Corbett thought. Both were having a good night.

Later, Corbett saw Peabody chatting with Haruyo while stuffing himself with dango, holding three striped candy canes tightly in his left hand. "Peabody, I thought you never came off your claim in the winter." Peabody's toothless smile was as wide as his face.

"I come down if I can. Sometimes the road is closed to Silverton." Peabody was as happy as a pony with a ripe apple. "Twice, I came down on the wrong day, damn it to hell." He laughed at himself.

"So, I gather it is all about the food."

"The sweets, Corbett, the sweets!" Peabody exclaimed, holding the three candy canes. "I love sweets. Mrs. Portman saved me a whole jar of honey. Ain't that something?"

"So, it is about the food."

"Ya think I came down to see your ugly mug?"

Several conversations later, Stanley Moore approached Corbett. Stanley, who worked at the lumber mill as a sawyer, donated wood to the church where he served an elder. Nearly bald under his stocking cap, he did have a nicely groomed beard and mustache that covered his rounded face. Not short and fat, he was, rather, short and solid. He and Corbett spent a few moments talking about the weather and a possible firewood shortage. Most of the dry stuff was gone at the mill, and the green wood would not burn.

"Corbett," Stanley said, not beating around the proverbial bush, "may I ask about your intentions toward Miss Wallace? I've seen you with her most of the night."

"Sure. We both work for Mrs. Portman. She's just a friend," Corbett said, his easy smile causing Stanley to relax. "She is not very comfortable in large groups, but I think she feels safe with me."

"I'm wondering whether Miss Wallace would consider me as a possible suitor. She caught my eye the first time I saw her." Stanley was quite anxious to get the embarrassing truth out and settle the question.

"Well, I can't answer that," replied Corbett. "But I think her to be lonely." Then Corbett broke out into a big laugh. Stanley stared. "It might be, Stanley, that a bit of chivalry is just what she needs." Then on second thought, he added, "How well do you know her?"

"I talked to her twice when she came down to the mill to pay the Portman bill."

"The dance starts in about an hour. Find me then. I will officially introduce you."

The days were so short and the nights so chilly that the burning of the Yule log for the children and families occurred about the time the sun was lost over the mountains. The Yule log showed signs that it would stay lit. The wooden planks the mill had hauled in to serve as the dance floor were being stomped together by the dancers in preparation.

"Jenny, come with me," said Corbett as he pulled her out of her chair near the Yule log. Miss Wallace commonly sat there to quietly finish the celebration. "You have an admirer." Jenny hadn't really held back while Corbett was walking her away from her seat until the word *admirer* was spoken. Jenny set her heels. *Me? An admirer? A man?* Confused thoughts ran through Jenny's mind.

"Corbett, what is this about?" asked Jenny, flying high on anxiety.

A harmonica, along with a banjo and guitar, began the dance with a lively tune. Lanterns hanging about added to the cheerfulness of the dance floor.

It was not a minute until Stanley Moore presented himself to Corbett and Jenny. He nodded to both and offered Jenny a special little chocolate cake purchased from the bakery yesterday. Chocolate was like gold in these mountains. For five months each winter, none could be brought in.

"Jenny, you remember Stanley from the mill?" Corbett's words would have sounded a lot like wedding nuptials to him if he had ever been to a wedding, but he had not ever attended such a ceremony. "He would like to be your escort this evening."

Both men looked at Jenny. Would she suddenly revert back to Miss Wallace, or would she listen to her heart? Jenny gave a look to Corbett that transmitted her message without sound: *You'd better come and get me if things go bad.* She offered her gloved hand to Stanley, who received it with his leather glove. To have a man who appreciated her, to be close enough to touch his skin, caused Jenny's heart to race.

The moment was awkward right up to Esther's loud voice saying, "Corbett, let's dance!" Without an affirmative answer, Corbett was dragged onto the dance floor. Corbett did not know how to dance, but for the first slow dance it did not matter much. Except for the growing baby between them, Esther and Corbett danced as one. She led.

Corbett saw Jenny twice during the dance. The first time, she was wide-eyed and quite stilted, leaning back a little from Stanley's beard. The second time, Corbett's and Jenny's eyes met as both were dancing, Corbett with Haruyo and Jenny with Stanley. Jenny smiled and held close to Stanley, a dream fulfilled.

The darkness and cold began to draw the Christmas party participants away to their homes. The Yule log was reduced to reddened embers as the lanterns began failing, one at a time.

Corbett, alone on the driver's seat of the carriage, listened to Jenny and the twins excitedly recap the night.

Mrs. Portman, utterly exhausted, leaned back on a cushion and watched the large, quiet snowflakes descend. "It was a good day."

4

In a blue suit and red tie, Corbett had the look of a prosperous businessman. Church had caused this. Sitting in the congregational church pew for the fourth Sunday in a row, he was this week learning about the burning bush. Corbett, judging from their solemn expressions, saw how important the message was to those in attendance. Stanley and Jenny, sitting close together, were the reason that Corbett was present. After Corbett had introduced them to each other, Jenny did a bit of whining until Corbett took her to church the next Sunday at Stanley's church. He had had to go in himself; the idea of his waiting at the carriage was dimly viewed by the women of the house.

Mrs. Portman had given Haruyo two of her late husband's suits to alter into church suits for Corbett. Dragging his feet was to no avail. Corbett normally spent Sunday mornings hurriedly doing chores and harnessing the carriage for church. The main problem with church was that it was on a Sunday. And Sunday constituted Corbett's only day off. The half day in and the half day out contradicted the whole premise of a day off work. The second Sunday, with head bowed, Corbett prayed that church be moved to a Tuesday. He was not against God; it was just that he and God had different ideas about Sunday.

Corbett's perfect Sunday would be to spend a late morning in bed and then pass the entire afternoon in the library. To be fair to God, Corbett spent time with the Bible. Starting at the beginning, he moved through the book rapidly, until the many names and *begat*s overran him. He finally concluded that the words printed in red were the most important. Church must be for the translation of thoughts to the people in the pews, he thought. At Saint Patrick's, he heard, they did this in some other language.

Three weeks later, Stanley, bless his soul, sauntered up to Corbett immediately after church. "If it would be okay with you, I would like to bring Jenny home later." To Corbett's good fortune, that afternoon led to Stanley's arrival at the mansion at exactly nine o'clock each Sunday morning thereafter.

Reading had become the passion of Corbett's life. Every book in the library appeared appealing; stories of characters and places influenced the thoughts of his day. *Moby-Dick* and *Treasure Island* transported him to places where there were adventures for him to experience and wonder about. The only other book besides the Bible to overwhelm Corbett happened to be over two hundred years old and from Spain: *Don Quixote*. Attacking windmills with his sidekick Sancho Panza was unrestrained fun. However, Cervantes's levels of hell were lost on Corbett.

Mrs. Portman, once the leader of the school, saw herself replaced within two months by her protégé. Corbett brought the room to life, writing words on the slate board that he, too, had just learned. Where she had been proper, he was playful. For some of the short stories that proved to be difficult, Corbett put on quick little one-act plays. It is said that for anything to be long remembered, emotion must be present, to give the thought longevity. Corbett imbued his readings with emotion.

Mrs. Portman laughed at her anomaly, a coal-hauling boy with a wretched past completely capable of mesmerizing two dozen small children. Each day with morning tea, she and Jenny watched him and the children in a frenzy to learn. Corbett's workload outside was ever a labor: snow, wood, coal, clinkers, ashes, hay, grain, and more road. His time with the children was a pleasure.

Haruyo, more than once, woke Corbett late at night sitting at a table in the library, a book at his side. His day was done.

It had been a week since the battle for the Silverton roads ensued. An angry late winter storm full of blowing snow had come in from the west. Each day a foot or more snow settled, not heavy and wet, but large flakes forming a huge volume. There was no more room for snow. Corbett fought for mere pathways to the coal shed, the woodshed, and the livery.

For enough coal and wood for the house, it took him half a day's hauling. The other half was spent dragging a sled full of hay to the livery. The hay for the three horses was in the barn. There were times when visibility was so poor that one building could not be distinguished from another. The grain might be gone in two or three weeks. The two draft horses, who were used constantly early on when it was thought the road could remain open, were now just happy to be inside.

Thomas, Mr. Portman's saddle horse, was part thoroughbred, so it was tall and quite high-strung. The sight of the high snow peeking over the Dutch doors of the livery made Thomas more skittish than ever. The horse had not been ridden since Mr. Portman's death. Mrs. Portman did not ride, and Corbett had not been asked to do so. He did not want the responsibility anyway. Thomas was becoming sour from all the inactivity and little attention.

Corbett had time. The children had not been collected because of the fear of becoming stranded along the mile stretch from Silverton to the mansion. Mrs. Portman worried as much about Silverton as the mansion. Concerned about wood, coal, and food, she began inventorying the mansion, asking Emi and Haruyo to evaluate the storehouse, and Jenny to provide calculations of daily use.

"Three crocks of pickled goods," reported Emi. "One of pickled eggs, one of pickled bologna, and one of pickled cucumbers." Mrs. Portman knew that the Japanese were crazy about pickled foods, but none among of the rest of the household would touch the pickled bologna. Jenny liked pickled eggs as a snack.

Haruyo picked up the thread, saying, "Four hams and half a venison hanging. Plenty of cornmeal, but just four sacks of flour. Some of it was buggy."

Jenny and Emi began determining what could be rationed if necessary. The train remained three to four weeks out.

Snowshoes and a wooden toboggan provided what little mechanization there was left to help with the snowfall. The snowplow had disappeared under a heavy blanket of white. The loose hay left a trail from the barn to the livery. Ashes and clinkers, seemingly in great amounts, barely fazed the snow in the battle for the road.

Meals, the two main ones, were served at the large formal table. Corbett read a passage in the Bible that represented his fondness relative to this group: "The blood of the covenant is thicker than the water of the womb." The covenant eating together under these conditions was, indeed, a family—a mother, a son, and three older daughters bound together for the health and safety of all.

Corbett complained to himself about the frosty morning, colder than the others had been. While he was on his second trip out hauling clinkers from the stoves, something caught his eye. An orb lay in the southwestern sky. The sun, sneaking out from behind Kendall Mountain, dazzled the mountain valley. The combination of sun and reflecting snow was hard to gaze at for long, but everyone wanted to see their long-lost friend.

Almost immediately, nature began dripping. Two days later, spots of green and brown dotted the white canvas. The snowplow arose from the dead. Footprints or any other marks in the snow provided the sun new places to attack.

"We have visitors!" shouted Corbett. A horse-drawn snowplow and a wagon crowded with shovelers approached, plying their way through the snow. The rescue team, or so they thought themselves to be, presented themselves right in front of the mansion. Through the door came the four women, giddy at having been saved.

"Welcome, welcome," yelled Mrs. Portman. "Come inside. We will make hot tea."

Stanley, sitting with and holding hands with Jenny, seemed to be the leader of the expedition. The other five were drying socks next to the fireplace.

"It sure is good to see you folks. In town it has been a struggle. Several of the wooden houses collapsed under the weight of the snow," Stanley said, speaking mostly to Mrs. Portman. "Steep-pitched roofs survived. Some of the others bore the load and failed. How are you folks doing?" He squeezed Jenny's hand and looked at Corbett, thinking maybe it was a man's question.

"I have never been so isolated in my life," answered Mrs. Portman, who honestly had been afraid at times during the blizzard.

"Well, I have good news and bad news," said Stanley, after a sip of ginger tea. "The snow is leaving in a hurry. Might even get the train up here a bit sooner." Everyone's face lit up; the train's arrival was always an exciting time. It meant that the miners were returning along with supplies—lots of supplies. "The bad news is, we are going to have a pretty bad spring flood. We have an incredible amount of snow up high." Stanley shrugged his shoulders and grimaced, implying the inevitability. "And it's going to come down in a hurry."

"How is it going to affect us?" asked Corbett.

"You're above the high-water mark of the river." Stanley turned his facial downward toward Jenny. "But you will be on the wrong side of the river, isolated again."

"What in the world is wrong with this country?" exclaimed Jenny.

"How long this time?" asked Mrs. Portman. "I've got some things to do in Silverton."

"We have to get back today. A flash flood might come tearing down the Animas in just a few hours or in two days. No one knows for sure."

"What's next?" Mrs. Portman said with sarcasm. "A forest fire?"

"We are ready for summer," said Jenny, convinced that if the proposition were put a vote, it would be unanimously agreed upon.

"So, there's nothing but snow holding up the train?" asked Corbett.

"Actually, there is." Stanley was just full of good news. "The train must cross the Animas River in the middle of Durango." Others in the rescue bunch began nodding their heads. "If that bridge should wash out, it will be months before the D&RG will arrive."

Most of the rescuers had decided to sit out on the porch and soak in the sun, but Stanley stayed back with Jenny. "You could ask to go back with us," said Stanley softly. "I'll find you a good place to stay. It would just be a week or so."

Jenny was surprised at the thought. She had always, since arriving in Silverton, stayed at the Portman house. What would Mrs. Portman say if she were to ask? What would the people in town think? Would Stanley and Jenny be the scandal for the summer? Would she be any different from Esther, thinking only about a man?

"Go ahead and ask Mrs. Portman." Jenny saw a smile through the beard. Love had come late for the pair; they both hoped it would never leave. Holding hands, and away from others, they kissed. Jenny's life was validated; Stanley's was complete.

Tears came to Jenny's eyes. "I have this one opportunity to do things right. I have a duty to help prepare the paperwork for the openings of the mines." At this point, another week might have just as well been a lifetime. "Come and get me for church when the river allows."

Corbett did not know what to call it. If he had known, he would have called it an inverse relationship. As the flooded stream left its banks in a rush, anxious to find lower ground, the world began to appear first as mud, then as dry ground. The faster the water, the quicker the world.

Although still on the wrong side of the river, the mansion began to climb out of its hibernation. Haruyo opened every window in the house, herding out the stale, musty air. Emi, knee-deep in the food storehouse, was sure that enough food was available until the train arrived. Once the buggy flour was sifted, the weevils went to the outside and the flour went into a clean crock. Musty cabbage, still hanging upside down, was shucked down to the shine.

Corbett could not get in the fields yet, so he cleaned the stalls. Manure and bad hay, all piled, was ready to be spread on the fields some summery day.

By the fifth day, the Animas River slipped back within its banks. The riffraff of uprooted trees and brush left by the river was as lost as the large number of rocks dislodged and set down in some new locale. The scouring of the river also had undercut its banks, changing the flow.

Tired of their winter diet, the twins were upriver looking for an equivalent to Japanese *sansai*, the shoots of various plants that grow high up in the mountains. Corbett was at the road entrance to the lane, fixing the broken fence posts that the snowplows had crashed into. They were too wet to really set, but at least they were in place.

"Corbett!" Haruyo was running down the road close to the river. "Corbett!"

Corbett turned and saw Haruyo pointing to the river. "Corbett! Emi is in river. *Wsh, wsh,* in the river." Her hands mimicking the flow downward.

"Where is she?" Corbett asked. He was down at the river's edge, searching the clear, cold Animas, named in 1765 as the River of Lost Souls. Corbett and Haruyo did not know that. They did know, by stopping and looking among the debris and brush while walking upstream, that the Animas had enveloped Emi.

"Emi, Emi!" Haruyo called, frantic with fear. The embankment caved in a hundred or so feet from where Haruyo and Corbett were searching. Haruyo changed her direction and began running again downstream. "She has passed." Out of her mind and racing downstream, Haruyo reckoned that her sister was gone forever.

Corbett turned to follow, when at the end of a fallen tree stump, sticking out toward the middle of the stream, he saw a bit of yellow material snagged there. At first, it looked like a beaver towing a yellow dress. *My God!* he thought. It was not a beaver. It was Emi's head, faceup, hooked by the nap of her linen dress. The water was breaking around Emi's head, causing an eddy just below the chin, her head bobbing like a cork as water flashed over her face.

"Haruyo, she's here!" Corbett shouted as loud as he could. Haruyo, long past the lane, could not hear over the noise of the river. The tree, free from the shore, bounced patiently against a wall of willows. Emi's body was aimlessly tossed about by the waist-high, fast-moving, water.

Corbett could not swim. He decided to wade in just behind

the willows and the tree, using them both to ease the flow of water against his legs. The water's origin was just ten miles upriver. A snowbank, nearly the temperature of ice, was beginning to be dislodged. Corbett's legs stung from the cold. When he crossed the demarcation line from legs to waist, he grabbed himself from the shock. A four-inch limb, attached to the bobbing tree, lay at the waterline between him and Emi. Judging that it was too high to straddle or to climb over, he, holding his breath, ducked under the limb then came up splashing and gasping, his chest tight from the cold. He looked closely at Emi: dead. He had seen dead before. Her face and lips were perhaps as blue as Ajai's had been. Corbett held the lifeless body above the water about midchest. He shut her mouth and pinched her nose, then both of them went beneath the limb. His energy gone, he stumbled to the bank, deposited Emi rather roughly, and flopped down beside her.

The next minute must have been a dream. Haruyo, screaming, ran toward her dead sister, then dragged the limp soul to lie facedown on some wet grass. She stepped over Emi's body, one foot on each side. To Corbett's amazement, Haruyo dropped to her knees, landing on Emi's back. Water spewed from Emi's mouth and nose. Haruyo repeated this act twice more.

"Corbett, hurry, bring Emi to the house." Half walking and half running to the wagon, carrying Emi, Corbett felt a little warmer.

"Haruyo, she's dead!" shouted Corbett repeatedly.

"No. Icy water," Haruyo returned, running ahead.

Each look at the white face he was carrying showed a different person each time. One time it was Emi; the next, Ajai. It didn't matter which; the pallor of death was there.

Mrs. Portman felt proud. The supply orders for the Gypsy Mine had been completed and were now in the file drawer. Mr.

Portman would have been proud too. Corbett sure was making a lot of noise in front of the house. The front door crashed open. Heavy feet barged though to the back of the house. Mrs. Portman pulled open the door to the study, where muddy tracks traced the route across her polished floor.

"What's happening?" asked Mrs. Portman, following the trail to the twins' bedroom. Lying in state was Emi, with Haruyo madly cutting away Emi's dirty dress. Corbett was near the bed where he had laid her. Corbett, stunned, just stood there.

"Corbett, go!" By the time Corbett left the room, Haruyo had pulled off her own dress and slipped in next to her sister.

Mrs. Portman stepped closer to the pair, examining Emi's face. "She is dead, Haruyo. She is dead." The poor woman would not accept the truth.

"No!" Haruyo screamed. "Ice water put her to sleep. Not dead."

Corbett sat on the chair next to his bed, his body sagging, a few drops of water still falling from his clothes.

"Corbett, what did you do? You're all wet and cold!" said Jenny, not knowing what she was seeing. "Get your shirt off!" she told him, unbuttoning his shirt and pulling at the sleeve. "Now your pants. You're freezing." She was at his belt, then at the buttons on his pants. Suddenly, Jenny jumped back, embarrassed. *What am I doing?* Looking at the area in question, she wondered if she had touched something or seen something. *What was I thinking?* "I'll get hot tea." *I will never be able to talk to him again.*

The evening report to the kitchen table, this time by Jenny, was: "She's breathing. It's so terrible." There were tears in her eyes. "She's breathing like a fish out of water!"

Two hours later, Haruyo, ever the one to appear a proper Japanese woman, came around the corner, her long, coarse hair disheveled and dirty, her robe far too open to be deemed proper by people of her culture. She was spent.

"You look terribly tired." A mother could not have said it better. Mrs. Portman was distraught over the slow, agonizing death of Emi. "What can we do?" Those were the exact words once spoken to her while she waited to hear the last breaths of her husband.

"She will live," stated Haruyo, tired of the comments to the contrary. "Her heart is beating next to me."

Corbett, in from the barn area for lunch, was met with smiles all around. "She is awake."

"You say that she is alive?" In Corbett's limited history, no one had come back from the dead.

"Come look!" Haruyo was seated beside Emi's bed, offering her sister egg drop soup.

"Emi, you're alive!" Corbett did something unusual. Moving quickly to the other side of the bed, he leaned and gave Emi a kiss on the forehead. "So happy to see you."

The meals without Haruyo were a disaster. Neither Jenny nor Mrs. Portman could cook. The morning meal was burned corn cakes. Only with butter and honey were they edible. Lunch was ham and cabbage, allowed to wither away without any fanfare.

The evolution of the reborn Emi went from a slow awakening in a soft chair in the main room to sunny afternoons covered with a fine quilt on the porch.

Time was passing for all Silverton too. Preparations for the influx of workers, mostly miners, sparked by the good weather, went on from daylight to dark. All roads were open and active. Trips to church and the mining office were as scheduled.

With the morning chores done, now was time for tea with Emi. Corbett, three steps up to the porch, stopped. His body immediately froze as he began listening more intently.

"Mrs. Portman, Jenny, hurry!"

Jenny, the first out the door, asked, "What is it?"

The others arrived in time to see Corbett holding his hand to his ear. "Listen!"

A sound was echoing up the canyon. Although it was still distant, they could hear the steam pushing hard against valves then releasing, the characteristic rhythm of the Silverton train. There were no great dancers on the porch, but everyone danced anyway.

Jubilation ensued. Everyone, including those from the mansion, met the train. Passenger cars, boxcars, and cattle cars were all full. There were no ore cars yet; the mines hadn't yet opened. Tents blossomed on every vacant lot. These miners, like miners of the past, were mostly broke, ready for big checks and maybe a nugget panned on their own. Men were hired on the spot to move supplies, herd cattle, or help with the food lines.

Mrs. Portman and Jenny counted the number of workers on this first train. Both were excited about the number; it was more than last year. Reports from scouts who had already been up to the mines were about the roads to the mines, many of which, the scouts said, had been damaged by the flood. The townspeople, happy to be relevant again, hit the bars and celebrated with the miners. The liquor was no longer in short supply.

Each day, more miners arrived. The tent city bulged. Small clumps of young women also appeared, disembarking from each train. Excited, and receiving proposals daily, they were the first to find work in restaurants or bars, or as housekeepers—any other occupation a woman might find to earn money in Silverton.

Miners came in all stripes. Hok'ee was using this fact to his advantage. The past winter, he had been a marked man. The United States Army actively sought the Navajo who had attacked a D&RG freight wagon in Durango. Other members of his renegade band wanted nothing to do with him. If the army found any evidence of his having been to their camp, the other Navajo were arrested and held. Ramona had disappeared right after her return to Chaco Canyon.

The blame for Ajai's pregnancy, the blame for the deaths of both Begay brothers, and the reason the army had been sent to track Hok'ee down all lay at the feet of a fair-haired bilagáana named Corbett.

Having seen Corbett traveling north on the train the past fall, Hok'ee knew he must go there. Watching miners buy tickets indiscriminately for the Silverton train, Hok'ee had stolen some miner's clothing and blended in. Displaying a negative attitude, he found that no one cared to make his acquaintance. Once in Silverton, he camped on the mountain west of town. This ideal location provided a view of most of the town and the well-traveled road to the north.

Hok'ee's first sighting of Corbett brought his formerly repressed anger to the forefront. A rifle shot from this distance might have killed him. However, the death must be hand to hand, to watch Corbett's eyes die and see blood spill from his mouth. The wagon came from the north road. Corbett was alone.

Hok'ee moved his camp closer to some brush near the bridge across the Animas. The second sighting of Corbett came by way of a fancy carriage, its team of horses trotting away from the mansion. During the night, Hok'ee crossed the bridge and made a hidden camp in the pines behind the house.

The following morning, Hok'ee watched Corbett doing chores. It was a pleasure to watch, knowing Corbett would die on this day. Carefully, he approached the back of the house and began to make ready.

Emi wanted the food storehouse ready for the next shipment up from Durango. There was an art to it, and she was the artist. She closed the heavy door and, in a slight opening to the back of the house, saw a big man with long hair. He removed his shirt. War paint had already been applied to his face. In a leather scabbard was the long knife he was carrying.

Emi rushed inside. "Bad man, *wsh, wsh*," she said, using two fingers to draw imaginary paint marks.

"What?" Mrs. Portman asked as she was pulled to a small side window, where she watched a powerfully built Native in war paint move silently from the back to the front.

"We've got to tell Corbett!" whispered Mrs. Portman. Emi was away.

"Corbett! Corbett!" shouted Emi from the porch. "Indian!" Hok'ee stepped to the edge of the porch, looking for Corbett to appear. Corbett looked out from behind the barn. The sight of Hok'ee just a few feet away from Emi startled Corbett. Where had he come from? How did he get here?

The area between them was an open space surrounded by buildings. Hok'ee began to cross, moving toward Corbett. If Corbett were to run, Hok'ee would have the advantage, for if Corbett ran, Hok'ee would be the predator and Corbett would be the helpless prey. Corbett stepped out of sight, returning with his hatchet.

Corbett was ready, and his enemy was just a few feet away. Having seen his young love's eyes become dull and empty because of their love, having seen his mother bleed to death, and having seen his friend crushed and torn beneath a pile of dead horses, he was ready.

Hok'ee was ready too, his enemy just a few feet away. With the embarrassment of having a white child inside his daughter's womb, the embarrassment of failing to kill Corbett in Durango, and the embarrassment of being an outcast in his own land, he was ready.

The pair circled, each with his eyes staring at the other. Hok'ee, his right hand holding the knife high, was ready to stab at any second. Bigger, older, stronger, and more experienced, Hok'ee was unafraid.

Corbett, no longer a little boy, held his hatchet with his right hand, ready to slash at any time.

Hok'ee lunged at Corbett, the knife aimed at Corbett's chest. Corbett stopped the motion of Hok'ee's arm but, overwhelmed by his charge, stumbled backward and down to the ground. Corbett's hatchet took one swipe on the way down. A long red line of blood, from Hok'ee's upper back to his lower back, appeared.

Rolling and turning their hips one way or another to acquire the advantage, the two men were like powerful bulls interlocked in combat. Corbett gained his feet, only to be heel-tripped backward. His movement ceased. Hok'ee came up slowly from his hands and knees. Corbett's head lay close to a bloody rock.

Hok'ee raised his arms and head to the sun and murmured a few words. He stepped toward Corbett's head.

"Leave the boy alone," bellowed Mrs. Portman, the large gun from the robbery dancing wildly in her hands. Hok'ee, amused at seeing the old white woman so near and so steadfast, laughed and bent down to gather a handful of yellow hair.

The first blast missed Hok'ee and the broad side of the barn. Hok'ee angrily charged Mrs. Portman. Shots two and three were point-blank. The knife tore at Mrs. Portman's dress. Hok'ee fell, still stumbling toward her, then was quiet. Mrs. Portman dropped to her knees and covered her face, sobbing.

When Corbett awoke, the earth was twirling. Any movement he made in any direction brought on a sharp pain. He was in his room. An audience was on hand. Peabody stood next to his bed, the three women sat nearby.

"Welcome back to the world," said Peabody. "Can you see?"

"Yeah. A little blurry, but I can see." Corbett stopped to think. "What are you doing here?"

"I was turning into the lane when I heard the shot," said Peabody. He wondered how soon it would be before Corbett recalled the fight with the Navajo.

"What shot?" It had been months since the robber shot at Corbett in the house. Corbett sat up, looking at the women. "Has somebody been shooting at you?"

Jenny stepped up. "Do you remember the Indian?" An hour ago, Corbett was fighting for his life. "Can you remember the fight?"

"Hok'ee. Where's Hok'ee?" Corbett could feel and see the strength and anger of Hok'ee as they had fought.

"He's dead. He won't bother you anymore," stated Peabody. "Mrs. Portman shot him." Corbett looked over at Mrs. Portman to see the status of her distress. She was sitting between Emi and Haruyo, clasping both their hands.

Corbett lay back. He had heard the words. Hok'ee had followed him? The fight kept wanting to be in a dream. Corbett drifted away.

Doctor Peabody treated both Corbett and Mrs. Portman with his favorite medication, willow leaves. Natives throughout the West, as well as Dr. Peabody, prescribed willow leaves for pain and arthritis. Mrs. Portman and Jenny both scoffed at Peabody's cure, but it worked on Corbett's headaches and softened Mrs. Portman's bad moments.

Peabody sat with Mrs. Portman in the evenings, before retreating to his stall. Her mines were doing fine; her husband would be proud. Mrs. Portman did struggle with her shooting of Hok'ee. On one side of the argument going on in her mind was the necessity to protect Corbett and even herself from death. On the other side was that she had taken a life.

Peabody gave no lecture, nor did he toy with any kind of homegrown psychology. He just listened. He rocked quietly back and forth, smoking his pipe and watching the day come to an end. Mrs. Portman was currently suffering the consequences of being such a powerful woman. She had no friends, just employees and business associates. There was no one to let into her heart, no one to see her vulnerabilities.

Periodically, she broke the silence with a statement of fact from one side of her brain or the other: "He was going to kill Corbett. I had no choice" or "He lay there dead, forever. I took away a life." It was as if there were two lawyers arguing for her soul. Peabody did not sympathize with or patronize either side. The evenings ended with Peabody's bidding Mrs. Portman a good night. Then she would sit for a few more minutes, aware of the conversation that was going on in her mind.

Corbett slowly returned to work, early in the morning until late in the afternoon. He could not believe the amount of work it took just to keep up with the property.

With the sawmill running, Peabody was, as usual, collecting slabs. The heavy snow the past winter nearly had killed Peabody and his pony. Both were condemned to the cabin and mine shaft. The pony had gone hungry for a week and a half, before brush and willow tips poked back out from under the snowdrifts.

Silverton was again about money. Freight wagons carrying ore from the various mining districts crisscrossed the town. Executive railcars from Durango were met by Miss Jenny Wallace. Many of the meetings were held at the Grand Imperial; others, at the mansion. George Ancell, a gold panner working the creeks to the west of Silverton, strutted into the Kendall Mountain Bar one day with a few flakes and one good-sized nugget of gold. A small frenzy of panners took off in that direction.

Corbett was busy as a carriage driver, driving down to the train station and back through Silverton and to the mansion. Peabody was there, periodically hauling and cutting slabs, and helping with the coal wagons that Mrs. Portman ordered.

"I can't believe how busy we are," Corbett reported one evening, sitting with a beer. Peabody was drinking cheap wine. "Jenny and Mrs. Portman are gone to Silverton nearly every day. I only get to see my students two, three times a week."

"I think Miss Wallace is going to get a lot busier," said Peabody, stopping to spit out some solids from his wine bottle. "She came down to the woodshed all excited. Stanley proposed to her at church yesterday."

"Why haven't I heard?" questioned Corbett, a bit put out.

"It takes awhile for it filter down." Peabody smiled a ragged smile.

Early the next day, a horse and rider came flying up the lane. Corbett set down his wash bucket and walked around the covered carriage to meet the driver.

"Whoa." The horse lathered and breathing heavily. "Trey, what's the matter?" Trey brushed by Corbett on his way to the porch.

"There's been a cave-in!" Trey shouted back as he entered the house. Corbett cooled the horse down with a wet rag and waited. Which mine was it? The biggest fear in the district was of dead or trapped miners.

"Corbett, harness the horses. The Gypsy has caved in. We've got to go right now." Mrs. Portman pulled at her shawl as she spoke.

Minutes later, the carriage was racing down the lane. Trey

had already left for Silverton; the people there did not yet know. Corbett was as experienced as any driver having freighted coal and driven wagons and carriages all spring. The carriage was light and quick. A buggy might have been faster but would have never withstood the trip. Passing through the Forks, Corbett felt the town seemed empty. Every saddle horse and wagon was already up the mine road, ahead of Corbett. Several saddle horses from Silverton flashed by, only to be passed later by Corbett and his steady hand. The road, new to Corbett, was as advertised, steep and rough. Twice, Corbett walked the horses gently along the side of the mountain, just feet from an edge that fell away hundreds of feet. The horses slowed down even more as the altitude and the distance took their toll.

Years ago, miners had found a cleft of gold and silver deposits in the iron-rich mountain. It lay between two powerful monoliths of red iron rock. Different sets of miners toyed with the front twenty feet of the degraded strata. Museum-quality crystals of quartz with gold and tarnished silver were present. With that evidence, Mr. Portman bought and financed the Gypsy Mine. The question was always whether the unstable crystalline river was worth the risk.

The gray to brown dust, so fine that it failed to yield to gravity, hung in the air a quarter mile ahead. "Oh my, look, Corbett!" cried Mrs. Portman. She had often witnessed dynamite explosions with her husband at the tunnel, but this cloud was larger. "Hurry, hurry!"

Corbett drove the wagon as far as he could, then pulled in behind a line of wagons at the side of the road. They beheld a panorama of reddish-gray dust blanketing the site and all things that moved or did not move. The dust seemed to be still bellowing out of the mine.

A young miner met the carriage, breathing heavily. "The Gypsy caved in again a few minutes ago."

"Did everyone get out okay?" called a man from another wagon, just arriving. His voice had the kind of urgency to it that implied a special need to know. Perhaps he was a father, a brother, or a friend who had left home for this mine weeks ago.

"Hell no. A rescue team went in about an hour ago." The miner's wide eyes were canvased all with dust. "Then all hell broke loose, and the entrance caved in." The messenger turned and started to rush back to the cave-in. "They're all dead. It even got Laddie!"

Laddie! Did he say Laddie? There must be some mistake, Corbett thought. "Laddie didn't work the Gypsy Mine. He's up at the Irish Rose," corrected Corbett.

Mrs. Portman rose to get out of the carriage, then slumped down in the seat after hearing the tragic news, stunned and defeated. Jenny got out immediately with pad and pencil, trying to get names of those who had gotten out and those unaccounted for.

Corbett dropped from the driver's seat. He needed to rectify the confusion about his father. The dust, the machinery, the men, the horses, all milling near the rocks, strewn from the mine, gave him no one to tell.

"Laddie works the Irish Rose!" Corbett shouted to a miner near to the front of the mine face.

"Yeah, he was the first one down here from the Rose. He gathered a rescue team from those milling about, grabbed a pick, and went right in." The miner who had spoken shook the dust and debris from his shirt, still holding a pickax with no place to dig. "Nobody could save nobody."

Corbett, at front of the mine, obeyed the reflex to pull at the jagged rocks. When he did so, others fell immediately into their place—the same result as others who had tried.

Near dark, members of the congregational church reached the mine with food and blankets. They lit candles and hung lanterns. They sang Christian songs and prayed.

Corbett sat at a makeshift table with Mrs. Portman, Jenny Wallace, and the Gypsy Mine boss, Mark Harold.

"We had the usual beam adjustments, but nothing serious," Mark stated in a matter-of-fact voice. "When you are digging in decomposed crystalline rock, you worry, but none was afraid to go in."

"We have eight miners inside, four from the Gypsy, two from the Rose, and two from the Sultan," said Jenny, checking and double-checking her notes. "You think that's right?"

"No, at least five from the Rose!" Mark turned to Corbett. "You should really be proud of Laddie. He represents what's good about us miners. I was in the bar the day you and your father had your fight. I feel bad about it because I don't think you ever knew your father." Corbett eyed Mark in surprise. "We would get him up here and dry him out. After that, he was the best miner up here." Mark finished his remarks, "The father you knew was alcohol; the father you didn't know was Laddie. I just wanted you to know."

The memorial service was held on the incline of Anvil Mountain, just west of Silverton and overlooking the town. The dead of Silverton's mining district were brought and laid to rest among their brethren. These, like the fallen members of the Gypsy Mine, were remembered even though their bodies remained entombed in the mine a few miles away. A small monument stood guard to forever comfort and protect the unfortunate resting there. The town and the miners wished sooner for a larger one.

The whole town had turned out; every business had closed. Both the pastor of the congregational church and the priest of Saint Patrick's gave eulogies, and people cried, including Corbett.

In less than a year, he had buried his mother and his father, as well as Ajai and Nick. He wondered if he was a carrier of bad luck. He sat between Jenny and Mrs. Portman, holding hands with both.

Mark, at the mine, had given Corbett something to think about. Corbett had never seen Laddie at a time when he was not drunk. Every sour memory of his father included whiskey breath and a personality of meanness. Laddie's gunslinger style of living would, of course, send him into the mine first, alcohol or no. Corbett needed to declare to his mind an epitaph for Laddie from this moment on. Corbett would commemorate Laddie as "the father he could have been."

"Young Mr. Jones," called a voice from an expensive black buggy that was passing by on the road dropping into Silverton. Corbett turned and recognized Mr. Williams and his wife.

"Yes, sir," Corbett responded, showing due respect to both age and money.

"First, I am very sorry about Laddie. My men say that he was a good miner. You be sure you are at the two o'clock meeting."

"I will, sir," replied Corbett. "Thank you."

Mr. Williams was a large man, bloated and wealthy. On this day, he was wearing a black custom suit and a silk-looking top hat, an uncommon sight in the high mountains of Colorado. Events like this allowed the mine owners to parade their financial status, wearing it on their sleeves. Mr. Williams owned several claims west of Silverton and recently had bought stock in Mrs. Portman's mining operation.

"Yes, we want to get past this," said Williams, his buggy swaying from side to side down the hill.

The reparations meeting, as it was called, was followed closely by all the miners. Given that there were no unions, the miners leaned hard on the mines, even threatening to strike if the surviving families did not receive some sort of proper reparation for their loved ones' having died in the mines. The miners, having seen or heard of wives with children leaving the mining communities with nothing more than pack rolls and tattered coats, already felt guilty about the conditions in which their families lived. The owners knew that good pay, decent housing, and reparations were key to keeping the mines open.

Promptly at two o'clock, with reporters from both the Durango and Silverton newspapers in place, Mr. Johnson stood to speak. Mrs. Portman and Mr. Williams were also sitting at the main table. Mr. Johnson, a former miner who had made his fortune placer mining in the Cripple Creek area, was respected by the miners as being one of them.

"Hard-rock mining is a difficult and dangerous business. Reparation meetings are a result of a sorrowful experience. Every one of us takes a risk, either physical or financial, when we get in this business."

Corbett knew nothing of reparations, but he did see the little children circled around their weeping mothers. To be on display at the most vulnerable time in their lives, even for the most positive of reasons, was a difficult matter. It caused them to lower their eyes as if subordinate creatures to be pitied.

Corbett rejoined the speech when the reparations were announced.

"For those wives wanting to leave Silverton, they will receive one hundred twenty-five dollars and tickets on the D&RG. Those wives wanting to stay will receive free housing for a year and ten dollars a month. After that, they must make their own plans."

The crowd applauded loudly, with some shouts of approval.

"Mr. Corbett Jones." The crowd turned to him. "We know that your father led an attempted rescue at the Gypsy Mine. Mr.

Williams and I had quite a conversation over you. It was not until Mrs. Portman made her suggestion that we knew what to do."

Corbett was unaware that he was at all involved in the meeting, being just a driver for Mrs. Portman.

"She said, and others have agreed, that you have a gift for teaching. That being said, we are sure, and your father would have agreed, that we will pay your tuition and fees at the new teaching school in Greeley—the Colorado State Normal School, I think it is called. Good luck to you, son."

5

The newness of college and of being in a city was unnerving to Corbett. By luck, he had found a good boarding house, run by Glen and Frances Casey. One of the other boarders was also a first year teacher-to-be named Howard. They walked the mile to the college that first morning not knowing anything about each other. They were just comrades in arms. They stayed together throughout the day. Standing in the sign-up lines side by side, both clearly out of place. Most of the other students were Corbett's age or slightly older. Howard, who had never made a decision in his life, followed Corbett blindly.

By the middle of the afternoon, both were registered in the teacher training courses. They were happy to escape the crowd back to their new home.

"Glen, you should have seen the mess of us at the first meeting." Howard was excited about the new college and about him being in it. "We filled the whole hall. Far more women than men. Isn't that right, Corbett?"

"Had to be," Corbett replied, laughing at Howard's giddiness. For a city kid, Howard was woefully immature. "I think Howard shook hands with every one of them."

"Corbett," The old man said, leaning back in his leisure chair, folding his newspaper. "It says right here that there might be a hundred of you. The *Tribune* even listed the instructors. Nobody I know, of course." Glen reached down and stubbed out his cigarette. "This college has been a long time coming, finally Greeley is on the map. By the way," He said, closing his eyes, "you remember you owe me ten hours a week around the place here, or I'll have to charge you more."

A few days after the start of the quarter at the Colorado Normal School, Mr. Ross was examining Corbett from his lectern. "Mr. Jones," he said. Corbett sat up, surprised to have had his name called. In the room of twenty, he was sitting in an outside row, the third seat back from the front. Howard was in the second row. "You seem to be a question mark. When we shook hands as you entered the room, your grip was strong. But even more interesting is how calloused your hands are. You seem too fit and stout to be a schoolmaster." Mr. Ross gave his unwarranted opinion: "You would be best served working in the sugar beets. More money there."

The college women, even on the first day, were winnowing away the old, the ugly, and the dumb. This was the population pool of men they would be with for more than a year. Corbett, handsome, blond, and shy, his biceps and triceps newly arrived and prominent, his chest tight in his shirt, was near the top of the list. This deposition of Corbett Jones might come in handy.

"Your prose on the first assignment was quite acceptable." Mr. Ross paced, one hand to his jaw, thinking. "But your cursive is no better than a third grader's."

Corbett, more than a bit embarrassed to be called out of his third day of college, responded, "Sorry, sir." *What else do you say?* he asked himself.

"What high school did you attend?" asked Mr. Ross.

"I've never gone to school." In unison, the audience looked at Corbett and gasped.

"Never?"

"Never."

"Can you read? Who did your assignment for you? Read something for me." Mr. Ross was incredulous at the fraud playing out in front of him.

Corbett reached to the bottom of his schoolbooks and opened the bottom-most book to the ribbon marker. He began to read: "'The air continued full of horrible cries and screams, such as man alone can utter, and only when in a state of the fiercest barbarity.'"

Mr. Ross, flabbergasted, pulled his chair near. "What is that out of?"

"Page one hundred fourteen of *The Last of the Mohicans.*"

"And you have never gone to school?"

"No, but I did teach young children for several months last year, and enjoyed it."

Mr. Ross rose as if he had just discovered a new island. He asked the students, "Can you believe this? We have ourselves an enigma. Welcome, Mr. Jones, welcome." Mr. Ross led the applause.

No matter how hard the librarian tried to quell the noise at one end of the library, it continued. At least a dozen students surrounded Howard and Corbett. Corbett was like a book of his own: handsome, never having been to school, but reading classics in his spare time. Coming from a small mining town, and having an interesting story about how he came to read, he was an enigma.

Howard could not believe his luck. He had all these young women perched all around him, listening to and watching Corbett, so he got to feast on their figures and faces. Howard and his parents lived in a most proper part of Denver. His father was a jeweler, spending each day quietly making expensive rings and necklaces.

After work, he and his wife would have a nice meal and some expensive wine and then read. Howard was there too, somewhere. He was heavy, bordering on obese. Quiet, he was invisible in class, except for his girth. At home, he watched the world go by around him while he would go to get another sandwich. Being friends with Corbett was as close as Howard had ever been to a celebrity. Corbett treated him as a good friend.

"How did you get enough money to come to school?" asked a blonde sitting in the group.

"My father tried to rescue some men in a mine cave-in. He was killed trying. The people there offered to pay for my college."

Unbelievable; now he was a victim. Corbett had it all. *Why couldn't I have been a victim?* Howard wondered. Corbett's admirers slipped closer to Howard to be closer to Corbett. What a great day!

"Frances, we need some more potatoes!" said Glen, who was on his second helping. With the two boys sharing a meal with the couple, there were four at the table. A fifth was needed to ensure the Caseys would have a positive bank balance. They were looking. "You boys think this is going to work for you? I hear that the pay is pretty poor for a schoolmaster."

"I enjoy it. Haven't thought about the money much. I've never had any to speak of," said Corbett between bites.

"I guess I'm just used to healthy young men out working in the fields. The reason we have so many Scandinavians here is because Meeker chose only the hardest-working families of those who applied. Now they've got all the irrigated fields and have gotten rich."

"Were you a farmer?" asked Howard.

"We had our three boys, and we farmed one hundred sixty acres of beets," Glen said proudly. "When they grew up and left, we couldn't find anybody to do the work. We sold out, then bought this place. Been working this boardinghouse since." He put his napkin on his plate and slid it to the side. "Frances, bring me my pipe."

Climbing the stairs to their rooms, Corbett said to Howard, "I think Mrs. Casey does all the work and that she has for a long time." Corbett had not seen one iota of effort thus far by Glen.

"My father isn't very handy around the house," Howard admitted. "But at least he helps with the dishes."

"I've never been in a real family, but I would guess that the wives carry the bigger part of the load." Corbett thought of the mansion, of Emi, the cook; Haruyo, the housekeeper; and Jenny, the secretary and organizer. "How could one woman do all those things—and with having kids?"

"Course, the man makes the money. That explains why there aren't many married schoolmasters." Howard never had thought of money as a need, but others, he thought, must have.

"People keep reminding me of that," Corbett said mildly. "I read somewhere that joining the circus cures all of this."

The class was US History. Terry Grimes, quite a homely woman but making the most of it, sat to Corbett's left, with Howard in front. Terry had no ulterior motives, unlike several of her college friends who murmured about Corbett. She knew he was a hot item, but she also subconsciously knew she could not compete for any man; she offered so little.

"What are you doing tomorrow?" asked Terry.

"If tomorrow's Saturday," said Corbett, "and I think it is, then Howard and I have to work at the boardinghouse."

"Yeah, I have to work too. I grade potatoes at Associated Farmers."

"You grade potatoes? Do they get As and Bs? Here is a girl

who grades potatoes on Saturdays," said Corbett, amused at the thought.

"I sort them by size and quality and throw out the ones that don't make the grade."

"Sounds like you will make a good teacher," responded Corbett with a smirk.

"I will if I don't run out of money."

"I know how that is. I'm a little light myself."

"I'm going to ride out to the Cattleman's on Sunday. I hear that they're hiring for the swing shift."

"All right, here we go again. Cattleman's? And what's a swing shift?"

"It's a big restaurant and bar, the biggest between here and Wyoming. Work would be evenings after we get out of school."

"Does that sound better than giving potatoes grades?"

"The job at Associates ends when the harvest ends. I need something for the winter, or else I go home."

"Howard," Corbett said, tapping Howard on the shoulder, "do you want to go job hunting Sunday?"

"Not if I can help it," Howard said, turning in his seat to look at Terry. Even though he was pear-shaped like Terry, and not the greatest of male specimens, his standard for women was quite high. He possessed calendar pictures in his room of women who met his expectations. And his chances of finding his perfect woman improved by his being around Corbett. Corbett was like a magnet, although he did not seem to care about any of the women who were interested in him. "Are you putting Corbett up to this?" asked Howard, putting on his squinty face while looking at Terry. "I need my weekends."

"Terry, count me in. I need to find something myself," replied Corbett, nodding his agreement.

Sunday, about two o'clock, Corbett, Terry, and Howard entered the Cattleman's and were directed to a dining table overflowing with paperwork. It seemed to be slack time after the Sunday rush. Dishes and silverware still littered the other tables.

Mel, the manager, looked up. "Can I help you?"

Corbett answered first, saying, "We're college students trying to find some part-time work."

"College students, huh?" Mel sized up the lot. "Haven't got much use for college. Have any of you done restaurant work before?" The three looked at each other and shook their heads no. "I thought not. I only hire experienced, reliable help."

"I can tell," observed Terry. A glance at the unworked tables told the story.

"What's that?" snarled Mel, a small Italian-looking man, his full head of hair streaked with white.

"I've never seen a restaurant in this condition during the day." Terry was not happy with Mel's attitude.

"Neither one of my omnibus boys showed up today." Mel was quite mad and embarrassed. "Go on. I'm not hiring today."

Corbett, surprisingly, sat down, his eyes on Mel. "Why don't you continue your paperwork while we college students bus your tables? Terry, you and I will clear the dishes. Howard, get some soap and water and wash the tables."

"You can't!" said Mel, not knowing what else to say.

"We can do as well as your experienced help did today." Corbett was already at the first table, scraping dishes.

"Whose tips are these?" asked Terry, holding up some coins. Three waitresses at a booth on lunch break were sitting in disbelief as the three young strangers cleaned their tables. Sunday's noon meal always kept the young women flying. Today, they were not looking to clean up the mess.

An older black-haired waitress pulled Corbett aside. "I'm not sure what's going on, but I do appreciate it," she said, patting Corbett on the shoulder. "And to tell the truth, it's good to see someone put Mel in his place."

"I can't believe what just happened," Howard said to the other two, once they were bouncing along in the wagon back to Greeley. "Those waitresses really got after that Mel fellow. Next thing, we got jobs." Howard was invigorated. "I got a job and I didn't really want one."

"At least I've got Sunday off. That's my day to study and read," said Corbett, quite satisfied with himself. "And we've got Saturday morning off too." Howard thought he might survive half a day.

"We have to work for Glen Saturday mornings," Howard reminded Corbett.

"Oh hell, I forgot that."

The class called Teaching Reading was also taught by Mr. Ross. "Phonics is the gateway to reading. If a student can sound a word out, then that student can read most words. The pages you made as part of the last assignment can be placed on the wall, to remind students of some of the reading rules. What other rules do we want to put on the wall?"

"I make mistakes in writing, going from one noun to many of the same noun," said Corbett. His poorest grades still came from his writing classes.

"Give me an example."

"I see one horse; I see three horses. I see one mouse; I see three mouses." The class chuckled.

"I see." Mr. Ross now understood the dilemma. "And it should be one mouse, three mice. Do you have another one?"

As Corbett thought, Julie Bjlack piped up from the back of the room, "One tooth and three tooths. One tooth and three teeth."

"Students, take notes. Are there any others?"

"Goose, geese."

Another student shouted, "Is the plural of *kiss*, *keese*?" Everyone laughed.

Mr. Ross waved his hands, trying to reenter the conversation. "Try these pronouns. For men, *he*, *his*, and *him*. For women, *she*, *shis*, and *shim*. English is a hard language. You teachers have yourselves quite a task in front of you. Good, class. See you tomorrow."

"Hi, Corbett. Can we sit here?" asked Julie, also done with classes for the day. Corbett knew her from class. He guessed that Bjlack was a Scandinavian name. She was a tall flaxen blonde, her face quite tanned. When she smiled, the world grew brighter. Martha, her companion, seemed to come from money or society. She did not flash it, but you could just tell.

Corbett did not have to work today, so he could linger a bit before going back to the boardinghouse to study. And sometimes he would be without Howard. That was okay too.

"Sure, you bet," Corbett replied. "Can I get both of you a phosphate?"

"Oh, that would be nice. Cherry if they've got it," said Martha.

"I'll take the same," answered Julie. Corbett paid his nickels and returned with the drinks.

"Did you get all your history done?" Corbett asked, quick to raise a topic. "Every little thing Mr. Williams talks about, I have to go to the library and find out what he means."

"No, I'm not done at all." Julie took a long sip of her drink. "We're shipping steers, so I've been down at the stockyards till after dark for the last three nights." She paused. "Our family knows

American history well, but I don't have time to get it down on paper."

"I might not pass the class even though I'm reading history every minute," Corbett admitted.

"Can I ask you a question?" Julie said, on to the real question at hand. "This is kind of embarrassing." Her face bore an expression of seeking forgiveness. "We farm girls are worse than the old ladies at a quilting bee."

"And?" Corbett was amused at the roundabout manner in which Julie was approaching her question.

"Martha and I have a bet."

"And?"

"This is terrible. Oh well, here goes." Her tanned face was now red. "We see you, Howard, and Terry leave up the Cheyenne road every day or so. Is Terry your girlfriend or Howard's?"

Corbett chuckled. "Neither. We all work evenings at the Cattleman's. She's a good friend of ours though. Why the question?"

"It's just silly," Martha explained. "Since you three are together so much, we figured she was a girlfriend, but none of us could believe that it was you and her. But she and Howard as a couple didn't make sense either. Do you have a girl back in Silverton?"

"No, afraid not."

"Did you ever have a girlfriend?"

"Yes. Why are you asking these questions?"

"You seem such a fine fellow, quiet, friendly, and handsome too." Julie tried to read Corbett's response to that. "I guess you really are our enigma. We all like you a lot. Now tell me about your last girlfriend."

Corbett sat for a moment, head down. Would the pain of reliving the Durango events ever leave? Would Ajai understand if he were to move on? He could not change anything. Maybe it was time to start a new life, just like his new life of being a teacher.

"Two years ago, my girlfriend was killed by her father because she was pregnant with my child." There, it was out. How many times in the future would he have to relive those moments, would it always be hanging over him, ready to ruin another day?

"My God!" The blood left Martha's face. Julie nearly fainted. The fun of the two college women, coyly playing on one of their favorite subjects, Corbett, now seemed to be cruel and callous. They stared, unable to speak.

"She was a Navajo girl. I loved her, and I always will."

"I am so sorry." To watch Corbett's face still suffer at his admission tore Julie's heart from her body. She reached over and held Corbett. He sat quietly for quite a time. "It was none of our business. I am so sorry." Martha was so embarrassed of her and Julie's nosiness, she could not speak or respond.

"I don't know whether she is not letting me go or I am not letting her go." Corbett realized that he again had failed to let Ajai go and to get on with his life.

"Oh, Corbett," Julie said, in tears. "I don't know what to tell you. She must know your love for her was proven again today." She hugged him tight one more time.

"Mr. Jones, it looks like you have never seen a slide rule." Everyone in the class slid the numbered wooden centerpiece back and forth with some knowledge of the instrument from high school.

"Nope, but from what I can tell, everyone else has." Corbett's honesty continually added to his popularity.

"All of us instructors are using Corbett's naivety and intelligence to demonstrate the instruction of one topic or another." The students loved when the instructors brought Corbett on stage to be the enigma.

"So, Corbett, do you know about square roots?"

"Some."

"To show the value of the slide rule, can you tell me the square root of sixty-five?"

"I don't know a thing about this slide rule, but the square root of sixty-five is about"—Corbett squinted his eyes as he figured—"eight-point-one or -two."

"That was pretty amazing!" said Mr. Anderson, laughing. "You're not supposed to figure that out so quickly. But since you got it, I have to ask, how did you do it?"

Corbett retraced the steps in his mind. "The square root of sixty-four is eight, and the square root of eighty-one is nine. Quite a difference between the two." Corbett put both hands out and spread them. "Sixty-five is very close to sixty-four," he said, wiggling the thumb of one hand to represent sixty-four and the thumb of his other hand to represent eighty-one. "Real close to eight, but a tiny bit more, so about eight-point-one or less." The students all slid the cursor over the A scale and the D scale, then looked at Corbett. He was right.

"Corbett, well done. Your classmates did it this way: Find your A line, put the cursor on sixty-five, and look down to the D your line, and there it is, eight-point-one or so."

"Many of you will be assigned to one-room schools serving students from kindergarten to twelfth grade. You must be able to teach sums to the little ones and square roots to your older students. Out in the country, it is important to know and teach measurements. Land is measured in chains. One chain is sixty-six feet, and eighty chains is a mile. We can teach all this advanced math, but out on the farms, those folks might prefer their children's math to be more relevant to their needs. So, for tomorrow, how many pecks in thirteen bushels?"

"Corbett," said Mel, exasperated, "can you get Howard to wash the dishes a little faster?" The Cattleman's was packed with the usual Friday crowd. When the place was this full, Mel depended on the dishwashers to replenish the serving area with clean plates. He had not many extras.

"The cooks need plates," Terry reported on the fly. She had moved up to waitress after her first week, and presently she was the best one Mel had.

"I'll trade him until we get caught up," said Corbett, busing some dirty glassware to the dishwashing area. Howard had liabilities, but his asset loyalty outweighed these. More than that was his ability to be honest. He took what life gave him and worked with it. Howard was meticulous. He could and would fix anything with his little fat fingers. He was very tight with his spending, but he would lend Terry money almost every week.

It was Martha's family's buggy, but Corbett was driving. Howard and Martha sat in the cushioned rear seats. The fall day had, by noon, warmed to a pleasant temperature. Julie had suggested the ride during the week. The plan included a picnic and looking for Native American circles outside Greeley. The Natives needed stones to hold the flaps of their tepees down. When the Natives left, the stones were left in circles. A little history, and fun to find.

"My gosh, Martha, this is nice," exclaimed Howard. "These prairie grasslands are so much different from the parks of Denver. You can see forever!"

"Howard," said Julie, looking down from her horse, "do you want to ride my horse for a while? I would offer you Jim's horse, but he would buck you off before you got on." Jim, Julie's brother, was always game for a Sunday ride. Although still in high school, he was heir apparent to the family ranch. Tall like his sister, long-limbed, and thin, he felt that being a rancher was going to be his line of trade and that racing horses was to be his game.

"Are we close to Pawnee Buttes?" Corbett strained to see something besides miles and miles of short-grass prairie.

"No," replied Jim. "A couple hours east of here, there's a high point." His pointing east gave Howard a bit of an idea which direction. "You can see them from there."

"I grew up in the mountains, where the horizon lies where the sun drops over the mountains," said Corbett, impressed and delighted to be on the ride. "Having the sun drop down over the edge of the horizon is incredible."

"There's a wagon coming up behind," said Jim, looking back. "I think it's Munley."

"Hi, folks," shouted Munley, waving as he passed by. "Got to go winterize a pump on a well out here before we get a hard freeze." Munley was the picture of what the easterners pictured cowboys to be, right up to the dangling of the string of the tobacco sack in his shirt pocket, never mind the stained cowboy hat, the red kerchief, and the sunburnt face. His was the face of a cowboy that made most people dream of yesteryear. He waved again as he and his wagon disappeared over the rise just ahead.

One shot, then two more. "What's that?!" Julie shouted to Jim.

"Probably coyote shooting," said Jim matter-of-factly. Then came three more shots in rapid succession.

"He wouldn't empty his gun like that. Something's up." Jim spurred his horse over the rise between him and the shooting. Corbett tapped the buggy horse and moved out in a trot.

"Corbett, what's happening?" Corbett and Julie saw the same

thing, but neither understood. Munley's team of horses were shrieking and spinning in a tight circle. Munley was standing inside the circle, trying to free the reins, which were knotted beneath the wagon.

Jim's horse reared and turned to run back to the group. "They're denning!" screamed Jim as he pulled up to the others. "There must be fifty rattlesnakes down where Munley's at. We've got to do something!"

Corbett could see that Munley was trying to free his horses from the reins tangled in the harnesses and the axle. Corbett flashed back to the freight wagon wreck in Durango. "Julie, give me your boots!" She did not hesitate. "Jim, throw me your knife. Jim, your knife!" Corbett quickly cut the stove top off both Julie's boots, sliced each open from top to bottom, and slipped them inside his pants legs, above his own boots.

"I'm not sure of this, but let's go!" Corbett knew that rattlesnakes, requiring heat to survive through the winter, gathered in a tight nest—nature's way of sharing body heat and increasing the body temperature of each creature in the nest.

By the time Corbett and Jim arrived, Munley, nauseous and played out, was lying down in the wagon. The lathered horses, still tangled, were nervously kicking and restlessly moving their feet. "Jim, stay right behind me. Don't shoot; we'll scare the horses more." The rattling of the snakes seemed everywhere. By the time Corbett cleared a path to the wagon, he had killed two snakes by striking them with a heavy stick. A third one struck Corbett's boot. The fangs caught in the leather and flopped about until Corbett cut off its head. Jim struck another with a big rock while it lay coiled, tail up and rattling.

"Munley! You okay?" asked Corbett. Hearing no answer, he

shouted to Jim, "Jump up into the wagon. Check on Munley, and reload his gun."

The harnesses and reins were a mess. Corbett slashed the reins, leaving them short, then climbed between the horses to the tongue with reins in hand. Released, the horses bolted onto the prairie grass with such power that the reins were lost from Corbett's hands. Jim fell to his back. He and Munley, sliding, bounced nearly as high as the side rails of the wagon. Jim finally recovered and set the wagon brake, which tired the horses, causing them to walk and then stop. Corbett worked his way free. The reason Corbett had not fallen between the horses was that he, too, had become enmeshed in the harness.

Jim saw Corbett flat on his back next to the wagon. "Corbett!"

"I'm dead, Jim. Bury me," Corbett said, trying to be humorous after the beating he had just taken. "Is Munley still in the wagon?" Corbett did not want to backtrack to find his patient.

"Jim thinks I'm alive, but he don't know shit." Munley, still in the horizontal position, was preparing to vomit. He had a headache and felt the pain of a swelling right leg.

"Sit him up," said Corbett. "Make that poison climb up to his heart." Corbett made ready to operate. "I'm going to bleed him out a little bit." He then gashed Munley's leg twice, one slice at each fang mark.

The buggy and Julie with both horses finally caught up with the runaway wagon. Howard looked over to the wagon. He was not about to get out. "Look at all the blood. He must have really got you?"

"He did," said Munley, pointing to Corbett.

"I'm going to go back over there and collect some skins," commented Jim. "I heard that a snakeskin coat is a mighty fine—"

"Like hell! I want to get out of here," Julie said. The rattling of the coiled rattlesnakes was still rattling around in Julie's head.

"We can take Munley and the wagon to our ranch."

"Wait a minute!" shouted Martha. "We've got water and some rags here. That leg is all bloody." Martha's parents owned a wheelwright shop in Greeley. The mother, quite feminine, had passed the trade along to her daughter, who was a nice, but a very uptown, young woman. Tall with big shoulders, and blonde with quite acceptable Scandinavian features, she, at first, had recoiled at the muddy, bloody leg. But given that she was a doer, she soon recovered and began to clean Munley's leg. The knife wound was still seeping blood, and the swelling was an indignant red.

The trip back to the ranch was slow. Munley's draft horses took small steps, their heads dropping to their knees. Corbett knew both horses had been bitten—both their noses were hot and dry, and their eyes were dull—but he knew of no other way to get them and Munley home.

The next day, Corbett saw Julie in the college dining room. "How's Munley? He looked terrible when your parents left with him to the hospital."

"My folks don't know yet. Dad said that denning season is a bad time to get bitten. In a way, the rattlesnakes this time of year are like the fat steers we sell in the fall, in good shape and healthy."

"It is just lucky we were there," said Martha. "I was so afraid of those snakes down in that den. You and Jim walked right into it."

"To be honest, I didn't understand what denning meant. Jim's the brave one." Corbett's eyes were wide. The memory of the snakes had raised his emotion a notch. "He knew what we were stepping into." Corbett, shaking his head, said, "I never saw so many snakes."

"Dad did say the horses will probably pull through. Their body weight is such that it spreads the poison around," explained Julie. "He said they would be off their feed and would be sick for a spell. He also said they would be worthless out on the prairie ever again—just too skittish."

Two weeks later at the boardinghouse, Glen asked Corbett, "You found all seven of these rattles right in that same place?" Glen was looking at the longest rattle. "I was told that each segment means a year of age, but others say two segments mean a year."

"Howard and I were afraid to go back out there, but like everyone said, the frost makes them all disappear underground," Corbett spoke in wonder.

"Jim got enough skins for a coat, I think," said Howard. "Even with the snakes dead, those fangs were too shuddery for me to touch. I'm glad I saw the wagon and the snakes, but I won't walk out there ever again. Not ever!" said Howard, making himself a solemn promise.

Leaves, leaves! Corbett and Howard had spent all morning raking the leaves under the trees on Glen and Frances's property. Glen had sat on a step of the porch, a fresh cup of coffee in his hand. Still looking for a third renter, he had figured that with the winter setting in, he might not get one until spring. Glen was watching Howard work, thinking the young man was slow and weak, although he did keep busy at that pace. However, Frances had told Glen that the kitchen stove and firebox had never been cleaner than the day Howard cleaned them. It took all morning, then all afternoon, for Howard to clean himself after that.

Corbett had impressed Glen from the beginning. The Saturday Corbett had cleaned out the chimneys was the first time the boardinghouse fires had been able to breathe in years. And Corbett had not complained about the soot and creosote all over his face and clothes. Although chimney cleaning was beneath him, Glen did admire someone who would take on such a task.

"Did you boys read that President Harrison is adding four more states?" asked Glen, reading about it firsthand in the *Tribune*. "The Dakotas are going to get split up into a North and a South. Then there's Montana and Washington." Glen fancied himself to be an expert on all things political. "I suppose that stops the British from having any thoughts of coming south.

"Corbett, are you a Democrat or a Republican?"

Corbett stopped his raking to think for a minute. "I don't suppose I'm either. Never needed to be." Corbett understood that politics had two sides with people on either side arguing with each other about the way the country should be run. But what side to be on? Who knew? Reconsidering that thought, Corbett knew that Glen would know and would give advice, asked for or not.

"If your parents came out of the South or Texas, you are probably a Democrat, a Rebel boy, like Governor Adams." Glen examined Corbett's expression. Nothing yet.

"If your family were Northerners and fought for Lincoln, then you are a Republican."

Corbett thought it through. "I guess that makes me a Democrat. We come from West Texas, but I can't talk for West Texans or speak ill of them."

"I would see to it that you learn your side." To Glen, partisanship held a higher status than perhaps working.

"Howard, how about you? Democrat or Republican?"

Howard cleared his throat. "I'm Jewish."

"And they send types like you out to teach the world," said Glen, throwing up his hands in disbelief.

After a long night at the Cattleman's, Howard and Terry sat in back of the wagon, both covered with blankets. "At home, leaving home was all I would think of." Howard stared at the stars. "Everything was so predictable and humdrum. My parents never knew or expected anything different." His present comfort was Terry, snuggled next to him for warmth. She was exhausted and meant nothing by it, but Howard took it for something grand. "It is better here. But to really live, you are obligated to work and risk it all. I'm not sure I can do that for the rest of my life."

"Howard." Corbett's eyes studied the glow of the newly installed city lights of Greeley. "Someday you will be sitting in front of your class watching your students do cursive and thinking how great it was to step away from a life of ease and take the harder road. Besides, you would've missed sitting next to a pretty girl in the back of a wagon, covered with blankets." Corbett looked back at Terry, who coyly winked. She knew she was not pretty, but tonight she was the prettiest woman present. Corbett had just said so.

The Saturday night crowd at the Cattleman's was wild and drunk as usual. There was less thought of food and more thought of getting drunk. The bar crowd spilled into the restaurant with regularity. Twin fiddles could be heard every time the door between the two areas opened. Howard, Terry, and Corbett were due to end their shift within the next half hour. Mel counted it as a good night, and his receipts proved it.

Three drunk cowboys were sprawled at a table. Coffee seemed a logical choice considering their condition, except that the flask being passed around, its contents poured into the coffee, contained Old Kentucky whiskey. The men were moving from being loud and obnoxious to being stupefied, but they were not there yet.

Howard was carrying the dirty dishware from one of the last tables. He stepped between an empty chair at an adjoining table and the cowboys. The nearest cowboy reached his foot out and tripped Howard. Howard and the dishes went crashing to the floor. All three cowboys at the table laughed. One offered a toast to the other two. Howard stayed on his hands and knees to gather the glassware.

The loud sound of broken glass caught the restaurant's attention. Mel jumped to his feet from the cash register. Terry came from wiping a table near the back, and Corbett emerged from the dishwashing area. As time would have it, all of them saw the same cowboy use his boot to push against Howard's side, causing him to fall on his side.

"Hold it! Hold it!" Mel reached down toward Howard to help him up.

"I'm thinking that he's a damned Jew, and that damned Jew got food on my boots!" said the cowboy, looking back to his friends, laughing.

"Leave him! Please leave him!" Mel, on one knee at Howard's side, held a hand up to protect them both.

"Are you a damned Jew too?" The cowboy stared at Mel.

Corbett's right hand knocked the cowboy into a post behind him. The blow landed squarely on the cowboy's nose, smashing it. The cowboy was out before he hit the post. However, hitting the post probably did not help his frame of mind.

A second cowboy rose to fight. The remaining cowboy was trapped on the floor by the upturned table Corbett had sent in his direction. Corbett tackled the standing cowboy, knocking him to the ground, and pounded his head against the floor until the cowboy's eyes rolled back in his head.

Only through the efforts of the bar manager and his bouncer, both arriving late to the scene, did Corbett stop. Laddie once said that the Marquess of Queensberry Rules of Boxing do not count in bar fights. "You beat them bad the first time, and you won't have to do it again," Laddie had said.

"Easy, Corbett!" said the manager, pulling him from atop the broken cowboy. "It's over."

The Cattleman's was empty and quiet. The bar manager, Mel, and the bar bouncer sat with coffee. It had been another long Saturday night.

"I can't believe that Corbett kid," said the bouncer, shaking his head. "You can tell by his looks that he's strong, but his quickness is amazing!"

"Mel," added the bar manager, "that boy, beneath his calm exterior, is very angry. I don't know anything about his background, but it must have been bad."

"A couple of times," Mel said, "I almost fired Howard, but since Corbett does the work of two, it works out."

"I know this much," said the bouncer, looking at the bar manager. "If I ever need help in a fight in the bar, I will get Corbett. I sure as hell wouldn't want to fight him!"

"Mrs. Casey, I sure appreciate your cooking, especially these beans and the bread," said Corbett, sitting down in the kitchen for an after-school snack. Anytime, day or night, Howard or Corbett could have a bowl of pintos and/or fresh bread with butter.

More than once Glen would say, "Frances, you are overfeeding these boys." But he never said anything about the beans at the back of the stove.

"Why, thank you, Corbett." Frances topped out at about five feet. Right below her wire-rimmed round glasses were two red cheeks and a sweet smile. Everyone knew her from her work ethic. Pies and cakes for the church socials, as well as baby quilts for every newborn, were only part of her reputation. Living with Glen was the other part.

"Good news or bad news?" asked Frances, seeing Corbett's deep concern over several papers on the table.

"My report scores for the first semester," commented Corbett, still reading in a serious manner. "I've never had a report card before."

"Well, like I said, good news or bad?"

"Three superiors and three above average."

"That's wonderful!" said Frances, reading over his shoulder, then patting him on the back. He sat back and dropped his chin to his chest. His mother would have said the same thing and would have patted his shoulder the same way, had they both had the chance.

"I hope you're proud," Corbett whispered, for his mother.

"So, you glad you came?" Frances was now sitting across from him. "You seem to be doing really well. Glen likes your spirit, always ready to pitch in."

"I kind of don't like it. I don't have any time to read my novels, only those things they want us to learn. And who knows whether students at a new school will be as nice as the ones in Silverton." He stopped and took stock of what he had just said. "My friend Julie says that her father would take me on at their ranch right now. I'd be making way more money than being a schoolmaster would ever get."

"Is Julie part of your thoughts?"

"No, just a friend."

"Does she know that?"

As Corbett rose to leave, he said with a sheepish grin, "I sure like cowboying!"

6

"Thanks for the ham and beans," said Terry. "It just fits the day."

"It's more like beans, beans, beans, and ham, but thank you anyway," replied Frances.

Corbett was looking out the window of the boardinghouse. "This is different from the heavy snows of Silverton. Up there, they have big flakes—and a million of them." The horses, hidden by a lean-to in their corral, were all pointed to the east; the blizzard was coming from the west. "Here the snow flies by sideways and sticks to anything facing west. A flatland blizzard. Amazing."

"Terry, you want to help make some sourdough bread?" offered Frances. "A good day to keep the oven hot."

"Corbett, I believe we could use some more wood from the porch," stated Glen from his chair next to the large ornate potbelly stove. He was waiting for Howard to set up the chessboard on the table next to him. "Probably need some moved from the woodshed as well."

The trip to Cattleman's for work that afternoon was canceled because the road was closed. The main road from Denver to Cheyenne through Fort Collins lay buried for miles, and more wind and snow was expected. With no college tomorrow, time was going to take a couple of days off.

"I'm glad there's no work tonight," said Terry. "I about froze last night on the way home. Howard and I were covered with blankets and were still cold." It was the clear, cold freeze before a storm. "The stars were clearly visible, and there was no wind, just cold. I don't know how Corbett stood it up in the driver's seat."

Bundled for the trip to the woodshed, Corbett laughed. "I heated three bricks from the Cattleman's sidewalk and put them in my coat as we left." Everyone thoughtfully approved. "That lasted about ten minutes. The rest of the way, I was poked and scraped by the bricks, keeping me from freezing in comfort."

Glen and Howard battled periodically at chess. Glen's temper tantrum after a loss was substantial. However, a win sent Glen into a pompous heaven. With Terry, Corbett, and Frances somewhat interested, it was a bloodbath. Castles fell, pawns were purged, and even the saintly bishops were castigated. Except for the pauses, the battle raged through the night.

The first pause centered on Terry.

"I guess I'd better get along," said Terry, her hands covered in flour. "I sure enjoyed spending time with you." Terry's small rental, about a mile away, had a fire going only after Terry had built one. Her meals consisted of the college noonday meal and supper at the Cattleman's. There was no money to fall back on; everything was day to day. She had saved for the opportunity to attend school, and the time to do that was now.

"You're not going anywhere," said Frances plainly. "I don't think you can get home," Frances stated with in a motherly tone. "And I would worry all night about it."

"Frances." Glen's voice was a little louder than necessary. "I don't—"

"No, Glen," Frances, who was always subservient, said coldly. "She is staying the night. Up in the extra room will do."

Howard, Terry, Corbett, and Frances scrambled upstairs to

prepare the empty room. Terry, usually invisible amid the goings-on in life, was, for the first time, the center of attention. She had heard about the other young women questioning why with her plain looks she was such close friends with Corbett and Howard, concluding that it was probably because she was filling the needs of both.

"I can't thank you enough," said Terry. "Every night I have to build a fire when I get home. I was not looking forward to it."

The next evening, snowed in and expecting more snow, Corbett was reading, his favorite pastime. Tonight, he got to open *The Scarlet Letter*, by Hawthorne. Glen and Howard were in game two of the chess battle of the century. Frances and Terry plotted the next item to be baked from Frances's old *Everyday Cookery*. It was a night spent quite cozily, safe from the raging storm.

Late that night or early the next morning, Glen, like most old men, got up to do what most old men do in the middle of the night. While he was standing there, he sensed something unusual from the window. Closer examination showed the snow still blowing viciously, but a glow of yellow and red had found its way through the flakes.

Glen could have shouted, "Frances! Ring up the fire department. The Mexicans' house is on fire!" Greeley had had crank telephones for about five years, but many, such as Glen, saw the device as too expensive. Besides, anyone on the party line could listen in on the conversation. Instead, he shouted, "Corbett! Frances! The Mexicans' house is on fire!"

Most houses built in the late 1880s were tinderboxes, especially those of the poor. Extreme cold forced the occupants to add more wood or coal to their fires. The Mexicans' home was a poorly insulated and highly vulnerable to fire around the stove area.

The boardinghouse came alive, Corbett wearing boots and

gloves not yet dry from hauling wood, Terry receiving gloves and a knitted scarf from Frances, and Howard carefully tying his boots.

"Frances! I need a couple of blankets."

Corbett, at the window, felt someone at his side. It was Terry.

"Let's go!" said Terry, opening the door. The wind blew her back until Corbett grabbed her by the shoulder of her coat.

"Follow my tracks," shouted Corbett through the wind. The eighteen-inch drifts slowed every step. The roof was entirely in flames, as was the sidewall close to the stovepipe. Several shadows were moving about the fire, shoveling snow at the flames. Then came the screams, horrible screams, just like those James Fennimore Cooper had written about in *The Last of the Mohicans*: "The air continued full of horrible cries and screams, such as man alone can utter, and only when in a state of the fiercest barbarity"—those kinds of screams.

"How many live here?" asked Corbett, seeing but one door, already lapped by flames dancing up from the bottom. Corbett did not know whether he wanted the horrible screams to stop or whether he wished for the Mexicans to wait out the agony with the hope of rescue.

"Don't know!" yelled a shadow flashing by with a scoop shovel full of snow.

Ten minutes later, the roof collapsed. Seconds later, the sounds ceased. To a man, everyone dropped and cried. Even those who were partial against Mexicans cried. Nearly every man had smoke trailing from his coat, carried away by the snow and wind.

Red embers were the only light, and they were fading. The crash of the roof an hour earlier had taken away all hope. The last of the men in shadows put his shovel on his slumped shoulder and walked away. By sunup, the ruins of the house would be covered like a burial mound of sorts.

"Corbett!" cried Terry. "Corbett, hurry!" The shouts came from the back of the shack. Corbett saw Howard kneeling just a few feet from the embers. Something had happened to Howard.

"Howard, what's the matter?" Howard made no attempt to raise his head. In the snowy pit, the walls of snow shoved aside, lay a baby, a cold, dead, blue baby.

"They must have thrown her out the tiny bathroom window," whispered Terry. "A mother's last gift to her child." Neither Terry nor Howard had touched the child. No one wants to touch a dead child. Terry was a wreck, in shock and shaking from the screams and now from the sight of a baby cradled and covered by icy snow.

Corbett reached down and carefully lifted the baby. "I'll cut a trail." He handed the baby to Howard. "Open your coat and protect the baby." As Howard pulled the baby to his chest, its head fell backward. Terry saw the limp baby's head then fall forward against Howard's chest. Until that moment, Howard had never held a baby. Both Terry and Howard stumbled onto the beaten path that Corbett had opened, weeping as they went.

Frances studied the dead child, a girl at that. The blueness of the lips and face, together with the absence of movement, seemed surreal to Frances. Tears came to her eyes. "We can pray over her and wrap her up properly." Glen, usually full of pronouncements, said nothing. His first sight of death had come at the Battle of Chancellorsville in Virginia. A young friend had died. Glen's first view of the young man was of the flies marching about his friend's opened eyes and mouth. Glen had walked away from the battle and the war. The vulnerability of the dead, leaving their bodies to be done with as others pleased, was too much for him.

Corbett was the last one in. "Terry, get all your clothes off and get into bed. Get it warm!" demanded Corbett. "I'll be in there in a minute." Terry stared at Corbett. "Do it. We are going to save this baby!"

Glen, sitting on a kitchen chair away from the others, said, "It's dead, Corbett."

"Frances, rub the baby with a dry towel," said Corbett as he dropped his head to pray. Haruyo had said a year ago in Silverton, "Cold water. Just asleep," when she brought Emi back to life. Could that still hold true?

Corbett carried the baby, its head and chest in one hand, face-down, with a leg on each side of his arm. Terry, looking frightened, had blankets pulled up to her neck. Corbett threw back the covers. Terry was nude and scared. She tried to cover herself.

"Stop it. We don't have time for this." He put the baby's head between her breasts. "You keep this baby warm."

Howard had just seen a woman's nipples for the first time. They were small, pert, and pointed. Terry surrounded the baby with her arms. A slight smile came across her face as she warmed the child. For the moment, it was her child. Then came the thought, which she gave voice to, "What if she comes alive?" Terry became stricken with fear.

"I don't know. What would you tell your daughter if she just woke up from a bad dream?" replied Corbett. "Her name is Emi. It means blessing in Japanese." Then he left, emotionally drained.

The morning window provided a hint of the day. *One thing about Colorado,* thought Corbett, *is that it is either sunshine or snow, not much gray.*

He stood up as if he had been shot from a cannon. *The baby.* Trying to dress quickly, he had run into a problem. Corbett's clothes were smoky, cold, and wet. He put on a soiled, wrinkled shirt and a pair of pants reeking of Cattleman's dishes.

The kitchen was bright, smelling of coffee and pancakes.

Frances sitting with her cup, and Terry was sitting with hers. Terry's shoulders were bare but for the blue quilt surrounding the rest of her. On this clear frosty morning, Terry's smile could have warmed everything. Against her body lay a baby's head, barely visible above the quilt.

Terry, her eyes wide with excitement, said, "I was asleep when I felt the movement of the baby. It startled me so much that I almost pushed her away. Then it happened again." Corbett had never seen Terry so animated. "You know how a pregnant woman talks about the first time she feels the baby move? It was just like that." Terry reached over and patted Frances's hand. Frances was in the room. She had been there all night, bless her heart. And the child was breathing!

"She hasn't opened her eyes yet, but her heart is beating faster," said Frances, like a proud new grandmother.

Glen plodded into the kitchen. He poured some coffee from the stove before he realized that there was a baby in the room. "She's alive?" he asked, sitting slowly, now making for four at the table.

"She is, Glen! She is."

"Oh damn, I was afraid of that." Glen shook his head, studying the surface of his coffee. "When things happen like this, the baby or adult usually ends up a moron. Worthless as hell."

"Glen Casey, don't sit here with us if you are going to think like that!" Frances was enraged. Her pink cheeks joined the rest of her face in turning a scalding red.

Corbett spent the morning outside clearing pathways, feeding the horses, and walking to the burn site. The few there were not interested in digging through the snow for bodies. That could wait. About noon, the priest from Saint Peter's arrived. After the priest had had a very quiet and prayerful walk-around, one of the onlookers asked, "Father, did you know them?"

"No. I have asked several Mexican members of our flock. We know very little about the family who perished. They say the man went from one farm job to another. Didn't even know he was married. But it is correct to assume they were Catholic. And we are here for them."

Corbett said nothing. His feeling was that Terry and Frances were as good as anyone the church could provide, but he went back and forth on the issue until he reached the boardinghouse. Maybe it was against the law to hide the baby from the community. Maybe she was going to be a moron. He also knew that Frances and Terry would put up a battle, at least at this point.

It was lunchtime. Corbett was kicking the snow off his boots on the steps of the boardinghouse, when he stopped and listened again. It sounded like a cry of a baby. Inside, Howard and Terry were spectators to the "sugar teat" method of feeding a baby, as demonstrated by Grandmother Frances.

"Look at this baby!" called Howard, watching the event with evident joy.

"Well, how is Emi?"

"We don't know Emi, but we do know Annie," said Terry slyly.

"Watch!" Frances held up a light brown baby squalling for food, her feet moving up and down and her fists pumping.

"Now, Terry, when you do this, put a pat of butter and a little sugar in the middle of a dishrag." Frances seemed at the height of her glory. "Twist and dip it into milk. If the baby is hungry—and this one is—she will suck on it."

The twisted rag was moved in a circle around Annie's mouth a couple of times before she snagged onto it. Everyone, including Glen, applauded. After several dips, Frances stopped. "We call this a sugar teat." Everyone watched until Annie's interest declined and she fell into slumber.

"We have to talk about Annie," said Corbett, as if the lawyer in the room. "The priest was at the Mexicans' house this morning. They don't know anything about the Mexicans or how many there were, except that the man did farm labor." Terry was rocking the baby. Howard was sitting next to her at the kitchen table. Both were listening intently. Frances and Glen were sitting off to the side. They, too, were very interested in where this was going. "They don't know that Annie exists."

"I want to keep her," said Howard. "I found her!"

"No, she's mine," piped Terry. "I birthed her!" Terry's face held a coquettish smirk. Everyone laughed.

"She belongs to all of us right now." Glen, the head of household, stunned the others with his pronouncement. "I am afraid for you folks that someday her people will come and get her. But for now, we can believe that Terry has had an 'immaculate conception.'" He waited for that concept to sink in. "And Annie will live here with us." Frances tilted her head with pride and amazement. It had been years since Glen had shown this much compassion toward anyone.

Corbett stepped in. "Terry, if you are to be the mother of this baby, at least for now, it will seem to others that you had the child with a Mexican. Can you handle that?"

"Everybody I know thinks that I am whoring with you and Howard because we are together all the time. My mother won't like it, but I don't care." The stress of fighting for her Annie showed on her face. "Look at me. Do you think I will get another chance to be a mother? I may be homely like they say, but I have the heart of a mother!"

"You've got me convinced," said Corbett jokingly, backing away with his hands up.

"What about me?" asked Howard, incredulous that he was being overlooked. "I found her."

"Unless you can prove that you produce brown babies, you're an uncle," said Frances, enjoying the little private society being formed around Annie.

College came back to life with assignment after assignment given to make up for the lost days. Because Cattleman's still took away hours of his study time, Corbett was behind. He contemplated quitting Cattleman's. Being an omnibus boy for the rest of his life was not in the cards for him. Corbett knew he would have to dig in. College would give him a future.

Howard always had some money—not much, but enough. Terry did not leave the Caseys' boardinghouse and rarely left Annie's side. Howard noted this when speaking to Mel, saying that Terry would not be back. Then, surprising even to Howard, Terry composed a letter to the dean of the college explaining her need to drop out. The explanation was light on details, but it was done. A new life, literally, had begun for her.

At the college lunch table, Howard sat playing with his meat and potatoes. "Corbett, I need your advice."

"This sounds serious," said Corbett, smiling back at his friend.

"What do you think about Terry?"

"What do you mean?" said Corbett. "I think she is wonderful—a very good friend and now a very good mother."

"Think she will ever marry? She's not at all pretty. Did you see those small teats?"

"Don't judge her by holding her up against your calendar girls. I think a wife is basically a good companion who keeps you warm at night. I loved Ajai, but she wasn't pretty. I would've moved to the reservation if that would have made her happy."

"Corbett," whispered Howard, leaning over the table, "I think I want to marry Terry."

"You had all that figured out before I made my big speech," Corbett replied, showing fake disdain to Howard.

"If she will have me. I don't offer much."

"That's for damn sure." Corbett, leaning back, laughed. "She probably wants a calendar man."

Corbett came down from his room to partake in Sunday dinner. Frances reveled in preparing the Sunday meal. That was before Terry. Now, with Terry as an empty vessel to be filled with all the nuances of cooking, it was more delightful. Glen, with the Sunday paper, sat at his post near the front window, wearing his favorite gray sweater, outwardly denouncing all the hubbub of Sunday mornings. Cracks were showing in his austere features. Although he refused to hold Annie per se, the rocking cradle he had found in the attic did require his attention every so often.

Howard was unusually late for the festivities. It was obvious to the entire boardinghouse that Terry and Howard were in love. The rebirth of Annie and the passion to love her and keep her safe had allowed both to move on from their feelings of inadequacy to a belief in themselves. Howard, at the onset of this relationship, had written home asking for more money. The reason he gave was that he had adopted two girls and needed an allowance each month to provide for their care. Obviously, he did not acknowledge the fact that one of the girls was his own age.

With all at the table, and Howard now present, he rose to speak, which was not normal for him. "I would like to take a moment." He looked to all at the table and then focused on Terry, who was sitting beside him. "I have explored many different ways to propose to Terry and marry her, knowing my Jewish family in Denver would never accept the result." The table grew desperately quiet. "I have decided to marry into my new family, and I will offer my Terry this ring." His chubby fingers opened a small velveteen box. A ring of blue sapphires surrounding three sparkling diamonds stole the breath of all at the table.

"I wrote my father just a few days ago and told him about Terry and Annie. He sent me this special ring made by him for Terry. There was also a note from him saying, 'Go with God.'" Terry, with tears in her eyes, stood and hugged her Jewish man. No one could see or hear her cry; the quiet heaving of her back and shoulders seemed to express her joy. Frances, tears falling, rocked Annie. "Terry, I promise to love and care for you and Annie as long as I live." Corbett was impressed with how manly Howard was acting. "I am trapped by the needs of my new family and the love of my Jewish family. My father has opened the door for me to leave my Jewish faith." Howard was not in tears, but he was deeply stressed. "But I can't." Howard held both of Terry's hands. "I am what I am, and I hope you and Annie know that I am yours."

It was another Saturday morning at Cattleman's. The place was known for its steak and eggs for breakfast. As per usual, Saturday was the day farmers and ranchers got duded up and went to town. What better way to start that day than to have steak and eggs at Cattleman's?

"Corbett!" called a female voice from across the room. Corbett set his tray of dirty dishes down and tried to locate the voice. "Corbett, over here!" Julie was sitting with an older handsome pair, probably her parents. "Come here a minute!"

"Hi, Julie. You look nice today." Indeed, Julie always looked good, but today, dressed up in a long frilly cotton dress, she was beautiful. He dried his hands on the dish towel and waited for an introduction.

"Corbett, these are my parents, Josh and Marty Bjlack." Josh stood to shake Corbett's hand. Josh's boots spoke of money. His silver belt buckle spoke of money, and his light brown Stetson, a touch newer than the Boss of the Plains model, usually worn by the established ranchers, spoke of money. Josh's gray eyes dominated the conversation, as they did any conversation. He was typical of Scandinavians, tall, thin, and well-ordered, except age had removed most of his hair.

"Happy to meet you, son." He looked directly through Corbett to gauge the young man's confidence level. "Julie talks about you every day." Then Josh remembered whom he was talking to. "Aren't you the rattlesnake kid who helped Munley?"

"Well, I was there," said Corbett modestly. "How is he doing, by the way?"

"I understand that he still has a little hitch in his giddyap, but he will make it."

"Good."

"Dad?" Julie looked up at her father, showing mock disdain.

"Yes, Corbett, I know you haven't a lot of time right now, but the reason we dropped in this morning was to offer you a part-time job at the ranch. Same amount of time as here, and a little more pay." That brought Corbett to a standstill. "Still want you to be going to college, like Julie does."

"Go tell Mel after work, and start Monday afternoon!" exclaimed Julie, moving things along.

It did not take long for Corbett to figure out that wrangling cattle outside in the open air beat pearl diving in the back of the Cattleman's Restaurant.

After the shift was over, Corbett found Mel deep in receipts.

"Mel, I guess I need to let you know that next week will be my last week," said Corbett, drying his hands. Giving Mel time to find a replacement was the right thing to do. "I'm going to work out at the Bjlack ranch for the spring and maybe the summer."

"Dang it, Corbett." Mel had known that at some point in time Corbett would find work more suited to his obvious talent. "Hell, you know you're going to be missed," said Mel, setting aside his paperwork. "You, Howard, and Terry really helped me through a rough spot. I'm thinking more highly of college kids. Tell me the truth about Terry. She up and quit one day, and that's all I've heard after all this time."

"I know," said Corbett. "The truth is that she adopted a little girl and quit school as well."

Now Mel had more questions. "How's she getting by? Did she get married?"

"Nope." Corbett winked. "She's with Howard."

"No shit!" said Mel, astonished at the answer. Both glanced over at Howard, who was at the cash register busy with paperwork. "How about that?" Mel smiled and shook his head slightly. "You know, he might own this place someday."

A lesson on teaching history: "At your school, geography and history will blend together. The youngest need to know that President Harrison, the ninth president of the United States, just added four states to the union, Washington, Montana, and the two Dakotas. That makes forty-two. Two new memorizations: Name the presidents in order, and name all the states and their capitals. Our youngest ones start here.

"History must be learned and understood. The British, French, and Dutch are racing to colonize Africa. Where's Africa? Closer to home, this last summer a dam broke in Pennsylvania and killed many in the Johnstown flood. Where's Pennsylvania? Five hundred miles from here, the US Army, a month ago, just won the Battle at Wounded Knee, opening huge new lands for mining and settlements. Where is South Dakota? I'm sorry," explained Mr. Anderson, wiping his brow and nearly frothing at the mouth, "I get very excited about our role in the dispersal of information not only to our students but also, in some cases, to the whole community. What a great time to be an educator!"

Corbett had never had a horse. Taking the freight wagons to the coal mines was his first time around horses. His lack of experience became evident the day he and Slater had searched for pregnant cows, either lost or birthing calves. The relationship between the horse and Corbett was not a pretty thing to witness. With the horse's back and saddle rising to meet Corbett's butt coming down, at a trot, was almost sorrowful.

Cows about to calve tended to separate themselves from the herd and find a quiet place in the brush or a grassy draw. The Bjlacks were mostly concerned with the two-year-old heifers trying to pass big-headed calves, only to wear out and die. Coyotes sometimes caught a heifer in the act of calving and ate the calf while it was being born. In both cases, the Bjlacks lost money.

"Here she is," shouted Slater, only his head and his horse's head showing above the tall brush. Jim was already on the ground, getting a sense of the heifer's struggle. Slater, tying his horse and standing to the rear of the heifer, said, "She's been at it for a while. About worn out." He sat down on his haunches, took out his makings, and twisted up a cigarette. "I usually wait till she heaves a time or two to see where we're at."

Corbett could see that the heifer was pretty well sprung with a watery excrement seeping out. He stepped back as she rolled a bit and groaned, then all her hip and abdominal muscles grew taut as she held herself still for several seconds. The cow's breath returned as she painfully relaxed.

"Oh hell, let's get on with it." Slater sighed, always impatient. He rolled up his sleeves. "I am glad you're here," he said to Corbett, "but in ten minutes, I bet you won't be." Corbett rolled up his sleeves to assist. "See those hooves sticking out? Walk your hands up those legs as far in as you can reach." Corbett stepped back. There was no way he was going to put his hands in there. "Damn it, Corbett, watch out!" Slater pushed Corbett aside. "Watch!" Slater grabbed both legs and slipped in, sliding deeper and deeper, spreading his arms as he went. "This usually gets 'em going." The cow began her strain. "Pull when she strains," Slater explained while he pulled and leaned back. A sharp pain erupted across Slater's lower back, which grew more unworthy each day. "Help me, Corbett!" Corbett stepped between Slater and the cow. He grabbed a leg with each hand, set his heels, and strained every muscle. As if on cue, a slimy white head popped out. "Good. Rest." Slater fell to his back, breathing hard.

"He's not breathing!" yelled Corbett.

"He's still breathing through his cord," said Slater, lying back, avoiding taking any deep breaths for fear of causing more pain to his back. "The next strain, we have to get the shoulders and chest out." The strain began. Corbett reset his feet, one on the cow's back leg and the other digging into the sandy soil. The calf's head moved back and forth a time or two. It was still trapped inside, from the shoulders down. A long moment later, the shiny, slick shoulders slipped out. "We got her!" Corbett wanted to wipe some spatters from his face, but after noticing the bloody mucous covering his hands, he decided against it. With the heifer's next strain, the calf flopped completely out. "You did it, Hoss!" Slater slapped Corbett on the back. Corbett could feel the wetness of the handprint.

Slater, with a rough rag, wiped off the calf's nose and mouth. The calf was breathing. "Funny damned thing. That cord breaks and the calf starts up the breathing. I couldn't have done it without you, Corbett. I'm just not strong enough anymore." The cowboy in him was very much alive, but he had disregarded his body for too many years. "I'll have to use a winch or something next time."

Learning to teach math at Colorado State Normal College, Corbett sat as Mr. Herving lectured: "All year we put forth our tools available for teaching: rote, recitation, and oral drilling. The length and depth of mathematics extends from rote to reasoning. Writing a multiplication fact ten times after class solidifies the rote. The next day, in front of the class, the recitation of multiplication facts memorized satisfies the oral drilling." Corbett was growing tired of observing the art of teaching rote. He disliked the classroom demonstrations of the same.

Mr. Herving continued, "Reasoning is taking the material learned by rote and, from it, providing an answer needed in real life. Example: Farmer Jones wants to buy one of these new metal silos to replace his old wooden granary. He wants the silo to hold more than his granary. The granary is sixteen by eight by six, so, seven hundred sixty-eight cubic feet. The silo is twelve feet in diameter and holds grain in a column eight feet high. Knowing the formula for the volume of a cylinder by rote and applying it, we get three-point-one-four by six-by-six-by-eight, for nine hundred four cubic feet. That is rote to reasoning."

The students shuffled about in their desks, ready to leave. "Don't forget that we start geometry tomorrow. The rote of Euclid's six postulates." The groaning was respectively low, but it was uniform throughout the group. All agreed that rote sucked the energy out of any classroom, but they were glad that another day was done.

Corbett loved the Bjlack ranch with its huge barns surrounded by fine old trees, and the nicely thought-out sets of corrals and tack buildings with hay equipment neatly in place. Best of all, he liked the cowboys and their horses coming and going from one task to another. Like in the pictures and drawings, nearly all the cowboys wore chaps, kerchiefs, and old leather vests for mornings like this. Individuality was expressed mostly in the cowboy's choice of hat. The creases to the crown, the shaping of the brim, and the height of the crown made the man. A good beaver pelt was often the most expensive item a cowboy owned. The last touch was the tilt of the hat. To wear it tilted showed cockiness. A man who wore his tilted back was a neighborly cuss who loved people and drinking. Corbett's Montgomery Ward hat showed him to be a poor pilgrim with little hope in cowboy country.

"Good Saturday morning to ya," shouted Jim. "Ready to buckaroo some? We have some cattle to move."

"Do I get to rope anything yet?"

Jim chuckled. "We aren't that desperate yet! Oh, the Basques have the lambs in." Jim waved Corbett's attention toward some low-slung sheds away from the rest of the buildings. "I want you to see something."

The sheep corral was full of white-faced ewes and their young lambs. The stirring of the Basques to collect the lambs the men wanted, and the constant bleating of lambs, made the situation seem chaotic. The Basques seemed to be of one family, olive-skinned with old light-colored shirts, and all with uncharacteristic noses. It looked as if all had been hit with the same punch.

Jim and Corbett followed one young man through a doorway, carrying a healthy male lamb. Sitting cross-legged on the floor was an old Basque moving another lamb off his lap. Corbett's body jerked back. The man had a sharp knife and a bloody chin.

Corbett's eyes grew wide with disbelief as he saw the man turn the lamb onto its back and slice its cod with the knife. He bent his face to the cod and, with his teeth, bit the cords to the testicles in two. The old man looked up at his visitors and smiled. Corbett lasted long enough to see the blood dripping from the man's beard, right before Jim pushed Corbett to the outside.

"Want to be a sheepman?" mocked Jim as he watched his friend vomit, heave, and vomit some more.

"What in the hell was that?" asked Corbett, not particularly enjoying the moment.

"You didn't stay long enough to see them dock the lamb's tail. Old country traditions, I guess."

"God, that was terrible!"

"My dad has sheep but is not a sheepman," stated Jim. "He says sheep stay up nights figuring out different ways to die."

Time was passing rapidly. Corbett felt that his schoolwork was done easier at the college, as the boardinghouse was just too busy. Not that having Terry and Annie living in the third bedroom made things worse; it just made the place busier. True to his word, Howard had not made any nightly forays into Terry's bedroom, but the pair were inseparable anytime Howard was home. Even though Howard's father had spent most of his life under the Haskalah movement, he saw the marriage of a Jew and non-Jew as being against the dogma of his faith. However, he continued to send money to Howard to help support his adopted family. Letters to his father from Howard turned Corbett into a dime novel hero, fighting rattlesnakes, fighting for the less able, and riding horses on the prairie. The elder Jew saw the freedom of the Gentiles as exciting, but he felt that he, like all Jews, must pass on the doctrines of Abraham for posterity to Abraham's children.

Annie was wonderfully happy with the adults in her life. She had jet-black hair and brown eyes, and was fresh-faced and a little roly-poly—just as a baby should look. Paranoia still existed with regard to Annie. Glen scoured the paper daily, looking for any news about Annie's Mexican parents. Terry was slow to take Annie into public view, but even her reluctance was lessening.

"That's the worst lasso loop I ever saw." Jim laughed. "Let me show you the difference. When you throw, you release the lariat with your hand, like a rock." A wild-moving misshapen loop hit the side of the post. "When I toss it, I let the lariat slide through my fingers. Next, I guide it until it gets where I want it to get, then I pull up the slack." His next loop sailed, the lasso gliding through Jim's gloved hand until it seemed to hesitate, momentarily, above the post and drop onto it, the slack taken up.

"You make it look so easy," said Corbett, shaking his head in admiration. Corbett thought maybe the difference was in Jim's rope, a rawhide Mexican riata, very expensive and very smooth. Now that he had a cowboy hat, a riata was next if he really wanted to be a cowboy.

"Now I don't think Dad will let you rope and dally today, anyway" Jim said. "Let's saddle up and see what you can do." The pair entered an empty corral. "Years ago, Dad put a wooden head on that sawhorse over there for me to practice." With wooden horns, a somewhat carved face, and a sawhorse for a body, and cemented to the ground, the wooden steer was ready to teach another class.

"Watch out now!" Jim spurred his horse forward. Casting a loop that grew smaller until it just fit over the horns, he snapped back on the slack and wrapped the rope around the saddle horn. Jim's roping horse, also very practiced at the motion, set all four feet and backed up until the rope was tight. "Ropers do that fifty times a day during branding." Jim, the young buckaroo, was quite proud of himself. "Now you make a big loop by twisting your wrist like this." The riata uncoiled in seconds, a wide loop now spinning over Jim's head. When it was released and guided, it landed still, a wide, flat loop.

Being that it was lunchtime, several cowboys on their horses were watching from outside the corral. For moral support, Slater and Jim, who had just come in from throwing a morning's full of loops during the early day's branding session, were in the center of the arena. Their loops were temporarily hanging over their saddle horns, resting.

"Make sure that if you miss the dally around the horn," Slater said, sounding serious, "you get your hands and fingers out of there." To illustrate the point for the umpteenth time, he pulled his right hand out of his glove to show that the index and middle fingers were missing because of a dally gone wrong. Fingers trapped in the rope between the horn and the roped calf are squeezed off. Slater's ugly scar, all that now remained of the wound that had been closed together by the camp cook, was a constant reminder of a bad dally.

"Okay, okay," said Corbett, anxious to prove his mettle as a cowboy. "Let me catch and throw this calf!"

The three calves, already pretty stirred up, squeezed against each other at the far side of the corral. Corbett's horse, a little high-headed with its front feet dancing, was spurred by Corbett to break up the group. One calf broke left from the other two. Corbett used his left spur and slapped the right rear of his horse with his loop.

The next second, Corbett's horse began to buck wildly. Corbett's loop had slipped under his horse's right rear hoof, going all the way up the leg, while a coil had tightened around the horn. Corbett, with reins and a whole lot of coiled rope in front of him, began to buckaroo.

Each time the horse bucked, Corbett fell forward, the saddle horn digging into his abdomen. Most of the rope fell away quite nicely, except the portion that was up high between his horse's hind legs. Corbett's newly purchased cowboy hat lay stomped and crumpled, to be visited twice more before the rodeo was over. It was becoming more of a cowboy hat with each stomp.

Cowboying is a boring day in, day out sort of thing, so to have a rodeo before lunch was outstanding. "Ride 'em, Corbett!" shouted one voice.

Rodeoing was Slater's life. "Sunfish, you sorry son of a bitch!" He had his hat in hand, above his head, cheering for more. Corbett was not a little boy anymore, yet he could not keep the horse from lowering its head and bucking forward. As the main attraction slammed against the side poles of the corrals, Corbett lost his stirrup. The next buck threw Corbett over the horse's head, crashing hard on his back and shoulder.

"How are you doing, Hoss?" Slater and Jim were both at Corbett's side. Slater examined Corbett's back, shoulder, and head. The pain was so bad that Corbett tried to avoid breathing in or out. "Well, old dog," said Slater, an expert at fallen cowboys, "if'n you were bleeding out of your ears, I'd say you're gonna die, which you ain't." Jim listened to the old seed. Slater knew everything. "If'n blood came bubblin' out of your nose or mouth, I'd wait a few days, then I would say you're gonna die, which you ain't." Corbett's pain was overriding Slater's doctoral advice. "I think you might make it."

"Jim." Corbett, with his good arm, pulled at Jim's collar. "Get in Slater's left saddlebag and bring that flat bottle of whiskey."

"Damn it, Slater!" Jim said, a bit upset. "Remember what Dad said about drinking?"

"I was savin' it for Corbett's first wreck, and this is it." Jim walked off, frustrated.

"This buckaroo life never ends well," said Slater. "You get hurt real bad, they'll take you to town, give five dollars, sit you next to the bar, and then ride away." Slater's gray stubble looked grizzled, more gray than brown. "I'm beat to hell. My only hope is to retire to the barns and brush horses, and stay there till I die."

Breathing was still a little difficult, but at least he was back at school. Corbett knew the speech given today would somehow be turned into an essay assignment by one of his instructors. Dr. Fisher, the dean, gave one of these speeches about once a month. Colorado Normal School was evolving. The demand for teachers in every little town in the West was far greater than the number of teachers being produced. The college had dropped the requirements for its four-year teaching degree to two years, mainly to get more schoolmasters out in the field. There were several in the class of one hundred with prior experience who needed to be degreed as teachers. They, it was rumored, could test out with their experience after just one year, again to get more teachers out and into the empty classrooms.

"Thank you, students, for being here this morning. I want us to ponder where we are as educators now, near the end of the nineteenth century. We rely on rote memorization, recitation, and oral drilling to teach readin', writin', and 'rithmetic to all our children. Those of you who are good at this and who have the ability to encourage your students to attend often and do well will have successful careers. A schoolmaster today must be a politician, knowing that crops come before learning sums, that bacon or potatoes might be your pay, that chalkboards and books will not exist in some of your schools, and that your employment will be tenuous at best.

You schoolmistresses will make considerably less than the schoolmasters. You might be forced to teach at more than one school a year. Some schools are open just two months, and some just in the winter, but never are any schools open at harvesttime. That being said, you will be looked upon as a pathway to the future by those families trying to provide a better life for their children …"

Corbett's mind wandered away from the speech. Dr. Fisher was giving a fair appraisal of a schoolmaster's career. In some ways, it was similar to Slater's appraisal of buckarooing. A wrong choice could be a disastrous move, maybe ones who aftereffects will last a lifetime. A couple of years ago in Durango, Corbett would have been happy to be the teamster driving the freight wagon to the mines three times a week forever. Corbett's mind produced images of the past two years. Exposure to life outside his mother's laundry, Ajai's companionship, and the streets of Durango had led Corbett to slip into a pensive sadness. Was life this hard for everyone, or was this his school of hardscrabble? The good side of this time for decision-making was that he had a full year before graduation.

Corbett's day at Colorado Normal School began with some excitement outside the office of Dr. Fisher.

"They say that Oregon country is the place to settle," said one student.

"It sounds like they want all of us," said Martha, nearest to the corkboard. "The state will pay your way to Oregon and guarantee twelve dollars a month the first year." Everyone knew of the great soils for farming, the timber, and the fishing in the Northwest. Corbett's first thought was of adventure, of seeing the ocean, and, curiously, of a new start. "It requires a teaching certificate from any state."

"I'll have that in a couple of weeks!" exclaimed Robert. He was one of six in the school with teaching experience, needing only one year of college for a certificate. "Where do I sign up?"

It struck Corbett that this Oregon thing might be worth more of his consideration. Corbett's love of cowboying was dampened every time he saw Slater hobble about with the bad back, the rheumatism, and the two missing fingers. The excitement of traveling, using schoolteaching as the avenue, gave the idea of teaching a bit of a lift, but that was still a year away.

That night, after helping with chores and feeding at the ranch, Corbett acted on an idea that had occurred to him while riding home. He wrote Mrs. Portman in Silverton, asking if she would verify that he had indeed taught there for a year. If his plan of action was accepted by the college, then he could claim one year of experience. The next letter he wrote was to the Oregon Department of Education in Salem.

"That is a good question!" Mr. Ross said, responding to a student question. "Since most of your small country schools are ungraded, what do you do with the fourteen-year-old raw-boned young man who walks into your school one day and says he wants to join the school?" All of Corbett's classmates knew that this scenario happened nearly every day somewhere.

"He must start the same place an eight-year-old starts, by learning sounds and letters, and putting them together to make words. He may not be back the next day, being too embarrassed and frustrated to be learning the same material as, and sitting next to, an eight-year-old.

"Corbett, your unusual background speaks to this situation. Tell us about those feelings."

"If a young man sees little to gain from school, he won't come through the front door in the first place. But if he should do so, then he won't come back after that first day." Most students readily nodded their heads in agreement. "But like Dr. Fisher said in his speech, if the boy senses that schooling will get him out of poverty, maybe get him a job in town, or instill him with the excitement of knowing that there is a whole world out there, you won't be able to run him off."

"Thanks, Corbett," Mr. Ross said, recognizing Corbett's mature understanding. "It could be at a new school where all the students of all ages are learning sounds at the same time." All the students were thinking of their upcoming roles out on the plains, some of them feeling trepidation. "The last thing I want to say today is that while your community may have twenty-five school-age children, you might get seven. They don't have to go to school. Their parents may need them at home more. Your job is to offer them a different future and see if they accept."

The letter from Mrs. Portman arrived, giving Corbett the verification of his having taught the previous year in Silverton. The second half of the letter was businesslike, saying that when the mine bosses in Silverton, primarily Mrs. Portman, provided the scholarship for Corbett, they had set up an escrow account at the Greeley Union National Bank to be used specifically for tuition and fees at Colorado Normal School. If indeed Corbett would be graduating after one year, Mrs. Portman would release the rest of the funds from escrow to Corbett.

Corbett could not believe his eyes. He knew Mrs. Portman saw him as the son she never had; she'd even shot Hok'ee to protect him. This gift of about sixty dollars, six months' wages, was love personified. It ended Corbett's worries about making a transition to Oregon. The letter sounded more like a mother writing to her son than a mine owner writing to an ex-employee.

The official Oregon Department of Education letter concerning placement reached Corbett two days later. Upon his arrival in

Portland, Corbett would be assigned to a school. Corbett took both letters as positive evidence that he had chosen the correct path.

Dr. Fisher posted the graduation list. Newly added to it was one Corbett Jones. Like the others, he was to be certified for one year of teaching and one year of college.

"You did it, Corbett!" said Howard. "You're going to Oregon!"

"You and Terry going with me?" asked a happy Corbett, already missing his friends.

"No," answered Howard. "Mel is training me to manage the restaurant. I'm going to do that full time."

"No more school?" asked Corbett.

"No. It will give me more time with my family. That's what I want." The squatty little man, for all practical purposes, was now a father and a husband.

"Did they tell you where in Oregon?" Howard changed the topic back to his hero. "I would want to be near the ocean."

"My biggest problem is telling the Bjlacks. I sort of told them that I would cowboy for them this summer and all next year. I don't want to leave on bad terms, especially with Julie. I think she likes me a little."

"I'm sure she does!" echoed Howard. "You have strong feeling for her?"

"I just can't go that far yet." Corbett's doors for romance were still closed. Shapely bodies that stirred other men were to be looked at, but he did not have the passion or the desire to partake.

"Come in, Corbett," shouted Josh. The family were all drinking their morning coffee before tackling the day's chores. "Have a chair. Had breakfast?"

"Thanks, I'm fine."

Julie had her chaps hanging over a chair. Her snap-buttoned

men's cowboy shirt brought out the best in her. Her long blonde hair in a flowing ponytail and her happy countenance were all that she would ever need. "Corbett, you look like just stole a brand-new pair of leather gloves."

"Well, I guess that's why I am here." Corbett liked these people very much and felt he was letting them down. He blurted out, "I've accepted a teaching job in Oregon and won't be able to help you folks this summer." Corbett scanned all three faces.

Josh turned to Julie with a suspicious grin. "You going to tell him, or do I?" Julie was suddenly on the spot, having shrunk into a little girl whose father must carry the burden. "The reason we are enjoying this minute with Julie is that she spent the last two days worrying about telling you that she is off to Dartmouth University in New Hampshire to attend law school."

Julie walked around the table and hugged Corbett tightly. "I'm sorry, but now I'm happy for both of us. I would never make a good schoolmarm!" She laughed.

"A lawyer?" quipped Corbett. "Lawyers are old fat men who smoke stogies!"

"That's just who I want to be!"

The ten o'clock graduation ceremony was the first for the college. Corbett Jones was the last to qualify and the only graduate to leave the state. Robert Hughes and Molly Junge would return to the Wray area. Jennifer Keenon was a recent hire at Lyons, up next to the mountains. Mark Mathews had been hired to start a new one-room school near Fort Morgan. He was the oldest at twenty-seven.

Governor Cooper spoke of the 1890 class as the precursor to the school's future. The event was well attended. Most of the students and many proud Greeley citizens listened and enjoyed the fine morning. Glen and Frances Casey looked on as proud parents.

Howard, Terry, and Annie sat in the front row. For many of the students, it was the coming out for Annie. Terry's classmates were unaware of the baby. Whispers of gossip erupted. Her beautiful brown skin brought stares to the family, but the couple took the looks as a compliment. They were no longer hidden from view, but were now upstanding citizens, he an assistant manager at the Cattleman's. The Bjlack family, as well as the Caseys, stood and cheered loudly when Corbett was presented.

Corbett's tickets were to Cheyenne and then on to Portland. The train was due to leave at two o'clock. After handshakes and good wishes, Corbett headed toward the boardinghouse for the last time. His adventure here had started with a pair of old people renting rooms to college students like him and Howard, a young, immature Jew from Denver. It seemed to Corbett that he had lived a lifetime in the last year.

"Hey there, schoolmaster!" yelled Julie. She, along with Terry and Howard, was waiting at the front gate.

"Did you kiss all the college girls goodbye?" asked Howard, always concerned with Corbett's love life.

Stepping down from the buggy, he replied, "I did the best I could. Hug 'em and leave 'em, I always say." Corbett grabbed Terry and lifted her completely off the ground in a hug. "And how did you do showing off Annie?"

"Oh, Corbett, it was wonderful to be free." Terry was in full bloom, her eyes sparkling. "Many of the girls came over to see Annie. They were really nice. I think Howard told them that Annie was adopted. That really helped."

Moving to Julie, Corbett said, "And this will be the prettiest lawyer in New Hampshire! Those boys out there won't know what hit them!" Then, in an unexpected gesture, he kissed her on the cheek. It surprised both him and her. "When you find that guy, just throw a loop and tie him to a tree until he says yes."

Howard was next. Corbett gave him a bear hug. "I understand the Cattleman's Restaurant," Corbett said jokingly, "will someday be called Howard's Steak House. I am really going to miss all of you." Corbett could not remember a better time. "Terry, I'll bring Annie back when she is twenty!"

"Like hell you will! You don't even know how to change a diaper!" replied Terry, loving the day.

"Don't learn," said Howard in a loud whisper. "It's a bad habit to get into."

The smell of roast beef, potatoes and gravy, and fresh rolls gave Frances a sense of family that had been missing for years. Her canned tomatoes and Dutch apple pie expressed part of the love she felt for these young people. Glen guided every movement in the kitchen until the women ran him out. The Bjlacks had provided the beef and were refilling the glasses of lemonade and ice from their icehouse. It was quite a thing to still have ice.

Corbett noticed that Josh had left the dinner table rather quickly to talk a couple of his hands who had arrived by wagon.

"You folks, bring your pie outside!" Josh recommended. Josh's hired hands were churning vanilla ice cream for all.

"Oh my!" said Frances, admiring such a luxury. "The meal now complete."

"I guess it's time for me to go." Corbett's next few minutes were filled with dichotomous thoughts. He wanted to stay but was anxious to go. Howard brought around the buggy. Corbett hugged everyone for the last time and then gave a wave goodbye.

It was quiet as Howard and Corbett rode along to the station, both young men deep in thought. Howard never had had a friend before Corbett and would never again have such a special one.

Corbett's mind wandered through all the times spent here. He asked himself, *Why can't I settle? For that matter, why can't I love?*

"Howard, I'm leaving you a gift of sorts." Corbett reached into a box and removed his cowboy hat. It was slightly trampled, but it had the bruises of a real cowboy hat. As he handed it to Howard, he said, "I don't even know if it fits you, but you deserve a cowboy hat."

"Oh, it fits." Howard smiled. "I've tried it on a time or two." He plopped it on his head. "Thanks." Howard smirked. "Now you can go in peace."

Corbett reached back, gathered his derby from Silverton, and did just that: left in peace.

7

The nighttime trip from Cheyenne to Ogden allowed Corbett to attempt the myriad ways to be uncomfortable on a wooden bench seat. The little boy two rows up from Corbett were the right size for train travel, short enough to lie completely across the bench seat when tired, yet tall enough to see out the windows. Corbett's derby was a constant nuisance. When off Corbett's head, it seemed to need a seat of its own, falling to the floor several times to prove the point. When it was on his head, Corbett could not lean his head against the side of the coach.

The whole night was one of stop and go. The train pulled off onto sidings twice to allow eastbound trains to fly by, using the same tracks. Water was taken on both times to fill the steam engine's boilers. Stops made at two small towns and one long, slow grade made the night feel like two.

As darkness settled when they three hours west of Cheyenne, Corbett dozed intermittently between thoughts of Greeley, Silverton, and Durango. Each had its emotional attachments, tied to both good times and bad.

The entertainment for the night were the conversations surrounding him in the darkness of the railcar. Three men behind him were talking gold, especially Winnemucca gold.

"Yeah, some of the biggest nuggets ever found were found up

there, lying on top of the ground," said an expert who had never been there. "We need to get there before the Chinese put claims down on everything."

"I went into the Black Hills right after Custer," said an older voice. "Even worked at the Homestake Mine to pay for grub. Don't like that underground digging. Let me walk along with an old mule and pick up nuggets, that's what I say. With Fort McDermott keeping the Paiutes off me, I believe I'll find some gold."

The first voice said, "Well, this will be placer mining, a lot of digging and panning. I just don't want to have to fight a bunch of Chinks for a claim."

A thin, weak voice concluded, "This will be my last go, so it'd better be good. After all these years, I got a gold pan back there in baggage that's not paid for itself yet."

The first voice said, "Floyd, you're gonna hit it this time."

Same talk, just different wildcatters. Those same conversations went on in Silverton constantly. Corbett even had heard mining talk in Greeley, something about Cripple Creek, south of Denver. It was not hard to get the fever, but most ended up working someone else's claim for crumbs.

"Gentlemen," a sweet female voice quietly said, "I overheard you discussing Winnemucca. My husband is working in McDermott."

"Fort McDermott, you mean?" the old voice said, correcting her in the darkness.

"No, the fort closed last summer. The soldiers are all gone," the female voice stated. "My husband has been there all winter. He is with the Indian Service to oversee the reservation."

"And they're going to keep the Paiutes and Shoshone in line?" the older voice snapped. "Like hell!"

The car grew quiet. The miners felt a spy in their midst. Natives in claim country would change everything. They were worse than the Chinese.

"Ogden, thirty minutes," announced the conductor, passing through the car.

Corbett looked from his window. His neck ached because of the unusual arrangement his head and neck had found themselves in the past few hours. The train, moving quickly down a gorge, slithered like a snake. The opening to the west seemed flat with the horizon, which itself was a mass of blue. If someone had said the blue was the ocean, Corbett would have taken it to be true. The Great Salt Lake was dead ahead.

The foothills had been broken out into farms and orchards, using the fresh runoff from the tall Wasatch Mountains. Corbett knew little of the towns they were passing by, but he did know success. Ogden's Union Station, new and mammoth, was another monument to the Mormons and, in this case, the Ogden Valley.

Switching trains for Portland gave Corbett time to mill about. Finding coffee was his main goal. Finally, after asking an employee, who laughed, he discovered that Mormons did not drink coffee. Then to show them, Corbett would not buy any. The Mormon world in Utah was one of temperance and internal pride stemming from the sacrifices made by those who had come before. Nearby, Corbett saw several prudent bonnets and the quality calico print of well-sewn dresses. The designs were severely drab, long, and figureless, many with collars, some with pointed collars.

Maybe looking for it, Corbett saw a man wearing a suit coat with a gaggle of women, nice-looking women, following him. Whether or not it was true in this case, Corbett took the group to be a polygamist man and his entourage of wives. All seemed comfortable and happy. *There must be plenty of men who would take up Mormonism just for that one benefit,* thought Corbett.

The West was full of beards. It seemed these men had such facial hair down to an art, maybe because they went to church so often. They were divided into those who had brought their style from Europe and those of the North American West. Corbett's late-developing shaving practices were centered on getting his soft, fine facial hair to stand up long enough to be cut.

Corbett smiled at a young woman who had caught him looking at her. She was wearing a starched white pinafore, covering a high-collared blue dress with long sleeves. Her features, under her bonnet, were soft. She was blonde, maybe eighteen, slightly taller and slightly younger than the rest of the women around her.

Corbett, feeling awkward for having been caught, stumbled into a conversation, saying, "Where are you off to?"

Smiling and unafraid, the young woman answered, "Sister Joanna is leading us to Oregon to help our sisters in their orchards in the Willamette Valley." She seemed quite comfortable talking to a stranger. "Are you traveling that way as well?"

"I am," Corbett said, impressed by her earnest interest in him. "I have a teaching job near Portland."

"Where have you …" The young woman saw the line of people begin to move. They had started to board the train car. "I'd better go." Picking up the hem of her dress, she began running to her group. She turned her head. "Nice meeting you."

Heavy, loud boots pounded out of the station door. The suddenness and loudness caused everyone to step back. A short, thin-mustachioed army sergeant wearing a blue infantry uniform with matching leggings stepped aggressively through the crowd. "Step aside!" he shouted. "We have a prisoner to board." His yellow leather gloves cleared the way. Corbett was not impressed with the show. That the sergeant was wearing leather gloves in early June to ride a train, and that he had a pin-line mustache and shiny sideburns, told Corbett that the sergeant was a dandy, a sure enough dandy.

Behind the sergeant trudged an old, small-boned Native, cuffed at the hands. His deerskin shirt was primitive and dirty. He had narrow shoulders and salt-and-pepper hair. His eyes were downcast; his face, expressionless.

At the end of this small parade walked another soldier, this one big and heavy. His single stripe indicated a corporal. He was pompous to the point of being irritating. Corbett chuckled. It was hard to be pompous and slovenly at the same time, but this fellow pulled it off quite well. Corbett's smile went away when he saw a gun in the corporal's hand. He looked back at the Native who had just passed by. If this was a Native uprising, then the corporal was going to need a bigger Native. Corbett could not believe the contradiction of the moment. The Native was bound, small, and nearly lifeless, yet the soldiers were maniacally displaying a pretense of combat status.

Two cowboys, with saddles at their hips, were the first in line to board. Given that they were obviously drunk and out of place, the sergeant pushed by them. "My God, men, didn't you hear me!" the corporal shouted, clearing the way for his prisoner.

"Hey, we were here first!" complained the drunker of the two cowboys, trying to move up the ladder.

"Step down or I will draw my weapon!" His right hand pointed to his service revolver.

"Whoa, whoa!" said the lead cowboy. His movements backward gave way to stumbling as he was at an advanced level of intoxication. He tripped backward over his partner's saddle.

The ruckus had completely unnerved the conductor. The previously polite people waiting in line erupted into chaos. Corbett ended up near the front of the line with the Mormon women, who were then bumped to the side and out of line. "Here, get in behind me!" Corbett shouted to the women. His little train of women entered the car to the shouts of the sergeant.

"You two, sit here," demanded the sergeant. "You other three, sit up there!" The seats were far from each other.

"We are all going to sit up there," said Corbett, pointing to seats farther up the aisle, his ire beginning to rise.

"Damn it, you will sit where I say!"

Corbett stood. He was a full head taller than the sergeant. He said, "We will sit up there." Corbett made way for the women to slip by to their seats. Both men were angry, but only one was big and angry.

The four Mormon women sat to Corbett's left in two seats in the middle of the car. The cowboys were near the front and already fading from reality. The corporal sat spraddled in the last seat, his boots off and smelling bad. The prisoner sat alone, two seats behind Corbett.

"I want to thank you for helping us on," said the young Mormon woman across from Corbett. "I don't know why that soldier is acting that way. My name is Johanna. The four of us are on our way to Oregon."

"That's what I understand." Corbett saw quiet excitement in the eyes of all four women. "Have you been out there before?"

"No, none of us," replied Johanna. "We are needed for the harvests. And each of us hopes to find a man to guide our lives."

"I'm sure you will find men there to court you," said Corbett confidently. "That one next to you had my head turned back at the station." All four women quietly chuckled.

"Yes, meet our Rebecca. She drives our elders crazy." Rebecca's coquettish smile looked as good next to Johanna as it had back at the Ogden terminal.

"What's your name?" asked Rebecca, knowing that all the young women wanted to know.

"I'm Corbett Jones," Corbett answered politely. "Going to be a schoolmaster somewhere out there in Oregon."

"You don't look like any schoolmaster I've ever seen," Rebecca said, seeking to embarrass Corbett a little. It worked.

"Rebecca!" Johanna chastised Rebecca with her eyes. That was Rebecca's thing, to challenge the boundaries and let the other women enjoy the ride.

Corbett's polite conversation with the young women gave way to reading and dozing. It was a pleasant ride on a sunlit day. One, when traveling to the massive forests of the Cascade Range, must first endure the constant view of sagebrush and more sagebrush all the way to the low-slung mountains on the horizon. In every gully grew wildflowers of yellow, white, and blue with a backdrop of tender spring grass.

Miles later, the corporal in back, bored and having looked at the backs of the four handsome women for some time, called, "Hey, Mormon! Are all those women yours?" Corbett did not realize the corporal assumed he was part of the same group as the women. "I'm going to need one pretty soon!"

"Bob, leave it be," said the sergeant to the corporal.

"Why should he have more than one when we don't have any?"

The young women bent down so as not to attract any more attention. Corbett, now aware of the comments, leaned forward to stand. Johanna put her hand on his knee. "Be calm," whispered Johanna. "We are used to this." Corbett was not calm, but he decided that he would honor Johanna's request.

"Bob, leave it."

The sergeant took full advantage of the La Grande stop. Corbett watched him make several entrances and exits into and out of the station washroom. Something was afoul. It might have been the sergeant's innards.

Corbett ate with the women, as did the cowboys. The women had brought bread, canned fruit, and cheese from Ogden and had urged others to join them. Johanna made a special sandwich for the Native, still chained to his seat in the railcar. Corporal Bob sat in the bar, oblivious to his Native prisoner in the railcar.

"I hope you are finding the trip comfortable and pleasing," said the sergeant, sitting down next to the women. His air of authority, he thought, gave him permission to interrupt and assert his presence anytime, anywhere.

"We are," replied Johanna politely, not forgetting Corporal Bob's comments.

"You will have to forgive my corporal for his language. He comes from a different background from the rest of us. My hope is that the military will guide him in his behaviors." The sergeant was making amends. "I assure you, it won't happen again."

Corbett, changing to topic, asked, "How come the Indian requires such attention? What did he do?"

"We are taking him back to Oregon to hang. He's considered to be quite dangerous," the sergeant said, sitting a little taller. "We were chosen to follow his trail and find him."

The women stopped their eating and considered the small-shouldered little man chained to his seat in the railcar. Whether it was right or not, their sympathies flowed his way.

"What did he do?" repeated Corbett. "He looks pretty harmless to me."

"He stole a horse down near Coos Bay." The sergeant, a little perturbed at being challenged by civilians, added, "The party from which he stole went right to the top commissioned officers in the area, so it must have been of high importance." The two cowboys listening in, whose lifestyles seemed to cross red lines each day, made themselves smaller. Their dealings with cattle and an occasional horse made the conversation a tad more relevant to them than to the others. Corbett wondered how the Bjlacks would react to someone stealing their stock. It would not be good, he was sure.

"That just seems too harsh," Rebecca said, spilling her thoughts. "Can't you jail him for a time?"

"Listen, missy, you take care of your Mormon ways. Let the United States Army take care of theirs!" With that, he got up and left.

"I do not like that man at all," said Rebecca.

"That's why we appreciate our Mormon men," added Johanna, gathering up the waste and cleaning the eating area. "They protect us from men like that." Corbett wished these women knew the soldiers at Fort Lewis, good neighbors to Durango, a good lot as he remembered. These two soldiers were poor examples of men in general.

"I think the sergeant, behind his uniform, is a little boy playing soldier," Corbett said, related his thoughts to the group. "I feel the Indian man is in for bad times from those two."

With everyone back in their seats, the sergeant, standing in the middle of the aisle, shouted, "Attention, everyone! Since I must be in the next car doing paperwork, you must move two seats forward, away from our prisoner." The corporal was still in the back seat, boots already off and souring the air.

"And don't talk to the heathen either!" said Corporal Bob, his speech somewhat slurred.

Corbett turned, irritated at the command. "Unless you commandeered the whole car from the Union Pacific, we are going to sit right here." His eyes challenged the officer.

The sergeant opened the holster of his gun, then faltered.

Corbett's stiff demeanor had battered down the soldier's confidence. "Stay away from my prisoner!" he said, his voice shaking and his head down as he fled into the first-class railcar, the one with a washroom. Corbett relaxed. The only paperwork that the sergeant would do in the next car centered on finding enough paper to support his washroom duties.

Oregon, Corbett expected, was a place of massive trees and fertile soils, especially in the Willamette Valley, but the precursor was the rolling hills of sagebrush and wheat fields of eastern Oregon. The farmhouses were scattered, but always detected amongst the sagebrush and the wheat by the large green shade trees surrounding the houses. Corbett could see the green stalks of winter wheat lifting their heads of grain toward the sun. The train's path passed through tiny towns, grown up around storage silos for the harvested wheat, soon to appear.

Bob, awake from his drunken nap, stepped clumsily up the aisle toward the first-class car. Corbett was sure that the corporal bumped every seat in every row. The corporal personified the idea that lifers in the military would never leave the service because they had no skills to offer the outside world.

After the front rail door had closed, Corbett moved back a seat and turned his shoulders toward the Native, who was surprised that Corbett would risk contact after all the warnings.

"What's your name?" asked Corbett, examining the old man closely.

The Native's eyes were sad and tired. "My name is Christopher."

"Is that an Indian name?"

The Native thought about it. "It is a Catholic name." Corbett smiled, as did the old man.

"Did you really steal a horse?" Corbett asked, showing increasing interest in the little man in front of him.

The Native seemed very measured in all he did. "I stole it back."

Corbett's eyes grew wide in disbelief. "You stole it back!"

Christopher spent a moment reading the strong white man, then spoke again. "Several years ago, the tribe gave each head of household land of his own for farming and grazing. It was mostly tidal grass and hillsides." This young man was brave enough to sit and talk, but also he was listening, observed Christopher. "I moved my horses and sheep to my property. A time later, the fish came from the sea. We spent days catching them and smoking them." Corbett could tell by the movement of Christopher's eyes as the Native stared at his feet that these moments happened. Then Christopher hesitated.

"It's okay, I want to hear the story," said Corbett. This man needed to tell his story. Even more importantly, he had to tell the story to a white man.

"When I returned, my best young mare—I guess you whites call them fillies—my best young filly was missing. I found her in a field owned by a white rancher. I asked for her back. He said she was not mine. He said the mark on the horse's hip meant she was his."

"You mean he branded her while you were gone?" Cattle rustling like this was always done in secret, but this brazen white rancher had no fear.

"In the night, I stole my mare back and gathered my other horses and took them to a safe valley known only to my family. I returned for my sheep, but the rancher's men were already after me. The army found me. Now I am to die before my return."

"Excuse me," said the conductor, standing over the pair, "should you be sitting there?" The look was supposed to intimidate Corbett in the same manner a schoolmaster's glare is meant to shush an unruly student.

"Everything's fine," said Corbett. "Christopher and I are old friends." The young women tittered, having been listening intently to Christopher's story. The conductor did not like the answer, but he was on a schedule.

"We are going to take on water one more time before Portland!" shouted the conductor as the large water tower came into view. "One more stretch before we start down the gorge."

"Hell yes, let's slow this damned train down one more time and let an eastbound have the rails!" exclaimed one of the cowboys, restless and ready to quit the travel.

As the train began to slow, the passengers began to stir. Fresh air, a walk, and a spell at the washroom was on everyone's minds.

The sergeant reentered the railcar to help the corporal with offloading Christopher. Neither said much. The sergeant was visibly unhappy with Bob. His dealings with the prisoner were again taking time from his first-class necessities. Bob pushed Christopher down the last two steps, causing him to lose his balance and fall upon landing. The sharp gravel bit into Christopher's forearms and knees as he tried to rise. Corbett bent to help the cuffed man to his feet.

"Leave him alone!" screamed the corporal, scowling. "Like I've said before, none of this is your damned business!" Corbett was tired. The rough handling of Christopher was no longer tolerable to him. He continued to help the bound fellow up.

"I'll arrest you, by God!" the corporal snapped, lifting the flap of his holster.

Corbett continued to lift. "Hey, just helping him up." Somewhere in Corbett's deep emotional center, his father, Laddie, was beside him in rage. That emotion tore at Corbett's mind. This was not over yet.

As Corbett and the others stretched and walked about, a new

smell and feel was in the air. The snow-topped Mount Hood loomed majestically a hundred or so miles to the west. The Columbia River, about an hour away, provided a cooling breeze, making the riders excited and the Mormon women quite giddy. Having lived all their lives in the austere and dry Utah country, their anticipation to see the Columbia was great.

"Hey, Mormon!" Bob, sitting two tables away, could not fathom the concept that he was the reason that no woman wanted him. "I hear them women of yours wear special undies, to be seen only by their men. Have them show me some undies, maybe even see some skin."

Corbett rose. He had had enough, but a glance from Johanna said that he should control himself. These women were too passive for Corbett's taste. However, this situation was theirs to handle. If Johanna were to give the word, Corbett's fists and Laddie's attitude would knock the hell out of this buffoon. Bob looked at Corbett, planted his feet, and rose, showing an inclination to fight, but then he staggered back onto his chair.

"How can you stand to allow him to belittle you folks?" asked Corbett, leaning toward the women in wonderment.

"Some say we are the latter-day Jews," said Johanna quietly. "Since our beginning, we have been persecuted and scorned, but we have stayed the course. We feel blessed to have you with us." The other women nodded their heads in agreement. To them, Corbett was the angel they had prayed for before starting their trip, someone to protect them. "Our men never want our women to have to stand alone. Our men may have several wives to love and protect."

History has a habit of erasing mistakes and the unused. Corbett wondered why this stop had ever existed. He could tell that history was erasing this mistake. The large, coarse wooden silo was dank and historic. Several sheets of roofing shingles flapped in the afternoon wind. The fir timbers were notched at the corners, log house style. The two houses seemed newer but were not lasting very well. A window was broken in one, and the front door was partially open on the other. Sagebrush and vine maple vines cluttered the space inside the broken-down picket fence. Several tables, under a cover, and six one-hole outhouses made up the welcoming committee, three one-holers for men and three for women. The telegraph line followed the tracks but had no access at the siding. This stop, once someone's dream, was now a graveyard for that dream.

Corbett saw he'd been wrong about the sergeant's intestinal diagnosis in first class. A richly dressed woman about thirty years old, standing at the sergeant's side, provided evidence of courtship in first class, rather than dietary distress. Her high standing required a stand-up collar atop a purple-bustled dress with ruffles on the sleeves. Although he twice looked in the direction of Christopher, the sergeant had moved his prisoner down his list of priorities.

The corporal should have been a priority of the sergeant, who was in complete disarray, his blue military shirt and his gun belt having been left on his seat aboard the train. Although he was close to the prisoner, just a few feet away, his total attention was on Rebecca. Looking at her through his bloodshot eyes, he was sure she had gazed romantically in his direction at least twice. If his ears had been closer, he would have heard her remarks about his constant staring.

As all could hear the steam being brought up in the engine, the passengers boarded hurriedly, anxious to continue. All shuffled to their seats.

Corporal Bob reentered the car, his army shirt off and his suspenders carrying a load. He delivered Christopher to his seat and continued to the front of the car. He turned, giving the car's occupants his best air of authority. On his return to his seat in the back, he stopped about six feet in front of the women. His inspection of each was precise, including the face, the chest, and the gathering of the skirts.

"Sit down, Corporal," said Corbett. The bottle in the corporal's hand was releasing the worst of his personality. He stumbled back to his lair before calling out, "Hey, tall one next to the window." Bob was no more than a drunken sod, swinging his bottle above his head as he spoke. "I'll meet you outside, and we can have a time!"

"Shut up, Bob!" Rebecca shouted back. This was a Mormon woman with an attitude. Corbett looked at Johanna. She shook her head slightly and appeared amused in her glance back at Corbett. Mormonism, for Rebecca, was a work in progress.

Corbett noticed the corporal's boots, again off and again in the middle of the aisle. He rose, patted Johanna on the shoulder, and quickly walked to the back of the passenger car, grabbing the corporal's boots on the way.

"What the hell?" said the shocked corporal, trying to follow the movement of his government-issued, size 12 military-grade boots. Corbett leaned back on the back handrail, holding up the boots for the corporal to see. Then, as the big man approached, Corbett calmly dropped them overboard. Transfixed on the boots, the corporal stepped down to the back platform. "No! My boots." The train was beginning to move.

Then, Corbett raised his boot, placed his foot in the middle of Bob's large backside, and booted him off as well. Impetuousness had never served him well. The women completely turned to the back, screaming as the soldier tumbled like a rock, rolling over and over. Bob's girl-like screech carried for a moment then dissipated, covered by the noise of the train. Corbett put his elbows on the back rail and watched the chase. The corporal's indecision was evident in the way he was running. He wanted desperately to put on his boots, but if he were to do so, the train would go out of sight. The bootless runner slammed down his boots and shouted ugly epitaphs at Corbett, who acknowledged him with a nod and went inside.

"He said he was going to take the next train."

"I'll be damned," one cowboy said to the other. "That takes testiculos!"

"You are definitely going to hell now!" said Rebecca, holding her head in both hands in disbelief. Johanna could not believe her eyes. Corbett was a crazy young fellow, but she liked him. The rest of the women, wide-eyed, looked at one another then broke out in a muffled chorus of laughter.

"I reckon," said Corbett, examining Bob's nest in the last seat. "Oh hell!" Bob's seat no longer contained Bob but, instead, was occupied by his shirt, an army gun belt, an empty whiskey bottle, and on the belt, curled up with other keys, Christopher's handcuff key.

"Corbett!" said Johanna loudly. She was disappointed. Every time she thought Corbett had the makings of a good Mormon, he had to go off and cuss some more. Of course, she, like the others, was waiting to see what "Oh hell!" would lead to.

"The keys for Christopher's cuffs are here." He picked up the key and dropped into his boot. If necessary, he would "find" it on the floor later.

"Turn the little chief loose!" shouted the younger of the cowboys from the front of the car, maybe because, being a horse thief himself, he thought the Native man was a kindred spirit.

"Yeah," agreed Rebecca. "Nobody should hang for stealing their own horse."

Christopher understood an opportunity existed, but he would not plead or beg for his release, especially from the whites. Corbett and the young white women had been kind; however, the army sergeant was in the next car. The whites would not go against the army. So, he said nothing, just listened. Without any emotion, Christopher viewed the Columbia River as it came into sight.

The sight of the massive Columbia River set aside, for the moment, any decision-making concerning Christopher. Even though the steep cliffs on the left side of the train were green with foliage and dominated by fir and hemlock trees in every possible cranny and usable outcropping, there were sharp crags. It was the wide blue ribbon of the Columbia that pulled everyone in the car to the windows on the right. The powerful waves ripped forward, challenging the banks to control them. No one on board had ever seen such a river, battering from one black basaltic shore to the other.

Everyone was spellbound, until the sergeant stepped in to check on Christopher and his unreliable corporal. He took several more steps, straining to see if Bob's empty seat might still contain a sprawled-out corporal. His movement increased markedly as he came closer and closer to the seat, which to him was becoming more and more empty. He raced back through the train, checking the two first-class railcar washrooms for his corporal. The sergeant's repeated and inconsistent movements revealed what he did not want to disclose to himself or to the Mormon women: he had just lost half his army.

"God damn it! Where is he?"

"Who?" asked the older cowboy with his nose to the glass. All those in attendance stopped gazing at the Columbia. The sergeant was very unhappy.

"The corporal, you stupid bastard!" The sergeant pushed the cowboy back into his seat. "Did you see him?" the sergeant snapped harshly. A bit of spit dampened Johanna's sleeve.

Johanna craned her neck, straining to the rear to see the drunk soldier. "He was here awhile ago," she said, not lying.

"We miss him," Rebecca said, snorting, loving her life right now. Maybe they would all go to jail.

"Sergeant, I believe that he is still back at the last water tank." Corbett, to some degree, regretted his impetuous decision to eject of Bob from the train. *How do Mormon women explain to their elders that they are in jail for being part of a plot to steal a soldier?*

"What?"

"Yes, I think so, sir."

The sergeant, pointing at Christopher, demanded, "You stay put!" Then he left the car, Christopher still chained.

The conductor, with perhaps better eyes, came rushing into the car. Soon it was evident that he'd had no better luck locating Bob.

The long, hard day had put Christopher to sleep. His head was back; his mouth, partially open. This view made him seem much older. He had demonstrated throughout the day a stoic attitude toward these last few days of his life.

"Corbett, gentlemen, come here," Johanna said, beckoning Corbett and the cowboys. All three men were played out. It was easier not to think about the key and Christopher than to address the problem. If the sergeant were to appear, the huddle in the middle of the car would set in motion the possible arrest of the lot.

"I'm going to stand at the front of the car in case the sergeant decides to have a look." Rebecca, at a run, was always ready. Christopher was awakened suddenly by Corbett, who nodded to the people tightly gathered, indicating that he should listen while the whites planned his escape.

"We have a plan," suggested Johanna. "I think we should be the jury to consider Christopher's innocence or guilt." Johanna studied the faces of the men. "If any one of us believes that he is guilty and should hang, then we let nature take its course, but if we all agree that he is telling the truth, we allow his escape."

"That's a good plan," cited the bearded older cowboy. "I don't know how much time we have to do something, but I vote for the chief."

"Me too," offered his young companion. The women flashed hopeful peeks at one another. Their attention turned to their de facto leader, Corbett.

"I've been thinking of the risk in what we are thinking of doing." Corbett's seriousness took away some of the excitement. "If we are rightly blamed, we could go to prison." Corbett could not deny that he wanted Christopher freed just like the others, but experience told him to take a last full measure of the group and not depend on his impetuousness, for which he was known. No one seemed uneasy about the plan. Satisfied, he said, "I didn't put the key in my boot to start a collection. But we had better do it now."

"It has to happen at the next stop," Johanna said, her mind racing.

"The sergeant will shoot him sure, if he's around," added the older cowboy. "He wants to shoot somebody."

"He won't get far in his leather shirt," Corbett said. He thought, *He will look like a renegade for sure.* "Do either of you boys have an extra shirt?"

"No," replied the young cowboy. "Mine are all dirty."

"Perfect!" said Corbett with a smirk. "I will give you two dollars for your dirtiest shirt." The young cowboy quickly found a wrinkled, smelly, cowboy-cut brown shirt. "Put it in the last seat."

"The conductor is coming!" Rebecca hollered, running back to her seat.

"There will be a five-minute stop at the Dalles!" stated the conductor full-throatedly. "Stay in your seats. This is not a rest stop." The conductor, having done his due diligence, made way for the sergeant to enter as the former was leaving the car.

"Ladies and gentlemen, we are almost to Portland." The sergeant, speaking as if to friends, said, "I am stopping the train to telegraph back down the line to discover what happened to my corporal. I can't be sure if you folks had anything to do with his disappearance, but his poor conduct overrides everything else." A screamer just an hour ago, this man was now a soldier's soldier, intent on not leaving any of his men behind. The sergeant waited at the back railing for the train to stop, then walked into the railway station to the telegraph office.

"It's gotta happen now," shouted Corbett. He unchained Christopher and handed him the open cuffs. "Act like you are still bound until the sergeant passes into first class, then run like hell!" From his boot, Corbett slipped Christopher five dollars.

Whether the sergeant were to come back through the railcar or not, Christopher was prepared to bolt with the movement of the train. "Thank you," he whispered as if the sergeant were on board. He also relayed his thanks through eye contact with his jury. The car was absolutely silent, waiting.

The sergeant appeared coming up the back steps of the car, puffing slightly. "I have telegraphed both back down the line and ahead to Portland." While speaking, the sergeant kept a firm base as the train was beginning to move. "We will find the corporal," he announced, turning himself back into the dominating army officer he thought himself to be. "And in Portland, we will meet up with the escort squad to take our prisoner to the state penitentiary in Salem, where he will be housed until his hanging." He tipped his hat to the women and went forward to sit with his admirer in a purple dress.

"Go!" yelled Rebecca, ahead of the others. Corbett pulled the deerskin shirt from Christopher's head and shoulders. As the little warrior ran to the back steps, he grabbed the brown shirt.

All seven of Christopher's accomplices watched the old man put on his brown shirt as he crossed the rails into the Dalles. The train tracks turned away from the Dallas, and the view was lost. Neither the cowboys nor Corbett had ever hugged a Mormon woman before, but the celebration seemed to require it. The three of them enjoyed the hugs from all four of the women. That alone made the planned escape worthwhile.

Corbett said to Rebecca, "Run forward and tell the sergeant that Christopher has escaped. We must seem cooperative in reporting the event to the authorities."

"Where did he go?" asked the sergeant, crashing through the car's front door, gun in hand. "How did he get away?" The sergeant was now at Christopher's seat, staring at the empty chains. "Who unlocked him?"

"I think he had his own key." Corbett was excited to help.

"He ran off the train at the last stop," said Rebecca with deep sincerity. "He may have had a gun." Johanna jabbed her talkative young companion in the side with her elbow, a gesture that was a little overdone.

"He may have," said the young cowboy, entering the conversation. This was better than a damned dime novel.

"I want your names," demanded the sergeant. "He couldn't have gotten away without your help. You are all under arrest. Don't leave this car." He had his gun on alert; any movement would be considered a hostile act.

Corbett and the others knew the sergeant was in breakdown mode. Corbett signaled with palms down to steady the situation.

"When we stop, I am going to have you taken to our headquarters. It may take days before you are tried. Nevertheless, you have aided in the escape of a horse thief, so you deserve no less." The lecture was directed mostly to Corbett, the sergeant thinking that surely the women were mere pawns.

Corbett stood and asked, "Sergeant, when were you ever in here to guard your prisoner? I will tell your commander how you spent your time. The floozy in the next car was the only thing you guarded." Corbett's intention was to throw the sergeant off the train. It seemed to be a good method of ridding oneself of poor soldiers.

Before Corbett's plan could take shape, Johanna pushed between the two men. "Yes, bring on your superior. I want him to know how you allowed that corporal Bob to harass my friends and me, saying sexual things to us." She poked her finger into the sergeant's chest.

"Now listen," the sergeant said, trying to change the momentum. If Corbett were to sense any movement of the sergeant toward Johanna, Corbett would carry the man kicking to the back of the train.

"You listen! The drunk you left to guard Christopher was your responsibility!" Corbett would have contributed more, but Johanna spoke like a jailhouse lawyer. Whatever Mormon man ended up with Johanna, for better or for worse, would be collecting himself a wildcat in a straight-lined dress.

"Christopher?" the sergeant asked.

"The prisoner!" Rebecca interrupted, frustrated that the sergeant did not even know his prisoner's first name. Although the warlike soldier was backing away, he hadn't given himself time enough to escape the brash young woman. "Our Corbett will have our elders down on you and your army. He knows those men." It took a minute for Corbett to understand that in Rebecca's false scenario, he was the Mormon man with his flock traveling with him. If a Mormon man were to end up with Rebecca as well, he had better carry a white flag around with him daily, because these two women never retreated.

The soldier retreated. His days of playing soldier and the confidence that came with it were both gone. Slump-shouldered, he walked to the back seat and put his head in his hands. He had lost his corporal and a wanted fugitive all in the same day. He was done for.

The remaining hour of the trip was one of reflection for all on board. The scenes that passed by the windows once again brought forth the excitement and purpose of their trip. The landscape showed a gentle flattening of the terrain to the west, the Willamette River to the north, and the Columbia River. The late afternoon shadows of the mammoth Douglas firs stole the sunlight from the train, the environment unlike anything they had ever seen before. The changes in green, between the sunlit green when available and the dark, foreboding green beneath the tall trees, made for pictures ready for the painting.

Rebecca and one of the other women had laid their heads on their chests, exhausted. The other two stared through the glass, seeing new orchards and small farms, taken from the forest at the cost of effort and perseverance. They had imagined this country, but they could not have imagined the wildness and potential that lay in every mile.

Corbett thought of Colorado and the turns and twists that had evolved to put him in this seat, in the middle of Oregon. To have Ajai in the seat beside him would have been wonderful, but Ajai would never see Oregon, the ocean, or the life that could have been. The moment she was forced to return to the reservation had ultimately ended her life and changed Corbett's forever.

Corbett glanced back at the sergeant, who was looking through the window and yet seeing nothing. His choice assignment had gone terribly wrong. The luck of finding the Native in jail for vagrancy in Salt Lake was like a gift from the gods. The sergeant had dreamed of the prospect of lieutenant bars, then of meeting Audrey in first class, a woman who would appreciate a lieutenant's arm at dances. All of it was now gone, all because of a corporal who, unable to find work on the outside, had become a worthless drunk in the army. The sergeant would seek revenge on Bob. The Mormons saw all his failings. There was nothing he could do to them.

Corbett noticed subtle changes. The Columbia moved out of sight to the north, and in its place was an expansion in the number of tracks, surrounded on both sides by rows of houses.

"Five minutes. Collect your gear!"

By the time the train lurched to a stop, the sergeant was gone.

It was if they had never met. Johanna, having stood to gather her satchels, bumped into Corbett. With the briefest of glances and a bit of embarrassment, she whispered a token "Sorry." The women stepped to the center aisle, in line with the back steps of the railcar platform, anticipating a new, exciting life ahead. Years from now, the story of this train ride would go on to be told a hundred times at Mormon quilting bees, but that would not happen for a while.

The older cowboy shook Corbett's hand. "Hell of a ride, this one. Are all your train trips like this?"

"Every time." Corbett smiled. He found his derby on the floor and dusted it off. Looking back at the seats and interior of the railcar, he saw that the car was empty.

8

The only good thing about getting up in the middle of the dark was the sausage gravy and biscuits chased by strong coffee. Corbett's view from the long bench in front of the Railroad Hotel consisted of warehouses, storage buildings, and rails, many rails. Whether it was true or not, Corbett believed he smelled a hint of the ocean in the morning breeze. The cannery down near the docks provided most of the ocean aroma.

His telegram from the education office of Oregon stated the plan for the day. Corbett was to be picked up at about eight o'clock from the hotel and transported to his new school. Weeks ago, when the telegram arrived in Greeley, it was not clear which school he would be assigned to. The thrill and the expectation of the day barely under his control. It was nearly eight. Except for a loaded wagon tied to a hitching post nearby, its driver enjoying coffee two benches away, probably a teamster of some type, little else was in sight.

"Nice morning," called Corbett. "Every day in Portland like this?"

The driver turned slightly. "In the summer." Under a blue knit sweater was a white dress shirt, a uniform perhaps. "We do like the summers here." His pleasant disposition went along with his relaxed body type, a little heavy and wide in the butt and well nourished in the front.

"I thought it rained here all the time."

The driver responded, "It does rain a lot here. We don't even tan in Oregon; we rust." He asked, "Did you come in on the train last night? I'm waiting for a lady. We have a long way to go today." He looked again back to the hotel doors. The woman he was waiting for was late.

"My people are late too." Corbett scanned the road from one end to the other. "I don't even know their names or what they look like."

"What are you in town for?" He looked Corbett over. "From your derby, I'm guessing that you are a salesman of some kind."

"Oh no." Corbett laughed. "I couldn't sell slop to hungry hogs." He had practiced the line but had never used it before. "I'm a schoolmaster."

The driver snapped to with a peculiar look. "Is your last name Jones?"

"Yes," said Corbett slowly. *How did this driver …?* Then he understood. "You're waiting for me?"

"I thought I was waiting for Corina Jones, a schoolmarm from Colorado. That's you?" He leaned back and belly laughed. "What do you know!"

"I'm Corbett, and I guess I'm waiting for you to haul me up somewhere to my new school."

The two shook hands. The driver introduced himself: "John, John Watkins."

"So, John, where are we off to?"

"We are going west, well past that hill you see across the river. We have a new little town at the railhead of the ORR&N called

Cedar Crossing. They're spending a lot of money to get to our logs. Cedar Crossing is right in the middle of it," said John proudly.

"How many kids in the school?" Corbett asked.

"We've never had a school before, but one got built last fall. Don't know how many students you'll have."

The closer the wagon got to the river, the worse Portland looked. The small houses were not kept up; trash and junk was everywhere. The buildings around the docks were unpainted and unattractive. Then there was the river, which showed the signs of every boom and every bust over the last forty years, including unused wharfs and docks with rotten timbers. Nothing was ever removed; the get-rich-quick occupants moved out during the night, and a new generation of entrepreneurs took their places, building up their own homes and businesses around the ruins of their predecessors.

"You don't have to worry about me trying to sell you on Portland," said John convincingly. "Across the river and two or three streets north is Whitechapel, a hellhole if there ever was one. Unemployed, beaten-down single men of all stripes find what they want: drugs, syphilis, and fights.

"This here is the Morrison Bridge. Been here about a year." The wagon stopped just before the bridge at a tiny little building. "Here you go." John handed a fellow some coins.

"What's that for?"

"This is a toll bridge, fifteen cents."

"It costs you money each time you cross the bridge?" questioned Corbett, voicing the same complaint others had heard every day for a year.

"Every day! Teamsters pay more for heavy loads and bigger wagons."

The buckboard clattered onto the bridge across the wide

north–south river. Corbett looked and looked again. "John, is this the Columbia?"

"No, the Willamette."

"It's the dirtiest river I ever saw." The surface was gray to brown in color, the river full of bottles, paper, and, if Corbett was seeing things right, human waste. There was a blue-green sheen that rode the tops of the waves in places; it was oil from shipping, unable to dissolve in the water.

John did not have to look down at the polluted river, but he did so. "The river starts way south, pure and clean, from the mountains, but because it then passes by the paper mills and canneries, then is run through by oily ships, you can see what you get. Even the sewers drain into the Willamette."

"My God, John, it's awful."

The climb up and over the mountain was slow and tedious, but the road was large enough for traffic in both directions. Flat farmland lay ahead; it was easy traveling west toward the coastal mountains.

"That's Martin's place right ahead," said John. "They change horses here 'cause the different routes into the mountains are hard on horses." John bumped Corbett. "Besides that, he has a surprise for you. Been planning it since we heard you were coming. But I reckon you'll be a surprise to him too." John was a little too eager to Corbett's way of thinking, but he was proving to be a solid and fair man, so Corbett figured the stage stop might be interesting.

"The way you're acting, I'm not sure I am going to like this," responded Corbett. John eyeballed Corbett and, with a goofy smile, winked.

Martin's Camp 12 seemed to Corbett to be a fortress. It was log style. The walls were two to three feet thick, and tall. The business itself was a restaurant, hotel, and mercantile, all within the same walls. The hay barn still had a few bales left. An accompanying wheelwright building was surrounded by wheels of all types and in all conditions. There were several fir and cedar stumps that still needed to be cleared; however, there was plenty of room to park, even corrals if needed.

"Martin's pushing hard to be a rail station when the time comes." John slowed the wagon to a stop a few yards past the front door of the restaurant. "But I'm not sure the railroad is even taking this route. It's all tied up in court anyway."

Out of what appeared to be Martin's private residence came a tall, handsome man in his forties. In his hand were three wine-glasses, and trapped in the bend of his elbow rested a bottle of white wine. He froze in his tracks, confounded.

John, standing in the front box of the wagon, pronounced, "Here's Corina!" pointing to Corbett.

Marvin, dumbfounded, just stared at Corbett, then he and John began to laugh uncontrollably. Corbett smiled at the joke he did not understand.

John, with tears running down his cheeks, directed his words to Corbett: "Martin was going to get the first shot at the new schoolmarm, wine and all." Then the laughs began again, this time with Corbett.

Corbett jumped to the ground. Martin, laughing at himself, said, "Want some wine?"

"Corina's not here, so I'll drink hers," replied Corbett.

"John, you got me good," said Martin, glancing around. "Now where's Corina?" The laughs started again.

"Martin, this is Cedar Crossing's new schoolmaster, Corbett Jones."

Looking Corbett right in the eye, Martin said, "You can't

believe how much stuff I did just to get the first chance at the new skirt from Colorado. Come to the back, and I'll show you."

In the large private patio, an oriental cook persevered around several light-colored crocks and two large pots of boiling water. Corbett saw work tools and ice picks in good supply on another table, as well as a pile of newspapers.

"Ever try one of these?" Martin asked, handing Corbett a cold, rough rock. Corbett held it at arm's length.

"What do you mean, try?"

"That's an oyster—comes right out of our Pacific Ocean. We usually eat ours raw."

"The hell you say." Corbett had heard of oysters, but raw? "You eat these?" Corbett was not sure that he had heard right.

"We'll shuck a few of these down before the main meal," said Martin, the host. "You and John sit right here. John, wine or scotch?"

"This white wine is fine, thanks."

"Corbett?" Corbett observed John's preparation, surrounding himself with newspapers, a knife, and a fork.

"You'd better hit me with some scotch. And I don't even like scotch." He added, "Raw, you say?"

"Just watch John while I'm pouring drinks." John used his knife to pry open an oyster, which he handed to Corbett. Trying to stay open-minded, Corbett saw nothing in the oyster's appearance that made it seem edible.

"How do you kill these things?"

"You don't. In fact, old, dead oysters are poisonous," replied John, prying on the second oyster. "You want them cold, fresh, and alive. Corbett, take your knife, go underneath the oyster, and cut it loose like this."

Corbett observed, but he was a few sentences behind. *Raw* and *alive* were the words that continued to roll around in his mind. John applied a little lemon juice and some pepper. It struck Corbett that John had forgotten the last step in eating a live oyster.

"How do you clean them?" Corbett asked, cross-checking with John and Martin.

"Oh, you eat them whole," said Martin, who'd just come back with the drinks. "Let me catch up with you two, and we'll down the first ones together." That did it. Corbett resolutely and categorically decided these coastal types were crazy, perhaps from the manure dredged up by a shellfish on its way to die inside a daft human.

"I'm telling you right now, my name is Corina, and I say to you that I'm too delicate for live shellfish. But if you show me to the whiskey bar, I will down my second while watching you two swallow down your first."

Fifteen minutes later, cooked Dungeness crabs as big as the plates they arrived on were served. Corbett soon understood the reasoning behind the work pliers and ice picks set up along the table. After a taste of the meat inside a crab's claw, he was hooked—and soon up to his eyeballs in the destruction of the rest of the crab.

"Now, you boys got something here," exclaimed Corbett, sliding his third carcass into the garbage can. "I thought seafood was just about fish. Boy, was I wrong."

"Corbett, you've been a good sport," declared John. "Most people cook their oysters in stews and the like, but we wanted to test your pluck."

"My cook had a nice stew for the schoolmarm. Then we saw you and decided to have some fun."

"Well, you did that. I need to take you boys back to Colorado for some Rocky Mountain oysters. Now there's a good oyster." Both Martin and John sat back, perplexed. Oceans in Colorado?

"On the days when we cull the bulls and make them steers, we have oysters fried outdoors over an open fire. Those parts we take off the bulls are sliced, flavored a bit, fried to a crisp, and served with beer. Corina wouldn't have one of those oysters either."

The next morning, about an hour away from Martin's, Corbett's head was aching. A taste of vertigo made him nauseous. Was he following the path of his father, an alcoholic to the end? He knew he deserved all the torment now upon him.

John and last afternoon's white wine seemed unfazed. "Ah, I see you are once again among the living. Don't let Edith catch you in your present condition, or I will be hauling you back down the hill!"

"Who's Edith?" Corbett's head pounded with each word.

"That's the family you're staying with. At least in the beginning. Her husband drinks like a fish, but you schoolmarms better not." John turned his head to Corbett and nodded. "Believe me, I am not kidding."

"Thanks for the warning," uttered Corbett, embarrassed that John had sensed the need to lecture.

"This is one of several roads to Cedar Crossing. I took this one because Martin wanted to meet you, but mostly so you will get to see the railroad's logging camp, and then up to Edith's."

"I can see that you love this place, but there are big trees everywhere," said Corbett, noting one large Douglas fir after another growing on each side of the road. "Why is the railroad spending so much money going deeper into the trees?"

"We have a special area where the land is flat and has thousands of perfect trees. You'll see." John remarked the map on the high plateau just northwest of Cedar Crossing. "The logging camp isn't cutting logs in order to ship them. They're clearing a path through the trees at railroad grade for the railroad to put down tracks and follow. It all ends at Cedar Crossing. And you're the schoolmarm."

"Are there any families up there?" Corbett was beginning to doubt a need for him. Maybe he could get on with the railroad if the schoolmaster job were to peter out.

"Oh no, there's people moving in every day. The railroad is anxious to have Cedar Crossing be a booming town. Right now, it's the Wild West, but it will get better with a school and all." At least John hoped so.

The left side of the road faded away into a deep canyon. The climbing turns finally took the pair over the top.

"Can you see the smoke in the clearing down there?" John pointed into an opening in the trees, barely visible from this distance. "We will be down there in just a few minutes." John was right; the road down was steep and rutted from wagon brakes in the past, some locked and skidding. Corbett deduced loggers were not bringing logs out this way. The roads were like those in Silverton, but in this case, you would not fall off; you would fall into a solid giant fir.

The camp was deserted except for the cooks, who could be seen moving about. The bunkhouses were of newly planed firs, the roofs made of mossed-over tin, covering the eating area. The corrals trailed down to the river, which bubbled and splashed just a few yards from camp.

"The good news for us is that they are close enough to Cedar Crossing to come up to us for goods and on the weekends to drink. We have some bad trouble at times, but it will get better. More families and all that."

"How many workers are there?" Corbett could see himself working as a logger, which was kind of like cowboying, masculine. And in some ways, he had fallen prey to the romantic notion of logging in the Northwest. Maybe schooling had gotten him here to Oregon so he would become a logger.

"Twenty to fifty, and many are the dredges of the earth," lamented John. "But we'll take their money. Heavens knows, they don't save any." *Similar to miners and cowboys*, reflected Corbett. "You'll see them soon enough. We were hoping a proper schoolmarm might settle them down a bit." John glanced toward Corbett and smirked.

The sky closed in around the road. The reason for the many twists and turns was that it was easier to build a road around these monster trees than to fell them and tear out the stumps. The vine maples and the thick canes of blackberries were already at work to reclaim the road. White-skinned alders indicated streams or boggy springs. White cow parsnips and lupines dotted the forest floor and crowded for space near to a multitude of ferns.

At a much-needed nature stop, Corbett began to plow through the foliage. "Stop, Corbett!" shouted John from nearby. "You're right in the middle of a bunch of nettles. Raise your hands and walk out the same way you walked in." Corbett retreated. John pointed out the tall plants, noting their arrow-shaped leaves and hairy underbodies. "These will sting and itch you for days. I hate 'em."

Even pee stops were treacherous. Corbett began looking for a new place and thinking how a schoolmarm would have handled the situation. "Makes you want to think twice about being out in the woods at night," said Corbett in amazement.

"The funny thing about the nettles"—John aimed one way and Corbett the other—"is that the Indians use the heck out those things, eatin' 'em, makin' rope with 'em, and using them as medicine."

This, thought Corbett, *is the longest short trip that could ever have been supposed.* "When do we get to see some more sky?" asked Corbett, his mind overwhelmed by the vast number of brown trunks located, like sentries, ahead and overhead.

"Edith's farm is the closest," said a drowsy John, his head rising from sleep. "They have about ten acres broke out and covered in sunshine. They came as farmers first, then became loggers. Been lots of loggers like them since." John smiled. "They and a few other homesteaders built these roads. Couldn't remove the big stumps and make it straight, so this is what we got."

A shot rang out. Corbett instinctively ducked while John leaned back and brought the horses to a halt.

"Where'd that come from?" asked John, searching ahead and to his left. Corbett pointed in the same general direction. A crashing and thrashing noise followed. The team's ears pointed nervously as the sound grew nearer. Corbett reached back for a weapon of some type. The horses were ready to break and run. John set the wagon brake, the wagon skidding a few feet.

Then a creature broke into sight, obviously the leader of its herd. It was wide-chested and powerful. Corbett had never seen such an elk. This one had its nose up, and its trailing antlers were nearly the length of his body. The crush of the other elk, both bulls and cows, thundered in front of the wagon and horses a mere twenty yards away. Corbett could not train his eyes on just one body as the mass blurred by.

Then it was quiet again, very quiet. "My gosh, that was something!" said John, for the both of them. "I have to catch my breath."

"I'm not much of a hunter," stated Corbett, "but blind luck would have gotten me one for sure."

"I have a pistol back there, but I would've probably shot one of the horses instead. Everyone who's got a gun out here shoots at them every time they get a chance, especially in the winter, when the meat keeps better."

Through and under the trees, Corbett could see bright green grasses and flowers in their best light. Sun, not shadows, lay ahead.

No one could have told Corbett of the thickness of these woods. The opening took him back to the first real poem he had ever read. He and Emi had read Longfellow's "A Gleam of Sunshine" from a book in Mrs. Portman's library.

It was amazing to Corbett that he could remember it. Its last verse was personified by this moment of breaking out into the sunshine:

> This memory brightens o'er the past,
> As when the sun, concealed
> behind some cloud that near us hangs, and
> shines on a distant field.

Corbett was missing his best friend, the written word. Maybe in the solace of these woods could he visit his friend often.

"Hello! The cabin!" shouted John. Two gardeners looked up from the large garden that was next to log cabin made of add-ons. Being relieved of the heavy canopy of trees and shade that had been their visual diet all morning was, to John and Corbett, like taking off a yoke of gloom.

Corbett and John, quick to the ground, stepped forward for introductions.

"Edith, look what I brought you!" said John proudly.

Edith was a heavy woman wearing a white homemade dress adorned with little red flowers all over it. Her threadbare apron advertised several different flour mills. One could see that just below her dress, thick ankles held up wide-placed stumps for legs. Her girth seemed ample for birthing; her chest, appropriate for afterbirthing. Her braided hair was like a thick, coarse rope, reddish, whitish, or brownish, according to individual hair which was chosen. The only item of note were the large black boots she wore, the tongue of each dangling gaily as she moved.

"Good afternoon, ma'am," Corbett said, shaking her hand. His hands seemed soft in comparison to Edith's calloused and rough handshake. With the grip of a vise, she pulled him in close.

"Do tell John that it seems you have brung us a certified suitor for my sweet Margaret." Turning to Margaret, who had just joined the group, Edith teasingly asked, "So does this dandy suit ya?" Margaret glanced at Corbett then looked away, blushing as only a teenage girl could blush.

With Corbett's first look into the garden, he had thought Margaret a tall, lanky boy. She looked to be sixteen or seventeen, but with women, who knew. Her breasts and hips were not yet pressing out against her faded bib overalls in those special places. Her fiery red hair and blue eyes were noticeable, but her smile was magic. Corbett caught a disarming coquettishness that was very pleasing.

"You will have to forgive my mother." Margaret flashed that smile. "We don't have folks out here very often, and—"

John interrupted, saying, "Meet Corbett Jones, a bright fellow who's easy to get to know. He has books and things here in the back." John started untying the tarp. Edith could not understand why this handsome man's things were any of her business. Then, with perfect timing, John said, "By the way, Edith, Corbett is the new schoolmarm."

The world stopped. Edith stared at John for a long time.

"So, I guess the schoolmarm won't be sleeping in my room after all," said Margaret, looking down at the statue that once was her mother.

"You're Miss Jones?" Edith's life dealt in facts and logistics. This new fact and the logistics thereof dazed her.

"Corbett to you, ma'am," said Corbett. "And Mr. Jones to you, Margaret," he added, laughing.

"I wondered how this introduction would go." John grinned. "Edith, you ought to have seen your face!"

"John Watkins!" Edith said, feigning anger. "You get out of here!"

"Good luck to you, Corbett." John was aboard and ready for home. "My prayers be with you." He gave a wave and a lighthearted smile.

"Lord, boy, let's get your things inside." Edith was now back in control. "We're a mess, but that is who we—"

They heard the sound of three shots, then yelling. From across the field and on the main road, a wagon came racing toward them. Corbett stepped back. First the elk, then a wagonful of madmen. Busy road.

"Them's my boys," Edith said, waving proudly.

The shot heard earlier might have been these boys hunting elk. Corbett's view indicated it must have been successful, as the boys were all smiles, hooting and hollering. Edith and Margaret walked toward the oncoming wagon as if this confusion occurred every day. Corbett was definitely intrigued.

"We got the sumbitch!" a tall, thin, young fellow announced.

"We got him!" A heavier bull of a boy jumped off the back of the wagon, while an older man stopped the horses.

"Edith, look what we got!" shouted the old man, pointing to the back of the wagon. All three reached in and produced first the head, then the midsection, and finally the tail of a monster cougar. "Robert got him down by the old snag. One shot!"

"Touch 'em, Margy!" The stocky boy grabbed Margaret by the hand and plunged her hand into the fur. "Ain't that something?"

"Sorry, son," said the driver. "I'm Joe. Who might you be?" Joe reminded Corbett of a skinny old miner he knew back in Silverton named Ollie Young. Both men rode hard and had past their prime before they'd entered their prime. Unshaven, with several teeth missing, they both had the complexion of dark leather.

"He's our new schoolmarm!" Margaret said, quoting the joke of the day.

"The hell you say!" Joe examined Corbett more closely, "Well, hell, you're a surprise." Joe would have had a broad smile if he'd had any teeth left. "Welcome. We need some elegance around here." Joe was scrutinizing Corbett's derby from Silverton.

"I'm Corbett Jones, here to do some teaching," said Corbett. "Hope this all works out."

"Ever see a cougar up close? Take a look." The tall boy waved Corbett toward the wagon. "Hi, I'm Robert. And this turd is Ernie."

Both boys shook hands with Corbett. "John has been filling me in on you logger boys." Robert was Joe, just a newer model, a string bean of sorts. He wore his hair combed back with a bit of grease. He had a girl out there somewhere. Ernie, muscular and proud of it, wore no shirt under his bib overalls to disrupt the view. His front teeth were badly gapped, but Corbett did not think Ernie cared. A mirror was probably a foreign object to him anyway.

Corbett stepped between the boys to see their prize. He had seen a cougar before, one crossing a canyon while he was hauling coal, but nothing like this. "Wow, what a nice pelt!" It was still early enough that the cougar had not shed its winter coat. Corbett could tell that while he was taking their score, the brothers were taking his.

"This damned cougar killed a heifer calf of ours a couple of weeks ago," Joe said, providing the historical background. "And when the hide's right, we will sell it down off the hill for what the calf was worth, maybe more."

"Gonna sell it to John?" This was a magic moment for Ernie. His life was hunting, fishing, and filling the firebox of the steam donkey, little else.

"You think I'm gonna sell it to that old grave robber!" This was a moment in Joe's life when he was actually in charge and winning. He deliberated with the reverence of a prayer. "I think I'll have Lewis see what he can do with it. He's the best around." To Corbett, John explained, "Lewis runs a tannery on the other side of the crossing."

"While the boys are gutting and trimming out the cat, I want to show you around," Edith said, turning Corbett to the garden. "Margaret and me hoped by having a dignified schoolmarm living with us, she could teach some outside manners to the boys." She stopped. "Are you dignified?"

"Probably not." Corbett smiled as he looked over Edith's head to Margaret, who began chuckling. "But I can speak highly of reading and learning like they do out in the world."

"That was a good answer," replied Margaret, teasing her reluctant mother.

Edith did not have to say a thing about the effort that had gone into the opening up of their homestead. Trees had been felled to open the ground to the sun. Stumps, big stumps, were everywhere except in the garden and down near the spring. Earlier, when Corbett and John were riding side by side up the hill, they had stopped at an unusually large red cedar. John had pointed, saying, "Out there are homesteaders living in hollowed-out trees just like the one we are examining, seeking to break ground rather than wasting precious time with a cabin."

"When we first got here, mustering up the effort to chop down one tree a week was our goal. Then it was a month to saw it up." Corbett knew from the pride and the emotion that Edith was reliving her experience with every tree that had been felled. "Where the first trees fell, the cabin was built. No one could see it because the other fallen trees were too tall to see over. There was meat everywhere—deer and fish in the summer, and elk after the freeze. See those tall plants there on the other side of the garden?"

"You mean those nettles?"

"In the spring, when the young tops are out, we would eat them every day—and miner's lettuce, of course."

Of course, thought Corbett.

"When the children came of age to help, things went much faster."

"So, Margaret, how much schooling have you had?"

"Mother knows how to read, so every book that came into the forest by homesteaders and the like, we've read from cover to cover." Margaret was proud of her very limited homestead education. "Now with the town growing so much, there are books everywhere. John even has a small library in the mercantile. Almost everyone moving in has more schooling than me."

"We will try to fix that." Corbett saw in her an eager student. "How old are you anyway?"

"Seventeen."

Edith grabbed Corbett's hand. The topic had gotten away from her homestead. Rarely had she been able to celebrate her hard work with an outsider; she was not going to waste this opportunity. The view to the south was the new topic of choice. Across the road and two hundred yards away, on a slight downslope, were willows and young alders. Edith pointed. "See our pond? Every year when the rains stop, the spring goes dry, so we collect the spring's water for the dry spell."

"Dry spell?" Corbett had heard a new term for the Oregon country: *dry*.

"Joe has a joke about that," said Edith.

Margaret wanted to tell it. "It doesn't rain often here in Oregon, but when it does, it's for six months."

At this latitude, about halfway from the equator to the North Pole, the cool summer nights started late. An outdoor table and a campfire away from the stuffy cabin were preferred. Joe's chair had arms covered with a beige-brown elk hide. His canning jar half filled with blackberry wine, he was living his dream, which he had given so much of himself to achieve.

"Margaret, you got any of that good bread left, maybe a little butter?" Joe sat like a monarch in full view of his domain.

"Corbett, you are getting here at a good time. The crossing is down the road about a mile. It's going to be the railhead for this part of the woods, A lot of money comin' in; going to be a big town." With his feet up, he continued to explain his good fortune. "Down California way, there are the big redwoods. They live in a perfect environment of constant mist and good soil. Well, we have that here, 'cept we have a red cedar grove." Pointing to the northwest, Joe could see it in his mind. "There is a high, wide plateau full of the best red cedars in the world. With the whole country needin' shakes and shingles for their houses, you can see why the railroad is thrusting itself up toward the crossing. The logging camp down yonder is clearing the rail line right up to us."

"Is that what you do?" asked Corbett.

"Naw, the boys and I work for a small shingle mill. We cut shingles and shakes out of the cedars and send them down to St. Helens."

"Yeah, I can tell you, I've never seen so many big trees in my life." Corbett felt very much an honored guest. "How long you been here? This clearing must have taken forever."

"Oh hell, we've been here a lifetime or two." Joe leaned back toward the door of the house. "Edith, how long we been here?"

"Too long!"

"We came into this country from Illinois. We were going to farm our way to riches." Joe needed to tell his story. "Couldn't afford to live down in the valley. The Willamette Valley was all picked over and too expensive for us'ns with no money to start. Then Edith heard that they were homesteadin' up here. Basically, it was nowhere—just a better place to starve."

"Thanks, Margaret." Joe handed Corbett a slice of bread, a pat of butter, and a nice taste of honey, as well as helping himself to the same exact snack. "She wants town. Been to Portland once and Beaverton a time or two. Yeah, she wants town."

"How about you?" Joe leaned forward, trying to keep the honey under control, pleased to have someone to talk to. "I didn't think they would ever find a schoolmarm to come out here." He mumbled through his sandwich, excitedly, "And we get you, and you ain't even a marm!"

"I saw an ad on the college bulletin about Oregon needing teachers hereabouts, so here I am."

Joe was not listening; he was smirking at his new joke. "Half the loggers down at the camp are ready to court the new schoolmarm. Won't you be a surprise?"

The conversation was interrupted by Robert and Ernie, who were carrying on their shoulders the heavy cougar pelt. "What do you think, Pa?"

The boys opened the underside for Joe's inspection. "I think it's about ready," concluded Robert. Corbett grinned at Robert. From the blood on Robert's clothing, one might have assumed that he'd spent the afternoon wrestling around inside the pelt.

"You still have some fat on that flank, but it looks like you can put it on the stretcher." It was obvious that Joe's approval was uppermost in the boys' lives.

It did not take Edith much coaxing to convince Ernie and Robert to sleep outside. Other, long-term arrangements would be figured out later. Ernie's bed was the bare minimum, an elk hide atop a wood slab, then two quilts, one filled with feathers of some type. Corbett could not help but feel he had gone back in time. The homestead and the family living in it could have been living in the 1840s instead of 1890s. They were good people, he thought, living a subsistence life that was passing them by.

"Corbett, time to get up." There was sunlight bouncing around somewhere in the cabin. "The boys have already left, and Margaret's out milking. "Thought you would like some breakfast." Edith was kind about it, but Corbett knew not to sleep in again.

"We got venison backstrap and grits fryin', which we'll put some butter and honey on."

"Sounds great, Edith," Corbett said, trying to gain favor. "I really slept well."

"I was hoping that you could go sponge hunting with us this morning," she said, the interpretation being, *You are going sponge hunting with us.*

"Sure. You bet." Corbett hoped his eagerness would help. His other hope was that this was not going to be a long year with Edith. "Tell me about these sponges," he said as his plate was set before him.

"Spring mushrooms. Other people call them morels." Edith obviously was an expert. "We'll get down to the burn and show you what they look like. We get tired of meat all the time, so let's go have a look."

Margaret met Edith and Corbett at the road. Her walk up from the spring had been a moneymaker. One bucket of milk was left at the cabin for the family, and one bucket was poured into a covered can and placed in a cooling box by the spring. Joe would take it to Grandma's little diner after supper. Milk, eggs, honey, and vegetables were making Edith more money every day.

Margaret might as well have been a boy. She'd been raised that way. Tall, agile, and strong, she led the way, with Corbett following and Edith bringing up the rear. Corbett could not help but be impressed with Margaret's skills moving through the forest. Joe had said she wanted to go town to live. While that might have been true, she was, at this moment, a girl of the woods.

"We made it." Margaret smiled. She was happy the family had a schoolmaster rather than a schoolmarm. Her emotion was subtly expressed, but it was there.

"These sponges love the shady north side, and they really do well in old burn areas." Edith was already scouring the ground by a crumbling blackened fir. Margaret was pursuing mushrooms in a direction of her own.

"Found one, Corbett!" Edith held up a light brown, cone-shaped object. The surface had wavy lines and indentations, causing it to look sort of like a sponge. "This is what we are looking for. My gracious, they are good. Look here. Where you find one, you'll find more."

The sponges were numerous and easy to find. Corbett contemplated, not knowing what he now knew, if he would have thought to pick up this strange-looking plant and start eating it. *These people are peculiar. They will eat raw, live, whole oysters and, as a side dish, nibble on a mysterious growth that is not even green.*

With the sun having already passed overhead, the three, each carrying a full bag of morels, retreated to the cabin. Margaret and Edith had also found tiny strawberries, not a lot, but a snack just the same.

It was nice to help the women, but Corbett was happy to see the dirty loggers arrive from a day's work. Robert and Ernie, though tired, were excited about showing Corbett Cedar Crossing after supper. Joe needed to deliver the milk and some fresh honey to Grandma. His pay would be a cold beer at Geri's.

The seared sponges, fried in butter, were like candy to Joe and the boys. Corbett tried not to like them, but he found them to be delicious. The boys ate them on the run, then took a quick wash down at the spring and drove to town in the wagon.

9

Entering Cedar Crossing, Corbett could not help but notice Watkins's Mercantile with its prime corner location, a lynchpin for the businesses down the main street. A board walkway extended past Grandma's, the eatery, and a lively indoor/outdoor bar, Geri's, according to the sign. All three businesses were connected and sectioned off from each other. Grandma's and Watkins's were both dark. A barmaid was lighting the oil lamps placed both inside and outside Geri's.

"Let me stop here," said Joe, bringing the wagon to a halt. "Grandma sits by the window until I pull in." Robert jumped down and collected the milk can from the back of the wagon. Ernie was already walking to the front door of Grandma's with three jars of honey. An older woman met the boys at the door. A bit of money changed hands. "She's a good old girl. Came in about the same time we did," said Joe. "Edith makes good money off her, selling milk, eggs, honey, vegetables, and sometimes my blackberry wine."

Joe drove past the horses and wagons hitched in front of Geri's to a vacant area on the side. The place was already packed and loud. "Geri doesn't have real walls on these two sides, just a heavy tent canvas, down in the winter and up in the summer. She pulls the canvas out and up. It's a roof of sorts, held up by poles and surrounded by spittoons."

Nearly all the clientele were loggers, some with the railroad and some not. Those sitting about were already drunk, planning on spending their week's wages on getting sloshed. Many a rail camp logger spent restless nights dreaming of the women Geri had on hand. Some loggers bathed at the hot springs before coming. Others just splashed their faces with lilac water as they left their camp.

"Well, butter my butt and call me a biscuit, what do we have here?" The blaring voice came from the poker table closest to the back wall. "Here is our cedar shingle gang!" It was obvious that the shingle gang were regulars and popular with the bar crowd.

A bleary-eyed sawyer at the bar waved at Joe. "You bastards are late. I done got drunk. And you can kiss my ass."

"Damn, Johnson, you stink!" said Joe as he muscled the drunk down the bar to make room for himself.

"I do believe I am, but the outhouse was too damned"—he burped—"far."

Corbett slipped under the flaps and into the bar. A long reddish-brown alder bar, to which Joe had proceeded, carried nearly the length of the building. Corbett saw that Joe was already entrenched at the end of the bar for the evening with a beer and friends. Three poker tables and a small dance floor made up the rest of the interior. Seeing how the chairs and tables had been placed outside under the large flaps, Corbett ascertained the darker setting provided privacy for talking or fondling.

"Robert, did you bring your weekly donation?" It was the same blaring voice from the same poker table. The speaker was a smallish fellow with slicked-down dark hair. His shirt was sleeveless, even though his arms should have never seen the light of day. His practiced slouch and the air of authority about him reminded Corbett of someone from his past: Laddie.

"And who is the new one ya brought with you?"

"This here is Corbett Jones!" announced Ernie rather brashly. "He is our new schoolmaster! He got here yesterday." With the introduction, Corbett noticed the bar become quiet. He nodded and waved to the different groups. Being introduced at a bar seemed contrary to a bar's purpose. This thought amused Corbett.

"Well, schoolmarm, welcome to the crossing. Sit down, and I will school your ass on some five-card draw. Ya play, don't ya, schoolmarm?"

"Lay off, Willie!" said a logger at the next table. "He will learn about you soon enough."

Corbett had come to see the town and meet some of Joe's friends. He had not planned on meeting the local ass within the first five minutes. He would not mind playing some cards. Robert and Ernie were excited to show him off. "Nice to meet you, Willie, but I see a space at the other table. I think I will play over there."

Willie stood, full of himself and working the crowd. "Robert, you and the schoolmarm sit here at the big kids' table." Willie's eyes were constantly eyeing those around him, seeking affirmation and status as the most cunning fox among them.

Robert, taken aback, looked at Corbett and shrugged his shoulders. They were both in a bind. Robert knew trouble at Geri's would end his trips to town. His father was no help; he was lost in conversation at the bar. Corbett had not thought it through. Schoolteachers were not even supposed to be in a bar. To allow Corbett to come to the bar, Joe had convinced Edith that Corbett was not technically a teacher yet. It was a fine line, but the logic had worked. Corbett and the boys had won the battle, but if anything were to go wrong, the war would be lost.

"Okay," Corbett said, sitting directly across from Willie, with Robert seated at his right. As the session began, Corbett followed what Laddie practiced: Spend little, watch a lot. Laddie was a great gambler. He never had a decent stake, and alcohol got him by the end of the night. Any winnings were either drunk away or given away, causing Laddie to again start over with the smallest of stakes. Corbett remembered his mother sending him out with his father, hoping the boy could guide Laddie home in the early morning hours. Once there, Corbett sat away from the table. He never saw the cards, but he did see the players' faces. Before the night was over, Corbett could pick the winner of the hand, based merely on the subtle changes in the man's eyes, face, or disposition.

Corbett grew tired of Willie's continued innuendo, disparaging either him or Robert. Robert was not a good player and did not have the money to ante up for many hands. The old logger to his left would bet money if he had the cards to back it up, but a bluff would send him to the sidelines. Tug, Willie's friend, was physically intimidating. His large blue flannel shirt with the sleeves rolled up made his dimensions seem even larger. Maybe he'd been a bad prizefighter in a former life. He played a lot of hands, but because he had so many giveaways, he could be read like a book. It was no wonder Willie was the big dog. The rest of the players were literally babes in the wood.

From time to time, an attractive young blonde came by and gathered up the empties, moving easily through the room as if she owned the place. Someone called her Geri. When Corbett heard that, it settled the matter: she did own the bar. Corbett watched how she played the different customers. Her peasant blouse fell open every time she cleared a table. Some loggers drank fast, looking for another peep. If one of the boys reached for a feel as she went by, Geri would dispatch one of her girls in that direction. She was young and a pro at running a bar.

Average players, like the loggers playing at Geri's, let the cards win or lose the hand. They rarely tempted the gods with concerted mind games. In five-card draw, the hand had little to do with who was to win. Every hand, in the right hands, was an opportunity. Good players often lost small hands on purpose, sowing seeds of amateurism. A bluff made on a small pot, then called and lost, set the stage for a big play later. Corbett had spent hours watching the seductive dance of the professionals in Durango.

Early on, Willie showed his winning ways, winning some hands with the luck of the draw or, at times, bluffing the other players out of the hand. Robert went out quickly, followed by the old logger. Both were replaced with better players. Corbett stayed, but he was losing. A crowd began to gather around the table. With money steadily flowing to Willie's pile, another set of replacement players took their seats at the table.

"Listen, son," said Willie to Corbett, "why do you even play? You're not in many hands, and when you are, you don't stay in long." After winning on bluffs, Willie would show his poor hand to embarrass and intimidate the losing players. Corbett let Willie override his hand on two or three bluffs. It was possible to Corbett that this might be the largest stage Willie had ever been on. His name was being called out by those in the crowd. It was easy to find those around him under his spell.

Finally, Corbett saw the telling feature provided by Willie. A toothpick in his mouth moved to the side of his mouth on a bluff, normally in the center. It was there every time. With this information, Corbett could lay a trap.

Corbett waited until the right series of events presented itself. Corbett was dealt five cards, three of which were threes. "I bet two dollars." It was the largest opening bet of the night for Corbett.

Willie, looking around and grinning to the crowd, said, "And I'll raise you two dollars." Most watchers knew that four dollars a week was average pay, and the bet was nearly that. The place got quiet. Geri made it to the front of the spectators.

Corbett threw down two cards. "I'll take two."

"I'll play these." It was the ultimate bluff. Willie's toothpick was tucked away in the corner of his mouth.

"Five dollars." Corbett could have heard a pin drop. Willie, seeing that his bluff had not scared Corbett off, figured the newcomer probably did have a strong hand. Willie would have to buy it.

Willie eyed Corbett and laughed. "Ten dollars to you, schoolmarm!" His tone was sarcastic and cold. His bluff had been called; he had just a pair of nines in his five cards.

Corbett knew the play was on, but was he strong enough to do it? He had left Greeley with seventy dollars, mostly from Mrs. Portman's scholarship money, and of that, he had about forty left.

"And I'll raise you twenty!"

Loud sounds of excitement filled the room. That was more than three weeks of pay!

Willie counted his winnings and came up short. Not to call would be an embarrassment to his ego. Willie's audience was expecting him to triumph like the slick gambler they thought he was. He could fold, but his vision of himself would not allow that.

"All in. And I'll throw in my silver pocketknife!" By this time, the other two tables had shut down, the men from those tables now among the spectators watching Willie and Corbett.

"I've got three of these," said Corbett, tossing down the three threes.

Willie's nightmare, to lose in front of all the loggers—and to a schoolmarm—had just come true. Without turning his cards over, he slid them over to the rest of the deck. He started to get up. "Come on, Tug, let's head back."

Corbett threw the knife back on the table. "I've got a better one." He put Willie into another dilemma, whether or not to pick up the handout. Willie chose not to.

The evening almost ended well. Edith and Margaret were still up. Edith was not particularly happy. Getting up late and coming home late had brought ire to Edith, lots of ire. Flames were fueled when Ernie whispered, loudly enough that the animals in the barn could hear, "The new schoolmaster just kicked Willie's ass at poker down at Geri's." Corbett, in bed when this took place, felt the roof raise a couple of times. Fortunately, Edith did not like Willie either. But the new schoolmaster was not supposed to be playing cards in a bar. Corbett knew there was going to be a price to pay.

The moment the first foot dropped the next morning, Corbett was up and dressed. He was surprised at Edith's shrewd intimidation of others, him included. In just two days, he was already afraid of her. He chuckled at the thought.

"Good morning, ladies," said Corbett in his best voice. "How are you two?" He waited to be invited to sit. Margaret looked tall in her overalls, compared to Edith in her squat dress, whose number of patches would give a quilt a run for the money.

"Here is some coffee, Mr. Jones," Margaret said, delicately starting the morning off with some fun.

"Yeah, we are going to need to work on this proper name deal." Margaret was right. Use of the term *mister*, at least at the house, was silly. "If it is all right with your mother, call me Corbett around here, Mister at school."

"It's fine with me," said Edith sternly, inviting Corbett to sit. "Tell me what happened last night!" She was right to the point. His apprehension was heightened by her directness.

"Joe and the boys introduced me to Geri's." *Just the truth. Say just the truth.* "A logger named Willie called me out almost immediately, not to fight, but to the poker table. I didn't take kindly to the way he was trying to embarrass me. Luck would have it that I won the big hand." That was the truth.

"I don't know how the ladies on the school board will take having a card shark instructing their children. We will see." Edith was steady and composed. "Take my key to the new school and see if it suits you. See what you might need. Might even have coffee at Grandma's. Present yourself by going around town so the gossip can begin."

"It seems like a challenge now," replied Corbett. "I'm sure the school will be perfect."

Joe and Robert were at breakfast on time, but they were walking on eggshells after the previous night's foray into town, saying little when Corbett left. Ernie was late to the table. He needn't have worried about breakfast; Edith hated tardiness.

Corbett, happy for a day alone, carried the key to his first school. A schoolmaster at last! It was still early. A mist surrounded the trees and danced between them. The one open field on the way to town was like a stage with the mist, albeit a curtain, rising to reveal a flowery display of Oregon beauty. It was a wonderful morning.

On his left, Corbett passed several small houses. The school and the mercantile were across from each other on Main Street. A left at the intersection took one to the rest of Main Street. Corbett instead walked past Watkins's to the river, which was very wide and shallow. It was like John had said during their trip to the crossing, a geological gift to those who wanted to pass over it. John said to imagine the rim of a large, smooth plate. In the summer, water slipped over the rim in a small stream—easy to walk through, pleasant, and safe for children. In the late fall, the water nearly created a holding pool. Cedar Crossing's gift was in the spring runoff. Instead of getting deep and dangerous, the river used the rim to become wider, not deeper. However, there were still days when it was impossible to cross its smooth bottom. Every road from one side of the mountain to the other passed over the crossing. St. Helens on the Columbia side crossed to Beaverton and the Willamette Valley on the other.

As Corbett walked back past Watkins's to the other side of the street, he saw a hand-chiseled sign proclaiming "The Crossing School." The exterior of the school was painted white shingles; the roof, rough reddish-brown cedar shakes. There were no windows along the back wall, but there were two each on the sides. On either side of the single front door was one window each.

Five rows of four student desks and a woodstove filled the otherwise empty schoolroom. The back wall was ready for either maps or a slate blackboard. It was evident to Corbett that the Douglas fir floor had garnered extra attention. It was glossy rich light browns and yellows planked with long, even runs of wood. The woodstove near the front seemed large and adequate. Corbett took his first turn at the alder desk and chair. He sat amazed. He was a schoolmaster entrusted with the care and learning of a whole community of children. The ebb and flow of confidence sent Corbett's mind in many directions, from *What am I doing here?* to *I can't believe my good fortune.*

It was just as they said: "Damned straight, Grandma's biscuits and gravy are top drawer!" The two large biscuits had a sweet buttery taste to them. They were split and covered with a white gravy loaded with pork sausage. There was no room for the two eggs, but they were there anyway, sunny-side up. Strong black coffee was included; the grounds at the bottom of the cup were free too.

It was a little past ten. Corbett had the place to himself. Five rough-cut tables with accompanying benches filled the room. The entertainment for the morning were the backsides of Grandma and

Geri in the back as they kneaded white flour dough on the bread-making table. The wood cookstove was black with shiny nickel plating down the sides and on the handles. The heat of the stove and the lack of ventilation caused the women to sweat as they bemoaned their situation.

"Damn, we are done for another day!" said Geri, wiping her hands on a white cloth. "I don't know how you can continue to bake like this on summer days."

"Ah, honey, it carries me along, you know." Grandma had come to the woods to cook at the different logging camps and had found her man, but he died soon afterward in a logging accident. At that time, she went to Portland to cook, finally gathering enough money for a little eating place by a stream in the woods.

"Hey there, need some more coffee?" Grandma asked.

"If you don't mind." Corbett suggested to himself that maybe Grandma's place could become a habit.

Geri, with coffeepot in hand, poured, then plopped down across from Corbett. "You sure as hell took Willie to the woodshed last night." She smirked. "I've never before seen Willie speechless."

"I, ah, the cards were running my way, I guess." Geri was better to look at up close than bustling around the bar as she'd been last night, and even then she'd looked pretty good.

"Don't try to 'poor boy' chickenshit me, Mr. Schoolmaster! I saw you set him up, letting him toy with the other players, making him believe he was invincible." Geri leaned forward, her eyes focused on Corbett's blue eyes. "Then in one hand, you took him down to whimper out the door like a whipped dog! Who in the hell are you?"

"Right now, to tell you the truth, I'm hiding out, kind of hoping I didn't lose my teaching job last night in the process. She wasn't too happy."

"Who is 'she'?"

"Edith." Corbett grimaced. It had taken him two years to get here, and he'd blundered it up in just two days.

"Oh hell!" Geri was genuinely amused. "You really stepped in it. She chews Joe out about once a week. With you, it won't take that long."

"Thanks. That makes me feel a lot better."

"How long do you need to be hidden?"

"All day, I'm guessing." Corbett reflected on his last conversation with Edith. He hated to cross a mean woman.

"A thought. Can you and your fancy derby keep me safe while I'm picking wild strawberries for Grandma?"

"I suppose. What am I up against?"

"Just bears and cougars." Geri was already to the door. "Wait here. I'll get the buggy." She shut the door then opened it. "By the way, I'm Geri!"

Crossing the crossing in the buggy gave Corbett a clear idea of how special this place was. A smooth basaltic flow millions of years before had left a perfect roadway, otherwise impassable for miles because of steep, rocky slopes and fast, deep water. Three small children were playing in the quiet pool. The buggy slowed at the wide space before the rim.

Geri's fine buggy was graced by a dappled gray mare. The top was down; the dirt road, lined by a small forest of light-barked alders and the thick canes of blackberry vines. Geri gabbled about first one thing, then another. She spoke of her Thursday trips to pick up her Portland girls, returning them Sunday mornings while others were either asleep or in church. Corbett, impressed with the that idea Geri wanted to take him on a buggy ride, sat comfortably with his good luck. Any of the logger boys at the bar would have given their left arm for this opportunity. She was nice, maybe five years older than Corbett, and she sparkled with both personality and looks.

The buggy suddenly left the main line and picked its way down and around, until coming to a stop at a small, barren flat. Two lonely hitching posts stood in this middle of nowhere, for no apparent reason Corbett could see.

"Welcome to Cedar Crossing's own hot springs!" Geri was quickly off the buggy seat. She tied up the mare and ran down the narrow lane. By the time Corbett caught up with Geri, she was at the roiling waters. He heard Geri saying in a giddy laugh, "Well, come on in, schoolmaster!" She was bent down, lifting her legs out from her skirt, underneath of which she wore nothing. Corbett had never seen that kind of nothing before. He was frozen, a pillar of salt like the woman in the Bible. "My God, Corbett, tell me you have never seen a naked woman." If he had, thought Corbett, he believed he would've remembered. This memory would be locked in forever, for sure. Then the peasant top dropped away, leaving Geri completely exposed.

"Whoa! Whoa!" She attacked the buttons on his shirt, quickly finishing and moving on to his pants.

"Come on! Come on!" shouted Geri, pulling him by the hand. She bounced along quite naked. Corbett, finally free of his denim pants, bounced along as well.

Geri stumbled forward into the water, dragging Corbett right in on top of her. The sulfur-laced mist covering the triangular-shaped pool of hot water shocked Corbett as he unwound himself from Geri. He sputtered to right himself.

"My God, this is hot!" Corbett gasped.

"Marvelous, don't you think?" Geri laughed, splashing around like a baby in her first bath.

As his body became acclimated to the soothing hot freshness of the pool, Corbett slowed his movements and began to relax. "Oh, this is nice." An observer might have wondered if he was referring to the water or to the fact that the waves were alternately covering and uncovering Geri's chest. "Never been in a hot bath before," Corbett related. "Like being in heaven." Again, he might have been referring to the heat of the water.

Geri and Corbett fell quiet, floating about in their mineral-laden bath, both taking private measure of their pleasure.

"I must ask," inquired Corbett. "Do you always provide the hot springs as part of your welcoming tour?"

"It must be you, Corbett," replied Geri. "It was a spur-of-the-moment idea. I've never done anything like this before. But you are the first man in ages with manners and clean fingernails to catch my eye this way." She hesitated, then rearranged the concept. "Don't think I am hot to trot; I'm not. I deem that most men pulling and tugging at my clothes want one thing: to be satisfied. They put the trophy on the wall and walk away, searching for a new conquest."

"I must admit, you're a looker. And I've looked," Corbett said.

"The difference is that you're a man, not someone who's trying to act like one." Suddenly Geri's eyes grew large. "Do you hear horses?"

If the pair could have quieted the water, they would have. Hearing nothing, they threw caution to the wind. Then reality rode in.

"Hey, that's Geri's rig!" called a voice. "I've got to see this!"

The second of the two riders followed the first down the lane to the water, where he was astounded to see Corbett drying off with his shirt.

"Where is she?"

"Who?"

"Geri. That's her buggy!" The first asked hurriedly, "Who are you?"

"Name's Corbett. I'm the new schoolmaster," Corbett said, needing to buy a little time while his naked new friend found her way through the briars and nettles to her clothes. "She loaned me her buggy for the day." That was Corbett's bluff for the day.

Anxious, not knowing to believe or not believe him, the two men wondered if this was a sign of a good bluff. Staring at each other, the pair made another survey of the steamy spring.

"Water's good this morning. It's all yours," Corbett said to them as he walked by. The riders knew they had been had, but what for and to what degree, they knew not.

Corbett, shirtless, had picked up a water-clad blonde in her buggy on his way back to the crossing. He wondered what Edith would have concluded, the new schoolmaster naked with the town barfly at the springs. He probably would not tell her.

"That was close!" Geri's clothes were still dripping. "That's the good and bad about me owning the bar. You know I like the attention, but it's for all the wrong reasons."

"I'd like to tell you it wasn't so, but it took me about a minute to see the main entertainment in the bar." Corbett took his eyes from his driving and smiled. "It was the cute barmaid with the short yellow hair and the peekaboo top."

"And you didn't make a move. Why is that?"

"If I had, you wouldn't have taken me bathing in the hot water today." The real reason haunted Corbett again. The stimulation at the hot springs was more than enough for the average fellow to push for physical activity. Was it gone forever?

"Maybe both of us are trying to find our way, and maybe neither knows how to go about it."

The buggy became quiet. The trees and flora passing by were

appraised in silence. Maybe it was the relaxation of the springs. Or was it the pieces of their lives still undone?

Crossing the crossing, a woman stood on the far shore watching two children float little sailboats in the calm water.

"Hi, Alice," shouted Geri brightly, consistent with her personality. "How are you doing?"

Alice, blocking the sun with her hand, hesitated as the mare and buggy stirred the water slightly as they crossed. "Hello, Geri." The tone seemed stoic and reserved.

"I want you to meet the new schoolmaster, Mr. Jones." It sounded strange to Geri saying it and strange to Corbett hearing it.

Alice was not forthcoming to break the awkward silence, Corbett spoke, shirtless, "Sorry about not being properly dressed for an introduction. My shirt is really wet from the hot springs."

"Corbett, this is Mrs. Arnold and her two children, Mike and Denise. Her husband is the preacher of the church over there.

"I think their kids will be in your school," said Geri, dragging the conversation along.

"I hope so," Corbett added. "How old are you two?"

Mike, having heard the word *schoolmaster*, splashed over to the buggy. "Are you going to teach in the new school? I'm eleven, and Denise is seven."

"Yep, I'll teach you to read and write and color pictures."

"We haven't many books for the school," Alice put in, almost implying that it was Corbett's fault. "Did you go to college?"

"Yes, ma'am," answered Corbett. "And we will do fine. Again, nice to meet all three of you. Better get on now." With that, he snapped the reins of the mare.

"My gosh, she seemed cold," said Corbett, not used to negative interactions with women.

"It's not you, Corbett." Geri grinned at him. "Have you ever seen a barmaid and the preacher's wife be best friends? You, being shirtless, and me soaking wet from the hot springs, wasn't exactly the best 'How do you do?' situation. I'm sorry, I didn't think."

"I will dazzle Mike and Denise with my teaching. Everything will work out."

Corbett did put the wet shirt on before their parade down Main Street to the livery stable.

Walking the mare around to the corral, Corbett asked, "You think I can rent the freight wagon over there for Thursday and Friday? I need to meet with the state school people."

"Sure, no problem. Talk to Buck," said Geri. Then she questioned, "The freight wagon?"

"I need to gather up supplies for my year here. I was thinking that if I followed you down, I wouldn't get lost." Corbett gave her the sheepish look of a fifth grader.

"Corbett, you're pathetic. I've never had a little brother before."

As Geri walked up the left side of the street to her bar, Corbett crossed over to stand in front of a large new house, two stories with a full-length porch, the whole edifice being yellow with white trim. "Mason's Boardinghouse" said the sign. Corbett wondered if living here might be better than living under Edith's thumb.

"Looking for a room?" The voice had come from a relaxed old man rocking on the porch.

"No, just new to town," Corbett answered. "Seeing the sights. You know how it is."

"Working for the railroad?"

"No, I'm the new schoolmaster!" Corbett was beginning to like the sound of it.

"Oh, the poker player!" The old man brightened up. "I've heard about you. Kind of a shark, are ya?" The telegraph could not move gossip faster than the people in this town.

"No. Let's say I was gathering up donations for new schoolbooks."

"Well, we donate every Tuesday night here with the railroad bosses and a couple of others. I'm Myron Mason, just so you know."

"Corbett Jones. Nice meeting you. Just might see you on one of those Tuesday nights." *If I am still here,* thought Corbett.

Corbett's last stop before heading back to Edith's was to see John at his mercantile. During the ride up from Portland, Corbett and John had become friends. John was someone Corbett could depend on.

John looked up from his display case. "Corbett, your shirt is wet." Corbett looked down at his shirt; it was drier than it had been.

"Long story. How are you, John?" asked Corbett, changing to topic. "You have everything!" The store was crowded to the ceiling with goods. On one wall were canned goods and basic food supplies. Another wall contained all types of farming and logging gear. The center of the store accommodated clothes on racks and tables of folded goods. Corbett could not see the back wall, but he did not need a gun anyway.

"Been busy," said John proudly. "Every time I return from Portland, customers drop in to see what's new. Heard about your adventures at Geri's place last night. Must've made an impression on Edith."

"Yeah, I'm pretty sure there's some barn cleaning in my future," Corbett surmised. The gossip moved faster than he could. "How do you know?"

"If the new baby down the street had colic last night, I will know by noon. Besides, poker is like horse racing; the story will linger for weeks."

"Great!" said Corbett with personal sarcasm. In his mind he

wondered, *John, what if I told you my wet shirt was from swimming nude with Geri this morning? How long would that linger?*

"For a smart, good-looking young rooster," John said, slipping in some advice, "your reputation is making the rounds."

"John, just have that team of yours harnessed. I could be needing a ride off the hill at any time." Both he and John laughed at the thought. "Give me some of those lemon drops, then I'd better be off."

Rustling sounds from a side door near the back got John's attention. "Oh, Corbett, wait!" John's face lit up as a woman and two young girls crowded around him. "These are my girls. They've been wanting to meet you since before I went to town to get you. That you are not a schoolmarm has intrigued them even more."

"Hello, ladies. I'm Corbett Jones." These were the kinds of meetings he had expected to occur as the days passed. John's wife, though wearing an apron, looked dressed for church. Smile lines were evident on her otherwise young face. Above the apron was a white scalloped lace collar covering a lime-colored linen dress. Her hair was in a tight bun. Corbett supposed that every town needed a clothes horse to set the standard.

"My wife, Mildred. My daughters, Edna and June." It was clear from the expression on John's face that he was delighted to show off his family. "Both girls had school before we came up here, but they've had none since. That's been two years."

"My goodness, I'm not sure I want these girls going to school with such a handsome schoolmaster in residence," Mildred said laughingly. "Regardless, we are happy you are here."

"Did you really go into Geri's and play cards?" June asked. "I think it was grand. It seems everyone wanted the schoolmarm to be a nun or something." There was excitement in her eyes. "I wanted someone to be alive and interesting." June was wearing a rather expensive rose-colored summer dress, displaying a little more neckline than proper for a teenage girl who was nearly mature.

"Well, I'm alive," Corbett responded. "Edna, you ready to get back to school?" Maybe twelve or thirteen, she was a tomboy, judging from her ponytail and the loose pinafore masking a plain blouse, which was a tad dirty.

"I reckon. I can't remember much from two years ago, but my mother says it's time."

"I'm excited and ready," said Corbett, flashing an honest smile at Edna.

After the long walk back to the clear-cut of Edith's farm, Corbett noted a buggy parked around to the side of the cabin, near to the garden. The closer he got, the angrier the two women seemed. They were parleying with Edith on some subject. He hid behind a stump and its neighboring vine maples and blackberry canes. The day had made him paranoid, but surely this was not about him.

"Margaret!" shouted Corbett. "What's happening over there?" Two cows were walking mindlessly ahead of Margaret to the milking area.

"No idea. I know them both. Mrs. Powell, the tall one, sews clothes in town, and the other one is Mrs. Russell. He manages the shingle mill. They are wound up about something." Corbett followed along.

"They sure are," said Corbett, taking a last look. "I met a girl named June at the mercantile. Is she a friend of yours?"

"Yes. There are four of us girls about the same age. We do things together when we can," said Margaret, opening the gate to the barn. "Angela's mother is Mrs. Powell. She sews with her mother to make enough to live up here. Her father died in a logging accident awhile back." She scanned Corbett's face for feedback. "You'll like her. She is a hard worker."

"What about June?" Margaret thought, standing for the moment, then sat to milk. "She thinks pretty highly of herself, and dresses that way, but is a lot of fun." In a more serious tone, she added, "I thought she would be the first one to get caught up with one of the loggers, but instead it was Ruth." Very serious now, she said, "She had a baby about a month ago."

"So, all four of you will be going to school?"

"I'm sure the board won't let Ruth attend. She's the smartest of us all."

"Probably not." Corbett should have known that. When Ajai left Durango for the reservation, it was to attend the government Indian school. Just a few months later, she returned to die in her mother's arms. Corbett's memories still drifted that way.

After returning from the past, he said, "I think we will have a great year. I think I'd better see if I can help Edith, before you rope me into milking the other cow. For your information, I've never milked a cow in my life."

"Corbett," shouted Edith, "go down to the spring and get in our cooler box. Bring up the crock and lid with the blue stripe around it."

The crock was heavy. From inside, Edith pulled out some light-colored, washed-out meat.

"Did water get in the crock?"

"No, it's good." Edith was satisfied. "I've only cooked this kind of meat a couple of times. Enough here for another meal. Take half of this back to the cooler in the crock."

"How come it's not red?"

"It's the cougar from yesterday. Meat goes bad in a hurry this time of year." Corbett contemplated whether it was a sin to eat a predator. "From what I remember, it's quite tasty."

Corbett remembered that Lewis and Clark ate dog every chance they got. A cougar for supper was something to ponder. This was the Wild West.

When the shingle mill boys arrived at the house, Robert and especially Ernie were thrilled at the prospect of eating cougar. Corbett volunteered to assist Edith in the kitchen, in part to keep track of the carnivore they were about to eat. The sight of the pale meat had set him back—and then throw in the fact that it was cougar. Something was not right with these people.

Corbett's mind began to ease. Edith treated the meal as if it were her finest hour. Robert was sent to gather fresh nettle tops. Corbett was to clean and slice a fistful of morels. Ernie was to find the bag of hazelnuts from the previous fall, and Margaret, in from milking, was asked to bring in some fresh, young wild onions. Since the cougar was lean, lard was added to the large cast-iron pot.

The smell had all parties in their seats, forks ready, when Edith presented her finished product. Initially, Corbett took small portions. Picking through those small portions was the rule for him when tasting unfamiliar food such as cougar. However, from the start, the aroma, the look, and the taste were all pleasing. Everyone in the group agreed: it was far better than the finest pot roast.

"Edith, this is a fine meal," stated Joe, going in for another round. "I told Corbett you could cook anything. You've proven me right again." Corbett tried to bring to his conscious mind that he was eating cougar, but it was too delicious for him to have any qualms.

With the meat in the huge black pot having been finished up by Ernie, the crew around the table began to rise. "Sit. We have an issue," said Edith in a tone neither loud nor emotional.

"Two members of the school board came to the cabin this afternoon." Margaret's eyes met Corbett's. "They have strong complaints against Corbett and are calling a meeting Saturday morning." Somehow, even while it was going on, Corbett knew the conversation between Edith and the two women had been about him. "If they get one more vote, Corbett, you will be done here."

"I'm sorry I'm causing so much confusion," answered Corbett. "The more I saw today of Cedar Crossing, the more I liked it. A schoolmarm would have a rough go here. Between the high expectations for her hair and her manners, and which men it would be appropriate for her to visit with, it would make her a constant item of gossip." Corbett then added, "Then there's the outhouse and the wood to haul."

"I think Mr. Jones needs to stay," said Margaret abruptly. "He gives me a sense that by being young himself, he might better understand our needs living out here."

"Yeah, I don't want some fancy woman telling me what to do." Ernie's comment interested Corbett. He had assumed Ernie was part of shingle mill gang and would not be going to school. Corbett was happy with that. It was good. Edith had lost Robert to the shingle mill forever, but Ernie was going to get an education.

"Maxine Powell told me that Alice saw you coming from the hot springs with Geri, with your shirt off and hers wet. Is that rumor true?"

"Yes. She was showing me around," Corbett replied. *In more ways than one.*

"You and Geri at the hot springs, in the pool, alone?" Alice Arnold's assumptions did not include the nakedness at the springs. *But why bring it up?* thought Corbett. "This is after you play cards in the bar?"

"We're not going to stand for that!" Corbett recognized the

word *we*. Those around the table were tense. The family always treated guests kindly. Joe was familiar with Edith's temper. Robert, Margaret, and Ernie were embarrassed by it, both when she expressed it at the table and when she directed it toward a guest.

"I have to go down off the hill to Portland tomorrow to check in with the state education people," said Corbett bluntly. "I will let them know you're looking for another teacher." Corbett knew he was handling the situation badly, but what the community wanted, he would never be able to provide. He was angry and frustrated. "I'm sorry I'm not meeting your expectations. I will be there for the Saturday meeting." Corbett got up and went into the boys' room. After recovering his belongings, he left.

10

"Looks like your stay at Edith's was short-lived," commented Myron, sipping coffee at his large kitchen table. "When Jeanette told me you had checked in, I got to wondering, did she throw you out, or did you retreat on your own?"

"I think I retreated before she threw me out," Corbett admitted, finishing his eggs and toast. "Her expectations and who I am don't match at all. I reckon I'll be gone by next week."

"That bad?"

"Yep, that bad. But I am glad you had a room available, or else I imagine I would have been sleeping in the shed behind John's store."

"When will you find out about your job?" asked Myron, just as another boarder entered the room. It was a young woman in a robe showing a dark, unpredictable mass of black hair. "Good morning, Minnie. Grab yourself some coffee. She did so, trying to cover herself better what with Corbett, a new person, being in the room.

"There's a meeting Saturday. I think I find out then."

"What's your plans until then?"

"I'm going to Portland this morning to check in with the school people there, probably let them know I'm available." Corbett shrugged his shoulders. "Be back Friday. So I guess if you have a room tomorrow night, I will take it."

"We can do that." Myron rose from his chair. "You'll have to excuse me. I need to see to Minnie's breakfast."

The buggy harnessed with Geri's gray mare was first in line, the rented freight wagon with its dual hitch positioned just behind it.

"Are you finally ready?" teased Geri. Her travel outfit was a red plaid flannel men's work shirt and San Francisco men's Levi's, tight against her well-designed rear parts.

"You said eight o'clock," answered Corbett, hurrying across the road from Myron's boardinghouse, derby in hand.

"Well, it's ten till. Let's go!"

From her house down the street from the corral, Maxine Powell watched Geri and Corbett trail south out of town in their respective rigs. Him with her? That would have to end.

Corbett was surprised to be going down the mountain on a different road from the one John had taken coming up, but then he remembered that Martin and his oysters were the reason for the detour on the way up. Corbett was happy to be on the road they were on; it was heavily traveled and smooth. Wagons carrying single twelve-foot sections of large fir trees passed periodically. The heavy weight put each of the log wagons at capacity. Ten to fifteen wagons would be needed for just one tree. An empty shingle wagon worked its way out and around the loads coming down. It was easy for Corbett to understand how a railroad would ease the burden.

About an hour into the trip, the caravan of two stopped for a "behind the bushes" moment. They washed up and drank some water out of the canvas bag Geri carried in her buggy.

"I know where I am going, but I don't know where you are going," said Geri, looking at Corbett's fine features, then at his eyes. "Do you have an address or anything?"

"I do," said Corbett, reaching into one breast pocket, then the other. Eventually, a rear pants pocket gave up the note.

"Are you like this all the time?" questioned Geri.

He thought, *Only when I am around you.*

"This will work out fine," said Geri, studying the piece of paper. "It's right next to the Pioneer Courthouse and not a long way from where I am going."

"Do you stay at a boardinghouse or a hotel down here?" Corbett asked. "I will need a room tonight."

"I stay at the same hotel every time down here." Geri's expression implied there was more to that answer.

"Think I can get a room there tonight?"

"Maybe. Nearly all the rooms rent by the hour, but I will see what I can do." With that, she climbed aboard her buggy and released the brake.

A whorehouse! Geri stayed at a whorehouse twice a week. Corbett could not get around the fact that Geri stayed at a whorehouse on her trips to Portland. Maybe she did so to make extra money, or maybe it was just to round up her women for the weekend. Corbett was not planning on rooming with Geri. That had never been the plan.

After several hours, civilization began replacing the forest along the sides of the road. Clear-cuts filled with homesteads and small orchards had found their way into stump-free areas. The soil was dark and healthy. Side roads turned into side streets, and houses in rows appeared from time to time. The newer, nicer houses that Corbett had not seen during his trip with John were now evident. Nice two-story houses with elms and maples gave Corbett a better opinion of Portland.

Geri pulled over to the side of the street and walked back to Corbett. She looked fine in her logger's plaid shirt and blue jeans.

"Doing okay, Corbett?"

"Yeah," he responded. "This is entirely different from the way John and I took. Much better."

"I'm going to pull off at the B Street Bar to eat, maybe get a beer." Geri was seemingly happy to have Corbett along. "I do this every Thursday. Kind of a habit."

"Sounds good to me. I need an outhouse anyway."

"Hi ya, Geri," hollered the barkeep. "Want your usual?"

"Two of them. I brought my bodyguard with me!"

"Be a minute!"

Settled, Geri immediately asked, "So, what's with the big wagon?"

"The brochure the state gave me when I signed my contract to teach out here said they offered a warehouse where little schools could buy school materials." Corbett hesitated, in thought. "Now with the meeting and everything, I'm not sure why I brought it."

"What meeting?" asked Geri. Corbett immediately wondered why, of all people, Geri was the only person in Cedar Crossing not aware of the meeting to fire Corbett.

"Well," Corbett said, laughing, "it's all your fault."

"My fault!"

"Yep. First, you opened a bar that, someday, a new schoolmaster might be enticed to enter to play and win the biggest poker game of all time." Corbett was keeping it light and without blame. "Then you took that handsome fellow to the hot springs so he could see your best side."

She slapped his shoulder. "I did not!"

"The school board Saturday will decide if those events represent the values they want in a schoolmaster."

"God, Corbett, I'm sorry!"

"Don't feel bad," replied a more serious Corbett. "I don't think I could ever meet their expectations anyway."

By chance, and at that moment, two plates of pink salmon fillets with fried potatoes arrived. It was a time to eat and ponder. "You going to the meeting?" Geri had posed the question knowing how cruel the people in Cedar Crossing could be. Her appearance, her choice of women, and the mystique of being a whorehouse madam were always with her, every day.

"I think I'm going to go," answered Corbett. "But I'm pretty sure I won't be there Saturday night."

"If they throw you out, come on over to the bar," declared Geri. "And we'll raise some hell!"

"Well, maybe. I guess I can't get fired if I have already been fired. Draw me a map to the school office and then to a hotel for the night."

"You're going to go through the middle of Chinatown. It's wild and crazy, day and night."

"Where will I meet you?"

"Whitechapel."

Four blocks from the Willamette River, Geri signaled Corbett to turn right as she turned left. Corbett debated whether to offer himself up for a different assignment or not. He settled on the school depository. He had come a long way, and despite his mistakes, he wanted to play out the hand, win or lose.

Just two blocks past the Pioneer Courthouse stood a nondescript light brown brick building, the Oregon School Depository. Corbett turned the team down the alley and pulled up to a tall cement loading dock. The big, wide double doors were open. An energetic young man was stacking student desks onto the loading platform.

"Hey, neighbor, move up about ten or so feet. The board chairman from Scio will be here any minute to pick up these desks."

Corbett obliged. "Is this where I could get some schoolbooks and other supplies?"

"Yeah. Go on in. Everything is out and marked. Where you from, anyway?"

"Cedar Crossing."

"I know the place. The new railroad spur is heading that way."

"Yep, new school and everything." How could this be? Corbett had just spoken about the crossing as if he had been born there. Saturday, he thought, he would probably think differently about the place.

As Corbett's eyes adjusted to the lackluster lighting, he could see piles of books and all sorts of school equipment. Corbett's mind saw no reason for him even to be in Portland. And what sense did it make to be buying schoolbooks when he was not even going to be using them? He wanted so much to buy. Walking around, he saw classic novels boxed in groups of ten. There were several he wanted to read. He figured he might buy them for himself.

Corbett was ready to walk back out into the sunshine, thinking that his practical side was right: He had lots of money, so forget the crossing. Then he saw them, McGuffey Readers. Mrs. Portman in Silverton had taught Corbett and his students to read out of this series of readers. Practicality having just been lost to him, Corbett spent more than one hundred dollars, six month's pay, on everything he saw. The scholarship money and the poker money—all spent for Cedar Crossing School. He had twenty-one dollars left, twenty of it in his boot.

Hours later, Corbett, with the freight wagon covered with a large brown tarp, stopped in back of the Pine Street Hotel. Geri, having been awaiting his arrival, ran to meet the wagon.

"Everything go okay?" she asked.

"Fine." Corbett looked at the large two-story hotel. He had heard of the Portland four-square design, but this one had an addition in front, a cozy bar. "So, this is the place!"

Waiting in the doorway was a logger's playground. She was buxom where she was supposed to be buxom. The slit halfway up her thigh gave a better look at her long, shapely legs.

"Come on, Corbett," Geri said, clasping his hand. "Come meet Darlene!" Her hurry was nearly too much for his derby, which bounced around, trying to find a way down off his head.

"God, Geri, he's handsome and rugged," whispered Darlene loudly. "My girls will pay for the room just to get him in it!" Although her body had not given in to age, her face seemed tired, the skin wrinkled at the corners.

"Nice to meet you," said Corbett. Probably twenty years older than Corbett, she was still quite sensual.

"Where did you get such a fine hat?"

"From a girl back in Colorado. She was a prostitute. One of her men had left it behind."

"The girls pay you? In hats?"

"When they don't have cash." Corbett laughed.

Inside, sitting in the side room off the main parlor, Darlene watched her women, through a curtain of beads, prepping the parlor for business. "Do I have girls for tomorrow?" asked Geri with excitement.

"Oh hell yes," commented Darlene. "They're worn out. A good rest will do wonders for them."

Corbett couldn't help but say impulsively, "Rest? I thought they were going up to work for you." Geri and Darlene looked at each other and laughed.

"You and all those boys up at the crossing have it wrong! These girls don't go up there to work. For them it is a holiday weekend. Sure, they get played with and fondled out on the bar floor, but I'm not paying them to turn tricks. If they wish to do so, it's up to them." Geri was excited by the idea that she and Darlene had put together years before. "It's their wild weekend too—free drinks and real flirting."

"That's hard to believe. The other night, they did look like they were having a good time." Corbett's eyes wandered through the beads to gaze at the scantily dressed women. He got caught.

"You want to have some fun tonight yourself?" Darlene asked, teasing the handsome young man.

"No. No thanks. But it sure looks doable."

Darlene grabbed Corbett by the elbow. "You don't have an older brother, do you?" Geri and Corbett had a good laugh. Darlene, like so many beautiful women, could have been dramatic and spoiled, but she was common and a joy to be around. She and Geri made a matched set.

"Corbett, you get my old room, number three," declared Geri. "I spent three years going in and out of there. It's right over there next to our room. Lock it, or you will have company all night."

"I've got a great idea," said Darlene. "Let's go down to the Jupiter and have supper. The girls can take care of things while I'm gone."

Whitechapel, in the early evening, was a bustling zoo. Men of all kinds and of sordid backgrounds crowded the streets. Nearly every business was either a bar or a whorehouse. As for the women, there wasn't decent one in sight, thought Corbett, except Geri and Darlene. He smiled at his own joke. Of the two women he referred to, one was the madam of a whorehouse, and the other was an alumna member of the whorehouse. If down and out had a capital, then Whitechapel would be it.

"I don't see any Chinese," Corbett remarked, surveying the street. "I passed through a whole herd of them getting here from the courthouse. There were Chinese everywhere."

"Chinatown. In '82, they passed a law banning new Chinese from coming into Portland. It helped everybody down here because the Chinese were taking over. We had Chinese girls selling themselves right in front of our houses. That all went away. No ID card, no stay."

"Hey! You Derby Jones?" shouted one of a pair of drunk soldiers. "Frankie, that's him, isn't it?" Both men were waving at Corbett and the women from across the street, standing at a wall cluttered with handbills.

"It is him, Corky! You are a legend, Derby Jones. I've never seen someone from a wanted poster before."

"What?" Geri asked, thoroughly perplexed.

"Yes, ma'am. Looky here. Look at this picture!" Corky exclaimed, pointing at an exact image of Corbett Jones.

"I'm on a wanted poster?" Corbett was stunned at seeing his own image.

Darlene pushed forward. "It says you threw a US Army sergeant off a moving train."

Geri echoed the charge in disbelief: "You threw a soldier off a train. You threw a soldier off a train?" She was incredulous.

"It says here he was a sergeant," corrected Corbett. "He was just a corporal."

"Wait, let me read the rest." Darlene found more charges. "Also, you are accused of aiding in the escape of a federal criminal sentenced to hang."

"You helped a criminal escape?" Geri was now beyond words.

"He got caught trying to steal his horse back." At the beginning,

Corbett had thought this was a fun joke, but now it was apparent that he was in real trouble.

"You threw a sergeant off a train. You are my hero." Corky took a bottle from Frankie and took a swig. After rocking back and forth for a second, he said, "I want to be just like you."

"First, get rid of that damn derby. If these two drunks can identify you from this poster, then about anybody could." Darlene grabbed the hat and threw it into the street. "That fancy damned hat could put you in prison." Both soldiers stumbled, racing after it.

"Who are you?" Geri had never met anyone like Corbett. The paradox to Geri was that this naive fellow was about to get fired as a schoolmaster and the board did not even know he was a wanted man. "Who does these things?" Geri asked, questioning herself mostly.

"The same guy you took strawberry picking, ending up naked in the hot springs. I guess I'm just lucky." Corbett did not know what to do next, whether to run or to relax, now that his derby was already in his past. He did know that his impetuousness was part of his bloodline. Laddie always had been held down by his own poor judgment.

"There's no law in Whitechapel, but let's get back to the hotel anyway." The little brother whom Geri had adopted yesterday was an enigma. Was he an outlaw hiding as a schoolteacher, or was he a lost soul living out a series of bad mistakes?

Back in Darlene's viewing room, Corbett was grilled about his ill-fated rail trip. Sitting at the small, round table, he realized that this was not a discussion. Both women, bent on learning the truth, fired question after question to get to the essence of the incident.

"You make it sound like you were somewhat a hero," said Geri. "But how will the court see it?"

Darlene jumped in, "The real question lies in your plan to stay out of court. Let me start the ball rolling. Wait a minute."

While waiting, Geri asked, "Are you still going to the meeting tomorrow?"

"My thought right now is to hightail it to Mexico or California. Darlene is right, I need to figure something out."

"I'm back." Darlene held two hats in her hands. "It seems every time Corbett Jones needs a fine hat, he looks around for a prostitute." Geri and Corbett laughed. "Which one?" The first was a brown fedora with a narrow brim; the second, a wide-brimmed Stetson, light brown with a two-pinch crown.

"I'll take the Stetson. If I'm going to be running like a western outlaw, I might as well look like one." Corbett tried it on.

"All you need is a herd of cows and a belt buckle." Geri had almost forgotten about Corbett's rugged good looks until she saw him in the cowboy hat. He was even more handsome than the cowboys on the handbills for the Wild West show.

"You leave before dawn and get up in those woods quickly," Darlene said, face-to-face with Corbett. "And don't come down till fall. Geri can find you work up there."

Geri agreed. Her adopted little brother was going to need her help. "You know the way back to the crossing? I won't leave so early. I try to give the girls time to sleep a little longer."

By afternoon the next day, Corbett was entering the south end of the crossing. He hesitated at the edge of town. At the moment the morning had begun, Corbett promised himself that he'd make a decision on whether to run immediately upon his arrival with the school supplies or else wait, with the remote chance that the meeting the next morning would go well. Maybe the shingle mill needed a hand. He tapped the reins and drove into town.

"I see you made it back," shouted Myron from his rocking chair.

His little hotel was nicely quiet. "Thought you might get lost, but judging from the new hat, it looks like you've just been moving cattle."

"Yeah, some hat," Corbett said, removing the hat and again examining its potential. He got down and stretched. His only companion had been the hard wooden bench seat of the large wagon.

"Where's Geri? I heard you were with her." Myron was tamping some new tobacco into his pipe.

"I keep getting the feeling that people up here are trying to put Geri and me together, but it ain't that way. I figure she's behind me by a couple of hours. She had planned on a late start." Corbett, showing a lack of sleep, asked, "You still got a room?"

"Yep."

"Good, I'll need it." With that, he stretched once more, then remounted the wagon and turned it across the street to the livery, where the horses could be unharnessed and the wagon could be stored until the next day.

At dusk, Corbett sat on the bench in front of the mercantile. He was hoping Joe and his boys would follow their normal Friday night routine, taking milk and honey to Grandma's and then moving on to Geri's for their Friday night beer. The canvas wall flaps were up, and the noise was loud. Corbett passed by the bar on his way to the mercantile. He did not need to stir up any more ruckus before the board meeting.

Like clockwork, Joe's wagon rattled its way to the front of Grandma's. Joe's toothless smile could be seen. The boys were waving as the wagon stopped.

"Hey, Corbett," shouted Robert, carrying the large canister of milk to Grandma's front door. "Goin' gamblin' tonight?"

"Not likely!" Corbett shouted back. Grandma's was between

Geri's and John's corner mercantile. Corbett, sitting at the merc, wanted to keep it that way.

Joe had walked over to Corbett and was shaking his hand. "Good to see you, Corbett. I wanted to apologize about the other day." Joe, always upbeat, had his serious face on. "Edith gets riled pretty easy and says things she regrets later."

Corbett had his own apology to make. "I'm sorry that I just got up and left. That's not who I am."

"Still goin' to the meeting in the morning?" It seemed important to Joe.

"Yes. That's why I needed to talk to you." By this time, both boys were standing near so they could hear. "Tomorrow morning, I am going to need some help at the school—heavy lifting and such. I was hoping you fellows could give me a hand." Corbett had worried all day that Joe would accept Edith's narrative and be angry at Corbett as well.

Speaking before his father could reply, Ernie belched out, "Hell yes, we'll be there!"

Joe, laughing at his rambunctious son, said, "Yeah, we'll be there. About eight, you think?"

"Just right."

"Comin' in for a beer?" Robert remembered the excitement of Corbett's last visit.

"Not this night," Corbett replied. "I'm going to be a good schoolmarm and go to my room and read." The shingle mill boys left, waving as they boarded their wagon for the short ride to Geri's.

The next morning, Edith and Margaret pulled the sweaty horses to a stop in front of the church, kicking up a cloud of dust. That was as close as she could see to park the horses. The meeting was supposed to be in the school across the street from the church. She saw Joe's wagon. Where was he and the boys? Edith could see a small crowd directly in front of the school's door. Were all the board members present? Myron Mason, Maxine Powell, and Wilma Russell all stood waiting at the door. There, in a wagon, was May Ludwig and her husband. What was his name?

Myron walked over to Edith. "They said we can go in pretty soon. They're just finishing up some volunteer work. Let's take everyone over to Grandma's for coffee."

"Good idea," mimicked Grandma. "It's Saturday. I have coffee and fresh-baked cinnamon rolls. Come on over!"

Grandma's little restaurant filled up. Grandma and Myron Mason poured coffee all around. Mildred, John's wife, sold cinnamon rolls near the back of the store.

"I wonder what they are doing over there?" asked Maxine Powell. "Nothing has gone on over there since it was finished four months ago. Now, when we need it, it's being worked on."

"Just relax and enjoy the good company," said Myron, calm and at his best. "Probably dusting and getting rid of the cobwebs."

Joe and the boys had left early without telling Edith even that they were going. Joe's wagon was now parked at the school. "Margaret, go on over to the school and see what your father is doing." There would be hell to pay when Edith got Joe home.

Margaret was gone for only a minute, when she reappeared at the front door. "They say we can go over now!" The big smile on Margaret's face stumped Edith. What was she thinking that made her so happy on this stressful morning?

As the first of the crowd entered the schoolhouse, the line of people stopped moving. Everyone behind heard sounds of surprise and astonishment. Slowly, the whole group made their way into the room. Where an empty wall at the front of the room had once stood, two large full-length slate boards, each with a polished frame and chalk tray, had taken up residence. Ernie and Mike

Arnold were drawing with colored chalk. A world globe of more than two feet in diameter sat on the teacher's desk. On the right wall, between the two windows, were roll-down maps. On the left wall were roll-ups showing historical events and famous men. Three desks contained stacks of McGuffey's Readers. One desk held a book on stenography, while on another desk sat a book on bookkeeping. Boxes of pencils and Big Chief tablets were scattered about.

"Sit, sit," said Myron loudly. "I know nothing of this." His grin, like that of the others in the room, went with the stunned look of amazement. "Whose idea was this?" Joe, in dirty work clothes and standing near the front, pointed at Corbett, just a few feet away.

"Corbett, tell us about this," said Myron in a friendly manner. Corbett had known from the beginning he would have to explain his purchases. Sensing the anger of Mrs. Powell and a couple of the others, one of these being Edith, Corbett changed his explanation into a farewell speech. He would not stay.

Stepping to position himself behind the teacher's desk, he looked at the crowd. John and Mildred were present, as were Mike and Denise Arnold and their mother, Alice. It was good to see Margaret and her friend June, John's eldest daughter, standing together.

"Good morning. First, I'm sure some of you must think that the money spent was somehow to bribe you into keeping me as the schoolmaster. That's not true. In fact, I don't want to stay here." Those in the room were taken aback, even looking at each other in surprise. "The other morning when I opened this door, I was saddened. The room was empty and lifeless. I promised myself that I would do what I could to make it feel warm and wonderful for the students who would attend here.

"You don't need prim and proper. And if you were to get

yourselves a prim and proper schoolmarm, you would find all kinds of faults with her, including how she wore her hair, how she dressed, who her friends were, and the way she cleaned the outhouse, until you drove her away." Both Mrs. Powell and Mrs. Russell dropped their eyes, knowing they would be the guilty ones.

"I could never be your prim and proper teacher. The most wonderful experience in my life was learning to read. The joy of passing that on to my little class in Colorado was marvelous." Geri slipped in and stood against the wall behind everyone, trying not to be seen.

"Mrs. Powell, you will miss the joy of being invited to the school and helping us make a community quilt. Mrs. Arnold, you will miss the joy of being invited to teach us all to sing. Grandma, in the fall, you will miss teaching the children to make pies for the annual pie social, to raise money for the school library. I don't know him yet, but the saddlemaker will miss being invited to teach the students leatherwork. You older girls, I want you to take these books on bookkeeping and stenography and learn from them to give yourselves a chance of getting down off the hill should you want to do so."

Corbett stopped. His voice had gotten louder as he spoke. It was time to say goodbye. "Don't try to be anything other than who you are, proud people surviving quite well in a tough and rugged country. I bid you goodbye."

With the room quiet, Corbett moved around to the aisle leading to the door. Those in the way made space for him to leave the building. Geri slipped out right behind him.

Myron Mason, president of the Cedar Crossing school board, stepped to the desk with a wooden mallet in his hand. "I'm bring this meeting to order. Let's say the Pledge of Allegiance with our new flag." That done, Myron began, "This meeting is solely for the purpose of voting for or against Mr. Jones as schoolmaster for this year. I have placed all five names of our board members in this bowl. The first name drawn will give comments and will mention how he or she will vote. Any questions?" Myron looked around. Nobody wanted to be first. "Good. June, will you come up and pick a name out of the bowl?" June walked tentatively to the front and reached into the bowl.

"Myron Mason!"

"Just my luck." He grinned sheepishly and nervously. "First, I don't know if we can get another teacher for this year—just don't know. Second, Corbett spent over one hundred dollars on the school, knowing he was not going to stay. That is six or seven months' wages. The third reason has to do with Geri. If she were to close up and leave, half the money this town earns would go away. She is a smart businesswoman who runs a clean bar. The railroad fellows and the loggers would either go to St. Helens or Beaverton to do business. And last, whether Mr. Jones and Geri have or will have a relationship, it is not any of our business. I like the young man. I vote to keep him." There was a murmur in the crowd, a couple of negative comments barely heard.

"June." She stepped forward once again and picked. The schoolroom was quiet and tense. Everyone seemed to have a horse in this race.

"May Ludwig." She moved to the front, away from her family, consisting of her husband, a school-aged son, two younger daughters, and a fourth child, very young, on her hip. The clothing on Mrs. Ludwig represented how the homestead was doing. Her skirt was threadbare with washed-out designs. Her top was a thin pale blouse with common buttons for ease of nursing.

"Thank you for letting me speak." She viewed the group with trepidation and nervousness. "My husband and I came with the thought that no young man Corbett's age could teach young children—no maternal instincts or anything." She stopped and looked at her husband for confidence. "But we watched as his eyes grew wide and a smile came over his face when he talked about teaching the little children." There were murmurs among the crowd as everyone awaited May's vote. "I want my boy Travis to enjoy school, not be prodded by an old spinster. We vote to keep Corbett."

With two votes in favor, Edith mulled over her vote. Standing in front of people was the last thing she had ever wanted to do. She hoped the matter would be decided before her turn came.

"Maxine Powell."

Maxine hurried to the desk in manlike strides. "I cannot believe what I am hearing! Corbett Jones has already been in Geri's. He has gone to hot springs with her, and he left with her Thursday night to go to Portland. He came back with her and three of the whores Geri generally brings." She looked around the room like a preacher on confession Sunday. "And that was just in one week. I'm surprised he doesn't have a bounty on him. I vote no." Returning to her seat, she gave May Ludwig an angry look.

"Wilma Russell."

Through no fault of her own, Mrs. Russell walked like a vulture, tall and long-necked, with her face looking down as if she were searching for small fishes. "With the growth of our mill and with the railroad coming, we will have families, lots of families. They will want a proper school like they are used to. A gambler and a cheeky rascal will not do. I vote no!"

Edith could not believe that she would be the deciding vote. Early in the process, she had demanded a strong woman teacher with impeccable morals, someone who would move through the town with grace and proper style, all the qualities she herself never had had. And now this.

"Edith Durham."

Her walk was like that of a plow horse, her years in the fields noticed by all. Being as uncomfortable as the scene would allow, Edith said, "Mr. Jones is not fit to be a schoolmaster. His relationship with Geri is not acceptable, not a good example. His age is a factor. How responsible is a twenty-year-old?" Edith looked down and rubbed the finish on the new desk. "There are some things that override all that. Robert never got to go to school—missed out on all his learning. I need Ernie to go to school. He says he will not go to school unless Corbett is the teacher. Simple as that." She waited for a second, then continued. "Margaret and June want him to teach them. Margaret told me that for sure on the way in.

"I vote to keep him!"

Geri caught up with Corbett as he crossed the street, seemingly headed for the corrals behind the feedstore. The night before, while unharnessing his freight wagon after his trip back from Portland, he had noticed a sign telling of the virtues of the big brown mule in the far corral.

"Corbett, that was quite a speech." Corbett was lost in another world, Geri almost trotting to keep up. "It sure was a shock to their systems when you didn't even give them the pleasure of firing you."

"I am so much like my father," said Corbett to no one in particular, even with Geri walking right beside him. "Always running to the next place, always the next place. Will I ever be able to set down roots, to love, to have a life?"

Looking through the poles of the corral that contained the big mule, Corbett peered at Geri. "I may be leaving town on a mule, a damned mule." Suddenly, it was visible that Corbett's mind had just changed directions. He took a firm grasp of each of Geri's shoulders. "I need to know something right now before I leave. Are you expecting romance from me? I don't want to let you down."

Geri, startled at the question and the seriousness of Corbett's demeanor replied, "I love you very much, but as the little brother I never had and just found this week." She kissed him on the cheek out of that same love. "You are very naive. Didn't you notice the happiness I enjoyed down in Whitechapel with Darlene? She is the love of my life." The emotion of finally releasing her most protected secret brought tears to her eyes.

Corbett took her tightly to his chest and squeezed her for some time. "I am happy for you. And for me too. I didn't want to let you down." Corbett was near tears himself. "I don't know if I will ever be able to give myself to love, real love." He squeezed her one more time.

"Damn it, Corbett," said Myron Mason, walking briskly toward him. "You are making this real hard on me." His eyebrows, long, shaggy, and old, gave away his every mood. Even though his words were on the angry side, his eyebrows were on the winsome side. "I look all over the place, trying to find you, and you are hiding behind the corrals, in the arms of Geri." Both Corbett and Geri were about to give Myron a piece of their conjoined minds, when he held up a key. "Here is the key to the school. Warts and all, they gave you the job."

"Even after I told them I didn't want it?"

"It was the children. They want you, and that's all that really matters." Myron was grinning. He shook Corbett's hand, then stopped. "What are you doing down here besides hugging on Geri?"

"I was getting ready to ride down the mountain on that mule."

11

"I never would have thought," said Otto from his smithy's shop.

"And the way they're measuring, it's going to fill the whole lot," added Corbett, standing next to Otto.

For two years, a large gap had existed between Otto's blacksmith shop and Geri's bar. Rumor early on had it that the new rail station would fill the vacancy. The proof had the townspeople, including Otto and Corbett, watching the two wagonfuls of surveyors and builders planting stakes and reading plans.

"From what Myron Mason said," Otto commented, pointing to an area behind the boardinghouse where two new cabins were being built, "there's going to be another street over that way. The crossing is really going to grow."

As both looked across past Mason's Boardinghouse, a large wagon crossed their view.

"Must be Friday," Corbett said, laughing. Geri and a new crop of women had arrived from Whitechapel, right on schedule.

"Hey, you two," called Geri as she drove by. "I need your help." Both men acted shocked. This had never happened before. Were they to help the women down or serve as bodyguards for the new beauties? Instead of parking on her side of the street, Geri parked in front of the school. Corbett and Otto did help the young women down. As usual, the Whitechapel women were excited and giggly.

"Quit drooling and lift this thing out of here." Lifting the brown tarp, Geri exposed a sizable gray bell. The mold had included human figures dancing around the bell, quite acceptable and heavy.

"What's this?" asked Otto. He knew his metals and the process of pouring molds. This bell was of high-quality metal.

"Where did you get this?" Corbett was always surprised by Geri. Their trip to the hot springs came to mind.

"Darlene saw an old church coming down and bought it on the spot," said Geri, proud of her best friend. "It took half the drunks in Whitechapel to load it." All three stared at the bell sitting quietly on the grass.

"Does it have a clapper?" Otto, interested in all things metal, was tipping the bell and trying to see under it.

Geri grinned. "Oh yeah, we woke most of Portland before we could get it under control."

Corbett's thoughts began to ramble. "The church doesn't have a bell, does it? This could be the town meeting bell, for church on Sunday and for emergencies." Corbett hugged Geri. "This is wonderful for the town!"

"Be sure and let Maxine know who brung it." Geri winked.

In the early evening, Joe and the boys came in for their Friday night beer. After delivering milk, eggs, and honey to Grandma's, they noticed Corbett, Otto, and Buck wrestling with some object in front of the school.

"Where did you get that?" remarked Joe as he and the boys took a gander at the bell.

"Geri and a friend of hers in Portland bought it for us," declared Corbett. "Then Buck remembered he had this yoke that he used years ago when he had his oxen."

Buck was one of the originals to the crossing. His homestead now was covered by the town of Cedar Crossing. His corrals, feed-store, and leatherworks were all remnants of the early homestead. Old, nearly ready to rest his skinny frame in the ground, Buck was a town favorite.

"The yoke and thick timbers look like a perfect match," said Joe, agreeing with the concept. "I'll bet you can hear this bell all the way out at our place."

"By the way, Corbett, you've got two weeks before school starts. I was wonderin' if you could help us out at the mill. We're a man short. It pays pretty well."

Corbett stood from his task, thinking for a moment. These people up here were purposely trying to keep him from his reading—were making a concerted effort to do so—but some extra money might allow him to buy a horse. He wanted a horse. "Sure, I could use the money." He looked at Ernie and Robert. "Do I have to work with either of these two?"

"Afraid so."

"I was afraid you would say that. Monday, what time?"

"Six o'clock at our house."

"I was afraid you would say that too."

The Monday morning walk, invigorating and crisp, held that it would be a fine day. Corbett learned as a matter of fact that at Cedar Crossing, a morning with a mild fog meant warm sunshine by lunchtime. It was nearly six when Corbett saw the lights of Joe's cabin. Edith would be putting the last touches on three lunches for the men, about to leave for a long day at the shingle mill. He hoped she would treat him kindly after the bitter meeting at the school where she had had to be the deciding vote on his serving as the schoolmaster.

"Mr. Jones!" called a pleasant voice from the back corner of the cabin. "Robert told me that you would be working with them today," said Margaret, Corbett's favorite long-legged milkmaid, bucket in hand, on the way to the barn.

"Are you going to laugh when I drag myself back tonight?"

"It will be a pleasure." Margaret laughed and continued toward the barn. Corbett thought it would be his pleasure to see her again in the evening. She was a delight. He would find it hard to remain "Mr. Jones" with Mary and Ernie during schooltime. Both were getting to be more like friends every day.

"There he is!" shouted Joe as the shingle mill gang piled out the front door. "Got a good lunch?" he said, holding his own cloth sack high. "I had Grandma make me some sandwiches just for the occasion." The feel was similar to the one he'd had the first day at the Bjlack ranch. It was a feeling of something new, surrounded by good people.

"We gotta wait a minute," said Ernie. "Ma wants to talk to ya."

During the wait, Robert toyed with a box in the back of the wagon. When he'd successfully found what he was searching for, he threw the pair of gloves at Corbett. Corbett was about to thank Robert, when Edith rushed out the door.

"Good, you haven't left yet." She eyed Corbett with a sly smile. "I just wanted you to know that we are all excited for school to start and that we are behind you." Corbett, to his own amazement, stepped forward and gave Edith a long hug. He needed that. Corbett always tried to act strong and confident, but sometimes he was like a kitten.

The road taken dropped away from the main stagecoach road after a mile or so. It began immediately making a slow, straight climb up onto a flat plateau. The timber, a little farther apart than in the country below, almost spoke of a need for more room for the trees, both outwardly and upwardly. The forest contained more red cedar each mile they traveled forward. These ancient cedars had wide bases driving downward and digging in, hoping to help balance the tremendous height.

About a half hour in, the wagon proceeded through a ghostly graveyard of cedar stumps and lonely snags serving as the grave markers for each magnificent cedar that once stood in that place. "They started clear-cutting here and cut everything all around the mill." Robert could see Corbett's interest in the foggy absence of timber. "Now we have to haul in from a mile or so in the winter to shingle them out in the summer." To the others in the wagon, this was merely the view seen every day. Corbett's view of the dark, misty openness was one of intrigue. He found the place to be almost spooky.

A stout old cedar sign stood at the entrance to a large assembly of wooden buildings, reading "Russell Shingle Mill." Several of the chiseled letters were filled with green moss. The brown sign blended in with the encroaching ferns and Scotch broom bushes.

A long row of tall wooden sheds, fully open to the south, made up the right margin of the mill site. Visible inside these sheds were fresh-cut dark red bundles of cedar shingles.

"The bundles you see in the sheds are drying and seasoning out of the weather. A wagonload goes out to St. Helens every day in the summer," said Joe.

On the left was the office, sided with water-stained shingles. The windows and front door, all new and painted white, made the shingles more obvious. Four closed sheds and a set of corrals finished the left edge of the mill. The hard, dusty center between the two sets of buildings was alive and surrounded by harnesses, heavy freight wagons, and workers going about their preparations for the day.

"There's Leonard and Pat," announced Ernie loudly and proudly. The two men seemed to be returning to the office from the corrals.

"The younger one without the arm is Pat. He was a shingle weaver for several years, then accidently cut off his arm." Corbett looked at Joe. The story was true, and had been told in front of Joe, the present shingle weaver. *The fear of losing an arm in that way must tangle with Joe's mind every day*, thought Corbett.

"They own the place," said Joe, finishing the thought and winding through the chaos to the corrals.

To Corbett, the buildings spoke not of money but rather of the will to survive. Any open seams of lumber were covered in moss and the black stains from weather, having accumulated of the course of just a winter or so.

"I'm the shingle weaver, and you'll be here with me in front of the shingle shed. They'll be a few minutes getting the steam up, so we'll go around in back, where I'll show you how it is done."

The shingle shed was as wide as the open area in front but not as tall. *Low slung* might be a better term. Corbett could see at least two metal chimneys sending the beginnings of today's smoke, billowing light brown, into the sky.

"Robert works down there." Joe pointed to a huge round saw blade, nearly as tall as a man. It sat on a covered rail cart. "They use a steam donkey to drag a measured log up into place. It has two winches that do all the work. Then the sawyer drives the saw along the log, cutting a flat surface." Joe was at home. He knew every step because he had been there. "They do it three more times until they have a long square timber." Corbett could see Robert and three others sizing up the first log.

"Once inside here, they use a steam-powered crosscut saw to chop the timber into two-foot chunks. Then I get the chunks and cut a thin slice off each, like off a loaf of bread." Joe looked at Corbett. "That's it! Ernie keeps both fireboxes full of wood all day—a terrible job," said Joe proudly. In the distance, Ernie had begun his task of splitting wood for the day's needs. He was near a cart specially designed to move a decent load quickly to the steam donkey or to the stationary engine that ran the saws. "Each pull by the steam donkey burns up the whole firebox full of wood. He is busy all day."

"I guess we're ready," said Joe, walking in between several humming machines and putting on a kerchief like a mask. "Matt will show you what to do."

Matt brought a wagon up broadside to Joe's location. "I expect you're Corbett. I'm Matt. I'll show you how to tie bundles and haul them over to the sheds." Matt's shoulders were evidence that he had definitely be doing this work for some time. Heavy slabs of muscle lay on each side of his neck. They were tied together at Matt's waist, which made him difficult to get around. Each leg was as big as a man's waist. Corbett had never seen such a thick individual. Matt's large jowls held his face together.

"As soon as Joe sets twenty shingles on the table, we tie them and put them in the wagon. Sixteen bundles later, we ride to the sheds."

A strange crash sent Corbett's eyes over to Joe, who was doing the same act he repeated hundreds of times every day. Taking a nearly square piece of cedar, Joe placed it under a heavy knife that sliced a thin shingle from the wood, cutting across the grain of the timber. When the knife raised up for the next slice, Joe grabbed the unfinished shingle and cut this way and that with a smaller circular saw to ensure a proper and uniform product. Over and over, Joe took every thin cedar sheet from the knife and squared the ends or cut off the extra, thus making him a shingle weaver.

By noon, Matt and Corbett had eleven bundles neatly tied and placed in the wagon. Joe had taken two small breaks, but his real break occurred when the wagon pulled away to the sheds. He would sit for a few minutes, then commence oiling the various shafts and sharpening the saws. The shingle weaver made more money. He deserved more money than any of the other workers, who eventually either burned out mentally or injured themselves physically.

Joe's appearance at the end of the day was one of mental exhaustion. Robert drove the wagon home with his father on the front seat with him, Corbett and Ernie sitting in back.

"Well, how was the first day?" Joe leaned back to Corbett.

"Lifting bundles all day was really hard on my hands," said Corbett, with his gloves off and looking at his hands. He had no blisters, but it was close. His back was sore, which he had expected.

"It's hard work all summer. Winter logging is entirely different," said Joe.

"Yeah," added Robert. "Pa and me run a crosscut saw together all winter. Fellin' a big cedar is a pretty wild moment. The earth shakes." Robert's face turned to Corbett, all smiles. "Beats sawdust in your face. I hate the mill." Robert was right about the sawdust. Joe's shirt was caked with the reddish dust; the boys each had endured a dusting too. Corbett's arms had collected dust under every hair. His cowboy hat was on the way to ruin.

"Yeah, it's as bad as a coal mine," added Joe. Corbett remembered the first time he'd seen Joe. It struck him that Joe was lean and lanky like the coal miners back in Colorado. Hard, dirty work, whether farming, logging, or mining, spit everyone out the same, beating them to hell by the time they were fifty.

Edith was tending her cucumbers when her gang rode in. Then a choreographed set of events took place. Joe found his way to his humble throne, and Edith, a woman in love, treated him to a jar of clear liquid that Joe slowly sipped over the next hour. The boys were sent away to care for the wagon, horse, and harness. That would be the last of their duties until it came time for their nightly chores, but the first hour home they enjoyed a settling down from the pace of the mill.

"Hey, Corbett, see you tomorrow?" Joe tipped his jar to Corbett, who was starting the walk to the crossing.

"Not if I can find some work that's not so much work!" He waved. *Nice people, but damn hard lives,* reflected Corbett, tired and dusty.

An afternoon breeze blew at Corbett's back as he turned down the main street from the school corner. He was looking to buy a hot water bath at the boardinghouse, but first things first. Across from the boardinghouse was the livery and the smithy, next to each other. Buck and Otto were sitting in front at the demarcation line between the two businesses, playing checkers. Buck's largest signs, old and barely legible, advertised cracked corn, rolled oats, and horse boarding. Otto's were newer and showed the prices: for horseshoeing, $1.50; to have a horse cleated, $3.

An empty chair invited Corbett to sit. "Who is winning today?" he asked, looking at the red and black painted board.

"Oh, he's cheatin' as usual," remarked Otto, not looking up. "How's the shingle mill?"

"Look at my hat. I brought most of it home!" Corbett took his hat off, freeing some of the red dust, which shook down onto the board.

Buck, a little irritated, said, "Go get cleaned up. I'm thinking you're trying to distract me!"

"Buck, you got any horses for sale?"

"Now I am done distracted." Buck looked at Corbett. A truce at the table became evident. "Tired of walking, are ya?" Buck's smirk was one of experience. "I've got a nice little mare out back, but you are just too big for her. Let me think."

"You wantin' a walker or a runner?" Otto had entered the fray. "Bill McElroy has a skittish thoroughbred-looking gelding down past Martin's store, but he'd be a nightmare to handle every day."

"Hell, Otto, sell him Ollie!" Buck looked at Otto for confirmation.

"What's Ollie?" asked Corbett.

"It's that brown Jack mule out in the back corral," replied Buck. "Hell, he's stout and walks out good." Buck was a horse trader. Everyone west of Pecos could tell stories about horse traders.

"Why did you name him Ollie?"

Otto smiled. "I named him after an uncle I didn't like." Corbett missed the wink from Otto to Buck. "Get that old Tex-Mex saddle on the fence out back and give him a go. Go on. He needs used."

The saddle was plain with its high, deep cantle and prominent pommel and horn. Corbett surmised that he could not fall out of it. He hoped it would sit well.

As at the Bjlack ranch, Corbett grabbed a bucketful of oats. Ollie, tall at the withers, was a powerfully built mule. Corbett looked him over closely. Ollie's ears and eyes studied Corbett while he ate. Corbett remembered the day when he'd stood at this spot waiting to be fired, thinking he would ride this big mule off the hill. Now, he was buying the mule to make it easier to stay up on the hill.

Ollie was interested in this new human, who was quiet and concerned about the saddle being just right. Once Corbett was on, Ollie could feel a calm strength and a confidence that made the mule feel at ease. A mule gets its athletic ability from the horse side of its family and gets its intelligence from the donkey side of its family. Satisfied that the donkey side of the family was now evident, Ollie would show Corbett his athletic side at some later time.

"I believe I'll take him," said Corbett, arriving back at the checkerboard table, "if he is not too much."

"Twelve dollars—and I'll throw in the saddle!"

"I'll take him." Corbett had thought he would have to pay more. To get the saddle as well seemed like a deal.

That done, Buck made his pitch: "A dollar a month to keep him in my back pasture, or two dollars a month to keep him where he always is, under that tree in the back corral." Buck thought a minute, then added, "You'll never catch him in the pasture. It's two dollars a month."

The next morning, Corbett was enjoying the walk out to Joe's. The mule had a nice gait and was quite aware of the nice morning stroll. Joe showed Corbett a grassy area where he could tie Ollie, and then the gang was off.

Corbett spent the first two hours at the mill helping Robert turn logs, using the steam donkey and dragging the nearly perfect cedars into place. Any trees with knots or damaged areas did not slice well. Two cables called chokers were worked under the log and connected together. Then the winches on the steam donkey dragged the heavy log up to the saw.

"Somedays it's a battle just to get the chokers under the log," said Robert, pleased to have the first log of the day on its way to the huge saw.

At the end of the day, the men's arrival back at Edith's presented a surprise: Ollie was missing. Edith, Mary, and the shingle gang looked all over the property and into the forest.

"How many days have you owned this mule?" asked Edith, already knowing the answer.

"One!" Corbett answered, returning from the uphill trip down around the spring.

"You have the worst luck." She could not help but laugh. "You know, if he's in my garden tonight, I'll shoot him.

"Is that to save your garden?" Corbett was laughing at his having made a poor selection in Ollie. Could it have been worse? "Or is it that you yearning for some fresh mule steak?"

Halfway up the street, Corbett heard the braying of his favorite mule. How Ollie had untied the rope would never be known. Corbett, as happy as he was to have a ride of his own, felt that a "come to Jesus" moment between him and Ollie was on the horizon.

The second day was like the first. After helping Robert for a spell, Corbett and Matt tied shingles and delivered them to the sheds. With the newness rubbing off, Corbett could not imagine tying shingles for the rest of his life. Was it laziness or boredom? Probably both. It was no wonder the shingle gang celebrated life outside work. There was no pleasure in the job they did.

"I wanted to come and see the schoolmaster at work," said Pat, the owner's son. "Word is that you're a pretty good hand. That so?" Corbett looked at Matt, knowing any work evaluation would have come from him. Matt, too far away to hear, stayed with tying the latest bundle.

"I hope so. It's a dusty mess, that's for sure," replied Corbett, reaching out to shake Pat's right hand. Pat turned his left elbow up and shook with his left.

Corbett immediately apologized. "God, I'm sorry!" He was white with embarrassment.

"Ah, don't worry. Sometimes I forget too. Started to shuffle a deck of cards the other day …" He laughed at his joke. Pat seemed easygoing, the missing arm not an issue for him at all. "My mother was hoping you were giving up the teaching. Said you are too rowdy to set a good example for the students."

It took a second for Corbett to understand what was being

said, then it struck. Russell Mill and Mrs. Russell, one of the angry school board members, were connected—and Pat's mother was Mrs. Russell. Acting as if he had understood the connection all along, Corbett said, "Yeah, she sure wasn't happy at the board meeting, but I'm looking forward to ring the school bell the first day and commencing teaching." He smiled respectfully. "And it will come to pass if I survive these bundles."

"It doesn't bother me at all that the male teacher isn't a sissy. I've got two kids. They'll be there."

Myron's Tuesday night poker night was a time for playing cards, not gambling. Myron and John from the mercantile were pretty good players, but it was penny poker, where no real money ever changed hands. Although invited to play, Corbett only watched for a few minutes, then went up to his room to read, where he promptly fell asleep.

Wednesday was a good day, cloudy and windy with a coastal flow. Corbett had tied Ollie securely to Joe's sturdy hitching post. With that issue cleared up, Corbett jumped into the back of Joe's wagon.

After bucking the first log into place with Robert, Corbett went to join Joe and Matt, making and shingling bundles. The boredom of repeating the same act over and over was the worst part. Matt groaned a lot but said little. Corbett's mind wandered to topics ranging from Peabody in Silverton to Terry and baby Annie in Greeley. To be living in this wonderful forest and earning his keep by logging had sounded richly rewarding, but the only thing that was richly rewarded were Corbett's muscles.

Corbett's feeling of exuberance ended later in the afternoon, when he and the shingle gang pulled to a stop in front of Joe's house. Ollie was gone. So was the hitching post. This time, interest in Ollie's antics caused Joe to tap the reins and head toward town.

Alice and her kids came running from the church lawn when they saw Corbett riding into town with Joe. She began laughing so hard, she could not speak.

"You ought to have seen that mule of yours drag the hitching post through town!" said Mike, standing beside his chortling mother. "Everyone came out to watch him. It was comical!"

June flew out the door to her father's mercantile and caught up with the wagon. "Mr. Jones, you should have been here! Ollie tugged, dragged, and backed the post all the way to the corrals. A Fourth of July parade would not have been more fun."

Otto, smithy apron and all, joined the group. "Yes, siree, that Ollie brought everybody out to watch. His braying and cussing was loud enough to raise the dead."

As the wagon and its entourage of townsfolk turned down to the back corral, Ollie was waiting at the gate, hitching post and halter rope still attached. The saddle that Ernie had picked up before leaving the farm was the only thing missing from the ensemble.

While Corbett was calmly detaching Ollie from his anchor and opening the gate, he remembered the ease of walking to and fro his first day going to work. He and Ollie were the town's clowns. Corbett was never unkind to animals, but if Ollie were to wake up dead the next day, Corbett would not mind the walk.

Ollie did not mind the morning jaunts with Corbett. The issue was that Ollie wanted to go home when Ollie wanted to go home. The trip the next morning found Joe waiting in the road upon their arrival. Corbett cleared his saddle's high cantle with his leg. It was a comfortable saddle, he had concluded. Joe motioned with a tilt of his head toward a large tree behind the milk barn. There would be shade all day, and the tree was not going anywhere. Corbett liked the location.

"My pa," Joe began, "had a stud that kept backing up and breaking loose. He used a weight like this to learn the horse over time." The weight was a large iron coupler, maybe a hundred pounds or more, from a ship or the railroad. "We get a good wrap around the tree and put this heavy rope through it, pulling it snug down to the halter." The weight lay on the ground beneath the tree, and when the horse or mule backed up, the weight was lifted.

Corbett removed the saddle and watched Joe put Ollie's new challenge together. "Every time the mule pulls back, he lifts the weight and also pulls on the tree. He'll tire of that soon enough. We'll see if that won't teach him a lesson."

At the mill, Joe and the boss were having a hurried conversation as Corbett came around the corner after helping Robert get started.

"Hi, Corbett. We're going to need you today," stated Leonard, the boss. An introduction would have just gotten in the way. "You're going to have to learn fast. We have an order for some shakes, and we haven't been doing them often." Leonard looked at Joe. "Good to go?"

"Yes, sir, boss."

Joe was joined by two other workers. He walked to shingle weaver station and grabbed a two-foot chunk he used for making shingles. "With shingles, we slice across the grain of the wood, thin and pretty as you please." He scanned the crew to gauge their understanding. "Shakes are cut following the grain. They're thicker and smaller. I take this knife, called a froe, and split a section along the grain. Be exact. Watch!"

Joe took the chunk of timber and split thinner, curved sections of cedar. Corbett had cut a lot of firewood, especially back in Silverton. Cedar was easy to split in comparison to other woods such as cottonwood, which would trap the ax forever in its tangled tissues. Corbett could do this.

By the time the shift was done, several bundles of shakes had been tied. Corbett was proud of his new skill. The day had been a good one.

All the way back to Edith's, the question was whether Ollie had taken the tree to town or just dragged the heavy weight to town like a trophy. The crew eased around to the back of the barn. Ollie brayed, quite irritated but still tied. Corbett got to ride home, quite quickly, for the first time.

Corbett finished the week at the mill quite pleased. His split cedar shakes came faster and became more uniform with each hour. By Friday afternoon, two wagons were loaded for transport down to St. Helens for use on a new house near the Columbia River. Corbett had enjoyed the meandering conversation of his fellow splitters and the craftsmanship each was trying to perfect. His muscles were coming alive. A good sense of manliness came with this feeling.

The gift every afternoon came during the ride home: the satisfaction of having a powerful animal to own and ride. Corbett's whim of the day was, instead of heading straight back to the crossing from Joe's farm, to take Ollie on long, slow ride down one wagon trail, then another. Corbett ate mountains of blackberries and spooked deer and elk that were out foraging for their evening quota of sweetgrass.

Corbett's work at the mill concluded on the following Friday afternoon, when a woman approached the splitters. Mrs. Russell paid every two weeks, personally handing each worker a small envelope containing their two weeks' pay. "Mr. Jones," said Mrs. Russell in a stately manner, "my husband says he could use you if you want to stay. And Pat put in a good word as well." For the first time, she had a chance to see the raucous young man she had voted against at the school board meeting. "I hope you take it."

"I thank you, but no, ma'am." Proper and appreciative, Corbett continued. "In fact, after work, I am going down to the school to work in there for a while."

"You're passing up better money."

"My long suit is reading and enjoying life. This job steals some of that."

Wilma Russell had never heard a man speak so succinctly. She stared in amazement. Corbett Jones was indeed unusual.

12

It was the first day of school. Corbett knew he had put it off long enough. He twisted a long piece of newsprint into a fuse of sorts and lit a match, placing the flame to the newspaper. Through one hole, he slipped in his head so he could see the abyss below in its entirety. Through another hole, he rammed his fiery wick down, all the way to his shoulder. It was worse than he'd thought. He continued to flash his paper torch until there was an unmistakable stench coming from that direction, the smell of burning hair, his. Corbett's head and arm exited the smelly cave at the same time. He had bested the task and still had about fifteen minutes to recover and clean up.

"Your stomach a little shaky this morning?" asked Myron, strolling to the back of the school and noticing Corbett coming out of the outhouse.

"Naw, I had to burn the spiderwebs out from under the two-holer." Grimacing at his smelly arm, he added, "Didn't see any snakes under there either."

"You could make a living diving into outhouse holes."

"Does it pay better than teaching?" Corbett laughed, washing up with a pan of water from the well. Seeing Myron glancing at his pocket watch, he got the message.

"Damn, I bet the kids are going to be showing up." Corbett

hurried around to the front of the school, where he saw a throng of students and parents.

"Ernie, ring the bell!" Corbett thought that for a schoolmaster absolutely ready for school, he sure was scurrying around a lot. The excitement of being a schoolmaster was nearly beyond what he could have ever imagined. "Go on in," he said, racing to the door himself. The door was unlocked. In a town where working men worked, education was a station above most. Waiting for permission to enter the school showed reverence to education, unassuming as the schoolhouse was.

Now at the door, Corbett made eye contact with each student, whether he knew them or not. Corbett did see a short teenage girl draw away from Mrs. Powell as June and Margaret came up the path.

"This is Angela!" Margaret beamed. "You'll like her!" It was obvious that her mother was a seamstress. She was wearing a tightly sewn dress of fine floral cloth adorned with tatted lace around the neck and cuffs. Angela gave a small respectful nod and went in with the others.

Corbett scanned one last time for students, when he did a double take. He saw a tiny woman with long black hair and long bangs, wearing a beautiful fawn-colored leather dress. Two little girls, small images of their mother, were standing beside her. The mother's eyes pleaded for at least a modicum of decency from Corbett. He hesitated not because they were Natives, but because he was wondering what to do about it.

"Ma'am, are your girls going to school too?" There was terror in the mother's eyes, but she was a mother, like all other mothers, willing to face hardship and embarrassment for the advancement of her children.

"Did Michael send you?" Myron asked the mother.

She bashfully nodded her head yes. Her eyes quickly dropped to the ground. Myron nodded as if he understood the situation, and signaled Corbett with a positive glance.

Using the nod as affirmation of what he thought was right, Corbett said to the woman, "Come in. Come in."

While the mother was handing each girl a tied handkerchief of food for lunch, Maxine Powell was apoplectic. The boiling rage she felt at the prospect that Corbett was going allow these Natives to go to school with her Angela had caused her to step toward the girls as if to physically stop them. She glanced at Myron for support. Getting an unsympathetic stare in response, she then looked to Corbett, whose stare was one of wrath. Corbett was done with this woman. It was his school.

"Alice, if you and the other mothers want to come in for a few minutes and watch us get started, you are always welcome." Myron and several of the mothers were excited and pleased to see what the school was and how it was going to work. The last one to enter was Mrs. Powell, sullen, but not sullen enough to miss the proceedings.

"First, we stand at our seats, right hands over our hearts, and say the Pledge of Allegiance. Since many of you don't know it, because it's brand new, I will say it, and you listen to what we are promising to our country.

"Now that everyone has their own seat, I want to tell you about what we are going to do. The most important thing we must learn to do is read. You older students, if you think you will be teaching these little ones all day, you're wrong. A good part of the day will be set aside for you to read exciting stories and historic adventures. I want to teach the little ones myself." Corbett sat and looked at the youngest children in the eye. "Three years ago," Corbett said, talking to the eager eyes, "I didn't know that there were twenty-six letters in the alphabet and that they talked! If you put them together, they say words." Corbett held up a McGuffey Reader. "These books tell us what they say and help us learn about things!"

Corbett stood and walked to the chalkboard. "We want you to write on the chalkboard. I didn't buy it for me to write on; I bought it for you to write on." Corbett looked at June and Margaret. "Get everybody one of those slates on the table over there. Angela, hand out the chalk."

"Everybody ready? Margaret, that tall girl, is going to write her name on the board. I want you to write it on your slate." Corbett had the first lesson under way.

That evening at supper, Corbett said, "Okay, tell me about Michael and these little Indians. Maxine about had a cow over my letting the kids in. We never talked about that."

"Regardless of what Maxine says or thinks, you did the right thing." Myron had contemplated this since last they'd met. "If she makes a big deal about it, her piety and pious nature will show right through." Myron became more calm than usual. "I think we have killed off enough Indians. These two little girls need an education."

"Now about the girls," Corbett insisted, knowing there had to be a story about Michael and the Natives.

"I'll tell you what I know," said Myron. "Several years ago, this Michael fellow bought a hillside down the mountain a ways and darned near burned up the forest to get enough acreage to put in a vineyard. He never comes out, and the road in is not inviting." Myron paused to get the story right. "When I opened up my boardinghouse, his man Louis brought me a case of white wine, then left."

Corbett was beginning to wonder what wine had to do with the girls. Myron continued, "I buy wine from him once a month or so. He has two or three Indian families working the vineyard.

It could be that he is going to do more business up here. This could be a sign of that."

"It was cute seeing them at the blackboard trying to scribble everyone's names, cute little rascals," said Corbett fondly. Corbett had not been able to get them to say a word at all during the day, but they had smiled whenever they dutifully completed a task.

The second day, the little preacher's daughter approached Corbett at his desk. "Mr. Jones, Chapoke and Chapana don't speak English."

"Who are Chapoke and Chapana?"

"The two Indian girls," said her brother, Mike. "I think they speak French like Violet, who comes to our church."

"Now that is interesting. You know their names, but I don't know their names, and you know they speak French, but I don't know that they speak French," Corbett said, laughing. "Maybe I ought to put you two in charge." First, Corbett did not know that Otto even had a wife, and second, he had no idea what to do about it.

The next day, while Ernie was ringing the morning bell, a tiny raisin of a woman was standing next to Otto at the door. Corbett reasoned that she was so much older than he that she might even be his mother. "Corbett, this here is my woman, Violet." Otto was not his usually loud self. In fact, he was a little timid at his task. "Little Mike came over last night and said you needed Violet to help with the French Indians."

Violet was the nearly invisible wife of Otto. She gardened, fed her chickens, and had a small vineyard. He was big, loud, and opinionated, so she seemed always to drift into the background. Violet's body was small and forgettable. Her hair, always covered by a bonnet, seemed to be graying nicely.

In Corbett's mind, it was one thing at a time. She was his

woman? They were not a match at all. Then the fact that Mike, a twelve-year-old, had taken it upon himself to solve the language issue by himself was, Corbett thought, quite a feat. Corbett would have never put the two and two together to get such a wonderful four.

"How do you do, Violet?" said Corbett in his most respectful tone. "Come in and meet the girls."

O the smile Violet got when she said, "Bonjour, les petits!"

The two little girls realized they now had someone who could speak their language. They each grabbed one of Violet's hands. One said, "Viens grand-mere." They carefully led her to their seats. Every school day after that, Violet waited for her girls to come outside and collect her for their time in class.

"On page three of McGuffey's second reader, there are four paragraphs of a story called 'An Early Riser.'" Corbett's work on action verbs with his middle group needed to be tested. "Count the number of action verbs, and then name them."

Little John was up before daylight. As soon as he was up, he went forth to behold the beauties of the morning scene. The first rays of the sun shone over the woods and hilltops. Soon the sun himself appeared in glory. He slowly rose and looked down with gladness upon the fields and little hills. Everything seemed to rejoice in his splendor.

Little John was glad. He thought of the goodness and greatness of God, who made the sun so bright and everything so lovely. And in the joy of his heart, he said, "I will praise God. His face will I seek. In the morning, I will call upon the name of the Lord, and in the evening, will sing His praises. For His mercies are fresh every hour. He keeps me all the day long."

It was Saturday morning. Geri was on her first cup of coffee. The bar had been packed the night before. Geri's focus was not yet on the bright sunshine coming through Grandma's windows. Corbett, bright and cheerful, needed no caffeine.

"Tell me about your night." His peppy demeanor was nearly an irritant. "I thought I heard music."

"Two of the girls were singers," said Geri. "They put on quite a show. I may have to bring up more musicians. Besides that, the construction crew that's putting down the floor for the rail station is camping behind the station, and they were all there."

"Complaining?"

"No, we are just overwhelmed. I see a new bar setting up just outside town, just big canvas tents. I bet they will be open next weekend. I thought it would be a problem, but the crossing is growing so fast that there's no way I can keep up."

"And another big night tonight?" Corbett saw from Geri's body language that she did not want to think about it.

"Let's talk about the new school and its captivating schoolmaster, Corbett Jones!"

"We had a good week. I didn't realize how hard it would be to have both little ones and teenagers, but I haven't lost any of them yet."

"What's Violet doing over there?"

"The two Indian girls speak only French. Violet has them laughing and studying for an hour or so each morning. Denise Arnold joins them, not understanding a word they say."

"Are the older girls in love with you yet? You're only two or three years older than they are." Corbett looked at Geri, knowing that at some point in time, this could be a problem. Margaret was adult and wonderful; June was beautiful and smart; and Angela was the most vulnerable. And Corbett was basically the only eligible young man who was not a logger.

"Oh, Lewis!" exclaimed Grandma from the cooking area in the back, speaking to a buckskin-clad man standing in the doorway. "Bring it on back! I am nearly out!"

Corbett watched as the man pulled a brown tarp from his pack horse and staggered toward the front door. Corbett jumped to his rescue, and together they hauled the heavy weight to Grandma's prep table.

"Thanks," said the man, smiling and opening the tarp to expose a clean, fresh deer carcass wrapped in white cloth. Corbett glanced at the fresh kill. It was not heavy with fat like the choice beef on the Bjlack ranch in Colorado, but instead it was sleek and muscular, the makings of some fine venison steaks.

"That's Lewis Lane," remarked Geri as Corbett returned to his chair. "He brings Grandma fresh meat every week. It's hard to keep it from going bad in the summer, so he brings her a young one, and she cooks with it all week. She has pickled fish and smoked ham, but the men come here for the venison, fresh venison with gravy."

"Mr. Lane," said Corbett, holding out his hand to shake. "I'm Corbett Jones, the new teacher here in town."

"Nice to meet you," replied Lewis with a slight smile and almost a bow. Lewis was taller and thinner than Corbett with much darker skin and hair. His dark eyes and mannerisms made him seem friendly and approachable.

"Could you be Ruth's father?"

Lewis's demeanor changed. "Yes." A look of defense and challenge came forward with the question about his daughter.

"The older girls at school worry about her. She seems to be a good friend. They ask if I couldn't give her some lessons somehow. I would if we could figure out how." Lewis was taken aback. It struck Corbett that not many folks had ever helped the family.

"Ida and I worry about her ourselves. We thought her boyfriend was going to take her, but he's gone, and now she's just got us." He said this not as a victim but simply in a matter-of-fact way. "You can come down and meet her and Ida anytime. That would be very nice." He shook Corbett's hand more energetically and bowed slightly to Geri on the way out.

"Boy, Corbett," said Geri, "you are smooth. You had better watch out for them girls!"

Back in the classroom, Corbett faced another day teaching proportions, Corbett's way of solving many day-to-day math problems. "Turn to page one hundred two. Let's solve some distance problems. First, as always, we must know the facts, such as those in the boxes above the problems. How many feet in a yard?"

"Three," the students answered together. This was becoming old hat.

"Good, a fact. Now, how many feet are in a chain?"

"Sixty-six!"

"Sure, another fact." Corbett smiled. "Okay, it's time to help Otto, our blacksmith. So, write down the question. Remember, we measure property in chains." The stage was set. Corbett loved the kids, so anxious to take on a challenge.

Corbett wrote on the board, "Otto's property line along the south side of his property is 8,118 feet long. He needs to record it with the state, but it has to be in chains." Corbett glanced back at the students, who were busily writing away on their Big Chief tablets. "What is our fact?"

One of the students, with all of them being almost too busy to answer such a mundane question, said, "Sixty-six feet equals one chain!" Foolish teacher.

Angela was first: "One hundred twenty-eight chains!" She was a teacher's delight, and also maybe Ernie's delight.

"I get one hundred twenty-three," said June. Others followed with that answer.

"Great! Proportions win again. Good job!" said Corbett, rewarding the class with a smile. "Okay, get after the ten problems on that page and the next. Good work today."

"Your feet are too big," screamed two of the little ones, laughing at Corbett's attempts at hopscotch. An alarming amount of chalk was being used up making and remaking the hopscotch squares, but the younger girls loved it. Coveted sacks of marbles were broken into at noon and at recess by the boys. John at the mercantile had been thinking ahead when he brought up from Portland a menagerie of cat-eyes, puries, aggies, and steelies. Corbett always surveyed the playground for any child who was alone or appeared sad. He worried about Chapoke and Chapana being neglected because they were Natives, but Denise Arnold, the preacher's daughter, treated them like her personal people. The three of them were always together and always whispering and giggling.

Even though the older girls seemed a bit old to be giggling at jump rope, Corbett figured most of the children, growing up in very small populations, had been missing out on group games. Ernie was as strong as an ox but was the worst skip-rope athlete in the world, Mary and Jenny Russell being the best. The older students were found most often at the picnic table under the big-leaf maple. Just being together with the chance to talk seemed a luxury. Without school, most would not have seen each other except at church.

There seemed to be some trouble at the picnic table. "You three, move along!" shouted Corbett. He left the game of annie over to approach three rather rough-looking young men who had walked in on June, Angela, and Mary's older group. Ernie's neck was already bowed. In a town like Cedar Crossing, pretty girls and young women were rare, so the need for female companionship was multiplied by the number of loggers and teamsters away from home for the summer.

"Buzz off," said the stout, curly-headed leader. "These girls want us here!" June, wide-eyed at the table, shook her head. A boy stood on each side of her, one of them flicking at her hair.

All the young men, hatless with unkempt long hair, were old enough to be out working, but they did not have jobs. Two were sleeveless, one of them wearing logging suspenders, the other wearing a rope for a belt. The brash leader was shirtless and wearing a necklace, a punched silver coin strung on a thin leather strand.

"Leave!" shouted Ernie, who had maneuvered to position himself at Corbett's side. All three stepped up. The leader, about Corbett's size, had his chest out to Corbett. The girls broke and ran.

"This is a school. Leave the girls alone!" Corbett warned for the second time. "Go on!"

"Hit 'em, Buster!" shouted one of the rowdies.

As Corbett's father had said a dozen times, a fight would always begin with an overhand right. Block it and then beat your opponent so bad that he will never try it again. That was his father's advice.

Buster's overhead was a wild roundhouse that took forever to reach Corbett. The young man obviously had not been trained to throw a sharp blow as Laddie had taught Corbett. Corbett's left-handed block was easy, but the right-handed blow to Buster's jaw was easier. As Buster slowly crumpled to the ground, Corbett delivered an even harder shot to Buster's ear. Buster was down, and he was out.

Ernie was by Corbett's side. Originally his aim had been to protect Corbett from a second entrant into the fight, but the violence of

Corbett's punches brought him and the two ruffians together in an attempt to pull Corbett away. Time stopped, but not for Grandma with her rolling pin in the middle of the road, not for Otto with his shoeing hammer at the edge of the school grounds, and not for Preacher Arnold, who'd left the telegraph office door open.

"I'm going to get my pa," declared the suspendered boy. He wanted to run, but his leader lay lifeless on the ground in front of him.

"You tell Elroy," exclaimed Otto, now stepping into the group, "that if he wants to come to town, I'm here for him!" It seemed that Otto knew suspenders' father. It also seemed Otto was ready to have a brief meeting with Elroy again.

An unwritten armistice took place, allowing for the collection of Buster's foggy head and body, to be extracted from the area. Corbett looked around, embarrassed that he had shown such a lack of control in front of the town and especially in front of the children. Maybe Laddie, while slapping Corbett around, teaching him to fight, knew he would not be there to protect his son, and that impetus alone was what drove Corbett to be so violent when protecting the children.

The next morning, Corbett was at the door of the school welcoming in the anxious and silly students, when a beautiful black Arabian carrying Mrs. Russell, riding sidesaddle, came up the road.

"Oh, Mr. Jones, can I have a word with you?"

"You bet, Mrs. Russell." Corbett stepped down from the school steps to meet her.

Arabian horses are famous for their classic high-head poses and elegant stances. Mrs. Russell had that kind of elegance as a rider.

"Mr. Jones, my daughter came home crying after the incident yesterday." Corbett's day was about to be ruined, or so he thought. "It took quite a long time to settle her down." Mrs. Russell stopped for effect. "She said that you protected her from some men. In her mind, it was the most gallant thing she had ever seen!" Corbett was speechless. Jenny had been among the seven or eight at the table, essentially a bystander, but in her mind, Corbett was personally protecting her. The violence was baked in with Corbett's forever being her hero.

"I wish to thank you." She bent from her horse to shake Corbett's hand. "By the way, they were right at the meeting: it is okay for you to be a bit manly as a schoolmaster!" She rode away.

Having drunk his coffee on this excellent Saturday morning, Corbett left the porch of the boardinghouse, wandered two doors down, and knocked. Corbett knew he could be impulsive, not thinking things through, and he figured this might be one of those times. That was his thought right after he knocked.

Maxine stepped back, a little startled. "Mr. Jones!" She was aware that she was his greatest critic and that he was surely aware of that. The fact that her daughter thought the sun rose and set with Mr. Jones was softening her slightly.

"I came to ask if you would make me some shirts? I came up here with a poor selection, and now they are a poor and old selection of shirts." Maxine and Corbett had never actually spoken as humans, as he was usually on the receiving end of one of her rants.

"Why don't you get them from the merc?" she asked, a little pious.

"Because yours are better. Preacher Arnold, John Watkins, and Myron all wear them. And I want to look good for my students."

Maxine hesitated. She knew it was true that she made the best shirts, but it was Mr. Jones who was asking. "Please come in." She would show her manners.

"Mr. Jones!" exclaimed Angela, excited that her favorite person was in her home. She stopped altogether at her treadle machine.

"Angela, you look like a seamstress over there!" It would not have mattered which student had been there, the genuine smile would have been the same, Corbett hoped. "You going to make me some shirts?"

He was too young and too handsome to be talking to Maxine's daughter that way. "Just what kind of shirt do you prefer?"

"I like the ones Mr. Arnold wears to preach in. I think a schoolmaster should wear ones like that."

"Mother, we could use that white cotton material we just got in for Grandma's new tablecloths. We will have plenty left over, and it's quite good." It was good material, and she thought this young man's physique would look good in it.

"That is a good idea, Angela! Let me get my tape measure. We'll start later today."

Corbett's neck was a little thicker than most, and his arms a little longer. Maxine had measured tens of men around their chests since her husband had died ten years prior, but she felt a tension within her as she reached around Corbett's chest with the cloth tape. He held a certain mystique. She could feel it.

It was a lesson on pronunciation. "Let's go to lesson twenty-six," directed Corbett. "You are doing so well." This little group of young ones had advanced to McGuffey's second reader at the onset. Corbett constantly pushed free reading at home and McGuffey's at school. "Look at the new words we will learn in this story. See the pronunciation marks above the words. Sound them out."

"Patty and the squire!" shouted Mike, always the first with the answer.

"Almost!" said Corbett, laughing at his prodigy.

"I've got it," answered Edna. "Course, I cheated. I looked at the picture on the next page." All of the others quickly turned the page.

"Patty and the squirrel." Mike lamented the fact that Edna had beaten him to the answer.

"Okay, read this story. And before you leave, tell me what book you are taking for free reading tonight." Corbett felt bad that some of his students lived in homes where only a bit of oil could be spared for reading. "Every spare minute today, read."

With the butter slowly melting into the hot creases of her cinnamon roll, Geri looked at the wonderment of Cedar Crossing. "You know, Grandma and I sit many mornings drinking coffee and seeing you and all the children at play. A big, strong husky fellow trying to win a hopscotch." Geri was showing pride in her little brother. "Seeing you on your hands and knees shooting marbles with the boys, and then sitting at a picnic table laughing with your young admirers, is pleasing to me."

"Thanks," said Corbett quietly. "I'm really enjoying myself." He felt slightly uncomfortable at such a compliment.

"I wasn't here the morning of the fight, but Grandma said you were magnificent protecting those girls. She said the message you sent to the world was 'Don't mess with my kids!'"

"Coming up in November, we have our election for president," said Corbett. "Who can tell me who's running?" The older five, sequestered in one corner, knew that history and civics was the topic of today's discussion.

"It's President Harrison and Grover Cleveland," answered June.

John had begun receiving the *Oregonian Weekly* by stage, and when he was finished reading his issue, he'd pass it on to Myron at the boardinghouse. June was one the few who read the weekly once it had passed through her father's hands.

"Margaret, how often do we have a presidential election?"

"I think it is every four years."

"Okay, today's lesson: Will the people of Oregon get to vote for president?" Corbett looked at the group.

June answered, somewhat confused, "Of course. That is why you have an election." Frowning at such a silly question, the students peeked at one another for support. Could that have been a trick question?

Corbett smiled, having hoped for just such a moment. "The answer is no." In unison, the students all gawped at each other in disbelief.

"Mike, how many states are there?" As was the case, the different-aged students listened to every lesson whether it was theirs or not. Mike was supposed to be learning states and capitals.

"Forty-four!"

"Great. What were the last two to be admitted to the union?"

"Idaho and Wyoming."

"Great!" Corbett was pleased at their interest. "Angela, from what we learned a few days ago, how many senators does each state have?"

"Two!" Angela was pleased that she knew the answer.

"Now pay attention," Corbett said, ready to raise the concept of the day. "Each state only gets to send a few votes to be counted for president. Each senator gives the state one vote, so Oregon has two votes so far."

Corbett, in love with teaching, asked, "How many House of Representatives congressmen does Oregon have?"

June raised her hand partway, out of habit. "Two!"

"Everyone agree?" Even the young ones raised their hands

in support so as to be like their older peers. "Two more votes for Oregon."

Corbett looked about as if telling a secret. "That's four votes. How many more votes do we get to send to Washington, DC, to elect the president?" For the first time in the lesson, the students were stumped.

Basically, June was the best candidate for providing the correct answer. She shrugged sheepishly. "We don't. Oregon only gets four votes for president."

"No," said Margaret, "a lot of people in Oregon vote for president."

"The people in Oregon vote to decide which candidate our four voters will vote for. California gets nine because they have more people and, thus, more representatives." Corbett saw the wheels turning in the heads of the older students, some of them not yet believers. "They call the voters we send to vote for the president the 'electoral college.'

"Here is your assignment: Who can vote, and who cannot vote, in this election?" Corbett was pleased to challenge the knowledge base of his students rather than have them constantly memorize information about the past.

Another day, another topic. "Ernie, go outside and close the shutters," said Corbett. Ernie gave him a puzzled look. "I need some dark." The younger students, otherwise engaged, squealed when the light from the windows went away. It was a new thing. Now everyone was attentive. Corbett brought together all the lamps and placed them all in one location at the back of the room. The big world globe sat on a student's desk toward the middle of the room.

"Everyone swing around and move to the back with me. It will be tight." Corbett had a mirror in his hand. "Margaret will hold the mirror and be the moonbeam that she is. The rest of us will hold lanterns." Corbett looked to all the students. He arranged the children so even the small ones could see. "Our lanterns are the sun. They shine brightly at the front of the globe, those people are having daytime. On the dark side of the globe they are all asleep, it is night. When the Sun's rays hit the mirror, which is the moon, the rays bounce down to the dark side. When the moon is shining, we are seeing the reflection of the sun's rays, reflecting like a mirror off the moon. So the moon doesn't actually shine, it just reflects."

"Would that be a full moon?" asked June.

"Yes," said Corbett, excited to have been asked such a good question. "If the moon is in front of the earth a little bit, it doesn't reflect down on earth at all. We call that a new moon, which we have on those dark nights when there is no light. Get out your slates. Let's draw an eclipse. No, let's draw two eclipses."

School had been over for thirty minutes. Corbett was overdue on fulfilling a promise he'd made to June and Margaret. As he saddled Ollie, something was nagging at his mind. Lewis Lane had seemed very receptive to the idea of Corbett making some kind of school visit. The girls had said that they had not seen Ruth for nearly two years. Was their close friend gravely ill, or was she mad at the girls for some reason? A promise was a promise. He would attempt to help with schooling and, at least, report back.

Corbett's first impression of the Lane homestead was that it stank. The smell was akin to rancid butter or bacon. The cabin itself blended in well with the two big-leaf maples surrounding it. A rough-hewn picket fence made it look very pleasing to the eye. It would have been a wonderful place if not for the stink. Corbett could see a girl or woman pouring some liquid at the downhill portion of the property. She had a long, well-maintained braid of sun-bleached light brown hair all the way down to her tiny waist.

So that is Ruth, thought Corbett. He was anxious to see the face that went with the body.

Corbett and Ollie were close now. The girl turned and waved. Seeing her from the front, Corbett saw that in fact she was not the girl, despite her youthful hair and figure. Perhaps she was an older sister.

"Hello," she said evenly. Her disposition was pleasant enough. "How can I help you?"

Still in the saddle, Corbett was not sure he was at Lewis Lane's homestead. Lewis did not have the kind of dapperness a man would need to catch such an attractive woman.

"Is this Lewis Lane's place?"

"Yes it is. I'm his wife, Ida. I'll get him." She entered the picketed area and aimed for a series of low sheds. "Lewis, someone's here for you."

Out of a wooden gate came Lewis, wearing an old, multistained leather apron. The shock, however, was his helper, a medium-sized young woman wearing a filthy, stained gray frock tight enough across her chest to see evidence of breasts. As the two of them got closer, Corbett wanted to acknowledge Lewis, but he kept looking at the young woman.

God! thought Corbett. *This must be Ruth.* Her hair, dirty, had been hacked by either a knife or sheep shears.

"Hello, Lewis. I'm here to see Ruth." Corbett looked to Lewis to make the next play.

"This here is our Ruth," said Lewis, putting his arm around his daughter and bringing her forward.

"Hi, Ruth. I'm Corbett Jones from Cedar Crossing." Corbett could see the embarrassment in Ruth's body language. This had been a bad idea. "June and Margaret miss you and asked me to come down and offer you some good books to read." Ruth looked up. Corbett almost cried. Her beautiful green eyes were full of sorrow and sadness the depths of which he had not seen for some time.

"Let me take Ruth for a few minutes," said Ida. "She's been working all day with her pa." The pair disappeared quickly into the house.

"Let me show you around," said Lewis, hoping to fill in some time. Lewis led the way to the same wooden gate where he and his daughter had come from earlier. "I bet you could smell us coming in! It's not always like this."

Behind the gate, Corbett saw four oaken barrels. All were full, and each smelled terrible.

"We're tanning two elk hides that I got recently. They're not great hides, but they can be used for harnesses and the like." In two barrels, whose stench took Corbett's stomach to the edge of disaster, Corbett saw a portion of a large hide with bits of hair hanging on. "You don't want to ask me what is in there," Lewis stated with a grin.

Corbett saw a deer hide lying flat on a table with the hair down, a scraper with fat still clinging to the blade. "That's what Ruth was working on. Lots of work, that, before tanning."

"Gosh, how can you stand the smell of these barrels?" At least the shingle mill did not stink like this.

"Just the life you lead. Let's go back out front."

In the shaded location under one of the big maples, Lewis stood close to Corbett. "Claude, the baby's father, promised her everything, then left ten days before the baby was born. It killed her." Lewis, speaking in a tone reflective of the seriousness of life itself, said, "She would have killed herself if it weren't for Leo. She would have!"

"Mr. Jones." Corbett turned around to see Ida and Ruth standing for inspection. The dirty hair, now a wet sun-bleached light brown, and the blunt cuts were still there. This was meaningless as the hair was surrounding a pretty, perky face and piercing emerald-colored eyes. The dress she was wearing, which had fit her a year or so ago, was now nicely tight, but clean. Ruth's face and figure were reflective of her mother's genetics. Except for the fact that Ruth was a little taller, the mother and daughter were a matched set. Lewis was lucky.

"The girls were right! You're as pretty as a picture." The girls never had said that, but it was clear that Ruth's mind was dwelling in a deep well and needed a way out.

"Thank you," said Ruth, unbelieving but wishing. Standing back from Ruth, Ida held a little boy on her hip.

"Now, is this the young man I've been hearing about?" Corbett's tone and body language were not his; he hadn't any experience in acting this old and mature.

"Yes," Ida replied. "His name is Leo." Corbett thought it a bit unusual for Ida to make the introduction, not Ruth.

"My gosh, Ruth, you did good!" Corbett was not doing the politician thing of holding the boy and all, but he'd come pretty close. "You are going to make a great mother. I brought over several books. A couple are romances, and several are mysteries. With your parents' permission, I'll come next week, and we can talk about them. Don't tell your parents, but they can read them too." Corbett saw a feature not seen for some time at the homestead, a sassy little smile.

"Say hello to Mr. Arnold," said Corbett to the class. "I'm sure you know him as Preacher Arnold or as Mike and Denise's pa." Corbett was expecting all but the youngest to understand the lesson. "He will tell us about the Morse code and how he takes messages off the telegraph wires. Look up here at the top of the board, where

I have written you a letter. Bring your answer up to me, but don't tell anyone the secret message. Okay, Mr. Arnold."

The Morse code message written on the board was as follows: (_._./._.../___/.._./._./._././/._/..)

"Hello, everyone. To do this properly, we need this little machine. It sends us the letters. It is called the telegraph key. If I make a short peck, we call that a dot. If I make a long push, we call that a dash." Corbett was impressed with Mr. Arnold's patience, which he'd probably developed from preaching to the hardheaded.

"*S*, for instance, is like this." He wrote the following on the board:

....

"Famously, *O* is like this." On the board, he wrote the following:

_ _ _

So, when have an emergency, we type this"—he wrote down the string of symbols ... _ _ _ ...—which is SOS, for distress. Write down the letters and the dots and dashes that go with them, then solve Mr. Jones's coded message and secretly take it up to him."

"You do this all day?" asked Edna. "I think it would be a fun job!"

On horseback, with a pack donkey tied behind it, Lewis Lane had waited for some time for Corbett to exit the boardinghouse.

"Well, good morning, Lewis. I see you have some venison for Grandma."

"It's freezing at night now, so the meat will stay good longer."

Corbett walked down to the horseman. "So how can I help you this day?"

Lewis leaned down to Corbett. "I want to thank you for what you're doing with Ruth. She reads every night so that you can be proud of her." Lewis, with a smirk, gave up a little secret: "I'm not sure, but I think she dresses up a little extra the days you come down."

The second snow in November did not dampen the spirit of the students. It was the last day of school for the fall. It would be four months before school would take up again. The dessert and hot chocolate were being passed around, when the older girls grabbed their coats and ran outside. With a steaming cup of cocoa in hand, Corbett went to the window. Ida Lane had driven Ruth and Leo to this final day celebration. June had sent a note, by way of Corbett, inviting them to attend. Margaret was covering Leo's head, protecting it from the snow. June and Ruth were together in a tight embrace. Angela pushed open the door and held it for Margaret, Leo, and the others. The happy brashness that ensued carried throughout the room.

Maxine normally would have thrown a fit and walked out, seeing the unmarried teen mother and child being celebrated thusly, but in the middle of the fray was Angela, laughing with Leo and having a great time. Standing next to Maxine was Wilma Russell, who had the same problem. Her daughter Jenny, although younger, had been accepted by the older girls as an equal and was modeling her efforts and thoughts to mimic those of her older peers.

Corbett was handing the youngest of his students small envelopes containing thank-you notes from him, telling them that they'd been good students and that he looked forward to seeing them in the spring. Violet and the two Native girls were reading their notes with great joy, having received their first letters ever.

Geri and Ida were visiting like long-lost friends, which they probably were. Very similar, both were petite, pretty, and smart.

Later, Corbett, sitting at his desk, realized he had a feeling of family and a sense of togetherness, things he often had wondered about. It was a good feeling.

Tomorrow morning, he would gather his things and ride down off the mountain to Martin's. Corbett wondered how Martin come to know he had experience with four-horse hitches. Martin had sent a note through John that they needed a good hand on the coast run, either as shotgun or as driver. Until the note, Corbett's winter was awash in maybes: shingle mill? trapping with Lewis? or snuggled up, mostly broke, with a good book? Besides, Corbett had never seen the ocean.

13

"Well, how's the schoolmarm?" Martin's loud voice confused several of the people seated and eating their meals.

"I made it through for the fall. We start up again in April," Corbett answered, proud to have the fall semester under his belt. "I heard you were desperate enough to send John a letter." He was happy to have short-term work between semesters of school. Lewis had invited him to trap with him all winter and share in the profits of the fur. Until John had told him of Martin's need for drivers, he'd consoled himself by thinking that the traplines seemed to be a good adventure, albeit at little pay.

"Well, we are." Martin pointed to a table away from the others. "The damned railroad has snagged every teamster in the country to haul freight for them. We even offer more pay now, but the teamsters see the stage as a thing of the past."

"I got nothing till April," said Corbett. He meant it.

"Got a good rifle?"

"No. Haven't needed one." Corbett thought about it for a moment. "I'm going to need a rifle?"

"We haven't been robbed yet, but you never know." Martin, now quite serious, asked, "Can you shoot?"

"Barely!"

"Well," Martin said, smiling, "I guess that's good enough.

Food's on you, 'cept at the relay station. Your whip is Bradley Peterson. He's seasoned and reliable. A dollar for each run. And you're scheduled to go every other day. Any questions?"

"No. We'll just see how it goes." Corbett had brought a dozen books to read. The fact that he would have every other day to read, he reckoned, was probably the best part of the job.

The next morning, Corbett examined the nearly new mud wagon, different from some he had seen. He was happy to see a pair of experienced lead horses at the front of the hitch. The wheelers looked ready, albeit young. Good leaders would teach and correct most of the young wheelers' mistakes.

"I'm Brad Peterson. Guess you're Corbett." Brad was paunchy and well-worn, probably not a big talker. He walked on by, checking the traces on both sides. "Help 'em on, then get on yourself."

Early mud wagons carried only three passengers, but this one carried four. This wagon was full of all men in heavy coats. The buffalo robes were already on board. Corbett loaded the riders' satchels and boxes into the boot and then buckled it down. The coach rolled and groaned with the weight as Corbett helped the men inside. This was not a Concord, but the leather thoroughbraces underneath looked new and would give a good ride.

Brad, one hand on the handrail and glancing inside at his passengers, asked, "Ready?" Next came a ritual that had occurred in Brad's life many times. He pulled up his pants, lifted his hat, swept his other hand over his balding head, took a step back, and reached his foot high upon the stage step. Corbett, having already noticed Brad's sunbaked hands and face, had smirked when, with his hat off, Brad's darkened tan gave way at the hat line to a baby-pink bald head.

This four-hitch set were quality horses similar to those purchased by the D&RG back in Durango. Corbett grimaced as he remembered the screams of his four-hitch that had been chased into the corral gate.

"What's the face for?"

"I had a wreck with a four-hitch a couple of years back and I killed all of them." Brad stared at Corbett for a long time, not saying a word.

Several miles passed. "Why did ya kill your horses?"

"Indians were chasing us and I couldn't control them," said Corbett. Again, he could feel a prolonged stare from Brad.

The river's valley floor was flat beneath the naked maples and alders. A snowstorm had come and gone in the recent past. The road was well-traveled—damp, but packed. The horses, relaxed, were moving at a good pace. As the stage traveled west, a constant breeze from the coast carried the smoke from the scattered homesteads eastward. Given the number of different billows of such gray smoke, Corbett was surprised to discover how settled the valley was. There were far more open fields than trees, entirely different from the hole in the trees that was Cedar Crossing.

"Will we get to the coast by dark?" Corbett was anxious to see the sea.

"Nah, this coach doesn't go that far," replied Brad, a stubby cigar at the corner of his mouth.

Corbett turned in his seat. "What did Brad just say?"

"I thought Martin said it went to the coast. Seaside, I think he said."

"Don't believe anything Martin tells you. This run goes through three little towns, carrying passengers and the mail. Right now, the mail contracts are the only way the line stays afloat." Corbett was stunned. The Coastal Stage Line was pure fantasy. Corbett wanted to ask a dozen new questions, but Brad's body language and the stern look he had on his face while staring ahead implied that the hourly quota of words had been met.

The incline of the road increased, and the hitch slowed. The road was on the north side of a rapidly closing valley. The south side valley walls were filled with ever-present forests of Douglas fir and hemlock, showing remnants of the past snow on the forest floor beneath the trees. The stream, no longer quiet and content, was tumbling and gurgling.

"Hey, up there!" shouted an angry voice from inside the coach. "I could walk faster than this!"

Brad showed no change in either his features or his view. "Then walk!"

"I paid four damned dollars to get to Granier—today!"

It made Corbett nervous not to try to appease the rider, but Brad was unimpressed. Corbett was angry at having been conned by Martin, but the pleasure of being a teamster again, riding in the open air and seeing the countryside, made up for it.

"How far to the relay station?" inquired Corbett. "Pulling this grade has the team about whipped."

"Not far."

The wagon trail left the stream that was flowing down from a tight canyon ahead and proceeded to move northward on a slight grade onto a grassy slope. Corbett had not been in such an open area for months. There were no trees. Even the brush was giving way to grassy knolls. Just past the summit, a two-story house sat nestled under some leafless trees. There was also a large corral, which held several horses, already hitched and ready for their turn in front of the whip. Around the crown of the hill was a huddle of cabins and sheep sheds. Against the background of green, one could see but two colors: small gray outcroppings of rock and the white fluff of sheep, the latter of which were everywhere.

"These boys will have some johnnycake, coffee, and prunes ready for us." Brad had the unique ability to leave his personality out of every sentence. "Go easy on the prunes!" That was his attempt at a joke.

Just before Brad pulled the team to a stop, he gave advice: "The tall one is Tim; the other, Jacob. They're both morons." Tim, a gawky sort, lifted his hat as Brad brought the team to a halt.

Smiling and glancing at his watch, Tim said, "You're four minutes behind."

Brad, on his way to the outhouse, answered, "Go piss on yourself."

The passengers were a little perturbed at having to unload themselves. "Sorry," apologized Corbett. He had taken to helping change out the teams, rather than attend to the passengers.

"Brad Peterson's an ass," said the smallest of the two men, his clothing better than the others', a sheepskin vest with gaily embroidered panels down the sides, and on top of his head, a dark wool beret. Noticing Corbett's attempt to lend a hand, he said, "Thanks, son, I can tend to it." Near to the corrals sat a bundled woman in a small two-wheeled cart. She seemed content and warm. A woolen hat covered her head and ears; a sheepskin blanket protected her legs and shoulders. The little Basque did a jig as Corbett approached the cart. Corbett thought to himself that the little jig seemed to say so much. He wondered what it was the sheep was trying to communicate.

The name was above the door: Granier Post Office and Stage Station. Inside, johnnycake with molasses was at the center of the table, along with the bowl of dried prunes. In the air was the aroma of coffee that had been left sitting on the stove too long. Regardless, Jacob was proud of his coffee and probably had been proud of it since breakfast.

"Jones, you're the one to bring in the mail, not me!" Corbett was learning the job the hard way. Brad threw down a small leather bag full of mail and sat himself next to fire, away from the others. Corbett drank down his coffee and wrapped his johnnycake in newsprint, before proceeding outside to help Tim with the new relay team.

A cold, brisk wind from the coast brought with it a sheet of low, gray clouds. The stage pulled away, now with just three already beneath the buffalo robes. Brad and Corbett were riding into a misty, damp cloud that was scraping its belly over the top of the grassy hill. Corbett lowered his head and let the drops of rain fall off the front of his cowboy hat. Brad faced the rain, letting the water drip off his chin.

The stage road made itself fit along the edge of a long U-shaped valley. Snow, hidden by the few trees and rocks that broke the surface of the green carpet, shared the valley with many small herds of sheep. A sheepherder's covered wagon presented itself on the valley floor, evidenced by the smoke coming from its stovepipe.

Wildflower consisted of a mile-long series of sheep ranches, each with a view of the valley in front and a cluster of fences and sheds behind. The mail drop was a tiny store, battered and beaten, with no sign at all. Two passengers got off there, where three packets of flour and sugar were unloaded. The houses seemed sorrowful, dark, and mossy from winters of constant rain. This was winter. Wildflower was a sorry place to be.

In the distance, Corbett saw two large buildings on the valley floor at the closed end of the valley. There was an orchard to the left and rows of grapevines to the right. The rain was now continuous and cold. At the entrance, two peeled logs held another log overhead across the muddy path to the buildings. There were two massive barns, but one seemed to be the house.

Three little girls waited in the lane and in the rain. One got the mail, one got a parcel, and one grabbed happily at the hand of the man who'd gotten off the stage. The man, a blond, older, had a sharp face and a narrow nose. He did not look Corbett in the eye, but instead set his gaze downward as he said, "Spa-c-ba." Which was obviously some sort of a thank you in the man's native tongue. With that, he turned to the little girl at his side and gave her a hug. As the four walked together up the path to the barns, Brad turned the stage in a wide circle for home. Corbett saw ten or so children spill out of the one barn, along with three or four women, all in the rain and all there to welcome the blond man. Even as the stage aimed away from the barns, Corbett kept watching. The dozen were gathered around the man happily.

"What was that place?"

"Newday!" Brad responded, unconcerned that Corbett's interest was piqued. Corbett needed more.

"There must be a dozen women and children. I didn't see any other men. How about the women? So many women all living in the same house?"

"Breeders," said Brad calmly. Many connotations rolled through Corbett's mind, the best of which was that the man they'd just dropped off was a polygamist Mormon coming home to his family of women living their lives in Newday.

Now with the rain at his back, Brad tried to light a cigar, a practiced art in the rain. Eventually, he succeeded. Corbett's coat was almost waterproof, but it had given up the ghost by the time the stage had reached the valley floor. Overall, the trip was well worth forgetting. The joke Margaret had told nearly a year ago was true: When it starts to rain in Oregon, it doesn't stop for six months. Brad was not a friendly soul, but Corbett figured that maybe having to make the stage run to Newday every other day throughout the year would turn a man into an unfriendly sort.

The next day, an off day for Corbett, he and Martin sat in Martin's bar watching the drizzle outside. Martin's hair was well under control with pomade. With his blue-collared shirt, pressed and tailored, no one would ever say Martin was not classy.

"Did you like the run?" asked Martin. The fact that he had sold it as a coastal stage route did not get in the way of his expecting to hear a positive evaluation.

"It is an easy enough run. Got to see a lot of country," said Corbett. "Brad is no gift, but he is not hard to ignore."

"As long as the railroads buy and sell and expand," Martin said, looking into his brandy-infested coffee. "The stagecoach business needs drivers like him, solid and dependable." *A lack of personality and poor social skills could be thrown in for nothing*, thought Corbett.

"Tell me about Newday." Corbett had slept little the night before, thinking about the little girls in the rain with no coats, and Brad pitching the idea that the blond man used the women as breeders. It did not sit right.

"Weiner, the owner, rode up with you yesterday. He's quite rich, I think. Generally, he sends down wagons of wine and cider in the fall. I buy from him."

"What about all the women and children! They his?"

"He ain't a Mormon, but I'll bet he enjoys his little harem. Keeps them all bred up pretty good, I'll bet. Brad thinks he's a Polack. Barely speaks American at all." Martin wanted to exploit a thought he had on the topic: "I believe he's a European, wanting to start over way up in that valley."

"You've got me scheduled for a run on Christmas Eve," Corbett reminded Martin. "We'll see either a tree with candles or one of those big candlesticks full of candles.

"A menorah?"

"This here is a Christmas Eve tradition," Martin announced to Corbett. Corbett and Brad were seated on stools at the bar, and Martin was pouring drinks behind the bar. The stage was to leave in thirty minutes. "Brad and me, and whoever we've got riding shotgun, knock down a couple of these before the Christmas Eve run. You and Santa both have a run today. I'll bet he has a couple of these before he starts out too."

In each glass was an egg, some honey, a few drops of vanilla, and cream. At this point, Corbett knew an eggnog when he saw one. "This is the most important ingredient, Caribbean rum. A slosh for each one of us!" Martin, the bartender, did not hold back.

The grassy mountain was cold, windless, and rainless. Brad and Corbett were both a little more than happy after celebrating the lighting of Tim and Jacob's Christmas tree with another glass of rum, this one warm and buttered, their second rum of the day. Time was beginning to fall apart, probably having started an hour ago, and neither man was missing it.

Ahead was a Basque celebration at Wildflower that had drifted into the road. Several Basque men were evidently feeling no cold, partly because they were wearing sheepskin coats and partly because they were holding up a bota of wine for each of the riders, yelling, "Cava! Cava!" Corbett was sure cava meant something like "I'm drunk!"

Newday was surely out there somewhere, but to Corbett, seeing through blurry eyes and the early winter darkness, the place seemed distant and drab. He could see two small lights coming into view, one at the road and another near the front door of the barn house. The lead horses shied away from the little shadows moving around a small fire next to the road. The three little girls who waited every other day for the post from the stagecoach stepped cautiously up to the horses and handed Brad and Corbett small delicate cups.

"Wassail! Wassail!" The sweet apple taste was wonderful, but the sweetness was far less than that of the servers who had sat in the cold, waiting for the coach to arrive. A menorah with its nine candles flickered quietly between the two barns. As the stage pulled out, Corbett dropped off a bag of taffy. This was his Christmas moment; the little girls were his for the moment.

Corbett hated getting up every morning to the different shades of gray, thinking about rain and dark clouds, yet another day of it. Corbett never missed his turn on the stage. He carried never the whip, always the shotgun. His off days were leisurely. He'd have coffee with Martin in the morning, read in his room until early afternoon, then read in a cafe-like setting in the late afternoon at a corner table next to the fire in the restaurant, supported by a beer or two.

"Here he is!" Martin was walking toward Corbett with a thick young man who had olive-colored skin, dark eyebrows, and a dark beard. "Sabino wants to meet you!" Corbett stood and shook Sabino's hand, a strong, calloused grip.

"Nice to meet you, Sabino," said Corbett, wondering why this strangely handsome man with the weather-beaten face would want to meet him.

Martin set the stage for the conversation. "Sabino is one of the Basques living in Wildflower. He's a teamster like you, hauls wine and cider down off the hill for Weiner, as well as bags of wool down to the woolen mills for the herders up there."

Sabino nodded, pleased with the introduction. "Yes, I met you at Christmas. I handed you a bota of cava."

Corbett laughed. "I don't remember much of that night, but it must have been good. Next time I will have to eat before making the Christmas run."

Sabino studied Corbett's book, opened and facedown on the table. "Are you a reader? I spend my snowbound times at my home reading." Sabino snuck a look at the title: *Around the World in Eighty Days*. Excited, he asked, "Is there any way I could borrow it after you finish it? I have been nowhere except from here to Portland."

"I'll leave it with Martin when I am finished." Corbett was surprised to find a reader in his present circumstance. "I've got some others here as well."

"I would be very pleased!"

Martin refocused the meeting, saying, "Sabino told me some unsettling news."

"I am a good friend of Weiner. In the summer, we work hard to keep the sheep and his goats separated. I help with the apple and grape harvest." Sabino, now serious, said, "He has been found out. He left Russia in fear of the Russians, then was chased out of New York City after being beaten and persecuted for being the wrong kind of Jew." Sabino leaned back in his chair, hesitating. Then he continued, saying, "His uncle and both his brothers were killed in New York. Now, his enemies are coming here."

Martin was perplexed. "Why would they come all the way out here?"

"I don't know. Could be money. Maybe even one of the women." Corbett sat back. Now there were questions to ponder.

"I see several women." Corbett felt a bit like the corporal on the train. Why did Weiner have so many women while he had none?

"Maybe it is the Jewish culture. Wherever you land, you plant." Sabino then brought up the topic for which the meeting had been scheduled: "Can you help us?"

"By God, yes we can!" Martin shouted, a little too loud for a far corner table. He looked around and hunched back down to resume the secret meeting. "Just signal us when you know they are coming."

The next two weeks were cold, often snowy, gray, and icy. The cleated horseshoes gave the four horses enough grip to make the run. The streams were barely contained in their banks. A warm day would release the stored-up ice to run itself over the banks. Corbett began to count the days until his escape back to Cedar Crossing.

"Look what just came in from Portland." Martin shifted his eyes from Corbett to two men sitting at the bar, waiting for the stage run to Newday. Both were wearing frock coats, unusual for the timber country of the Northwest. One wore a bowler. His broad butt was matched by his wide shoulders, and his eyes were permanently squinted, or so it seemed. The other had darker, more Middle Eastern features and black shoulder-length hair. He was thin and anxious.

"That be them," agreed Corbett. The only plan of action was to notify Sabino that the New Yorkers were on board.

Brad, sipping at the same table, imparted his thoughts: "They're just ass-grabbers going up to do some stud work." Corbett clenched his jaw. Someday he would knock the hell out of that bitter excuse of a man.

While Brad was at the stagecoach door, aiding the men inside, Corbett picked up the large trunk belonging to the men. It was too light. What could be in this too large a trunk that could not have been packed in a smaller suitcase?

"Wait up, Brad!" called Corbett. "Got a problem with the boot!" Corbett reached into the station's toolbox and brought out a thin pry bar, which he used to snap open the trunk's lock. Inside was a pistol and a large two-piece rifle with a box of ammunition. He threw the guns into some bushes next to the windows of the restaurant. Martin, through the window, solemnly nodded his approval.

Corbett had felt the stress and apprehension from the onset. Was there a time when he might have interceded? He'd had his rifle. Maybe the stop at Granier was one of those points. Corbett carried his rifle off the stage, which he never had done before. Brad was always first to the outhouse, given his old man condition. The passengers were next. Upon their return, the thinner of the two stopped at the boot and toyed a second with one of the buckles, then patted the leather boot and boarded. Corbett wished he knew for sure that these were the New Yorkers. What if they were Weiner's relatives? The opportunity had passed. Corbett cursed.

Corbett had hoped Sabino would be standing outside the stage stop in Wildflower, but such was not the case. Martin had tied a note to the mail pouch to alert whoever first gathered the mail.

Corbett, now in a sweat, focused on the far end of the valley. Big flakes of snow made the view difficult. He hoped that the three little girls were not at the gate.

A rash of ideas passed quickly through Corbett's mind as the minutes passed. He thought to have Brad drive by without stopping. But what if they were friends or relatives? Brad would not stop even if he knew what was up. Corbett wrestled with shooting both the Jews as they got off, but there was a chance, just a chance, that they were friends or bodyguards coming to protect Weiner and Newday. Besides, their guns were in the bushes at Martin's. Corbett would just have to wait for a clue.

Standing beneath the tall-poled entrance were the three little girls. Corbett's hope lay in having an adult come out of the barn and identify the men as friends or foes. Stopped, Corbett got down with his rifle, which he set by one of the rear wheels. Delaying every act, Corbett watched the scene. The girls seemed unafraid.

A woman came out the front door and carefully began to pick her way through the snow, walking down to the stage.

"Let's get on, Corbett," said Brad, ready to turn into the wind and light a cigar. Through the snow, Corbett could barely see the woman, nor she them.

Brad slapped the reins. The stage started the long turn for home. Corbett saw the woman stop and scream. He viewed the horror that was about to overtake the woman. The heavier of the men drew a pistol from inside his coat and started firing. The woman was frozen in the dilemma: flee or attend to the sacred responsibility of motherhood. She chose to run and collect the girls. Two of the girls ran toward the woman. The third was being held against the thigh of the shooter. The other New Yorker was throwing the contents of the trunk about, shrieking for the missing guns.

"Stop!" shouted Corbett to Brad.

"No, sir, I will not." Corbett hit Brad with the butt of his rifle. Corbett jumped off, yelling for the girls. Brad fell onto the floor of the driver's box, thus tightening the reins, bringing the stage to a stop.

Corbett took three strides, when he saw the woman fall face-first into the snow. The two girls stopped and stared at the fallen woman, frozen. Corbett pulled up to shoot. The third girl was still in the grasp of the shooter, too close for him to risk taking a shot. The thin New Yorker, stunned, stood and glared at the empty trunk. He had nothing.

There was more shooting. Coming down the other road were three carts carrying sheepherders, who were shooting in the air. The New Yorker with the gun was slapping his pockets. He was out of ammunition. He yelled at his partner, then saw the empty trunk. Both men tried to hide behind the girl. The thin man was holding a knife at her throat.

Weiner started down the path from the house, shotgun in hand. The Basques and Corbett closed in and around the two. Sabino represented the group. "Nothing you do to that poor child will change what we are going to do to you!" The press of angry men closed to just a few feet. Suddenly, the nervousness of the thinner man gave way. He pushed the little girl to Corbett, and both New Yorkers raised their hands.

"Shoot us! Shoot us! That's what you do to Jews!"

"No, that would be too easy for you." Sabino nodded to his men, who wrestled the other men down the stage road toward the long, open field of deepening snow. The gang of sheepherders continued to drive the New Yorkers farther and farther into the field.

Corbett held the girl tightly as he walked toward the women, who were flowing out of the house. A young woman, gathering up the girl, cried, "Spa-c-ba, spa-c-ba!" He looked attentively at the other women from the house, all gathered around the fallen woman. They were common, loving women, not breeders or captives.

Corbett turned to watch the wood being carried down into the field, following the men. "Are you going to burn them?"

"No, the wood is for the guards. They will camp there and guard the men from New York, who will freeze." *No wonder,* thought Corbett, *that there seems to be no crime amongst these people. The punishments are brutal.*

"I want to thank you," said an older woman with long hair, quite shaken. "They came for Yegor and killed another." Little did she know, Corbett had walked that same trail once.

Ready for home, Corbett climbed into the stage box. Brad drew back. He did not look good. He had a frightened look on his face.

"You can light your cigar," said Corbett, not a bit sorry for Brad's clipped jaw, which was in sorry shape. Brad did not move. "Get in back. I'll be the whip. Just remember, the next time someone needs you to stop so a life can be saved," Corbett explained, "you damned well better stop!"

Tired both mentally and physically, Corbett finally brought the team to a stop at Martin's. Martin rushed out to the stage, where he saw Brad crawl out the door and limp away.

"Did they do that to him?"

Corbett's answer was a surprise: "No, I did."

As Corbett opened the boot and removed the mail and boxes from the snow-swept Wildflower country, he explained the day's events, finishing with a sad afterthought: "I should have shot them as they left the stage in Granier. It would have saved a woman's life."

Before sunup, Corbett and Ollie were on the road, the very route Corbett had taken hours earlier. On his own and on his off day, he was eager to find Sabino and see what had gone on after he and Brad had left. Corbett was intrigued with Weiner after having met with him but briefly. Sabino had given Weiner a positive recommendation even though it was across two cultures. The arrival of the Basques the previous night probably had prevented more deaths.

Ollie loved trips. He was high-stepping, with his ears turning and chasing every sound. Corbett believed the morning's dark and heavy clouds were being brushed away by a thin, high-level sheet. The sun poking though one of the holes would be a gladdening sight; however, Corbett had given up the notion that winter in northwest Oregon ever allowed more than merely a possibility of sunshine.

Arriving at Granier, Corbett asked, "Tim, reckon Jacob has any coffee made?" Tim was brushing down the big draft horses that would make up the relay for tomorrow's stagecoach run. Even though Brad thought him a moron and his oddness made him a comedic figure, Corbett saw Tim as playing a valuable role in spite of the visual impression he left.

"He's got johnnycake on the stove!" Tim shouted back. "Did you hear, the Basques got in a shootout with them men you brought up yesterday. They're chasing them across the far side of the valley!"

"What do you know?" Corbett said, acting surprised. One of the reasons for his trip was to see if the Basque campers were still needed in the snowy field.

"See ya, Tim. Grabbing coffee and going!"

Passing through Wildflower, Corbett noted that the Basques were busy tending their sheep, feeding them grass hay that had been gathered throughout the summer. Corbett hoped to see Sabino but did not. Two miles toward Newday, Corbett saw a small band of men in the middle of the snowy carpet of the valley floor. Obviously, the herders weren't finished with the intruders from New York.

Newday seemed quiet. Corbett could see two women on the hillside above the barns, spreading hay for the goats. At the gate was a packed and scrambled mix of tracks, some leading toward the barns and some following the road into the lower field. Only after he had turned into the Newday path did Corbett see the blood. A sacrifice, maybe not on the same scale as Jesus's, but a sacrifice just the same.

To his surprise, Weiner stood at the front door. He did not move until Ollie had completed the short trip to the barns. A woman, her long black dress sweeping across the snow, ran quickly to Corbett. "He wants you in!" she said nervously. Weiner was waving—not a grand wave, but a measured, proper wave. Two small children were looking from behind his legs. Visitors were rare, but after the events of the past evening, visitors provided new layers of danger.

"Come sit," said the woman, taking Corbett's coat. The room

was large. It held a massive stone fireplace with seating all along the front. In the same room, but at the other end, were two nickel-plated iron stoves with accompanying alder cupboard doors. The dining area held three rough-hewn tables of fir with wooden chairs neatly tucked in on each. Little ones passed back and forth through a large doorway into the other half of the barn—sleeping quarters, probably. The backdrop was solemn. The children, a respectable distance away, were watching intently.

"This is our leader, Yegor Weiner!" said the woman, about forty, in the black dress of mourning and matching head covering. Yegor was also wearing black—a vest and some type of custom pant. On his head was a black kippah.

"My name is Corbett Jones," Corbett said, trying to figure out whom to talk to, the woman interpreter or Weiner. "I ride the stagecoach!" It was not much of an introduction, but that was all he had. "I came to mourn the woman who died last night." Tears came to the woman's eyes. Was she a sister or a good friend? It did not matter; she'd suffered a great loss.

"Spa-c-ba, thank you!" said Yegor, shaking Corbett's hand. Then, putting both his hands around Corbett's, he prayed earnestly for a time. When finished, he looked at the woman and spoke to her in a foreign language.

"He must go in a few minutes," said the woman quietly. "But he wants to tell our story. Sabino says you are a trusted man."

"Marja," Weiner said, pointing to the translator. She bowed politely and listened to Weiner as he began his story. Weiner nodded as Corbett heard the translation:

"We are not here because of religion, but we try to maintain our religion here. My family in Russia was wealthy, and because we were Jewish, the Russians decided to take our wealth. We sent our silver and jewels to France. There, it was taken by members of the family we thought we could trust. Before we fled, my three brothers and an uncle made a pact: we would all flee to America. If anything should happen, we would do everything possible to keep our bloodline alive—everything and anything." Marja, strained and stressed, making the translation accurate and full. Marja was not as old as the crow's-feet at the edge of her eyes and the furrowed lines across her forehead would indicate. Her light complexion was similar to Weiner's, but no other similarities were evident.

"His uncle was shot the night of the pact, and both brothers were ambushed as they walked along a street in New York City a few weeks later. A rabbi told Yegor to flee all the way to the other side of the United States with the family that was left. We are here, and still they come." Tears were in her eyes once again. Weiner stood and bowed, then left to lament the passing of another member of his bloodline.

Ollie was in a hurry, tail in the air. Brown to purple clouds were boiling up from the coast. Corbett's thoughts lay with the women and children of Newday. Could Yegor keep his family safe? Could Sabino keep his neighbor safe?

Whether it was the potent wind or Ollie trying to run, Corbett got the message. A big storm was trying to climb the coastal range. Maybe it would arrive by tomorrow. The billowing wind and the tortured blackened clouds finally took away Corbett's thoughts of Newday.

The following morning, Corbett walked in to have his morning coffee. Martin stood and yelled, "What else did you do to Brad? He packed up and left last night!"

"I fired him," said Corbett, turning over his cup and setting it upright for coffee. Martin, already gathering the attention of the rest of the restaurant, eased himself down into his chair. His part-time shotgun had fired his whip of fifteen years. Corbett added,

"He is an ass!" Not expecting any reaction from the local coffee crowd, he heard loud clapping.

"Today's going to be a hell of a run. Who's going to do it?" Martin, a little quieter now, added, "There's a storm coming, and we have mail to deliver!"

"I can whip if you can find someone to shotgun."

The restaurant door opened. A man and woman appeared in the doorway, sharing it with a strong influx of blowing snow.

"Jocko! Come on over." The woman headed through the back doors for the outhouse.

"Is the stage to Portland still going?" asked Jocko, shaking out his wool scarf.

"Sure, both are!" There was no doubt in Martin's mind.

"No, you can't send the stage to Granier. We barely outraced the snow from there to get here!" Jocko's stern view settled the argument before it had started. "It's going to be a hell of a blizzard. And if you don't get the Portland stage under way, it won't be going anywhere either."

The storm blackened the entire sky to the west and appeared to be rolling downhill as it moved at a remarkable rate. The tumbling avalanche of wet, heavy snow was deposited on the west side of trees and buildings and on stretches of road. Martin had closed up shop by noon. Recognizing that it might be days before the Granier run would be attempted, Corbett helped get the draft horses into the barns, out of the biting snow. Ollie had demanded special consideration the afternoon before, having been chased off the mountain by the leading edge of the blizzard, Corbett made sure Ollie's stall had new straw and hay for the day.

Martin's was hit at the last moment by locals wanting supplies for the duration. He opened up briefly to accommodate his neighbors. After that, the place was empty. Martin was in a dither, glancing at the storm periodically through the window and marching back and forth, mumbling about his ruination. Corbett observed the breakdown for a few minutes, then left for his room to begin packing. The road to Cedar Crossing was in the same fix, but all the same, Corbett was planning on being the first on the road home, whenever that might be.

14

Spring Term

"Usually we read in the afternoon and learn about life, the history of life, the romance of life, the adventure of life, all of it." Corbett appreciated Ernie, who was building up the fire. The constant dampness could only be beaten back by good dry wood heat. "Starting today, in the afternoons, we will read and write. You older students, order a new or different catalog for your family. You may already have a Sears or Montgomery catalog, so how about a new seed catalog?" Corbett noticed a nod of approval from the group. Then, prepare a letter to a student at my college, telling them about yourself. My professor back there is going to give these letters to those learning to teach. They will write back and talk about themselves." Corbett smiled. "More than a page on yourself. Get busy!"

The younger students were always absorbed in all that the older students did. Their eyes grew wide with the thought of ordering a catalog, maybe even a Sears catalog, Oh, to be a big student!

"Okay, my little tigers, get out your Big Chief tablets." Writing on their slate boards was common, but an assignment on the Big Chief was special. Cursive again. The little ones groaned, then laughed at their groaning. "Today we will practice with the letters that almost fall off the line." Corbett, at the board, drew a cursive *p, g, j, q,* and *y*. "Let's do *pig*. The *p* head stays above the line, but his dangle is dangling." They laughed. "Now the *i* with the dot on top. Poor *g* almost falls off the line. His head is above, but his dangle is dangling! Now carefully write on your lined paper *pig* ten times, then add *dig, jig, joy,* and *quip,* all ten times. Make sure their dangles dangle." Such a silly word.

Denise and the two little Natives would laugh at anything. Violet, sitting with them, responded with a funny look. *You are a crazy man,* she thought of Corbett.

High clouds and a touch of sun had been the order of the day. It was Friday afternoon. Wagons were picking up some students. Other students were walking in all directions, which made an already busy street appear even more confused. Unusual in the mix was Lewis, calmly sitting sidesaddle, picking his teeth. When Corbett saw him, Lewis flopped his leg over to resume his regular riding style and rode forward.

"Are all the schoolmarms in this country as pretty as you?"

Corbett responded, "If I'd known you were coming, I would have powdered my face." He grinned. "What do you want, Lewis?"

"The boar's out!"

"What in the hell does that mean?"

"I've been baitin' a big boar," said Lewis excitedly, "and he showed yesterday. His hibernation is over!"

"I gather now is the time to get after him?" Corbett thought, then said, "I thought the fall was the time to hunt bear and elk, not the spring."

"It all depends. In the fall, bears are fat like hogs. There's a lot of meat to keep cold, but the hair on the hide is thin because of the summer's heat. Now, if you want a great hide, thick and warm, spring's the time." Lewis had it all figured out. "The bad part is that the fat is gone, and keepin' that much meat good is hard." Then he got to the point of the conversation: "Do you want to go get him in the morning?"

"Well, I sure do!" So much for sleeping in. "Where, and what time?"

"My place at noon." The sleep-in was back on.

"I'll have to borrow a gun from Otto. I'd better go get it now."

As Corbett started his walk to the smithy, Lewis put forth his last comment: "Have him give you some ammunition as well!"

Just my luck, thought Corbett, whose contemplations of a bear hunt overran his ability to sleep. He'd seen a bear once near Durango. It had run back into the pinyon trees, skittish and cinnamon in color. When he was a little kid in Alpine, Texas, using sticks for guns, he would have never thought of bear hunting for real. It was foolish to be too excited to sleep, but such was the case for Corbett today.

Walking along behind Lewis with a mix of mud and snow beneath his feet, Corbett saw how easy it would be to track a bear or elk. Claws and hooves would sink deeply into the trail. This was new country for Corbett, long basaltic stretches of gray to black rock with no logical arrangement, covered by a few inches of mud and decayed organic material. Deep plunges of dark rock were punctuated by craggy uplifts. Deer and elk trails funneled themselves into the flat, neutral corridors that happened quite by accident. This was country wilder than the high-canopied fir forests just a few miles away.

"I hope he is up near the bait. A lot easier to get him out." Lewis, now down in a stalk, said, "If he drops down to the streambed, we can get him easier, but it would be hell getting him up out of the canyon."

Corbett was about ask to Lewis a question, but he changed his mind once he saw Lewis motion for him to stop and slip behind a rock. Ahead and slightly below was a flat rocky opening with several trees standing alone. A nature-made brushy path following a wide crack led up from the canyon below, a natural walkway to the higher ground.

Lewis slipped in beside Corbett. "He's not here. See that bucket hanging in the tree?" Lewis whispered, "I rendered down some elk fat and filled the leaky bucket, then hung it in that tree. As it gets warmer, the fat melts and drips. At night, the cold freezes it back up, so it lasts a long time."

The first hour, Corbett was intent, watching and listening to every leaf move, imagining the bear's appearance. The second hour, Corbett was quietly snoring the snore that he had missed earlier, anxious for the hunt. Every few minutes, he would peek at Lewis, who was silently surveying the scene. The sky was gray, not wanting to rain, but not eager to yield to the sun. They called it spring.

Lewis bumped his partner gently. Corbett was immediately awake, looking for the reason for the bump. Lewis held one finger to his lips and pointed to the brush north of the rocky opening. A grunt and the movement of newly sprouted leaves at the tops of the brush indicated something large inside. "They are like pigs," Lewis whispered. "They act just like pigs."

After ten minutes of rooting in the thicket, a big black bear appeared, its eyes drab, its claws big, and its nose to the air. To Corbett, it seemed that the eyes were unseeing and the nose, the main guide. Smelling and licking the droplets of fat on the rock floor, the bear felt several fat droplets plop onto its head. It quizzically looked up at the bucket, raising its nose higher and higher, until the creature was standing tall on both hind legs.

The shot fired right next to Corbett dazed him. Lewis was to his feet and aiming once again. His first shot had been enough; the bear had fallen immediately.

"Nice shot!" yelled Corbett to Lewis, standing right beside him. "Got him on the first shot. Congratulations!"

"Now the hard part," said a grinning Lewis. Examining the sky, he saw that the gray had given way to the beginnings of darkness. "We won't have him dressed out before dark." Corbett was wordless at the size of the beast. His imagination had not conceived of such a large animal. The fangs were two inches long; the claws, long and strong; and the body, four hundred pounds or more. "We'll have to spend the night and start packing it out tomorrow. We can get to within a quarter mile of here with a horse, but I haven't had much luck putting bear meat or hide on a horse."

"I'll build a fire under the big cedar there. It looks dry enough," said Corbett, trying to be helpful. Ever since the time of his arrival in Oregon, it amazed Corbett how some trees repelled rain and snow outward so well that even in the rainy season, under those trees, the ground remained dry. Corbett gathered some dry punk into a fluffy pile and, with his flint and steel striker, made a fire, which started snapping and popping, the smoke filtering its way upward though the flattened needles.

"Corbett, I believe I told you a lie," said Lewis, on one knee with his bloody skinning knife in hand. "This meat has plenty grease in it. If we can keep it cold, we can pass some of it around. Help me put him on his back. I've got to make a straight, even cut right down the middle from just below his chin, all the way to the bottom." Corbett saw the symmetry Lewis was trying to obtain.

"Looks like you've done this before!" Corbett had sharpened his knife the previous night in preparation of helping dress out a bear, but as he dropped down on both knees, neither he nor his knife was prepared for the exactness and precision of Lewis's skinning. A man who deals in tanning and finished leather makes few nicks or mistakes.

"Yeah. Both our bedrooms have rugs. This'n will go in the main room." Lewis did not often have reasons to smile; however, now he had such a reason.

Between the two men, the bear was completely skinned and gutted, the last details completed by feeling their way in the darkness.

"Whittle us a pair of sticks," said Lewis, checking the loin for two proper steaks. "I'll cut us some prime supper."

Minutes later, he was saying, "Look at the fat drip into the fire!" Corbett watched and listened to the delicious sizzling.

"Yeah, this one wintered good. So now we have more than the hide to haul out. Corbett, I'm really glad you're here now. Your muscles are goin' to get a workout in the morning." The hide flat, the hair down, and the meat covered with snow by Lewis and Corbett, the day was finally done. Corbett had gorged on fresh meat. The trunk of the tree was his pillow.

"Corbett, wake up. We have visitors!" Corbett looked around the fire, expecting a soul but hearing a low-pitched growl.

"I think there's at least four, maybe five. As you get up, kick some punk into the fire. It'll spark up some. That'll help." Both men slowly rose and turned this way and that, their rifles pointing outward.

"I'm going to drag the big limb over there into the fire." Corbett set his gun against the trunk. A bigger fire might discourage the wolves some and maybe make them easier to see.

A tormented kind of howl made a jump toward the meat, still outside the bright area lit up by the fire. Corbett fired. There was no sense that he had hit anything, but the act of shooting made him feel safer.

"Wait for the fire to build," advised Lewis. "We'll see some shiny eyes if they come any closer." The fire caught the lower branches on fire. They lit brightly, then faltered.

The meat, not the men, was the goal. A young wolf eased forward and tore at the meat when Lewis fired. A squabble of howls lit up the quiet. The wolves, more confused than Lewis or Corbett, attacked the young wolf and the meat in a frenzy. A wide-set pair of shiny eyes came from behind the meat. The wolf went down for a sniff, then rose to an attack position. Corbett saw the wolf and shot. The passion for the meat slowed instantly. The wolves, previously coordinated with regard to their purpose and plan, lost focus, scattering about and whining loudly.

"I think you got the alpha!" shouted Lewis, nervously looking for the next attack. After ten minutes, the pack, far away, began howling a lonesome song, perhaps for a fallen leader.

The cool, misty morning gave hope of a high-sky gray day. The first fifteen feet of the cedar tree above the fire had been blackened and burned from the night battle for the meat.

"This here is going to make a dandy wall hide," said Lewis, finishing the cape and head of the dead wolf. "It was a barren female, for sure the alpha. Just too big not to be."

Corbett and Lewis relayed the hides and meat out two hundred yards at a time. To keep the meat somewhat guarded, they would carry what they could, cache it, then go back for another load. Thankfully, the bear had been boned out, making the load lighter.

By early afternoon, the hunters were close enough to a wagon path that Lewis could go for his wagon. Upon his return, the floor of the wagon was full of snow, gathered hither and yon from the shaded areas between trees. Corbett could barely carry a hind quarter on his shoulder to the wagon, while Lewis bagged up the boned meat from the ribs, back, and shoulders. Lastly, the bear hide, hair up, was settled on the pile. Corbett's wolf hide lay hair down to cap off the load.

Lewis, not one to brag, went straight to his home. Ida and Ruth, worried about Lewis's absence overnight, came out quickly to meet the pair.

"Did you get him?" Ida asked, rushing to the back of the wagon. "You did! And you kept the meat!" As the women looked beneath the hides, Corbett could not help but be envious. Ida was not only pert and pretty; she was also practical and loyal. She lived and worked among the slop and smell of the tannery. Because of this, Corbett continued to feel sorry for Ruth. Her few trips to the crossing had given her, her only exposure to life and to men.

Lewis smiled. "Let's get the hides to the back. Then I'll take the loin and one hind quarter up to Grandma's to sell."

Ruth was looking at the head of the wolf. "That's the biggest wolf head I have ever seen!"

"Your Mr. Jones got that rascal last night," Lewis said, giving full credit to Corbett. "A pack of them attacked us last night. He got that alpha female."

"Are you going to let us tan her?" Ruth asked. She was Ida all over again.

"I expect so. I've never shot anything worth keeping before!"

"Before the snow melts in the wagon, Corbett and I are going to run this meat to town. This will pay down the bill at the mercantile."

Coming into town, Corbett and Ollie turned off at the corrals, leaving Lewis to deliver his prized meat. It would not take long for word to get around that Grandma's had bear steak.

"We have two reports this morning about money. Ernie will be first." Corbett started out the new school day. John at the mercantile had lent Corbett several different coins for Ernie to use in his presentation. His lesson was primarily for the younger students. However, Ernie did get the attention of his older classmates.

"I got some help from Mr. Watkins at the store. He gave me lots of coins to talk about. Miss Violet over there gave me some French coins for us to look at. I did some looking in the *Century Dictionary and Cyclopedia* for extra information." Ernie spread a white cloth on the desk, then pulled a red cloth bag from his pocket and set it on the table.

"This here is the Indian head penny. We use it a lot 'cause it's worth one cent." Ernie showed it off, as he'd done with all the others. "It is made of copper mostly.

"All the coins have the year they were born on one side."

"Minted!" corrected Mike.

"Minted!

"Next, I have two coins called nickels, 'cause they have a metal called nickel in them. They are still mostly copper. Here is the three-cent nickel and the five-cent nickel." Ernie held one in each hand. Corbett was proud of Ernie's efforts on this report. There was no way last fall that Ernie would have stood in front of the class.

"Now I have four silver coins. The littlest is the old half-dime, worth five cents. I'd never seen one of these before."

Ernie picked up two coins. "A ten-cent silver liberty and a twenty-five cent silver liberty." Ernie held the twenty-five cent coin higher. "This one is called two bits. I looked it up. Some Mexican money was worth twelve and a half cents, and this coin was worth twice the Mexican bit, so two bits." No one else in the room, including Corbett, had known that bit of information, which made Ernie feel like a scholar.

"And look at this big thing!" Ernie displayed the Morgan silver dollar and then let everyone hold it for a few seconds. "It is almost all silver. Places where they have banks, you can trade your little coins in for a silver dollar.

"These coins belong to Miss Violet and are called francs. They are very old money from France." Ernie began to look up at his audience. Always boisterous and loud when away from the classroom, he sensed the possibility of drawing this crowd to him.

"June gave me this to show you this morning. I don't know anything about it, 'cept she said that it is a twenty-dollar silver certificate. You take it to the government, and they will give you twenty silver dollars."

Corbett saw that Ernie was done. "Let's give Ernie a big hand."

"Jenny, come on up, it's your turn!" Corbett appreciated Jenny Russell's status in the school population. She was not old enough to be in concert with Margaret, June, and Angela, but she was further in her adolescence than Edna Watkins, her best friend. At the mill, Jenny was surrounded by masculinity and maturity, raw jokes, and little peeks at her by the young loggers. She did not want to slow down for Edna but would not probably catch up with the older girls.

"Okay, everyone, quiet. Jenny is going to recite her memory poem."

Stately and mature, and dressed like a seventeen-year-old, Jenny began, saying, "From *A Child's Garden of Verses* by Robert Louis Stevenson." Then she read the poem:

My Bed Is a Boat

My bed is like a little boat.
Nurse helps me in when I embark;
She girds me in my sailor's coat
And starts me in the dark.

> At night, I go on board and say
> Good night to all my friends on shore;
> I shut my eyes and sail away
> And see and hear no more.
>
> And sometimes things to bed I take,
> As prudent sailors have to do;
> Perhaps a slice of wedding cake,
> Perhaps a toy or two.
> All night across the dark we steer;
> But when the day returns at last,
> Safe in my room, beside the pier,
> I find my vessel fast.

Corbett was applauding with the others. "Jenny, that was marvelous, It was a good choice to memorize." Jenny looked to the older girls for their approval, which she received with broad smiles and vigorous clapping. "Why did you choose that poem to recite?"

"I dream sometimes of living far away, Portland or maybe on the coast. Sometimes, I listen to Violet talk about France. I guess sometimes my bed is my boat."

"Don't shoot any more bears or wolves!" said Geri as Corbett sat down for Saturday morning coffee. "Otto spent an hour telling me all about it while he and I ate bear steak that Grandma had cooked up. The two hides seem to be right nice. Otto rode all the way down to the tannery to see them."

"I found out real quick that there's a difference between a man going out to shoot some supper and Lewis, a true trapper and hunter." Corbett shook his head at the difference. "His house may smell like a toilet on days he's tanning, but he's good at his trade."

"I've never seen a wolf," said Geri. "And it was at night?"

"It was quite a night, those wolves growling around us in the dark," Corbett said with a smirk. "I was ready to give them the meat, if they would just leave us with the bear hide and our lives." A little embarrassed, Corbett admitted his cowardice.

"I wanted to ask you: How is Ruth doing?"

"She's reading now. The first time I saw her, she reminded me of a cave woman or something. It was a sad case of melancholy. I wish one of these white-shirted railroaders would come in and sweep her off her feet. She is so much like your friend Ida. But they would probably appear on a day when they're tanning and smelling the place up."

"She fall for you yet?" Geri's eyes widened at the premise.

"I suppose. A little bit," replied Corbett. "I am actually looking for an attractive woman to bathe naked with me at the hot springs!" Corbett grinned. As funny as it seemed, there was an awkward silence that followed.

It was a Sunday morning full of sun. Everyone but Myron and Corbett were along the river below the crossing, catching and netting salmon. The weather and the day off made it a delightful day for families. Looking across at the rail station, which was nearly done, Corbett said, "This town is really going to grow this summer." He was pleased that the fine building was reaching completion.

"Yeah, with the loggers hauling out prime fir and cedar, there will be a lot of loggers and railroaders building homes here in town and round about." Myron's mind gave away a secret. "I'm going to put a bank in the house next to the telegraph office. Already bought the safe. It'll be up here in a month or so."

Corbett's response: "A bank in Cedar Crossing? My gosh, can you imagine that?" The thought of a bank set Corbett's mind in another direction. *We would be a town then, with a big school. How great would that be!*

"It will be midsummer before we open. And as much as they have other plans, I want June and Margaret to manage it. I know they want to go off the mountain, but with their having to wear fancy store-bought dresses and being courted by the proper men of Cedar Crossing, maybe I can get them to stay." Corbett studied Myron closely. Myron was always clean-shaven and was young for his age, regardless of what it might be. His common dress of a collared white shirt and brown tweed wool waistcoat spoke of maybe a lawyer or banker in his earlier life.

"In conversation with Union Pacific representatives, I'm trying to get them to add a passenger car several times a week." Quietly, Myron pointed out the negative. "The stagecoach runs would no longer have a purpose." Myron took a second to bemoan the passing of the stagecoach. "By the way, you wouldn't be interested in selling that wolf hide? Lewis and Otto both told me it is the best they have ever seen," Myron said, watching the churchgoers pass by. Preacher Arnold was getting quite a passel each Sunday.

"I hadn't thought of selling it," replied Corbett. He had not made any plans. The hide was still down with Lewis. "I might. What would you do with an old flea-bitten rug?"

Myron, raising and dropping his eyebrows, grinned. "I would put it on the wall of the new bank!"

Corbett hated being impulsive, but this fact did not keep him from being impulsive. "Okay, so what you offering?" He would sell the hide to Myron no matter the offer. Myron had helped Corbett in so many ways.

"Thirty silver dollars!" Myron was doing business, so he was serious. Corbett leaned back, away from Myron, and studied him carefully. *Thirty dollars.* "You in?" asked Myron.

"Oh, I'm in. Is the hide made of gold or something?" The realization was coming to Corbett that he was to be the proud owner of thirty silver dollars.

"Good. I'll have Lewis deliver it to me when it is ready."

With the heavy rain having precluded the afternoon recess out of doors, the students were not at all unhappy. The seats were arranged for wider aisles. Mr. Jones's desk was pushed all the way against the slate chalkboard.

"Is Angela playing?" asked one of the little girls.

"I think everyone is playing!" said Angela with a bright smile aimed at her little friend. Then she looked at Mr. Jones, waiting in the corner for the field of play to be secured. "Who goes first?"

Corbett covered his eyes with one hand as if hiding from his eager students and in deep contact with a mysterious being. "I choose Mike, Chapoke, and Margaret!" Cheers and squeals went up for Margaret. The older girls and Ernie did not often play, so to have them play today was thrilling.

"Okay!" hollered Corbett. "Heads down and thumbs up!" It would be and had been embarrassing to cheat, so the students at their seats even closed their eyes. The chosen three moved silently throughout the room, seeking out a victim. Once they had one located, they pushed down on the victim's thumb.

"Heads up!" Corbett enjoyed the closeness of the group. Margaret and June mothered the little ones as if their own. "Stand up if you got touched!"

Jenny, Denise, and Ernie all stood.

"Ernie!"

"I think it was Mike!" Chapoke, who was supposed to be quiet until all three had been picked, jumped up and down in joy. She had tricked one of the big ones!

"Well, so now you know whom Chapoke picked!"

"Jenny, how about you?"

"Mike!"

"And Denise?"

Denise hoped it was Margaret. She idolized Margaret. She could not imagine Margaret picking her, so she said, "Mike!"

"Okay, Mike, whom did you touch?" Mike took his hand and moved it back and forth like a wand, pointing at the two girls. "Jenny!"

"Well then, Margaret, whom did you touch?"

"Denise," said Margaret, smiling broadly at her little friend.

Chapoke and Margaret both got to stay in the front of the room and pick again. Jenny replaced Mike, and Denise sat. The rest of the day, Denise was in heaven. Margaret had picked her.

"I need a pound of those peppermints."

"Corbett, I think you're hooked," said John, reaching into the large apothecary jar where the mints were kept.

"I think you're right. Got it down at Martin's. Before every trip, I would snag a few."

John stopped, looking at Corbett with a questioning face. "Has the little Ludwig boy been at school?"

"Travis?" Corbett thought of the fourth grader, who had curly black hair, was big for his size, and was backward in his dealings with other students. "No. He has missed a lot. Haven't seen him for the last couple of weeks."

"May was in this morning and paid off her bill completely," said John, weighing the peppermints. "When I asked her how things were going, she said, 'Not good.' The part that has me wondering is that she said they had just sold their milk cow."

Corbett grimaced. "Who sells a milk cow with that many

young ones? I'd better ride out there and see what's going on. Maybe I can figure out a way to get him back in school."

John smiled and nodded. "Thanks, Corbett. Something's wrong."

The smells and his memories of the hot springs came and went as Corbett passed by. If his life had been normal, the dip with Geri would have been the highlight of Corbett's life up until that moment. As it stood, it was not bad.

The Ludwigs were one of a few homesteaders on this side of the crossing. As Corbett dropped into the homestead, he could tell that a good part of the farm was boggy with springs leaking out of the earth in many places. The house and barns sat on four to six acres of land, positioned above the swampy ground.

Corbett could see the family gathered outside under a tree near the barn. In front of them sat a buckboard with stakes at the four corners of the bed. Travis stood and walked up the lane, waving at the mule and rider. Travis had outgrown his pants, and the shirt looked more like what his father would wear. A quiet emptiness prevailed. The only animal in sight was an old roan mare.

"Hello, teacher," said Travis, seemingly concerned that his teacher had come to his farm.

"Travis, good to see you." Corbett smiled. "How have you been doing?"

"My father lost his arm." Travis needed to explain his absences. "We're movin' out." He looked as if he had done something wrong. He did not want to be in trouble with the teacher.

May rose as Corbett came to a stop under the same shade tree. Two tiny children and a baby lay on a quilt nearby. The mister was sitting in a rocking chair next to May. "Mr. Jones, can I help you?" It was obvious that she was tired. Her face and hands were covered in grease, and her dress was torn and showing leg up to her knee. "We're resting a bit," she said apologetically.

"I just came out to check on Travis." Corbett tried to lessen the stress that seemed abundant. "He is one of my best students."

"We are about to leave this country," announced May. "My husband lost his arm and is still quite ill." Corbett looked over at Irish Ludwig. He was frail and dying, thought Corbett. Irish's eyes were looking at Corbett but were not following Corbett's actions. He wiped away some spittle from the corner of his mouth with his kerchief. He had not blinked during his vacant stare at Corbett.

Corbett did not know whether to address Irish or not. Was he capable of conversation or just watching to see what might happen? "Sorry about your bad luck. I hope things will work out." Corbett did the best he could.

"He can't hear you," stated Travis. "We are going to take him back to his mama and papa in Kansas City." Corbett did not know a lot, but in the last three years he had learned about death—and Irish was dying.

Corbett turned to May. "When might you be going?"

"We would have left yesterday, but the back wheel is broken." May pointed to the rear wheel. The felly had escaped the steel band surrounding the wheel, taking two spokes with it. The axle was being held up by the other three wheels of the wagon.

"Let me lift the axle onto a stump and see if we can get the wheel off." Corbett handed Travis Ollie's reins and walked to the back of the wagon. May followed. On Corbett's third attempt, he lifted the axle high enough to slip the stump underneath.

"Thank you very much," whispered May, tears tracing their way down her tired and dirty face.

"Looks pretty bad to me." Corbett had seen worse buckboard

wheels in junk piles, but never still on a wagon. "Do you have another one?"

"I have been trying to get a wheel off that two-wheeled cart over there," answered May. "But I don't think it would work."

"No, I don't think so," commented Corbett.

"We have a little one on the old planter. It's iron and smaller."

"I'm going back to town. Maybe I can find one." Corbett looked at May. She was really in a fix. Three babies and a husband dying, the farm an afterthought. "Travis, you keep care of your mama and papa. I'll see if there's a wheel in Cedar Crossing." A last survey of the property by Corbett showed a forgotten garden and the belongings ready to be packed. His mind walked away from him. *Where will they dig the grave?*

As Corbett and Ollie crossed the cool waters of the crossing, Corbett's only thought was to find a used wagon wheel by the time school was over tomorrow. He hoped Buck or Otto could be found to direct his search. Relief showed on Corbett's face when two checker players came into view. The old men at play was a good sight indeed.

"How's the game going?" Corbett stayed on Ollie, thinking the conversation would go quickly.

Buck lamented, "He's cheatin' like a wild man."

"Buck, you know where I can get a back wheel for a buckboard?" Corbett realized that Buck was on the short list of two men who could help him. Otto was the other. "I was out at the Ludwigs'. They need one bad."

"How is Irish doin'? I heard they took it off at the shoulder," said Otto as he jumped two of Buck's black checkers.

"He's dying!" replied Corbett. He did not think he was lying.

"That can't be. He's just a young buck." Otto's surprised look stopped the game. "Back in the big war, just a few days after the amputation, we'd send them walkin' for home."

Buck entered the conversation. "He's had the damnedest luck. That homestead he got into is just a bog all year round. Now this."

"They're leaving as soon as they can find a wheel. She's aiming for Kansas City, where his folks are." Corbett kept seeing Irish's frail cheekbones and vacant eyes. "It's a four-footer for the back axle. If you find one, I'll probably try to buy it off ya." Corbett had done all he could. Both men were looking at each other, seeing just the problem, not each other.

The next afternoon, while June read the students a story, Corbett was thinking of the Ludwig wagon. No one could travel all the way back across the country as ill prepared as May was. Irish Ludwig would not even make it to Portland. Corbett was waiting out the clock so he could find a wheel and get back out to Irish's homestead.

Buck was not at the livery, and neither Otto nor Violet was at the smithy, Corbett was beside himself with anxiety. He knew both were busy this time of year, but he had hoped a wheel would be leaning against the hitching post. Alas, he'd found nothing. He had just himself.

All the worry did not go away when Corbett saw the Ludwig house. There were several wagons and horses tied about, and at the dry north end was a gathering. With all that help, the family might get on their way after all.

Mike Arnold, who had missed school, was sitting on the tailgate of his parents' surrey, idly moving his feet back and forth.

"Are you all right?" asked Corbett, who thought the Ludwigs ought to feel good about all the help getting them off.

"Mr. Ludwig died last night. We've been here the whole time." His eyes were tired and red.

What response do you give to a fifth grader who has just said that? Corbett could think of none. He tied Ollie to Ludwig's wagon, which had yet to be fixed, and started the walk toward the crowd. They were dispersing. Men were donning their hats, and the women were tight to their hankies.

"Corbett, you were right," said Otto, walking with Buck back to the house. "We came out early with a wheel, and the Arnolds were already here." Otto pointed to Preacher Arnold. "He just finished talking over Irish—a good talk too."

"That girl is in the worst fix I've ever seen," said Buck, putting his left foot on a spoke of the broken wagon. "Otto and I can get the wheel on and get her on her way, but with three babies and young Travis, how far could she get?"

Violet entered the group. She had spent much of the day with May. Corbett knew her to be softhearted from her interactions with the Native twins. She loved them, and they adored her. "May is going to take a nap. Alice will watch the babies." Violet looked at the three men, all problem solvers, none with answers. "The trip to Kansas City was to get Irish back home. She said she has a sister in Portland who might take them in."

"Why didn't she say that sooner?" asked Otto. Her sister was obviously the answer. "Why did she wait to tell us about her sister?"

"Women take care of their men. She followed Irish all the way out here by wagon," said Violet, a little peeved at her husband. "She would take him all the way home if necessary." Corbett was impressed with the answer. Many women, over the years, left their families and churches and set aside their own well-being to follow their men west.

"So, Portland is where she wants to go?" Otto was trying to come up with a quick solution. "We could get her down there."

"The problem is that May's sister and her husband are just getting by themselves."

"And there's no one up here to take them in for more than a few nights," said Buck, holding up his hand for silence. "Let's get the wheel on while May is resting, and then go with what she wants to do."

That evening, the shade of the big maple expressed itself across the wide grassy area next to the house. Women from the church had food spread on a quilt. The murmurings were quiet. May was nursing the baby. The men, showing due respect, were in the barn, seeing what could be sold quickly to aid May.

"A few hours ago, we prayed for Irish's deliverance. Now we must pray for May and her family. She has decided to go to her sister." May's pride made it nearly impossible for her to face those on whom she now must depend. "Sunday, we will take an offering to help provide for May and the children. It's a new start for her."

"I don't know if this is the right time, but if need be, I will take May and the young'ns to Portland in this wagon," said Buck, standing with his hat in hand, "then pay her sixteen dollars for the wagon, then bring it back up here." Everyone knew the wagon was worth no more than ten dollars. The gesture was appreciated by all.

Otto stood. "I have seen some things in the barn here that I can sell and get the money down to May." A churchwoman Corbett did not know said she was going to ask around for diapers and quilts for the family.

Corbett knew what he was going to do, but selfishness on his part was making it difficult. He knew what it was like to be a young boy, poor and lonely. Corbett scanned the area and found Travis sitting with Mike Arnold. Unfocused and looking at the family home, Travis was evidently grappling with the fact that his childhood had disappeared.

"I want to help," stated Corbett, stepping forward. "Not long ago, Myron paid me thirty dollars for my wolf hide. I wasn't expecting it and didn't earn it. I'm not too far into the church teachings, but I think I was given the money to pass on to someone in need." Corbett walked through the small circle gathered and handed May a small sack, kissing her on the cheek.

The days were getting longer. The sun was pushing through more often, and the rain was done for the spring. Corbett and Ollie were nearly to Joe's farm, where they noticed a change had taken place in the field between the spring below the house and the house itself. It was plowed. The dark volcanic soil had been turned completely over. Corbett could see where Joe had burned out three more massive stumps. A fire glowed far down in the roots of another.

"What do you think of that?" Joe's toothless grin went from ear to ear. He stood at the small corral where he kept the horse that pulled the wagon with the boys to work every day. Robert was not in sight. Corbett knew Ernie would be along directly. He'd seen Ernie and the girls go into Grandma's right after school.

"Looks to me that you are getting a little uppity," replied Corbett. "When did you get a plow?"

"Winter loggin' puts a lot of hours on ya." Joe stepped forward to greet Corbett. "I used the money to buy the plow over there, new." The plow lay on its side. The shine on the blade came through, even when muddy.

"Come, sit. Robert's getting a jar of wine."

Corbett looked at Joe's shirt, which was covered in sawdust, not mud. "Joe, I see that you're back at the mill." Joe examined his shirt, scattering some sawdust away with his hand.

"How soon can I get Ernie back? There's some money to be had." Joe sipped away his thirst. "Do you think this year of school has done him much good? He missed out on a lot of work."

"I'm thinking for the long haul," answered Corbett. "He's gained confidence. He's always been in the background, with you and Robert ahead of him by a few years." Corbett observed how that bit of truth was taken. "You ought to be proud of him. He is going to be a good man. He will need more responsibilities to bring it out."

"Yeah, you and Edith are probably right. Look at Robert over there checking out our stump fire. He's the hardest worker I know, but what girl will ever see him, 'cept Friday nights? And them girls aren't the right ones anyway. He'll be fifty and lonely before you know it."

"Look at the way he combs his hair. There's a girl out there somewhere."

"We appreciate you lettin' Margaret work in the afternoons at the mercantile. I know she wants to get out of here, and you've given her some tools to do so."

"Oh, she's a dandy, Joe. She'll make it."

"Myron wants to meet her and June next week. A summer job maybe, I don't know. How is the wine?"

"I'm generally a beer man, but this is tasting mighty good. You didn't think I rode all the way out here just to see you?" Corbett smiled. "It's the wine I came for."

The first annual end-of-school picnic was taking place, the attendees filling the grassy area around the school. New bonnets and light-colored blouses gave the scene a carnival-like feel.

"Looks like you made the year," said Buck, passing by with two plates of fried chicken, potato salad, and corn bread.

"Believe I did, Buck. I'm celebrating more than the students are."

Corbett scanned the grassy yard. Buck was sitting down with his longtime friend Grandma. Maybe forty or fifty were present, and he knew them all. The Arnolds had just about adopted Chapoke and Chapana. Denise had taken to them the first day.

The older students were where they always were, at the picnic table under the tree. June and Margaret, as well as Ernie, would be gone. Angela, Edna, Jenny, and Mike would be the picnic table group for next year. With all the construction and predictions, the school might even double in size.

Myron, Otto, and John would still be the cornerstones of the community. Geri and Ida, forever friends and always talking, would probably have an easier year next year. Corbett saw Ruth and Lewis sitting in the grass, drinking lemonade and watching Leo chase a butterfly. Corbett had never seen Ruth looking lovelier. She had grit and would someday leave her parents and the tannery behind and ride off with Leo, looking for a better future.

Geri looked marvelous. Her short blonde hair, her pleasingly petite frame, and her white peasant top and blue skirt made the beautiful day brighter. She and Corbett sat on the school steps and watched. It had been less than a year since the opening of the school, yet everyone treated the occasion as if it were a tradition many years ongoing.

"I really feel bad for June and Margaret," said Geri. "This pond doesn't have many fish in it. Their parents don't want them chasing after a logger, but there's not much else. You and a couple of others—that's it."

"For a town making its mark as a logging town, the young fellows shouldn't chase after your bar girls, and the town girls are off-limits." Corbett had stated the paradox: love was in the air, but the air was thin. "I sure like being part of this town and having a pretty barmaid as my best friend and older sister."

"Can you imagine the excitement these little kids will be part of the next few years? I know it's been a few weeks since May Ludwig moved on, but I'm thinking of getting on the school board."

"You haven't got any kids," Corbett reminded her. "And you own a bar."

Geri, with sparks coming from her eyes, said, "Who do you think is paying your way, mister?!" Her look was hard to read, but Corbett knew he had stepped in it. How badly, he was about to find out. "Grandma and I watch the first recess every day while having our coffee. We both wish that we had a child of our own to watch, but we don't. So we watch all of them."

Corbett had not known that nerve was there. "Sorry, Geri. I wasn't thinking."

"Damned right you weren't thinking. You want to know why I want on that board?" Corbett did not want to guess; he wanted to retreat. "Because if next year you even make a sideways glance at that vulnerable little Angela, I will fire your ass!" She smiled and winked.

Women! thought Corbett. *There must be a book of rules somewhere on how to understand them. And I must find one soon.*

Later, with his feet on his teacher's desk, Corbett felt satisfaction. He was finally a man. He thought he might travel down the coast for a good part of the summer. What would Ollie think of the ocean? Then reality eased its way into the conversation he was having with himself. He had money to survive the summer. That was all. Was Corbett that much like his father, always starting anew with an empty plate? In the morning, he would get up early enough to catch Joe and see if he could get on at the shingle mill.

15

As Ollie obligingly headed back to the corrals at the crossing, Corbett was chuckling at Leo's crazy antics. When Ruth tried to feed him something he didn't like, he would cross his arms, turn his head away, and say, "No! No! No!" Corbett chuckled some more. Ida again had asked him to stay for supper, but he knew they were just barely making it with their food supply, so he declined the invitation. Lewis was very spontaneous with Ida, always playing around, sometimes embarrassing Ruth. Corbett's judgment was that families could have a good life even if they were just getting by.

Two, then two more, muffled shots rang out ahead. Two typical rhythms of shots were common in and around the crossing. Any deer wandering out of the woods in view of the town was literally free game to any of the town's inhabitants. There would be a first shot to down the animal and, a minute later, the kill shot if needed. The second rhythm was Otto either practicing his shooting himself or selling a new model to someone else. Several shots, equal in their distance apart from one another. This seemed different though. There was a fifth shot. Something was wrong.

Corbett booted Ollie into a trot. After slipping over the last rise, Corbett could see down the main street, where he observed two horsemen riding hard in his direction. A bullet whistled by, not by the riders. It was Otto shooting at the riders from the center of Main Street. Corbett ducked down behind Ollie's neck. As he looked again at the horsemen, one stopped and, with a pistol, fired at Corbett. It was Willie.

The riders turned into the woods, riding along an old path. Otto took one more shot before the horsemen disappeared. Ollie, sensing the danger of being shot at, had chosen to leave the road and run at full speed over, under, and around any brush and trees in the way. Corbett would have stopped Ollie earlier if he could have. Ollie was in firm control of the bridle bit, and in Ollie's opinion, Corbett was just along for the ride. The pair ended up in a clearing behind the town. Ollie was breathing hard and ready to run farther away from the shooting if necessary. Cussing and holding on had been the only avenues left to Corbett. Anyone watching would have concluded that Corbett had run. Corbett himself was thinking how best to kill Ollie. Every time Corbett needed Ollie to perform in a positive manner, Ollie thought otherwise.

Trotting down Main Street, Corbett's thoughts became centered on the mercantile. Everyone in town was milling around the front door. He piled off Ollie, tied the reins to the saddle horn, and shooed the mule away. He knew Ollie would head to the corrals and then bitch and moan until someone opened his corral gate. Ollie was the most barn-soured animal Corbett had ever seen.

"They killed John, and Mildred is in there dying!" cried one of the women loudly, leaving the store. Corbett fought through the crowd to the back of the store. John lay on his back, his chest blood-soaked, his eyes looking up at the ceiling. To the left, Alice Arnold and Grandma were pressing cloths against the holes in Mildred Watkins's body. Corbett knew the colors of death: pink, alive; white, dying; and blue, dead. Mildred was a pale blue. Corbett left the building, trying to process the deaths. How many dead faces would he have to see before it would be enough?

"Corbett, I'm going after them. I saw them head down the Missionary Trail," said Otto, surrounded by two young bucks with guns in their hands. "Pete and Jimmy are the only men coming so far. The stupid bastards must not know much about the trail. It will tear them up and spit them out." Otto looked at Corbett with some apprehension. He did not want to be turned down. He needed Corbett to go. "Corbett, can you come?" The request was one of need. Corbett took it as a compliment, knowing he would have gone anyway, asked or not. "Got a gun?"

"No."

"Yeah, he does!" Myron Mason, running up to Corbett, handed him a holster containing a .32-caliber Colt, rarely used. Corbett turned to thank Myron. "You just get those sons of bitches!" Usually calm, Myron was angry, most evident from his eyes, which snapped with fire and resoluteness. Thirty years earlier, he would have been leading the posse.

"I've got a Winchester rifle that uses the same-sized bullet. I'll get it." Otto turned rapidly for his smithy hut. Looking back, he yelled at Corbett, "Bring the brown mule! You'll need him!"

Corbett began running down the street behind Otto, on past the smithy, to the corrals. Ollie was standing at the corral gate, ready to be let in.

"Ollie, we've got to go," said Corbett, grasping the reins from the saddle horn. Already Corbett's left foot was in the stirrup. The first several steps toward the street marked a battle of wills with Ollie crab-walking in protest. Corbett did not wear spurs, but a pair of sharp blows to Ollie's ribs with Corbett's heels ended the debate.

Within thirty minutes, Ollie was packed with a bedroll, a scabbard for the rifle, and saddlebags with food from Grandma's. Corbett was astounded at the quickness exhibited by everyone in preparation for the chase. Two hours prior, Corbett was looking forward to finishing Steven Crane's *Red Badge of Courage* in his room after supper. Now, he was part of a posse trying to capture—no, to kill—two murderers.

The face of John, solemn, staring at the ceiling, wondering why he had just been killed, was locked in Corbett's mind, sending him into a silent rage. John was such a fair man that some of the loggers gave him their pay on Friday to hold for the weekend, retrieving it on Sunday, rather than blowing it all on one weekend.

"Why are you taking so long?" asked Maxine Powell, nervous for the posse to leave. "You will never catch them at this rate!"

"They have maybe four more hours of daylight, and then they will be trapped on a bitch of a trail on top of a mountain. We'll get 'em!" Otto, a big man, turned his horse and headed south at a trot, his bulk dwarfing the saddle. Buck, standing in front of his livery, waving his lever-action Winchester above his head, shouted and waved them ahead. His anger was new and complete, but his old body was unable to saddle up and follow.

Otto stopped briefly at the edge of the forest for introductions. "Corbett, this here is Jimmy, and that one is Pete. Their steam donkey has a broken winch and is down for the day. We're lucky they were in town today. Good hands to have around," It was obvious they were brothers. Both were of average height and were heavily bearded. Of particular interest was the genetic gift to both men, large ears sticking out, quite noticeable. Jimmy was wearing a red flannel shirt.

Ollie took offense as the riders negotiated their horses around for handshakes. With his long ears folded back, he was going to kick himself a horse if they did not back off. All three horses, knowing the body language of an angry mule, danced about, adding a new dimension to the sharing of handshakes.

"My plan is to keep them at least an hour ahead. I don't want an ambush," said Otto quickly. "Let 'em sleep on top of the mountain without blankets or food." Otto led the way onto the trail, which was little more than a deer path. Corbett was behind him, with the two brothers bringing up the rear.

"Where does this trail go?" Corbett asked.

"If you stay on it, it rides the mountains all the way to Astoria," explained Otto. "If they get that far, they'll disappear."

"I thought we would run them down today," shouted Jimmy from the back. His idea of a posse was to have a grand chase through the woods with pistols and rifles blazing.

Otto, quite satisfied with his leadership, said, "We are going to walk them down. They will push their horses the rest of the day, then tie them up snug with no grass and probably no water. Tomorrow, between the trail wearing them out and a long, sleepless night, they will be ours if we play it right." Otto was visualizing his thoughts.

The trail was so tight that Corbett wished he had chaps, like the ones he used back in Greeley for brush popping. Fallen alders and a steady deployment of vine maples across the path made travel slow and tedious. Periodically they'd hear an old ax cut into a fir, blazed by a trapper or even the missionary, confirming that they were still on the trail.

"Just remember, those two up there are breaking trail for us," said Otto. "Tracking them—hell, a blind man could track them." Broken tree limbs and trampled blackberry canes led the way.

"Why would they try this trail?" Corbett could not believe how arduous and slow the travel was. Blackberry canes, an inch thick or more, spent their lives trying to close roads and paths made by human beings—and this path was full of them.

"They probably just heard it would get them to Astoria without anyone seeing them," replied Otto. "That was all they needed. Look, their horses are getting all cut up by the blackberry canes." Horsehair strands hung from a broken cane ahead of them.

"This trail we are on came about in the 1840s. Some trapper stumbled into an Indian village closed to any canoe traffic up from the traveled rivers, a wide flat valley hidden from a world that wanted to change them." Otto stopped to negotiate over another fallen alder. "Damn this trail!" Every little jump or steep rivulet added to their energy spent. "After a couple of years, some missionary, wanting a village to convert, turned the little village into his private sideshow. He brought in Christianity and smallpox, and now the remnants are dead or gone." Otto looked back to present his final point. "He moved on to find another village to convert."

Besides the weaving between the firs and hemlocks, the horses were tiring because of the constant lunging up a slope with rider on board or bracing themselves to go down another endless slope. White foamy sweat around the edges of the saddles and along the horses' necks where the reins rode back and forth were witness to the constant struggle to stay at altitude.

After three hours, Corbett noticed that Otto's push and eagerness were ebbing away as the sweat spot on his back grew larger. Nearly everyone in Cedar Crossing took it for granted that Otto was as close to being the law in town as anyone. Bar fights at Geri's were generally Otto's domain, and he knew guns. Otto's age, about fifty, had given him heavy legs and a bulge in front. It didn't show in Otto's everyday movements, but it did here.

As the sun faded to the west, dropping among the heavy forest canopy, Otto stopped. "We're going to have to stop here in this clearing. The horses are done. Jimmy, take your rifle and watch the trail ahead of us." Otto guided his horse off the trail into some tall grass. Corbett noticed Otto's horse was very tired, but not as tired as its sweat-soaked rider. Otto could just barely clear leather. He stood holding onto the fender of the saddle and the back cinch.

"Otto, you okay?" asked Pete, walking his horse in the same direction.

Corbett, tying Ollie some distance away from the horses, heard Pete and called to him. "Pete, everything all right?"

"Hell yeah, I'm all right!" snapped Otto. "Just fat and tired!"

"Well, if it's any consolation," lamented Pete, "I'm half your age and beat like a drum. My legs will be bowlegged for the rest of my life. This trail of yours is getting worse and worse. If those two are moving through this country faster than us, they must be some kind of cowboys."

"They're not," said Corbett, removing the saddle from Otto's horse. Just like the others, this horse's back was slick with sweat and was steaming in the mountain air.

Otto, sitting against a tree, took a long swig of water from his canteen, then two long breaths. "Boys, we got ourselves a problem. Jimmy, come on in." As Otto waited, Corbett sat down. For the first time in his life, he was wearing a holster. It did not sit as well as he did.

"I've put us in a bad position. They are just a ridge or two ahead of us and in worse shape than we are." Looking up through the trees, he said, "It will be dark in an hour. I thought they would've gotten further ahead than they are, being on the run and all."

"I don't understand," said Jimmie. "Isn't that good? I mean, we've caught up with them."

"Ever watch a snake that's trapped? It coils and attacks." Corbett thought of Munley and his wagon stuck among the rattlesnakes back in Colorado. After about it a second, he removed the memory from his mind.

"A gunfight up here would be hell. We would move forward

thinking they were still runnin', then, *bam*, them shootin' us down from behind all this brush and trees." Otto sipped from his canteen. "I just want to push them until they drop."

"As soon as they know we are right behind them, there's going to be a gunfight. They can't escape. Our horses are sweated down to nothing. Their horses have got to be worse. I was hoping to surprise them a day from now while they are asleep in some grass next to a stream."

"Don't you think they could be sneaking up on us before dark tonight?"

"Notice that I am watching that mule." Otto put out a slight smile. "If anything moves, that mule will hear it. If his ears hear something, grab your rifle and slide into the brush. Also, no fires tonight."

Late into the night, Corbett was tired but unable to sleep. He heard Otto, turning and restless, a few feet away. "How are you doing over there, Otto?"

"Still out of breath from the ride," said Otto in a tired, hoarse breath. "Sashaying around on horseback is one thing, but fighting through timber in a hurry is another. Your mule is the only one of us unaffected by this posse chase."

"You seem to like Ollie. Why did you sell her to me?"

"A mule's hoof is smaller than a horse's hoof." Otto looked over at Ollie. "Hard to do a good job of shoein' them. That mule there kicked me three times. Even bit me once." Although Corbett could not see it, Otto had a smirk on his face. "Probably the best animal in the country, but me and him don't see eye to eye."

Just an hour or two later, "Corbett!" was the whispered cry. Corbett awoke and grabbed his Winchester. He could neither see anything nor hear anything but Otto's labored breathing.

"Otto, what did you hear?"

"It's me, Corbett," mouthed a breath-starved Otto. "I can't breathe." Corbett crawled the few feet to Otto, his closest hand touching Otto's bedroll. It was drenched in sweat.

"How can I help?" asked Corbett, his eyes a little better adjusted to the modest bit of light beginning to brighten the darkness.

"Somebody put an anvil on my chest. Can you go over to the stream and bring me a cold rag?"

"I don't see anything," murmured Jimmie as he closed the distance between him and Otto in a bent Indian-style approach. "What did you hear?"

"Wake Pete. Get him over here." Otto, sitting forward, bent at the waist, was working for every breath.

Three minutes later, a council of sorts was convened.

"I can't go on," Otto said softly. "You fellows go on if you want."

Corbett was the youngest, but he already had assessed the brothers. They seemed hours behind in changes and decision-making. "We'll get you back." The brothers seemed satisfied with the decision and were soon ready to lift Otto onto his horse.

"These boys can get me back," Otto said, focusing on Corbett. "You follow them. It'll be easy. They will either drop off to the south, Young's River country, or follow the path to the right, the Columbia." Otto was out of breath. He inhaled deeply to recover so he could continue with his instructions. "Follow 'em off, and contact the sheriff wherever they land."

The morning sun broke as Otto, Jimmy, and Pete were finally packed and on horseback. The question was becoming moot: Was Otto going to make it back astride the saddle or over the saddle? Corbett was not betting on his making it back. Otto motioned to Corbett to bring Ollie closer. "If they try for Astoria, just bring back their bones!"

Corbett cautiously began to follow the Missionary Trail, now a path. With the morning sun at his back, he knew anyone looking back would be squinting into the brightness of sun, giving him a small advantage. Otto had been right: Corbett found Willie's camp less than a mile from where the posse had camped. It was nothing special, just stamped-out grass where the horses had been tied. Corbett was about to move on, when he noticed bloodstains against the white background of alder bark where the horses had been tied. One of their horses was bleeding badly either from its shoulder or its chest.

At this high elevation, among thousands of identical trees, the forest floor seemed nearly empty. The sun could not get through to feed the heavy brush and deciduous saplings. Just ferns and mosses grew. Corbett knew that he was close. Ollie's ears were pointed ahead. Corbett felt a new eagerness in Ollie's gait. He was depending on Ollie as another set of eyes. Soon a deep ravine pulled the trail upstream to stay at elevation. Dropping straight down was possible, but the climb out would be almost impossible. The detour the path took upstream lessened the depth of the ravine. The narrow, winding path was steep and difficult for Ollie—and treacherous as well.

They finally crossed the stream that had worn its way down from above, when several shots rang out farther up the crooked path, coming from around an outcropping, out of sight. Ollie almost fell off the steep embankment. One hoof slipped down through the soft edge of the trail, but then the mule recovered. Corbett pulled out his pistol. His accuracy with a handgun was like that of most men, all talk. If a target was more than fifty feet away, luck would be the determining factor. The Winchester rifle would be unwieldy. Ollie was another variable Corbett could not depend on. Whatever was ahead, Corbett felt better on the ground, on foot, leading Ollie. As he snuck around the rocky bend, he heard screaming.

Tug was writhing in pain. A few feet off the path, he was not aware of Corbett's approach. A horse lay crumpled and quiet next to Tug. Corbett dropped to a knee. Willie was there somewhere.

Without moving, Corbett called out to Tug, "Where's Willie?"

Tug, surprised to hear a voice, said, "Help me. Oh God, help me!"

"Where's Willie?"

In extreme pain, Tug replied, "His horse gave out. He shot it, then the son of a bitch shot me and took off with my horse! The bastard shot me. Oh God!" Tug tried to sit up but failed. "Don't let me die!" Then came more moaning.

Corbett's first thought was of quick action to step forward and attend to Tug. But what if Willie was finally aware of Corbett's presence and was waiting just yards ahead?

"Did he ride or walk off?"

"Hell, he didn't even change saddles," said Tug, trying to stand. "Just jumped on and took off."

Corbett saw Tug standing and trying to hold together what remained of his right elbow. Corbett noted that the blue flannel shirt was the same one Tug had worn the night of the big poker game. The closer Corbett got, the more the left rolled-up sleeve showed a dangling forearm and hand. Ollie was not getting closer. Either Tug or the shot-up horse had put him off. Corbett tied Ollie and hobbled him over to a red cedar. He did not need Ollie to escape and run all the way back to his corral in Cedar Crossing.

Tug's gun had fallen near the dead horse, but Tug was not in the frame of mind or in good enough shape to get into a gunfight. Corbett retrieved the weapon and put it in his saddlebag. While making room for the gun, he discovered a gift, probably from Geri. A metal flask lay half buried. Corbett surmised that Geri thought

Corbett might forget the most essential item in any posse chase, whiskey.

"Half now, half later." Corbett gave Tug a good swallow. Tug, head back, was relishing the drink, when alcohol struck the torn nerves of his elbow. Corbett had poured a goodly amount on the bloody arm. The scream grew even louder as Corbett took off his belt and cinched it tight just above the bloody elbow. Whether it was the alcohol or lack of blood, Tug's scream became an animalistic shriek as he reached with his good arm for the flask.

Over the screaming, Corbett shouted, "If you're alive when I get back, you can have the rest!" Ollie made boarding difficult, backing away rapidly from the man with the dangling arm.

Ollie and Corbett crept forward slowly, bringing Corbett's greatest fear to bear, the fear of cowardice. He was not a gunman, although it seemed that every two years or so, somebody shot at him. Corbett wanted to do what Otto had instructed, follow but do not confront. He never shot either gun; he would get ambushed sure. No one would know if he had surrendered to the call of a coward and turned back. His blood rose. The anger at himself could only be satisfied in one way.

Corbett's teeth were clenched. The pot was going to be brought to a boil as soon as Corbett could make it happen. He recklessly bolted forward, the rifle in his hand, now ready to kill. Willie and his horse had left the same signs to follow: hoofprints in the grass, broken twigs, and fallen branches. Ollie was looking far ahead, nervous and jumpy.

From just a few feet away, Willie emerged from behind a tangle of vine maples and shot twice. Ollie turned quickly, his body slipping out from under Corbett, whose rifle, hat, and body tumbled to the ground.

Although unhurt, Corbett was thoroughly stunned—and at the pleasure of the scratched and weary killer.

"Don't move or I'll kill you!" The gun was aimed at Corbett from no farther away than ten feet. Willie, nervously eyeing Corbett's rifle, edged toward it. "Don't move!" Corbett knew he could never draw his pistol fast enough to shoot Willie. He had been had. As Willie took small measured steps to the Winchester, a thought ruminated through Corbett's mind. Then it hit him: Willie was bluffing. His gun was empty. He needed the rifle.

Corbett made for his pistol. To him, it seemed to take forever to clear the pistol from the holster. Willie ran the final steps to the rifle, but it was too late. Corbett Jones completed his task with one shot. Corbett rose from the ground. He wanted to rant at the dying man but did not do so. Watching as Willie took his last breath, he reflected on the moment's events. He had killed a man, a sorry excuse for a man. How should he feel? Corbett knew what it was like to be on the other side, victimhood, especially when thinking of Ajai, his mother, Nick, John, and Mildred. This shooting did not resurrect them, but it did give Corbett's memories a bit of closure.

To Corbett's surprise, Ollie was in residence behind some leaves of a small alder, waiting, watching. Together, they rounded up Tug's horse. Corbett was in a fog and could not shake it. Should he load Willie on the horse and spend a day and a half getting him back to the crossing? Maybe he should do like in the old days, cut off his ears and return home with them as trophies.

Corbett's actions, without thought, took over. After walking around the body several times, he shouldered the body and flopped it across the horse's saddle between the horn and cantle. The horse moved little. As long as it could finally eat its fill, it did not care. Corbett cut one of the reins of the bridle of Willie's horse and tied

Willie on like cargo. That done, his composure returned. He had killed a murderer and was taking him in.

Five minutes later, Corbett saw Tug, newly positioned, leaning back on Willie's dead horse. Tug's head was down, unmoving, his right arm shot to hell, with a belt tightly affixed above the bloody mess.

"Tug, you alive?" said Corbett, walking toward him with his canteen in one hand and the whiskey flask in the other. Tug's head jerked a couple times before he stabilized it. "Here, drink this." Tug drank thirstily, water dripping off his beard.

"Where's the damn whiskey?" Corbett picked up the end piece of the belt. Lifting Tug's upper arm, the lower arm barely following, he again poured alcohol onto the inflamed tissues.

Tug groaned and strained but did not utter a sound.

"There's quite a bit left," warned Corbett, but Tug emptied the flask in several long pulls.

Corbett had been thinking while taking the short trip back to Tug. If Tug were still alive, he would have to build a travois. He found two poles, of which one end of each would be put through a stirrup and tied off. He then cut the cinches of the saddle of the dead horse and pushed the saddle over. By luck, the saddle blanket was a double-folded wool Native blanket just large enough to serve as the bed of the travois. He cut the reins of the dead horse to use for tying the blanket on. A spur-of-the-moment thought caused Corbett to cut the leather fender off the saddle as well.

Ollie did not like the chest protector Corbett had made for him but did not argue. Whether he knew the reason that the trail back caused him less pain, because of the leather fender blocking the sharp barbs of the blackberry canes, he did not say.

Corbett figured the way back would take at least a day and a half. The travois would have to be dealt with, lifting it over or around fallen logs that the horses merely stepped over, slowing the whole process. The one feature that made things better was that two horses and a mule had already broken the trail coming in. Indeed, it was much better heading back.

While Corbett dozed, Ollie led the way toward home. As the hours passed, Corbett stopped for water twice. Tug, who seemed dead the rest of the time, drank heartily. Corbett did not like the way flies were gathering around Tug's sleeve-covered elbow, but there was little he could do about it. The only bit of good news was that the offshore breezes were billowing overhead, relieving some of the impact of the sun's rays.

The day was nearly gone. Corbett would have to stop soon; he would not make it home today. His hips were stiff and in pain. Three hard days in the saddle had caused Corbett to decide to get out of the saddle and walk more. Corbett's head was down, watching the endless path, when Ollie stopped behind him, nearly jerking the lead rope out of Corbett's hand.

The mule's ears were forward; its eyes, on the forest ahead. The path trailed into a grove of alders just before reaching a stream. Corbett tugged at the rope, but Ollie would not budge. Finally, Corbett got the idea. There was smoke in the air. Corbett cleared his head and gathered himself. Ollie moved forward cautiously. Corbett, with rifle in hand, advanced toward the smoke.

"Hello, the camp!" shouted Corbett. Several figures appeared from the center of the grove. The sun setting behind him gave him the advantage. He could tell by the thin frames, seemingly identical, that the brothers had returned to the trail. He closed the distance, then shouted, "This trail is gettin' a little crowded, don't you think?"

"Hell yes," replied Jimmy. "We have tramps coming through all the time!"

As Corbett rode into camp, he immediately became aware of the posture of the camp. Perhaps it was a militia encampment. A tight rope had been strung between two trees, and a large brown tent sprang forth. A picket line held four horses. A separate one, a few yards from the first, showed three pack mules tied. Around the fire were four fold-up chairs, and barely visible inside the tent was at least one wooden cot.

A young uniformed man, probably a soldier, and the brothers, Jimmy and Pete, came to pause next to the travois and the body draped across the saddle. The astonishing sight froze the men.

"Which one is on the travois? He still looks alive." The soldier, small and broad, exhibited signs of concern. He tilted his head downward to examine a bloody sleeve. Tug's head was turned and lying against the wool saddle blanket, motionless, unaware of those viewing him.

"Name's Tug." Corbett checked the lettering on the soldier's shirt, where his US Marshal deputy's badge stood out. So, he was not a soldier, but he acted like one. "Willie shot him and then stole his horse. I hope he made it. He has really suffered." Jimmy, or was it Pete—whichever was not wearing the red shirt was Jimmy—tapped on Tug's good shoulder. Tug responded, lifting his head slightly, then letting it flop down again.

The deputy said, "Help me get him to a cot so I can work on him." That sentence alone took a measure of stress off Corbett. What do you do when an arm is shot off? Who knows, it might have been better to let Tug die back there rather than have him hang in for a month or so. It was the price Tug had paid to be Willie's friend.

The other brother was bent down, untying Willie from the saddle. He jumped back. "What in the hell did you do to him?" The blood, which could have run right after the shooting, followed gravity southward as Willie's head, hanging down from the saddle, collected the congealed black and red mass. It was seen most easily in Willie's face. Corbett bent down and peeked, then drew away. The bloated face was unrecognizable.

"That happens every time you slump one over a saddle." A tall, handsome man wearing the same style of shirt as the deputy, but wearing it much better, said, "You'll find that when you take him off the horse, he won't unbend. Rigor has set in." Sure enough, Willie remained U-shaped when a brother hauled him off the horse.

"I assume you're Corbett Jones. Come into camp so we can talk." The marshal, so it said on his badge, was already heading back toward the camp.

"I'm going to take care of my animals first," said Corbett casually, turning Tug's horse to a rivulet surrounded by foot-high grass and casting quietly down between two cedars on its trip to sea.

The marshal turned quickly. "The boys can take care of them," he said, insinuating that Corbett should follow.

"No, I'll do it. This gelding has been through a tough three days, and nobody can handle Ollie but me." Again he'd said this casually. The marshal's glare at Corbett would have melted a glacier. Corbett turned and walked toward the horse. He had planned, since loading Willie and the travois onto the bay, to rub the wearied animal down when finished. Ollie too. The others, the deputy, and the brothers stopped their doings and watched. Corbett, without knowing it, had challenged the authority of the marshal. They waited as the marshal stared at Corbett's back as he continued on to the water.

Corbett tied Ollie to a tree. After pulling his saddle, Corbett would rub him down, this after taking care of Tug's gelding. Corbett lifted the saddle from the tired horse, which was young and tall, about sixteen hands, and had suffered two rips in his skin from the chase. The one across the chest was fairly deep and was covered with dried blood and flies. Blackberry thorns also had slashed a cut high on one leg. While rubbing down the bay with a rag and cool water, Corbett saw a saddle sore on the horse's back. Corbett had never owned a horse, but if ever he were to do so, he would want one like this gentle but strong bay.

Done with the horse, he looked at Ollie. Twice Ollie had called to the mules tied across the camp. The mule was wearing out the grass where he was tied. Though it was nearly dark out, Corbett figured out the dilemma, namely that one the mules tied yonder was a Molly and was in heat. Ollie was beside himself, stamping and stirring. Corbett, unable to rub Ollie down, left him to deal with his love life with both a bridle and a halter tied short to the tree.

"Your Jack is going to cause us problems all night," said the marshal sarcastically as Corbett entered the circle of firelight.

"Yeah, I'm afraid so," said Corbett apologetically. "I guess it's been awhile for him." All but the marshal laughed.

"Marvin, get this fellow some coffee, and dish him up a plate of food as well." The deputy, seeming always eager to help, jumped to his assignment.

"I'm Marshal Harmon. I was sent up from Portland to capture these two murderers," the marshal said, relaying the information to Corbett. "I didn't realize we would get it done so quickly."

The brothers and Corbett, hearing the "we" part, each relived the maddening chase through the forest and the death of Otto. Corbett also relived the shootings of just today. The man was pious and was scraping Corbett's fur the wrong way, doing it as if it were his custom.

"They brought me in because of my experience in chasing down renegades these past few years. I was with Major Baker when he chased the Blackfeet into Canada." The marshal stopped and sipped at his coffee cup. All was quiet with everyone listening to him. "I was a sergeant at the time. Right after that, I switched over to the US Marshal's Office. Years later, here I am."

Corbett was right, this fellow was a pompous ass, all full of himself. What Corbett did not know was that Harmon had been a sergeant in the army ten years ago and, along with a drunken Major Baker, had attacked the wrong Blackfoot camp and killed over one hundred fifty women, children, and elderly people. It was called the Marias Massacre. When the truth finally came out, Harmon was drummed out of the military.

"Now, Corbett, tell me your story." Harmon adjusted himself in his chair as if he were a judge passing judgment on what was about to be said.

Corbett's story seemed short. How could he express the hardships of the chase, the anguish of watching Otto struggle with a heart attack, the crashing through thickets, and the stress of the constant, looming danger?

"So, Willie shot Tug, and soon after, you shot Willie. Is that correct?" Harmon studied Corbett's face with a touch of disdain.

"Yes," said Corbett, feeling the marshal was questioning his honesty and integrity. "If Tug ever comes around, you can ask him."

"I might have to." Harmon lifted himself above the rest.

"I guess then you have to decide whether you are going to believe a murderer or me." Corbett's voice was tight and unyielding. The brothers giggled. Corbett had taken the marshal to the woodshed.

"In the morning, you and your confounded mule will start out an hour behind our party. I don't want to hear that mule all the way to Cedar Crossing."

"Sounds good," said Corbett, approving. He rose to his feet and walked toward the deputy, who was scrubbing the metal plates with sand before dipping them into the stream to rinse. To the brothers, Marshal Harmon's angered face was better than a good drink. Harmon had not dismissed Corbett as he had presumed he would. The brothers knew Corbett's absence of protocol had lit Harmon's torch, but the marshal seemed unable to decide what to do about it.

"Marvin, I saw you were carrying some honey for the marshal's coffee. Is there a chance I could have a spoonful?"

"Got a sweet tooth, do ya, Corbett?" said Martin with a smirk.

"No. The bay over there got cut up pretty bad. I want to tend it tonight."

"With honey?"

"Yeah. I lived with a couple of Japanese women for a year. They used it all the time for cuts and such."

"Well, here's a spoonful." Martin smiled as he gave the honey to Corbett.

Harmon, who happened by as Corbett walked off with his honey, just stared.

The night was forever long between Ollie's dancing around and braying and Corbett's getting up to check on the ropes. Corbett thought about the hour delay for him and Ollie in the morning. If Ollie were to go first, he would be turning and dancing all the way home, an hour behind, and he'd be hard to hold back.

The morning came. The marshal's camp loaded up and left. Nobody was happy with Ollie or Corbett. Harmon led the group away from camp, followed by Marvin, who led Willie's and Tug's horses. Jimmy and Pete brought up the rear with the pack mules.

Corbett wished he had a bridle with a more severe bit, one that would help him control Ollie. Their pace was directly related to how far Corbett leaned back and put on the brakes. Both rider and mule were worn out after about an hour, at which time the walk became more pleasant.

Corbett turned onto the main road just below town about the same time the US marshal made a parade of his latest conquest. He, in the lead, slowly moved up the main street with two murderers in tow. Nearly all the townspeople had emptied into the street, some shouting and cheering. Buck and others shouted their hurrahs to the marshal.

Corbett eased Ollie to his corral, where he threw the saddle on a hitching post and watched Ollie wander to the creek for a well-deserved drink. The mule was done in.

Myron, from his viewpoint on his porch, had watched the parade. He walked to the corral. "That didn't take him long!" Myron shouted as he approached Corbett.

Looking to see Myron on his left, Corbett replied, "Yeah, he hasn't had a drink all day." Corbett did not mention that Ollie had been fighting Corbett's hold for a good portion of the day's ride.

"No, I mean the marshal," said Myron, impressed. Corbett had not seen the parade and did not understand why the marshal's quick campout the night before was so enthralling. Myron and Corbett turned their attention to the riders coming to the corrals.

"Now, that was a pile of cow manure!" one of the brothers said, fighting mad.

"No, sir, that ain't right!" said the other one. "All he did out there was boss us around while we were makin' camp. Corbett here brought Willie and Tug into camp. Harmon didn't have anything to do with it."

"That so?" asked Myron, looking at Corbett, baffled at the talk.

"Hell yes, it's true!" said the first brother. "He had better not be in Geri's tonight, 'cause I'm settin' things right tonight!"

"Why didn't you say something?" wondered Myron to Corbett. "There's a hundred-dollar reward for the two!"

"Strange, the bastard didn't mention that yesterday," said the first twin. "I'll bet he will try to get the reward for himself."

A fire was building in Myron's mind. "I'll take care of it." He started walking purposely toward the telegraph office.

"If there's a reward," called Corbett to Myron, still within earshot, "make sure Violet gets it!" Myron did not turn, but he waved to indicate that he had heard and understood.

Otto's funeral was as dignified as Cedar Crossing could make it. It was the first time Preacher Arnold's church was full, and he did not waste the opportunity to preach the Lord while honoring Otto as he lay in state. Alice sang and played the piano. Otto and Violet had been early to the crossing. Both were seen as benevolent and caring people, even though Otto's rough actions said otherwise.

As soon as the funeral was over, Corbett leaned toward Myron, in the seat ahead of him. "Who is that fellow?" He pointed with a nod and tilt of his head in the direction of a short man, partly bald, the rest of his hair in a well-kept ponytail. A dark silk shirt went well with his polished black suit coat. The gentleman's light olive skin, tanned to perfection, showed a few weathered wrinkles when he smiled.

"I think that might be. Yes, yes it is!" Myron noticed and remembered Louis, Michael's right-hand man, standing just behind him. "That's Michael. Remember, I told you about his vineyard. The little Indian girls come from there."

Louis and Michael waited until most of the mourners had left, then approached Violet. Little Chapoke and Chapana were at Michael's side. Condolences were always solemn and difficult.

"Madame Bogan, je suis désolée pour votre perte."

"Merci. Je te benisse," Violet said quietly.

"C'est si agréable de parler en francais. E'tait Otto French?"

"Il était beaucoup irlandais." She smiled.

Corbett and Myron leaned in to ask Louis, "What are they saying?"

"They are happy to be speaking French. And Otto was Irish."

"O'u en France?"

"Nouveau Bordeaux. Je me brûle la peaudans le vignoble."

"Ah, je suis alsacien. Beaucoup de bon vin."

"Now they are talking about the French wine country they came from."

"S'il vous plait, vivre a ma vigne. Chaque a besoin d'une femme."

Louis's eyes opened wide. "He just asked her to live at his vineyard. He said it needs a woman who can speak French!"

"Merci beaucoup. Je vais y réfléchir."

"Oh my," Louis quickly whispered. "She said she would consider it. Ai yai yai!"

"Les enfants adorent la grand-mere!" said Michael. "Au revoir, ma jolie!" Then he kissed her hand.

"The little girls are like their grandmother. Goodbye, sweet woman," said Louis quietly.

Not every funeral ended in that manner.

16

Thank God for Myron Mason, thought Corbett. "That was quite a confab," said Corbett, watching out from the schoolhouse window at four silk-top-hatted men boarding an expensive surrey. Myron was sitting at the teacher's desk looking over some formal papers. The three girls were whispering in chairs next to one of the windows. They had done well listening to the men negotiate. Margaret sat between June and Edna, her fingers interlaced throughout the two-hour proceedings. Corbett sat with them as well, but his influence was not nearly as important. Rearranging the chairs on his way back to Myron, Corbett wondered how all this would have worked out had Myron not been involved.

"It looked to me that you are quite the negotiator."

"Well, I think we did all right. Even though the damned vultures contacted the girls just two days after John's and Mildred's funerals, it's probably turned out the best for June and Edna. They don't live there anymore, and June won't go into the store unless you or I are there."

"When will they take over?"

"Thursday."

"They were sure taken aback when you said you were negotiating with the girls yourself to buy the place."

"These railroad top hats are used to just running over the top of anybody they deal with. Just look at the section of land that they're tearing up just across the river. They got it from the state. You can see how they're going to use it, for the roundhouse and log landing." Corbett knew Myron was beginning to come down from the emotional high of dealing face-to-face with the railroad honchos. "They not only want the logs, but also Cedar Crossing as a company town, and Watkins's Mercantile as the company store.

"You girls, come on up!" Myron and Corbett arranged chairs for the three. "Thursday, it's theirs." June began to weep openly. "Edna, if you want anything out of your house or the store, let your sister know so we can get it out for you." Edna had not returned to the store since the shooting, staying with her sister in a room at the boardinghouse. "Corbett and I will be there every day to help you and Margaret finish things up."

A week after the murders, June and Margaret had reopened the merc. Corbett and Myron were in and out, but the young women had worked there long enough. The bookkeeping skills they'd learned from keeping Corbett's books made them quite competent.

"Does June have to go back?" asked Margaret. "This is just too hard on her. If Mr. Jones will help, I can close out the accounts, and maybe he can do inventory." Corbett nodded. He had been over there most every day anyway.

"I agree. She needs to spend time with Edna, maybe figure out what they are going to do next," stated Myron in a calm, sympathetic voice. "June, you and Edna now have money, quite a lot of money." June broke down once again.

Geri sat alone, waiting for morning coffee with Corbett, who had yet to arrive. The arrival of so many people into town had changed the place considerably. The railroad was painting the exterior of the new station. The dirt scrapers across the crossing had brought in a dozen more workers to the bar last evening. Geri surprised herself by appreciating the bar that was doing business down the street, the Landing. It had taken pressure off her bar. They did not have the same type of girls; they sold cheap, watered-down liquor; and they seemed to attract a lower class of drunk.

Finally, Corbett came into sight. Geri could not believe how manly he seemed, wide-shouldered and tall. "Is that dirt from yesterday?" asked Geri with a frown.

"I believe it is," replied Corbett, looking down at his dirty knees. Having coffee with Geri these late summer mornings was special. He wondered what it would have been like to have a relaxed coffee with his mother just once, but the situation was always too stressed, and she was always too tired.

"You don't usually get this dirty," stated Geri, waiting for the cinnamon to cool and the butter to melt.

"I'm digging a new outhouse for the school. It's either dig out the old one or dig a new one and move the two-holer over it."

"Are you saying your students are full of it?"

"They were. That's the problem."

"Let's move on to something more important." Geri leaned in. "I saw you and Margaret working pretty close together closing down the merc."

"And?"

"You going to let her go?"

Corbett leaned back. Geri always toyed with his mind.

"You mean Margaret and me?"

"What else do think I am talking about, digging outhouses? You've thought about it. You've had to. She's only three years younger than you."

"Oh, I love being around her. She's very special, but she's going to need a man who rides a better mule."

"Better mule, my ass! Every girl and woman in this town has thoughts about you."

"I admire everything about her, but I don't love her or want to hold her!"

"Kind of an older brother sort of thing?"

"No." Corbett deliberated. "Maybe just her teacher."

That afternoon, Corbett looked out from his waist-high hole behind the school to see Preacher Arnold leave the telegraph office at a run. It was not ten seconds before the school bell began to ring and continue to ring. Corbett and others took it as an emergency.

Mr. Arnold avoided any questions, concerned only with the ringing of the bell. Except for the robbery and shooting at the mercantile, Cedar Crossing had never seen so many people gathered, townspeople and railroaders closely mixing in with the same tight crowd.

"I know I am not supposed to read you someone else's telegraph, but you need to know!" The preacher, usually quiet and soulful with his congregation, was shouting loudly. "Negotiations have ended. The Union Pacific is bankrupt!"

There were murmurs and questions. After a pause, Arnold shouted for silence. "All work is shut down. All railroaders are to receive their final pay Friday at noon at the new station across the street."

Corbett and Myron found themselves together at the back of the milling crowd.

"Could this be right?" asked Corbett, thinking of the many railroaders working at the crossing and also of the men laying rail nearly to Cedar Crossing.

"I've been trying to keep up with it in *The Oregon Weekly*. Banks and railroads seem to be their own worst enemies. The railroaders borrowed on speculation, and the banks gave the money to them on speculation. Now they are all broke." Myron lowered his head then shook it slowly from side to side. "Cedar Crossing will disappear off the map."

"The school will stay open, don't you think?"

"The merc will be closed. So will both bars. And all the money the railroad brought in will disappear. No, the school won't survive. No money to keep it going." Myron glanced at Corbett. "I could be wrong."

A crash caused everyone to look toward the new, never used railway station. One of the railroad painters had thrown a paint bucket through one of the front windows. Then a new conflict was developing at the mercantile. From what Corbett could see, the new manager and employees of the mercantile had locked the front door and gone down to Geri's to drink, leaving customers standing at the door.

"Is she waving at you or me?" asked Myron. Geri was frantically waving at the pair.

"I think it's me!" said Corbett, running across the street.

"They're going to tear the place up," screamed Geri. Corbett needed to hear no more. He pushed over a table just outside, under the flaps. With his foot, he kicked a leg loose and picked it up. He pushed through to the front of the bar, where a host of railroaders were angry, wanting to get drunk on free drinks and hoping to take their anger about the message of the day out on someone or something.

"Listen up!" yelled Corbett loudly. "This is not Geri's fault. If you want a beer, quiet down and settle down!"

"Up your arse, schoolmarm!"

Caught in a trap of his own making, Corbett knew a fight would break out into a brawl. Therefore, he believed, holding a chair leg and ready to swing, that what he was doing served no great purpose.

"You gonna beat me to death like you did poor old Willie?" asked the loudest logger. At the same time, he was measuring Corbett's size and strength and the chair leg, but most of all, he remembered Corbett was the one who had brought in Willie and Tug.

One of the railroad foremen pushed his way through the crowd of drinkers, saying, "Let's go down to the Landing. It's better anyway!" He pushed several of his men toward the door. The others followed.

As things settled, Corbett stood behind the bar with Geri. "Corbett, thank you. Weren't you scared?"

"Biggest bluff I ever ran," he said quietly. "That railroader bailed me out."

"Your reputation comes from dropping that pinhead right across there on the schoolyard, then tending to Willie and Tug." Geri went on, "Those railroaders still think Willie's blackened face was the result of you beating him to death. Your father made you tough, and your mother made you pretty." She rubbed his hair then kissed him on the cheek.

Ida and Ruth had come to town to sell three new leather holsters and shoelaces, only to find the mercantile closed for good. By chance, Corbett had come out of the schoolhouse, carrying a box, at about the same time.

"Mr. Jones!" called Ruth as Ida pulled the wagon near. "I'm scared. What happened?"

"Hi, ladies. They announced that the railroad went bankrupt and they're all done here."

"Forever?" Ida was crushed. "Where will I go to buy goods and to sell ours?" Both Ida and Ruth were wearing nice dresses. Ruth's dress was dark red with a high collar and frilly sleeves. Her hair was long, her natural curls showing the best of their highlights.

"Down off the mountain like you used to do."

"Oh no!" complained Ida, remembering their times of poverty. "Oh no, that will be dreadful!"

"We, I mean they, will still have school?" Ruth asked. Surely Corbett would stay.

"Nope, all done. I'm cleaning up inside today." The moment of silence seemed to last forever. "Ida, you and Lewis are strong. You will make out okay." That probably was not true, but Corbett did not know what else to say.

Ida looked wonderful. It seemed that the nice dresses had a meaning. Leo, standing in the back of the wagon watching Corbett, hoped Corbett would lift him up as he always did.

"I give up. Do you three always come to town looking this good? And does Lewis know?"

Ida brightened. "Today is Ruth's eighteenth birthday!" It seemed today that Ruth looked to be a woman, whereas only yesterday, when Corbett first saw her, she had looked to be a sad, broken child.

"If that's the case, then let me help such beauties down. Leo and I will escort you across the street to Grandma's!" Both were feminine to the touch, far different from the tough lives they lived.

With Leo devouring the frosted cinnamon roll—he had wanted the one with the candle—Ida asked Grandma the big question: "Are you going to stay?"

Grandma began to tear up. "Geri wants me to go down with her, but—"

Ida interrupted, "You mean Geri is shutting down? We can't have you two leave. We can't!"

"Yeah, Ida, she's all but gone." The sadness in Grandma's voice said it all. Grandma might be staying.

The rest of the conversation was a trip down memory lane. Neither Leo nor Corbett had been there in those days, so Leo, sitting on Corbett's lap, played a made-up blinking game with Corbett. Many of the events had occurred before Ruth had Leo, as she was just a young girl then. First came Buck and his homestead, then Grandma, then the mercantile, followed by the church, Myron Mason, Geri, and finally the school, all in a few short years.

There was a hard, continuous knock at the boardinghouse door. The misty morning had yet to rouse anyone. Myron, usually an early riser, had yet to awaken.

"Maxine, what's the trouble?" This was not like Maxine at all.

"Something has happened to Angela!" Her loud, emotional voice had Corbett on his feet and fighting with his boots, which he soon took off to put on his pants.

"Where is she?" asked Myron, putting on his shoes and wrapping his robe tighter around his body.

"I don't know. I think all night!" Myron hugged Maxine tight to keep her from shaking herself off the porch.

"Sit, sit," Myron said to his frantic neighbor. "I'll get …" Corbett had quickly stepped through the opened door.

Trying to catch up, he asked, "Where's Angela?"

"She's not in her bed! I don't know!" Maxine brushed back her unbrushed hair with her hand. Her eyes were following her thoughts of the evening past.

"I'll go upstairs and ask the girls if they know anything!" Edna and June, since the night after the shooting, lived in a room at Myron's boardinghouse. "June!" Corbett knocked and called again. "June, I need to talk to you!"

After a loud rustling, June opened the door. Her nightgown was wrinkled and sat crookedly on her body. One eye was still trying to rise to the occasion. "Mr. Jones?"

"Angela is missing!" Corbett sensed his voice was traveling through a fog. "Is Angela with you?"

"I haven't seen Angela in two days," answered June, now with Edna at her side.

"Well, think on it!" Corbett was already at the stairs. These woods were full of bad endings. Both he and Geri routinely saw small groups of unemployed railroaders and loggers coming and going all times of the day, sometimes at night too. They were looking, for what they were not sure, but a woman would work. Geri was fearful at the bar but kept Shorty nearby. Shorty was a sawed-off shotgun that Otto had made just for Geri. She never had used it, but were she to do so, she would not miss.

A concerned group began to form in front of the boardinghouse, each with their own idea as to Angela's location. Some, like Buck, were fatalists. "Nothing good ever happens to young girls in these forests."

Grandma, holding Maxine's hand, said, "She's here somewhere safe. The whole town will be looking."

Geri pitched in with her plan, saying, "I'm going to take my buggy and cross the crossing where the railroad was scraping ground before it all ended."

Corbett fell in step with Geri. "I'll get Ollie and stay on this side of the river. I'll check Edith's first. If anyone would know something about Angela, it would be Margaret. She'll know."

When Corbett approached, he hoped to see either Edith or Margaret outside doing chores. The milk cow was lounging, a sign that she had already been milked. The breakfast stove fire was down to a mere blue haze, indicating that breakfast was done. Maybe

Edith was around on the other side of the house, weeding in the cool morning air.

"Mr. Jones!" Margaret and Edith were both down at their spring. Corbett let Ollie gallop a little in the soft sod. Both women were muddy up to their calves.

"Every year, we fight this spring down to a dribble." Edith's thoughts were on her problem.

"Angela's missing!" Their eyes quickly went from the dribble to Corbett. "Margaret, know anything?"

"After spending so much time closing down the merc, I've been out here catching up." Margaret, a problem solver, was trying to solve this problem. "Did you ask June?"

"Yeah, nothing there." Corbett sensed a dead end. "How about Ernie? They're pretty friendly."

Edith, worried and thinking, said, "No. Joe gave him the week off to go camping." Then her eyes narrowed. "You had better go out to the Van Beques'. Even before your fight with Buster, they've been eyeing our girls."

"They scare me," agreed Margaret.

"They don't let anyone on their property," warned Edith. "They raise rabbits and goats—eat them raw, I bet!"

"I'm going back to town. I'll get some help." After hearing Edith and Margaret make their case against the Van Beques, Corbett knew that was his next stop.

On the way back, Corbett reflected on Angela. The most naive of the three girls, she was also the truest of friends. June was the smartest and most mature. Margaret stood as the hardest worker and the most pragmatic, whereas Angela was as delectable as her mother was a crank. Corbett, once in an honest moment, said to himself, "Too bad she's so young." The thought of finding a wife sometimes struck, then his memory of Ajai, and a sad, cold wind from Colorado, would fall over it.

In town, the bustle of a few weeks ago was gone. Myron and Maxine were sitting on the steps of the school. Both stood upon seeing Corbett ride up at a trot.

"Did you find her?" asked Maxine, running out to the mule and rider, placing her hope upon hope.

"No, but Edith thought I ought to check out at Van Beque's. She said those Van Beque boys have been favoring our girls for some time."

"Until you took Buster down, over yonder at the school," remembered Myron. It was a good moment for the town.

"You want to ride out there with me?"

Myron considered it. "No. I'm not sure you should be going out there either."

"Got to find out!"

"Well, wait a minute. If you are going to go, let me get that Colt you used on Willie."

The Van Beques lived up to their reputation. The road in was full of everyone else's junk, including axles, broken spring seats, stolen parts from the shingle mill, and the same used wood that patched up a long, low hovel of a home.

A Van Beque whom Corbett did not know had just snapped the neck of a large gray rabbit in front of the house. The man, a little older than Corbett and dressed in logger's gear, saw Corbett but continued to pull the soft hide off without the aid of a knife.

Corbett figured this to be Buster's older brother, Elroy. "I need to talk to the boys," said Corbett flatly. Ollie, sidestepping a bit, regarded the bloody rabbit with apprehension, both ears focused.

"You wouldn't be that teacher fellow, would ya?"

"I am. One of the town girls is missing, and I need to talk to them." The sad status of the property made Corbett eerily aware that a girl could be stored there.

"Can't!"

"I'm not going anywhere," said Corbett casually.

Elroy Van Beque grabbed a pitchfork and poked at Ollie. "Get off our property, before I stab ya!" Then he thrust the fork even closer. "Get out!"

Corbett reached back along his waistline and drew out the Colt. He wondered if it was loaded.

"Whoa, whoa, teacher man." Elroy's eyes coming to rest on the crazy man's gun, he quietly set the pitchfork aside. "Buster!" Louder, he said again, "Buster!"

Buster stepped out of the house. Upon seeing Corbett and Corbett's gun, he ducked back in.

"Buster, get out here before I shoot Elroy!" Corbett thought about the next step, backing up his bluff.

Tentatively, Buster came out with his hands up.

"Angela, one of our town girls, is missing. What do you know about it?" The gun was now pointed at Buster.

"I know her, but I don't anything about her being gone." Although the same size and age as Corbett, Buster was spooked by the fight with Corbett and by the fact that Corbett was carrying a gun this time. Corbett noticed.

Corbett replaced his gun. "Anything at all. I don't imagine you did anything, but Angela doesn't deserve to be missing."

"Ernie told a kid down at the shingle mill that he wouldn't be back. Goin' off the mountain, he said. Him and her maybe."

No, that could not be, Ernie and Angela running away together. Ernie would not know what to do with a girl if he had one. Angela seemed very young, but on the other hand, she did not want to be a seamstress like her mother, who was a frustrated and bitter woman.

"Buster, I think you hit on it! I'll bet Ernie and Angela left together last night. Thanks to ya."

Buster looked at Elroy. Could it be that he had done something right?

"By the way," said Corbett, "just lettin' you know, your roundhouse swing takes forever to land. I had to wait to block it. If you're going to throw an overhand right, at least make it straight!" With that, Corbett turned Ollie for the crossing.

"Thanks," said Buster, not sure what had just happened.

"Come on over!" said Myron, waving from the front of Grandma's. The waiting party had moved. Maxine, Myron, Buck, Margaret, and Grandma had put two tables together. Margaret had recently arrived. Geri had not yet returned from across the river.

"Hello, all," said Corbett, happy to possibly have the answer for the worried group. The tone caught everyone off guard.

"You found her!" Myron exclaimed, sensing Corbett's mood.

"Not exactly."

"But you know where she is?"

"Not exactly." He sat. "I'm pretty sure Angela and Ernie have run off together!"

Margaret jumped in. "No, he's out camping!" She then stopped to analyze the potential of what she had just said. "Oh my God, Ernie, Ma's going to kill you." Then she stopped to think about that. "He's got our only extra horse, and he's got Robert's thirty-thirty. They're all going to kill him!"

"Are you sure?" Maxine would have never thought that possible. "She's not that type!"

"No, I'm not sure, but if go back over to your house, I'll bet you'll find a note somewhere. She would have done that!" Maxine and Myron rose from the table at the same time.

"I'll go with you," said Myron.

"Me too!" added Margaret.

Geri met the trio coming out After a short exchange, Geri, wearing a sheepish grin, entered the restaurant.

"Well, how about that!" She laughed, relieved at the result. "That cute little thing and the little bull!" Then she started laughing again.

A few minutes later, while Grandma's chicken-fried steaks were being devoured by Geri and Corbett, Margaret pushed through the door. "We found the note!"

It was time for Corbett to leave Cedar Crossing, and he found himself faced with quite a conundrum: whether to use a pack horse and not have enough room or to use a wagon, where a lot of room would not be needed. Corbett settled on the wagon, with Ollie tied to the back of it, fully aware a bucket of oats was on board to be issued, probably at the next stop or two.

Since Corbett had purchased nearly everything in the school, he and Myron negotiated what should go and what should stay. Someday, school would begin again in Cedar Crossing, so the McGuffey's Readers and the Ray's math books were boxed and packed for the future. Corbett wanted to keep the library books he had yet to read. Most items stayed, but Corbett picked some things he had a fondness for. The historical maps on the wall went with him. These were expensive and probably would not be at his next school, if there was to be a next school.

The springboard wagon felt new and comfortable. John had purchased it just before his death, and June wanted Corbett to have it. The nearly new leather backrest was a luxury Corbett fully appreciated. Tug's horse would lead the way, harnessed and ready for a new life.

When the railroad stormed in to buy the mercantile, Myron's ability to help June pull many items out of the sale helped many in the community. Corbett got a gun of his own. Myron was happy to have his back. Corbett was given, as a gift by Geri, a new felt hat called the Gambler, wide-brimmed and handsome just like she thought he was.

The mercantile was closed and boarded up. It was a sad statement to the status of the fallen little town. Now, because of its gluttonous appetite, the railroad owned the biggest empty building in an empty little town.

Corbett had been surprised when Martin offered Margaret, June, and Edna jobs working for him at his restaurant and stagecoach stop. It did not hurt that the young women knew the rudiments of bookkeeping and stenography. Of course, Corbett remembered the roundabout trip to Martin's so Martin could be the first to see the new schoolmarm of Cedar Crossing. The young women might have been hired just because they were females.

Grandma and Buck were staying. Their location at the top of a long stage run would keep them both in groceries. Buck had the corrals to change out teams of horses, and Grandma's was a place to eat. They had been the early comers. They would eventually have stones planted above their heads somewhere near the crossing in the future.

Violet was escorted by surrey to her new home at Michael's vineyard. She seemed ready for a change.

The church bell had not been rung for a few Sundays. Preacher Arnold had been called to preach in Westport, on the Columbia.

Myron Mason had tried to get Maxine to stay. She was so shocked that her best friend had taken off with Edith's shingle gang boy that she packed up and moved to Portland, where her sister lived.

Corbett had visited Joe and Edith the previous evening. Margaret was gone now with June, off the mountain. Edith had sent Ernie to school so that he might find a way from the shingle mill and off the mountain. She had not realized that running away with a pretty schoolgirl would be the method. She, Joe, and Robert would stay on the homestead, their money coming in from the mill.

Every goodbye was hard. For these good, common folk, it was especially hard.

Geri's stayed open for a spell, until the loggers clearing the right-of-way for the railroad and the railroaders alike disappeared. She let down the canvas walls and secured them permanently. Inside, Geri sold all the bottled drinks and sold out the beer. She helped Grandma rearrange her little restaurant into a more usable stage stop. Whitechapel was to be her address, not as the operator out of room 4, but as part owner, sharing the master suite with her best friend, Darlene. Her final act was to go into the empty schoolhouse, where the schoolmaster was packing for his own departure. She kissed him and held him for a long time.

"I thought you had already left," said a surprised Corbett.

"I took a long walk this morning," replied Geri. "I waded the crossing and looked back at the town. I cried and cried. So many dreams have disappeared with the railroad."

"I know. Just a few weeks ago, Myron bought the wolf hide off me to put on the wall of his new bank." Corbett's head dropped. He shook his head slowly in sorrow. "I thought I was finally home."

"I'm not sure you and me are supposed to ever settle down," said Geri sadly. "I hope Darlene and I can live a good life in that rotten Whitechapel. It's our only hope."

Corbett looked at Geri with a broad smile. "You are a rose

living in a world of thorns. You will always do well." He reached out and held both Geri's hands. "I'll find time to find my Geri every now and then. You're my only next of kin."

Geri giggled through her tears. "And you, mister, bring your wife and children when you come. Find that woman. You were born to care for a woman. Your life will be wasted if you don't find her."

Geri released one hand and gently pulled Corbett out the schoolhouse door and toward her wagon. Silently, they hugged again. Then Corbett helped Geri onto her wagon. Without shedding any more tears, she looked forward and snapped the reins.

After all the thoughts concerning Geri and the rest of Corbett's Cedar Crossing family, he turned to the school building. It looked lonesome. With only one year of kids, it was now done.

Corbett would ride down to Martin's to see June, Margaret, and Edna one more time, and then be off. Corbett was not sure where he would go. Surely there were teaching jobs still unfilled out in the country. His first year had done nothing to vanquish his love of teaching. Maybe he would get on with one of the stage companies. Maybe he'd find a coastal stage. Every year, it would be another place.

Corbett saw the turn into Lewis and Ida's homestead. He had taken that turn many times. With the railroad gone and the crossing nearly empty, the couple would have a rough time of it. Ruth was such a good woman, imprisoned by a total lack of opportunity. The logger who had left her and Leo had killed her dreams.

Corbett remembered that the first time he'd seen Ruth, she looked like a wild woman. Now, this last time, she had her hair in a bun and was wearing a handsome dress Lewis had bought for her. She was very easy on the eyes. Corbett wanted to drive by the turn-off, thinking it would be too hard to say another goodbye.

Ollie started braying. He had carried Corbett down that lane many times. The mule pulled at his lead rope in preparation. Corbett unconsciously made the turn down the lane. The homestead smelled as it always did. Corbett could see Ida pushing Leo on his swing. Lewis and Ruth were under a tree watching. As they heard Corbett's wagon come into view, each broke into a smile.

"Hello there," called Lewis. "I thought you had left already!"

Corbett stayed in the wagon. "It looks like Leo has grown a foot." Leo looked up at Corbett from behind Ida.

"I'm thinkin' you're right," replied Lewis. "He's eating us out of house and home."

Corbett stepped down and shook Lewis's hand. "Ladies, you are looking good on this warm morning." Corbett moved to Ida and gave her a hug. "I miss that venison backstrap and pancakes for breakfast. And this must be Leo's mother." Corbett pulled Ruth to him slightly. "I am going to miss all of you!" Leo stepped forward to be lifted up by Corbett, a common thing between the two. Leo hugged Corbett around the neck. A tear came to Corbett's eye. He abruptly handed Leo to Ruth. *This kind boy will be without a father for probably the rest of his life, and his loving mother may never have a chance to find a good man.*

"Lewis, can I talk business with you a minute?"

The two moved away from the women. "Sure. Hides or pelts?" asked Lewis with a chuckle.

Corbett looked at Lewis, a serious expression on his face. "Lewis," whispered Corbett. "I want to take Ruth and Leo with me." Lewis was stunned, as was Corbett. This revelation had come from deep down. Corbett's mind had been unaware. "I will take them as my own."

Lewis put his hand to his face and pondered what had just been said. Then, attempting to disguise his smile, he said, "Then ask her."

Ruth was petting Ollie when Corbett spun her around and kissed her sweetly on the lips. Startled, Ruth backed away a step. "Ruth, I want you and Leo to leave with me!"

Ruth looked at her mother and then at her pa. A dream too good to be true had just come into Ruth's life. Corbett would never joke like that, Ruth thought. Frozen, not knowing what to say or do, she thought, *Corbett Jones wants me!*

"Ruth, I think you'd better start gathering your things. Your man's not going to wait all day."

Ruth grabbed Leo and raced into the house.

Ida, tears streaming from her eyes, kissed Corbett on his cheek. "That is the greatest gift you could have ever given any of us."

With the wagon packed and Corbett waiting to help his new family on board, Ruth ran to him and kissed him the way she always had wanted to kiss him, long and slow. She had never even called him Corbett, but now she was his.

After all this time, Corbett had again succumbed to love.

About the Author

Steve Whiteman has lived a full life. He has driven cattle through Durango, jumped mining claims near Telluride, and taught in a one-room school. He lived and taught on the Southern Ute reservation for fourteen years. He and his wife live in a small logging town in Oregon.

Printed in the United States
by Baker & Taylor Publisher Services